BAIT AND WITCH

Praise for Clifford Mae Henderson

Perfect Little Worlds

"A literary gem…Humour mixed with pathos is a powerful and memorable combination."—*Late Night Lesbian Reads*

"I love this novel. Clifford Henderson is funny and smart and a terrific storyteller, and her empathy for these flawed but loveable characters is boundlessly entertaining. And there's rage just under the surface that gives the narrative great edge. *Perfect Little Worlds* is a delight."—Elizabeth Mckenzie, Author of *Dog Of The North*

Rest Home Runaways

"A search for one last shot at freedom leads four elderly runaways on an adventure that at once touches the heart and leaves readers rooting for the 'escapees.' This is a beautiful, heartfelt story."
—Randy Peyser, author of *Crappy to Happy* as seen in the movie *Eat Pray Love*

"Geriatric anarchy breaks out in this poignant and funny new novel by Clifford Henderson, who writes with verve and compassion about the loss of self-determination that comes to the elderly and the difficulties that descend on their children. Underlying this fast-paced story is one clear message to our older selves: Do what you need to do. Give them hell."—Elizabeth McKenzie, author of *Stop That Girl*

"As much as anything this is about exploration, finding out who we are and who we are capable of being. Life can put us in boxes to do with our age that we aren't ready for. In this charming story we watch as each group fights against those restraints and chooses who they want to be—old and consigned to the scrap heap, or living life as an adventure to be taken. This isn't a romance, but it is full of romance nonetheless."—*Curve Magazine*

Maye's Request

"Henderson has a way with oddball families…The novel's serious subject matter—shattered families, religious fundamentalism, emotional instability—is balanced nicely by Henderson's flair for lighthearted prose that carries the narrative without undercutting the serious issues she explores."—*Richard Labonté, Book Marks*

"Clifford Henderson takes the reader on a frightening journey of physical, emotional, and spiritual illness to a place of love, enlightenment, healing, and forgiveness. There are times in this story that will be difficult to read, but you will feel no choice but to continue because the writing gently nudges you forward to come out the other side, hopefully unscathed. *Maye's Request* is Clifford Henderson's third novel, and like the others before, she continues to excite, enthrall, and entice."—*Out in Jersey*

"*Maye's Request* simmers throughout the story as the author delves into the family's past. These memories are not warm fuzzy moments of familial bliss; but rather, abusive and dark situations that are meant to disturb the reader…If you like complex family dramas, you will like *Maye's Request*."—*Queer Magazine Online*

"I truly laughed out loud at some passages and cried at others. A beautifully written and touching story of love, healing, family, and truth. Ms. Henderson has made me an instant fan!" —*Bibliophilic Book Blog*

Spanking New

"Clifford Henderson has written a masterpiece in *Spanking New*… Henderson's clever exploration of her protagonists' feelings leads the reader into a world where gender and identity are fluid. *Spanking New* should be a required reading for all gender and queer study courses. While the author addresses serious issues, her book is fun, fun, fun! The playfulness, curiosity, and fresh naivety as portrayed through the eyes of the storyteller is refreshing and often humorous.

It is pure genius on Henderson's part to write from this perspective. The protagonists are endearing and very human as you follow their struggles to navigate through life. The reader is able to sympathize with the antagonist's feelings as well in this richly developed exploration of human beings' struggles to make sense of their worlds."—*Anita Kelly, LGBT Coordinator, Muhlenberg College*

"*Spanking New* is a book that brings the fantasy of what happened before I was born, to life. If you have ever wondered what you were, or where you came from, Clifford Henderson gives you an interesting, oft times hilarious answer. The gender benders in this book are lovable characters, the most memorable being 'Spanky' the 'floating soul' that is looking to attach to his parents. When Spanky finally does manage to finagle a meeting of his soon-to-be parents Nina and Rick, the sparks fly, and all seems right with the world that he is about to enter, until Spanky finds out he is a girl! Other than being hilarious, this a poignant point of view, and makes for a fun and interesting read."—*Out In Jersey*

"Spanky, the narrator of this delicious novel, is an unborn baby who can flit from one character's thoughts and emotions to another's—a storytelling perspective that, from a less able author, might have come off as a diaper-load of a gimmick. But Henderson, in only her second book, handles the unorthodox point of view with inventive style and charm. Spanky's parents-to-be are Nina, an aspiring actress without a role in sight, and Rick, a musician paying the rent changing tires in a garage…These are just a few of a fabulous novel's well-rounded characters, which also include…a queer dog. And, of course, Spanky—who thinks she's going to be born a boy."—*Richard Labonté, Book Marks*

"Clifford Henderson took a warm look at people in her first novel, *The Middle of Somewhere*. She continues her warm looks in *Spanking New. Spanking New* is a book I found myself talking about with others, and one which I won't soon forget. This is a wise and funny book."—*Just About Write*

The Middle of Somewhere

"The characters in this book are easy to relate to, I found myself caring about their struggles, and celebrating their triumphs... Clifford Henderson writes with depth and ease. Her writing gives you the sense that her muse was not only visiting, but had moved in."—*Out in Jersey*

"Henderson grabs her readers in a firm grip and never lets go. *The Middle of Somewhere* is a wonderful laugh-out-loud read filled with pathos, hope, and new beginnings."—*Just About Write*

"I loved this book. I was laughing from the first paragraph all the way to the end, and in the meantime fell in love with all the characters. Although this is Henderson's first published novel, her writing is replete with complex characters and a full-bodied plot, sort of like a well-rounded Merlot. I can't help but give this book a hearty two thumbs up review and hope that you'll read it. I know you'll enjoy it just as much as I did."—*Kissed by Venus*

By the Author

The Middle of Somewhere

Spanking New

Maye's Request

Rest Home Runaways

Perfect Little Worlds

Bait and Witch

Visit us at www.boldstrokesbooks.com

BAIT AND WITCH

by
Clifford Mae Henderson

2023

ISBN 13: 978-1-63679-535-5

THIS TRADE PAPERBACK ORIGINAL IS PUBLISHED BY
BOLD STROKES BOOKS, INC.
P.O. BOX 249
VALLEY FALLS, NY 12185

FIRST EDITION: NOVEMBER 2023

CREDITS
EDITOR: JENNY HARMON
PRODUCTION DESIGN: STACIA SEAMAN
COVER DESIGN BY HOUSTON GRAPHICS

Acknowledgments

Dear Reader,

My first thank you goes to you for picking up *Bait and Witch*! It means the world to me.

My next thank you goes to the many creative people who helped you and me share this experience. Leading the pack, Len Barot, who had this glorious idea to start a publishing company and then did it. Sandy Lowe, Ruth Sternglantz, Cindy Cresap, and the rest of the Bold Strokes Books posse who somehow manage to keep from drowning in all the varied details it takes to keep the books coming to you. And of course, a ginormous shoutout goes to my fabulous editor, Jenny Harmon, whose editing wisdom made this a much better book.

And then there are all my brilliant peeps who were willing to give feedback on earlier versions: Lara Love Hardin, Debra Ryll, Jennifer Cass, Peggy Townsend, Martha Allison, Gino Danna, Duke Houston, Eileen Burke Woodward, and Elizabeth McKenzie. Also, Houston Graphics, who designed my cool cover and website graphics, and Eileen, who helps me maintain the website and never tires of all my technical questions. Thank you all.

But the biggest thanks goes to my wife, Dixie Cox, who hears every version of everything I ever write and still somehow loves me.

For my mom, who studies the earthly magic of bird migration.

Chapter One

To make one hundred percent sure Mags was dead, Zeddi stepped around the old woman's slippered feet to check her breathing, her pulse. It was a strange intimacy to share with one of the few friends she'd made since moving to Tres Ojos. The papery skin of Mags' wrist and neck was cool and waxy, exposed, vulnerable. Not that anything worse could happen to a person besides dying, Zeddi supposed. Then again, it was only her second experience with a dead body—the first, a homophobic grandmother whom she barely knew because her grandmother thought her son (Zeddi's dad) and his husband (Zeddi's other dad) were sinners and had no business raising a child, much less a daughter. Zeddi had expected her to be dead. Knew she'd be dead. It was the only reason she'd made the trip to Ohio—because Nana was dead.

Nothing like this.

Nothing like arriving for her weekly housecleaning job and finding her eighty-six-year-old client dressed and ready for the day. Loose hemp-fabric slacks, soft sage-green cardigan, short white hair in its usual tussle, sitting in her frayed green overstuffed chair as if any minute she might get up and take a walk along the river or reach for the cordless landline on the coffee-cup-ringed table next to her. The dullness in her eyes was unnerving, the one eyelid stuck all the way open, the other at half-mast, as if Mags was mid-wink when she died. But she didn't stink the way dead people did in cop shows. Just smelled slightly…fermented.

Outside the sliding glass doors, the drizzling rain fell on the tiny fenced-in backyard garden. Besides that, the world was eerily quiet.

Zeddi slipped her phone from the pocket of her sticker-covered cleaning caddy. How could Mags be dead? She'd been so full of life just last week.

A fly circled Mags' nostril. Landed. Zeddi waved it away, the tears finally pushing their way past her shock. What were she and Olive going to do without Mags? She'd been such a lifeline in the ten weeks they'd known her! Offering to hang out with Olive on those days when Zeddi had to work late. Mags and Olive would do things like grow mushrooms from a kit, or pick up trash along the river, or there was that time they'd spent the afternoon watching praying mantises hatch. *You should have seen them, Mom!* Olive had whooped. *They all started fighting and eating each other!* Or that day Zeddi had found them in the garden singing and water coloring. *We're painting what the songs look like*, Olive had said offhandedly, like this was just something people did. But Mags was like that. Creative, a free thinker, a warm heart.

Not anymore.

The fly landed on the inside of Mags' eye, then started to crawl across her open eyeball. Zeddi sprang toward her and waved it off, the suddenness of the action letting loose a torrent of tears. "I'm sorry, Mags," she sobbed while waving frantically at the fly. "I should have…"

She jabbed 9-1-1 into her phone.

Just three days ago she'd called to reschedule the weekly cleaning. Olive had woken up with a stomach bug. Mags was unhappy about the change. *There's something I need to talk to you about*, she'd said. *Something best talked about in person. How soon can you come? Tomorrow?* But there was no way. Zeddi had three houses to clean, a pile of personal laundry, grocery shopping. Zeddi had suggested the day after, Wednesday, late afternoon. The sound of Olive puking had prompted her to add, *that is, if Olive's over this*. And now here it was, Wednesday, and Mags was dead.

Zeddi heard herself answering the dispatcher's questions. *Who what where when*, the exchange so mechanical, so careless, so nothing to do with the end of a beautiful life. Still, Zeddi felt better having made the call. It was in someone else's hands now.

Unsure what to do next, she settled onto one of the barstools at the kitchen counter to wait.

One thing about being dead, it meant you were no longer accountable. Wasn't that a depressing thought. It's just that things had gone so sour since the move to Tres Ojos. Since the sublet falling through. But they had Turtle, and that was so much more than some people had. Turtle, the '91 Chevy conversion van that had been their home for the last ten weeks. And Olive's school was working out well. And the cleaning business Zeddi had purchased before moving from Sacramento was doing well. Still, a couple miles down the river, a homeless camp was spreading like COVID. Every day, there were more tents, more city-provided trash cans and porta-potties. She tried not to think about it. She'd find them a home. They didn't need much. A small apartment. Even a studio would work. But on top of being super expensive, the Silicon Valley outpost also had a severe housing shortage.

The fly found its way back. Or was it another one? She waved it away. Rolled up a page of newspaper and whapped the fly against the leg of the small round table. The fly fell to the carpet, then just lay there wiggling its little legs in the air, crying for help. She whapped it again and again and again, her eyes brimming with tears, then picked the tiny carcass up with a tissue and tossed it in Mags' kitchen trash.

Where were the first responders? Shouldn't they have shown up by now? Had she not been clear over the phone? Given the wrong address? She checked the Kit Cat clock. Not ten minutes had passed since she'd called 9-1-1. Still. She slid off the stool and walked over to the door. Cracked it. Outside the world was carrying on as if nothing of consequence had happened. As if it were just another ordinary day.

She blew her nose again. Wiped her tear-streaked face. Returned to the barstool. Rubbed the tattoo on the inside of her right wrist. *Trust*, it said. She'd gotten the word inked onto her skin the day she'd decided to keep Olive. It hadn't been an easy decision, not under the circumstances, but it had been the right one. Olive was her everything. She plucked a hair from her jeans. Her stress was making her lose hair. How bad was that? She held it to the light. Could hardly see the blue dye. But who had the time or the money to redye it? Let alone a bathroom. She took a deep breath.

Outside, the drizzle turned to a downpour. It was the first real rain of the season. She'd known it was coming. Even so, it was inconvenient. Maybe Dan would let her put a patio umbrella in the driveway next to where he'd let her park the van. That would help. If she angled the umbrella just right, they could leave the van's barn doors cracked while it rained. It would keep it from getting too steamy inside. He'd been so generous, the combat veteran, charging them next to nothing for the use of his driveway, giving them bathroom and kitchen privileges. But there were limits to people's generosity.

She stared at the moisture collecting on the feathery fronds of a giant fern in Mags' small herb garden. It turned into a strand of pearls as the droplets made their way toward the mound of thyme below. It was a beautiful garden, tiny and bursting with life. Who would care for it now? Would anyone? She knew so little about Mags' private life. But there was no time to worry about Mags' garden. Olive would be getting out of school soon, and with the rain Zeddi would have to pick her up—her and her bike. Only now she had to be there for the paramedics too, or whoever it was they sent in these situations. She really had no idea. Should she call the school? Ask if there was someone who could wait with Olive? Then, as abruptly as the rain had begun, it stopped, which solved at least one problem: Olive could ride. She had a good warm jacket—if she remembered it.

A flattened dust bunny was stuck to the sole of her white PF. Flyers high tops. She peeled it off. Rolled it into a ball along with her strand of hair. She loved how Olive had decorated the sneakers one night while they were hanging out in the van. She'd penned *You Da Boss Lady! Chillax! Enjoy The Ride, Man! Keep It Clean!* on the canvas along with colorful lightning bolts, snakes, and of course Olive's favorite: skulls and crossbones. She'd done it to cheer Zeddi up, which was a worry. The last thing she wanted was to be one of those mothers who needed their kid looking after them. Still, the sneakers made her smile.

She tossed the balled-up dust and hair into the trash. Waved away yet another fly. They were the real first responders. Flies. She shook the gruesome thought from her head. Another gloomy one replaced it. Mags' account would be the second she'd lost this month. Actually, third if she counted the one she'd quit after the woman said, "But I thought you'd be Mexican!"

Another breath.

Another reminder to trust.

She looked back at Mags. This old lesbian who'd been so good to her and Olive. But it wasn't Mags. Mags was gone to wherever it was the dead went. Which was where exactly? It was too big a question for the moment, but it was unsettling the way she could still kind of feel

Mags, even though she had so obviously vacated her body. "So, what do you think, Mags?" she asked the emptiness. "What should I do about Olive? Would it be okay for her to see you like this? Would it help her understand you being gone? Because she's going to miss you—bad. Or would seeing you dead be just one more thing I've subjected her to? Should I try to soften the blow, meet her outside and explain to her about you dying? What do you think?"

Olive's flinging open of the trailer door mooted the question. "Mom! Mags!" she shouted, barely able to get the words out she was so out of breath. "Great news! We got out of school early because all the toilets in the girls' bathroom overflowed. All at once! It was awesome!"

CHAPTER TWO

C"an I touch her?"

Zeddi lay a hand on her daughter's shoulder. Damp. She'd been caught in the rain after all. Strike one for her parenting skills. As for Olive's request, how best to respond? Parenting 101 hadn't covered what to do when your nine-year-old wanted to touch a dead body. Not that she'd ever taken a parenting class. Who had the time? Still, the question remained: Would touching Mags scar Olive for life or help her deal with the loss? "Well…" she said finally, tentatively. "I touched her. That's how I knew for sure she was dead."

"Because you checked her breathing?"

Olive stood a few feet shy of touching range, her soft pale hands tightly gripping the straps of her owl backpack. A gift from her grandpas, the backpack was filled with books and rode low on her back, pulling her purple puffy jacket with it.

"Yup. I checked her pulse too." Zeddi waved at a fly. Where were they coming from? "She definitely feels dead."

"She does?"

Zeddi finger-combed a tangle out of Olive's short chestnut ponytail. Also damp.

"Uh-huh. But you don't have to touch her if you don't want to. We can hang out in the van until the paramedics show up. Get you into some dry clothes. Did you remember to lock up your bike?"

"And just *leave* her here?"

It was a miracle Olive could see. Her tortoiseshell glasses were hideously smudged. Normally, Zeddi would mention it, or clean them herself. "She *is* dead. She wouldn't know."

"What did she feel like?" Olive asked.

"Dead."

"Mo-*om*!"

"I don't know what you want me to say."

Zeddi peered out the door. Still no sign of an ambulance.

"If I touch her, where should I touch her?"

"That's up to you, honey."

What had Mags wanted to tell her? She'd seemed so keyed up when they'd talked on the phone. Zeddi stared at Mags' painting above the couch. Five crows huddled secretively in a golden field, one with its wings spread open. The colors were intense, the palette-knife strokes bold, thick. Zeddi tore her eyes from the painting. Whatever it was Mags had wanted to say would remain what Papa Alan called any unanswerable question: an eternal busy signal.

Olive squinted, huffed a breath.

"Olive, once they get here, you might miss your chance. So, if you really want to—"

"She *looks* dead."

Zeddi sighed. "Yes, she does."

"Her eyes, why are they like that? One half closed."

"I don't know."

"Maybe she was blinking when she died."

"Maybe."

"Remember that bird I found that time? How I knew it was dead before you did?"

"I do."

Zeddi waited for her to elaborate. Olive really loved the old woman, had made so many memories with her in the last ten weeks. Zeddi had lost a client, yes; a good one, yes; a helpful ally, yes. But Olive had lost a friend, a buddy. Zeddi bit down on her lip. Why couldn't life ever be easy for Olive?

"I'm going to touch her," Olive said finally.

"Okay. Want me to take your backpack?"

Olive peeled the pack from her shoulders and let it clunk to the floor. Arms limp at her sides, fingertips twitching nervously, she placed one sneakered foot cautiously in front of the other.

Zeddi tried to snatch another circling fly but missed. How had they gotten in?

Olive adjusted her glasses, a nervous habit, then carefully pressed a single finger onto Mags' hand—the same way she touched newly baked muffin tops for doneness.

"What do you think?" Zeddi asked.

Olive did it a second time, then said softly, "Definitely dead."

Zeddi squeezed the shoulders of the person she loved more than anyone in the world. "That's what I thought."

Olive's chin trembled.

"Oh, honey. I know you cared about her. I did too."

"She was going to show me"—Olive hiccupped—"where barn owls"—she hiccupped again—"are nesting in a palm tree by the river. We were going to see how they can't move their eyes, how they have to turn their whole heads to see…"

Zeddi drew her into a hug. "Maybe after they take her away, we can walk the levee, see if we can find that palm tree."

"She said the owls are hard to spot," Olive sniffed into Zeddi's chest. "I bet we won't be able to find them."

Zeddi rested her head on Olive's. "Maybe just this once we'll get lucky."

❖

"I'm just the cleaning lady," Zeddi said for the third time.

She was talking to the nicer of the two paramedics, Ricardo, a balding man with a slight paunch. Pleasant as he was, the uniform made her nervous—*all* the uniforms did. In making her statement to the police, she'd been asked for her address. She'd given them Dan's while silently praying there'd be no reason to check up on her and find out what a terrible mother she was. Making her nine-year-old live in a van in a driveway, who did that? Thankfully, the investigation seemed to be winding down. The bottle-blond coroner, now crammed in the tiny kitchen conferring with two police officers and the other paramedic, had unceremoniously pronounced Mags dead from natural causes. The men seemed more interested in the blond coroner than they were in Mags. Zeddi shoved her hands into her jean pockets. Mags deserved more. So much more.

"It's pretty sad, huh?" Ricardo said to Olive.

"Yeah," Olive said. She was clinging to Zeddi's leg. "She was my friend. We hung out together after school sometimes. We liked to sing together. And paint."

"Is that right?"

"Uh-huh. That's her painting there." Olive pointed at the five crows.

"Interesting."

"Lately she's been into plein air. Do you know what that is?"

"Can't say I do."

"Landscapes."

"Ah. Nice."

"Painted outside. Not from a photo."

"Okay."

He was good with kids. Probably had some of his own. "Olive knew her better than me," Zeddi clarified. "We haven't been in town that long."

"Almost two months!" Olive objected.

Zeddi and Ricardo exchanged sad smiles. Two months was a long time for a kid.

In the kitchen, the coroner peeled a large magnetic card with Mags' emergency contact information from the refrigerator. "I'm going to take this outside. Make some calls."

"Okay," Zeddi said. She'd cleaned around the File of Life card so many times, never giving it a thought. Now, though, it was hard *not* to think about it. Who had Mags left behind?

"Four days ago I saw her," Olive said to Ricardo. "And she didn't have a cold or anything. She was fine."

Ricardo nodded. "You know, sometimes people, especially old people, can seem fine on the outside, but not be fine on the inside."

"What killed her, then?"

He shrugged. "She may have had a stroke. Or maybe her heart just got tired."

"She *was* old," Zeddi said.

"It looks like she died peacefully," he added kindly, "so it probably happened quickly. She probably just drifted off in her sleep."

"I touched her," Olive confessed.

Ricardo smiled. "What did you think?"

"That she was dead."

"There you go then. You should have my job. Now, just so you know, pretty soon someone's going to come with a stretcher, and take her—"

"Where?"

"Honey, we need to let these guys do their job."

"WHERE?" Olive demanded.

"The morgue?" Zeddi guessed. She looked to Ricardo for confirmation.

"Probably, but it depends on who the coroner gets ahold of. If she reaches a family member it could be a funeral home."

"But what if we're the only people she's got?" Olive said, not so much a question as a gauntlet tossed to the floor.

"I doubt that," Zeddi said. "It seemed to me she had lots of friends."

"But what *if*?"

"I don't know, Olive. I guess—"

A loud yowl came from outside the sliding glass door.

"Barnaby!" Olive cried, and rushed to let him in. "What are you doing outside? Mom! Mags never lets him outside!!! She doesn't believe in it! She says cats kill birds!"

"He must have gotten out when the police got here, or…"

Ricardo ran a self-conscious hand over his bald head. "I don't think we let him out…"

Olive hefted the obese orange and white cat into her arms. He was soaked, legs dangling and dripping onto the floor. "You couldn't have. It wasn't raining by the time you got here."

As usual, Olive was right. Barnaby wouldn't be wet if the police or paramedics had let him out. And he was definitely an indoor cat. In all her weeks of cleaning Mags' trailer, the overfed, over-pampered feline had never once shown even the slightest inclination to go outside, let alone hunt birds. The closest Barnaby ever got to the outside world was lying in a patch of sunlight by the sliding glass doors and lazily slapping his tail at a squirrel. He liked to nap and eat, that was pretty much it. "That is odd," she said.

"Odd?" Olive struggled to hold Barnaby off the ground. "I'd say it's more than odd! I'd say it's a…" She paused to remember her new vocabulary word. "An anomaly!"

CHAPTER THREE

Once Mags was whisked away and everyone gone, Zeddi just stood there stunned. Now what? There had been no family members to call, just a friend, a funeral home, a lawyer—or that's who was listed on her File of Life card. The police had also spoken with several concerned neighbors of the mobile-home cooperative. They seemed a close-knit community, and hopefully helped to shed some light on Mags' affairs.

A small gold pillow, knocked down in the hubbub, lay on the carpet a few feet from the green chair where Zeddi, not ninety minutes ago, had found Mags, dead. The pillow looked so lonely on the floor all by itself, forgotten. Zeddi hugged it to her chest, then returned it to its place on the chair. It was so quiet with everyone gone, just the sound of Barnaby purring as Olive petted him by the fireless wood-burning stove. That and the ticking of the Kit Cat clock.

Zeddi had been given the okay by the authorities to go ahead and clean if she wanted to, though the pointlessness of the endeavor obviously baffled them. Why clean? The woman was dead. Zeddi rubbed her tight shoulders. Why indeed? She was exhausted. But that envelope tucked between the flour and sugar tins, as it always was— her name written on it in Mags' unmistakable left-slanting cursive, *i*'s dotted with slashes rather than dots, the words themselves suggesting they might, given the chance, conga-line off the left side of the page— gave her little choice. It was the last thing Mags had asked of her.

Still.

She gnawed on the ragged cuticle of her thumb. She couldn't take the money without cleaning. That would be wrong. And she needed the money, that was for sure. It was the end of the month, bills were due.

Her cuticle began to bleed. She stanched the blood by pressing on it with her finger. One of these days she had to quit chewing on herself.

"Mom," Olive said flatly. "You're just standing there staring into space."

"Am I?"

"Yes, and we still have to clean."

We? Olive never offered to help on cleaning jobs. Zeddi never expected her to either, never wanted her to. Olive was a kid, and being a kid meant trusting your mom would take care of you. "What about your homework?"

Olive gave Barnaby a final pat and joined Zeddi at the kitchen counter. "Mom, our friend died. Homework is the least of our worries."

Zeddi laughed.

"What?"

"You're right. But you don't have to."

"I *want* to."

Olive's concern made her heart hurt. "So let's get to it. Clean it the best we've ever cleaned it."

Olive lifted a fist in the air. "For Mags!"

Startled by Olive's enthusiasm, Barnaby flipped onto all fours and peeled down the hallway toward the bedroom.

"Wow! I didn't know he could run that fast," Olive said.

Neither did Zeddi. "He's really spooked."

"I know, right?"

"I guess he's not used to so many people in his space." But why had he been outside? Another eternal busy signal. Zeddi picked up her cleaning caddy. "Shall we?"

Olive grabbed the feather duster and headed for the bookshelf. No doubt she'd spend the whole time on it, dusting around the books, shells, rocks, bird nests and fossils. It would be good for her, give her some closure. Just as cleaning the trailer one last time would give Zeddi some closure. Fighting back a lump in her throat, Zeddi set her small wireless speaker on the kitchen counter and started scrolling for an upbeat playlist. *Hawaiian? Zydeco?* She settled on Cuban. Perfect. Sad and happy at the same time.

Olive shouted, "Spider alert!"

"Well, you know what to do."

Mags was adamant about saving spiders. Olive grabbed the four-by-five card and small plastic cup Mags kept on her kitchen counter, her Spider Catcher.

What did she ever do to deserve such a great kid?

"It's a daddy longlegs," Olive reported, setting the cup over the spider. "Have you ever noticed how they spin when you touch them?"

"Can't say that I have."

"Mags showed me. Would you open the door for me? My hands are full."

Outside, they watched the spider crawl from the cup into a potted rosemary bush.

If only finding a new home were this easy.

❖

Standing on a straight-backed chair by the bookshelf, Olive raised the feather duster above her head, Olympic-torch style. "Done, done, and doner!"

Zeddi peeled off her favorite Dollar Store elbow-length rubber gloves decorated with pink flamingos. "Perfect timing. Me too."

It was a relief to be finished. The whole time she'd been cleaning, Zeddi couldn't shake the feeling that Mags was there in the room too, especially when she'd stuck Mags' bananas and apples into her cleaning caddy. But fruit was perishable, and who knew when anyone else would be by? Still, it felt scavenger-y so she'd put the fruit back. She'd felt Mags too when she washed the two china teacups in the sink. Who had she entertained? What had they talked about? Did Mags have any inkling she was about to die, or were her last words *Let's do this again soon*? And what to do about the key. Should she leave it? Take it? She plucked a pen from Mags' cup of pens and jotted a note on the back of a piece of unopened junk mail, wrote: *To whom it may concern...*

She explained that she'd been the one to find Mags, left her phone number, left the key with its beaded mermaid fob, and mentioned if they needed further services she was available. So mercenary. But you never knew. Wiping back the tears, she centered the note on the sun-faded countertop where anyone would see it first thing, then grabbed the envelope with her check and turned to Olive, who was sprawled out next to Barnaby on the floor. "What do you say we splurge for dinner? Pick up a couple of burgers? We can grab one for Dan too."

"What about Barnaby?"

Right. Barnaby. They couldn't very well leave the cat. But they sure couldn't take him, the poor guy would freak being locked in the van. Dan? No. Dan had asthma issues. *Never had 'em before Iraq,* he'd told her once while toking his vape. Besides, it was too much to ask.

"How about this?" she said. "How about I swing by in the morning, make sure he's fed, has some water, and scoop his poop. By then we'll probably know more about what's happening with the trailer."

Olive frowned. Hard.

"It's one night, honey. And tomorrow, if we haven't found out anything, we'll...well...we'll figure something out."

Olive held up a finger. "One night."

"Right."

"Promise?"

"Olive. If we can't—"

"Promise?"

Zeddi sighed. "Okay. I promise." Then plucked the little mermaid from the kitchen counter and tossed it in her caddy. "I'm sure we'll think of something." She just hoped it didn't involve the SPCA. But that's what happened to homeless kitties.

Outside, Zeddi strapped Olive's bike onto the van's back ladder, stowed her cleaning caddy under the bed, and closed Turtle's side barn doors. Living in a van meant everything in its place. Period. By the time she climbed into the driver's seat, Olive was already seat-belted in and doing homework, the seat pulled up to its most forward position, her sneakers resting on the dashboard.

Zeddi flipped open Mags' envelope. The check was folded inside a sheet of lined yellow paper. Three numbers were written on the paper. Three, thirty-two, sixteen. Was she supposed to understand, or was it just a random scrap of paper?

"Do you have any idea what three, thirty-two, sixteen might mean?"

Math workbook propped up on her knees, Olive grunted, "Nuh-uh."

"Hm." Zeddi tossed the slip of paper in the catch-all basket between the two front seats. "You have a lot of homework?"

"Nope. I already wrote my report on Harriet Tubman, so it's just math and science, and science is easy. I just have to read some stuff. I'll have it done before we get home."

Home. It hurt that Olive considered Dan's driveway home.

❖

"You shouldn't have," Dan said, eagerly unwrapping his burger. "But I'm sure glad you did."

"Me too," Olive said. "I'm sta-a-ar-ar-*ving!*"

Zeddi dumped the three packs of curly fries into a big pile on the flattened-out burger bag in the center of the table. She didn't usually indulge in fast food, but sometimes it was necessary, and fun, and today they really needed some fun. They sat at the cluttered table in the dimly lit dining room, a concession on Dan's part. He usually ate at his computer or out in his garage where he was restoring a '66 Camaro. Along with asthma, Dan had an aversion to light. Photophobia, he called it. Another thing he attributed to his time in Iraq. *All that sand, all that sun, burned the fuck out of my eyes*, he'd told her. A moody guy, he was just a couple of years older than her but had a world-weariness that made him seem older. They'd met him at a thing called Dance Church two weeks into their van life.

She and Olive had been getting on each other's last nerves. The van was too small, and it was too chilly to hang outside at the campground, and they were sick of hiking, and they both loved to dance, so when Zeddi saw a flyer on a coffee shop bulletin board— *Join us for a morning worship where the DJ is the minister, the music the sermon, and the dancers the congregation*—they'd checked it out. Turned out to be the perfect cure for van-fever. They'd gone a second Sunday too, and a third, and each time in the corner, a bearded, heavily inked guy danced wildly by himself. *Dancing is how I release my demons*, he'd told her on a break. When he'd asked about what brought her there, she'd mentioned that she and Olive were temporarily campground-hopping in their van, and about the sublet falling through. He'd generously offered up his driveway. *It's not much*, he'd said, *but you're welcome to it if it would help you save some bucks and get back on your feet.* He'd parked his own car out on the street to accommodate Turtle.

She popped a curly fry in her mouth.

One of these days she and Olive were going to wear out their welcome. Or more was going to be expected of her. Or was it? She'd told him she was gay; he'd barely blinked. And he never acted like he expected more. Still, you never knew with guys.

Another curly fry.

He wasn't big on decor, that was for sure. The house's main design element was an unwillingness on his part to have his back to doors and windows. It made for an odd furniture arrangement: everything facing out. And the furniture itself, once plush and belonging to his parents, was worn and stained: the floral couch, overstuffed chairs, the piano that never got played. The fringed lampshades were dusty with cobwebs, the kitchen counter smothered in piles of newspapers and junk mail. More than once, Zeddi had offered to help him clean up the place, but as he put it, *people fucking with his stuff made him nervous.*

Not the ideal place for a child, but Dan was a good guy, and like every other perceptive adult, he really liked Olive. Why was it kids rarely did?

She tuned back into Dan who was patiently listening to Olive's overly dramatic account of finding Mags. "...and her eyelids! One was half closed..." She was talking with her mouth full. Zeddi sat back and stared out the window. Today was not the day to get picky. The cheeseburger *was* delicious. She took another bite. Across the street, the warm glow of people's porch lights shone through the mist. The apartment they'd left behind in Sacramento had a porch light. It hadn't seemed like much at the time.

She worried about the rain. The inside of the van was already starting to feel damp, and they'd get soaked using the garage toilet at night in the rain. She'd have to come up with some kind of pee-pot. Empty it each morning. Dan said it was fine for them to shower in the house, and store some food in his fridge, but it was awkward. He slept until noon most days.

She took a paper napkin off the stack and blotted a bit of ketchup from Olive's cheek. Maybe it was time to send that SOS to her dads, admit she'd made a huge mistake, ask if she and Olive could come live with them temporarily in Yucca Valley. But there was Papa Alan's Parkinson's to consider. He'd been getting worse—not that he'd ever say so, but she could hear it when they talked on the phone, the slurring of his speech, the delay of his responses. Papa Glen was beside himself with worry. They didn't need one more thing to stress about. Besides, their place was too small. She also hadn't mentioned the slight detail that the sublet had fallen through. They didn't know she was making their granddaughter live in a van. So there was that.

A bite of cheeseburger.

Tomorrow she'd hear back on an apartment listing she'd seen on Craigslist. It sounded tiny and depressing, the description using the words *rustic* and *charming,* but maybe they'd get lucky. Maybe.

The room went suddenly quiet. Or had it been, and she just now noticed? Dan was looking at Olive. Olive was staring at her half-eaten cheeseburger.

"This your first dead body?" he asked her gently.

Olive slid a pickle from the burger and set it on the wrapper. "Uh-huh."

"It's kind of strange, huh?"

"Yup."

Dan wiped his chest-length beard with the back of his hand, dislodging a rogue strip of lettuce. "The thing to remember is, something can't turn into nothing. It's plain science."

"So?"

"So, she's not gone. Not really. She just changed form."

Olive looked up from her burger. "You mean like gone to heaven? Because I don't believe in heaven. Or hell."

Dan smiled. "I didn't say that. And for the record, neither do I. Unless you're talking about here on earth. Then I definitely believe in both. I'm talking about matter. Inanimate or animate. It can't become nothing."

Olive scowled. "So, what are you saying?"

"Just that the dead are never really gone."

"So Mags is like…what?"

He shrugged. "Hard to say. But she hasn't left the planet. She couldn't have."

Zeddi couldn't help herself. "Are you talking reincarnation? Because we've talked about that, haven't we, Olive?"

"Yep," Olive said. "It's what Buddhists believe."

"Other people too. Hindus. And I think there are some others."

"That's not exactly what I'm talking about," Dan clarified. "I don't think people come back as one specific thing or person or animal or whatever."

"So, what *are* you talking about?" Olive asked.

"I believe the dead scatter and become a part of everything. Maybe parts of them get swept up into new creatures, people, cats, birds. But other parts get swept up into trees and clouds."

Olive thought about this. Outside, a wind chime chimed. Her eyes grew wide. "Maybe that's her!"

Dan laughed. "Maybe."

Then, like the nine-year old she was, Olive switched topics with no warning. "Oh, and did we tell you about Barnaby? How he was outside? When he's *never* outside?"

"No. I didn't hear that part."

So of course, Olive had to tell him.

On the mantel, Dan's collection of "therapy" lava lamps undulated.

CHAPTER FOUR

"Lost my home, made a mess, all alone, what comes next?" Zeddi whisper-sang into the darkness. Bundled against the damp night, crouch-sitting on a low beach chair in the driveway, she accompanied herself on her new thrift-store ukulele. It was going on midnight and Olive was asleep in the van. Zeddi was mindful to keep it down, her fingers barely brushing past the strings. Dan, a night owl, wouldn't be bothered by her strumming. It was the retired couple next door she worried about. So far, they hadn't made a fuss about her living in his driveway. Lately, though, when she smiled at them, they didn't smile back. She couldn't blame them. The houses in the harbor district were packed in like condos.

She released the back of the lawn chair so she could stare at the sky. No moon. No stars. Just a thick layer of fog.

She slowed the tempo. Leaned into the minor chords. "Lost a friend today…And lost my way…My heart is aching…On this sad day…" The ukulele, turquoise with a single decorative shark, had been one of her many bribes to keep Olive from whining about living in Turtle. Fortunately, they were still sort of in Adventure Mode, but the nights were getting colder and wetter, and the fun was fading fast. And the ukulele hadn't helped. Olive strummed it a few times pretending to be a wild rock star, flinging her hair, yowling *yeah yeah yeah, oh baby baby*, then never picked it up again. So Zeddi did. Taught herself a few chords. Made up some others.

The profile of the elderly man next door silhouetted on the backlit curtain. Her hand froze mid-strum. She imagined herself invisible. He walked past. Phew. Living under the radar was stressful. She hugged the ukulele to her chest. God, she wished she had someone to talk to. She thought about Sylvie. Again. Wild Card Sylvie who'd showed up in her life at exactly the wrong moment: three days before she and Olive were set to move.

Burlesque Night. Her friend Daria was debuting as a dancer. Zeddi had gotten the neighbor to look after Olive so she could cheer Daria on. Daria was amazing. She'd made this crazy sexy taco costume. Off came the lettuce, the tomatoes, the tortilla. And that was just the beginning. The other dancers were amazing too. Or maybe it was just that she was getting to hang out with adults—feel sexy for a change. Or maybe it was just a magic night, because after the show, when Daria introduced her to Sylvie, the lighting and sound tech, she'd fallen hard. Sylvie was so cute in her plaid retro pantsuit and black Doc Martens, her green eyes sparking with mischief. And she was funny too. Smart. By the end of the night, Zeddi and the Irish librarian-slash-lighter-of-burlesque dancers were finishing each other's sentences—and laughing and laughing. They were *so* connected. And then it got even better because they'd kissed and kissed and kissed. It was crazy. Spontaneous. And so so good.

Why couldn't they have met earlier? Or was the appeal that the relationship had no future. Sacramento was a hundred and fifty impossible miles away. She'd FaceTimed with her a couple of times since the move, but it was awkward. Mostly because she was feeling like a loser. Living in a van with her daughter. Who did that? Still, she couldn't quit thinking about her. About those kisses.

She dared another faint strum. Then another.

She'd thought having a kid wouldn't change her life that much. What a bonehead! Olive changed everything. It was such a fluke she'd even slept with a guy, but after a series of backfired relationships she'd thought it was time to give up on women. Or that's what her tequila-soaked brain had come up with at the bar that night. Why not try a guy? They were so much simpler to understand. So rudimentary.

It took just the one hookup to prove that theory wrong. The night had been highly unsatisfactory. What's more, she'd gotten pregnant, despite her insistence that the guy use protection. In retrospect, the unlikely conception should have been her first sign that one very stubborn spirit had an eye on her. The second came five weeks later when she realized, to her horror, that she'd actually gotten herself pregnant, got wild-ass drunk, and wrapped her Toyota around a tree. She'd had to get five glass shards removed from her head and eight stiches. But Olive, little trouper that she was, had hung on. Then, not two days later, Papa Alan was diagnosed with Parkinson's. That's what really did it. She'd panicked. They'd all panicked. And suddenly going ahead with a child seemed the only sane thing for her to do: grow the family, give her dads a grandchild, give her own life meaning. So much of that time was a blur now, how she'd shut the door on partying, gotten her shit together, chosen not to tell the father. She'd been so naive, thinking having a child would force her to grow up, that all she had to do was stay one step ahead of the baby. What a joke. Olive had pushed into the world two weeks early. Zeddi was still trying to catch up.

Something rustled in the bush at the end of the driveway. Zeddi prayed it wasn't the skunk she'd seen the night before. Last thing she needed was to get sprayed. She held her breath until whatever it was took off.

Olive's head poked out the side door of the van. "Mom?"

"Oh, honey." Zeddi set down the ukulele. "Did I wake you?"

"Nooo," Olive said, drawing out the vowel in sleepy annoyance.

"Shh," Zeddi whispered. "We don't want to wake the neighbors. What's up? Do you have to pee?"

"I can't stop thinking about Barnaby."

Zeddi rose from the chair. "Honey, he's fine. We left him some food. Cats aren't like dogs. They know how to take care of themselves."

"But Mags told me he sleeps with her. He's probably wondering where she is."

"Well, he probably is."

"Can we go check on him?"

"Now? Sweetie, it's late, and a school night."

"I know, but…"

"How about I come in there with you, and we go to sleep. In the morning, we can go check on him, together. Before I take you to school."

"Okay." Olive yawned. "I just can't figure out why he was out…" She yawned again, a big shuddering one, then disappeared back inside the van.

Inside the van, Zeddi hung up the ukulele, stripped out of her hoodie and jeans, stuck them in the cubby over the driver's seat, and climbed between the two captain's chairs to the bed, where she crawled in beside Olive, who lay curled under a pile of blankets in her favorite glow-in-the-dark skeleton pajamas. She flicked off the foldable solar light and wrapped an arm around her small, warm girl. "Everything's going to be okay," she whispered into the curl of her ear. "You'll see. I'm looking at a place tomorrow."

Olive snuggled up next to her. "I know."

Outside the rain returned, pinging the roof of the van.

"You still like Tres Ojos?"

"Yeah. But I sure hope we find a place soon."

Zeddi reached up to the curtain by Olive's head and tugged it shut. "We will. You'll see."

Olive dropped off quickly, leaving Zeddi alone with the light drumbeat of rain.

Turtle's engine light had flashed on earlier in the day. Who knew what that was going to cost? And where were they going to stay while it got fixed? Zeddi rolled onto her back, tried not to think about the people living in tents down the river from Mags'. The sprawl even had a name. Last Stop Camp, they called it.

CHAPTER FIVE

L unch money? Homework?"

Olive nodded. "Affirmative." She was in a mood.

So was Zeddi.

Neither had slept well. The rubber seal around the van's windshield had sprung a small leak around three a.m. and now they were running late. Zeddi banged the van door shut and walked around to the driver's side. She hated driving around with an unmade bed. It seemed so irresponsible.

"Are you nervous about your oral report?"

"No."

It took a few tries and a concentrated prayer to get Turtle's engine to fire. The logistics of taking Turtle in, the repair costs, made her brain hurt. "I think I should just take you to school so you're not late. Then I'll go feed Barnaby."

"You said I could go! You promised!"

Ten Mississippi, nine Mississippi, eight Mississippi... "Okay. But we need to make it quick." Zeddi backed around Dan's old Lincoln parked on the street. "This is the Harriet Tubman report, right?"

"You already know, so why are you asking me?"

Because she couldn't very well ask *Have you made any friends yet?* which was what she wanted to ask. Olive killed academically. Always had. Friends were another story. As far as Zeddi could tell, Olive hadn't made a single one since arriving in Tres Ojos. It was starting to feel like a rerun of her school in Sacramento, where, at a parent/teacher night, she'd been informed that Olive grew impatient with the other students.

"I'll pick you up today. Hopefully, I'll be done by three. If not, I'll bring you back to the Donaldsons' and you can do your homework there while I finish up. Sound good?"

"I guess."

"I know it's not perfect but—"

"It's o-kaaay." Turning her back to Zeddi, Olive flattened her nose and mouth against the passenger window.

"Olive, that's just plain gross." She was clenching her jaw again. "How about next week, when I have a little time, we get you signed up at the Boys and Girls Club?"

"What, so I can get involved in afterschool programs that promote good character, academic success, and personal responsibility?"

"You read the website."

Olive went back to smashing her face against the window.

"Olive, hanging out with kids your own age doesn't have to be awful."

"And you would know that, how?"

"Hey, I was a kid once."

"Yeah, that was a long, long, looong time ago. Things have changed."

Zeddi laughed. "Okay, well, we'll think of something. But for now, count on me picking you up."

"Bet."

Zeddi's phone buzzed. She tossed it into Olive's lap. "Check that for me? Would you?"

"Caller unknown."

"In other words, robocall."

"I don't get why you won't let me ride my bike. Then I could just go to Dan's after school. He's fine with it."

Zeddi pulled alongside the slim grassy patch in front of Mags' trailer and left the engine running. "We'll talk about this later. For now, let's check on Barnaby and get you to school."

Olive hopped out of the van and charged up the two steps to the trailer door.

Zeddi followed. Knocked.

"Just use the key," Olive said.

"We don't know for sure no one's here. A family member could have shown up."

"No car."

Zeddi knocked again.

"I told you," Olive said. "No one's here."

Zeddi pulled the mermaid key fob from her jeans pocket. "Would it kill you to be nice to me?"

Olive bounced up and down on her toes. "Come on! Come on! He's probably starving."

"It's been one night, Olive. One. He's not starving."

"You don't know that."

The lock was finicky, but Mags had shown her how to wiggle the key around until it engaged. She cracked the door and called out, "Hello? Hello?"

"Mom, there's no one here."

"Olive—"

"What?" Olive pushed past her into the trailer. "Baaarnaby! Baaarnaby!"

"It's okay, neighbors," Zeddi said over her shoulder, "we're just feeding the cat." She shut the door behind them. But something was off. A smell. That was it. Not a bad smell, a different smell, a smell that hadn't been there the day before. Cologne? Scented hair product? Had someone else been there? Were she and Olive trespassing?

A loud yowl came from the back of the trailer. Olive raced toward it. Zeddi glanced at the counter where she'd left the note the day before. It was still there. Maybe the unidentified caller in the van had been next of kin? She jotted: *Thursday AM, came to check on Barnaby*. She underlined her phone number.

"Found him!" Olive shouted.

"Oh yeah? Where?"

"Under the bed, way back in the corner!"

Zeddi walked down the narrow hallway to the bedroom, pausing to peer into the bathroom on the left, the small office on the right. *Wait.* There were fresh footprints in the plush, green office carpet.

It was the only carpet in the house where she could get that just-vacuumed effect. It was newer than the rest of the carpet, so she always made a point to back her way out, erasing even her own footprints, leaving the nap unblemished as fresh snow. It was that extra touch that made clients feel the love, like folding the top sheet on a roll of toilet paper into a point, or wiping down the chrome sink fixtures with glass cleaner. The footprints went straight to the desk and back. Someone had been there. Someone with big feet. She backed into the hallway. "Olive? How's it going?"

"He won't come out. He's like way back there."

"Get some dry food from the kitchen. See if you can persuade him."

"He seems kind of freaked out."

Zeddi walked back to the living room and scanned for other clues that someone had been there. The rain started up again. *Crap.* "I'm going to check on the windshield," she called out to Olive. "But we need to get a move on."

Olive came into the kitchen and scooped dry food into Barnaby's bowl. "I'm going to take some back. See if I can get him to come out." She said it as if Zeddi hadn't just suggested it.

"Okay. But please be quick about it."

Outside, Zeddi paused under the trailer's overhang. It was the kind of day that Papa Alan used to take her rainbow hunting, sunny and rainy at the same time. They'd jump in as many puddles as they could find. Her dads had been such good parents...

"Excuse me," a woman's voice called out. "You're the cleaning lady, right? The one who found her?" The woman wore a sporty Barbie-pink tracksuit and stood under the awning of the trailer next door. Her blond hair was pulled into a tight ponytail, and she was aerobics-instructor fit. "I'm sorry. I didn't mean to startle you. I was just stepping out to see if I could get my run in any time soon."

"Um, yeah," Zeddi replied too defensively. "My daughter and I were just coming by to check on her cat. She's in there now, feeding him. We weren't sure if anyone else would come by."

The woman crossed her arms in front of her chest. Shifted her weight from one foot to the other. "It's such a shame, her dying like that. She seemed like such a nice person. And to go so quickly after her sister! I hope she had all her affairs in order."

The woman wasn't the El Rio trailer park type. Not nearly eccentric enough, and her exercise wear looked designer. The Lexus in the driveway was wrong too. People in the park drove beater cars or fantastic art cars. "I didn't know she had a sister," Zeddi said. "I mean, like I said, I didn't know her all that well. She's kind of a new friend."

The woman trotted over. "I don't live here either. I'm just staying with my son, Jeff—er, Dante. Helping him"—she smiled a tight smile—"get back on track." She held out a hand with clean, short, French-tipped nails. "I'm Lorna Doyle. And I didn't know her at all. Not really."

Zeddi took her hand. "Zeddi Osborne. Nice to meet you." What was taking Olive so long?

"I asked about her affairs because Mags was so frustrated by her sister's. Apparently, they were a mess. She talked to me about her at length about a week ago. It was kind of odd actually. She was on the way to her lawyer to get her own affairs in order—"

"Unlike her sister."

"Right, but she went on and on about her sister's death, about it not sitting right or something. I'm not going to say she sounded paranoid, but to talk to me, a stranger really, about her concerns, it was odd. That's all."

"Doesn't really sound like the Mags I know," Zeddi offered. "To be paranoid."

"It doesn't?"

"Not really. No." Zeddi glanced over her shoulder. "Is that it? Because I really do have to go. I mean, once we finish feeding the cat."

"Of course. I didn't mean to take up your time. It's just—"

"It's fine. We're just running a little late. And look, the rain is letting up, you can go for your run."

Lorna chuckled awkwardly. "I hope I haven't overstepped. I just don't really know anybody down here. As I said—"

"You're just visiting your son. I get it. And I'm just the cleaning lady. And now I really do have to round up my daughter."

"Oh, I'm sorry if I—"

"Seriously, think nothing of it." Zeddi's phone buzzed in her hoodie pocket. She pulled it out. Same number as before. "Um, do you mind?"

"No. No. Go ahead. And, ah, nice to meet you. Maybe I'll see you around?"

"You never know." Maybe she'd need her son's place cleaned.

Zeddi watched as Lorna trotted off down the one-way access road, then checked her phone. A voicemail notification.

"Mom!" Olive said, sticking her head out the door. "I got him to come out."

"Great!"

"I poured him some cream too. I hope that's okay. It was in the fridge. Mags gives it to him sometimes for a treat."

Olive referring to Mags in present tense was worrisome. "I'm sure it's fine. Now we really do need to go."

Olive disappeared back into the trailer to say goodbye to Barnaby.

Zeddi read the voicemail's transcript. A lawyer, Ari Miller, asking her to contact him immediately. What could that be about? "Check the windshield, would you? See if the paper towel needs changing."

Back in the van, Olive rested her wet feet on the dash. "We're going to check on Barnaby later, right? Until we know who's responsible?"

Responsible. The word held such weight. "We'll see."

CHAPTER SIX

Turtle all but drove itself to Zeddi's favorite coffee shop where Zeddi managed to wrangle from her caffeine-deprived brain the words, "Large house blend to go, please." She added a single splash of half and half to the paper cup, stirred it, lidded it, then exited the coffee shop. After giving Turtle a few grateful pats for once again coughing to life, she headed to Dan's. Her bottles needed topping off, her rags changing out, and Dan had graciously let her store her supplies in the corner of his cobwebby garage.

Minutes later, she sat on an overturned, empty five-gallon paint bucket crammed between the back bumper of Dan's semi-restored '66 Camaro and her half dozen gallon bottles of cleaning solution. Why would a lawyer be calling her? It wasn't illegal to live in a van with a child, was it? She googled Ari Miller's website. Saw that he specialized in custody cases. She dropped her head into her hands, silent screamed. No! She'd been so careful. Only a couple of her besties knew who the father was, and the only reason they knew was because she hadn't planned to keep the baby at first.

Stomach in knots, she began refilling her solution bottles, trading out the old sponges in her caddy for new ones, sorting through her rag box, sorting her thoughts. She'd feared this for so long.

The task calmed her. Gave her time to talk herself down. By the time she was done, she'd almost convinced herself it was a wrong number.

As she stood, she noticed her jeans were fitting loosely. There was something positive to focus on. The unexpected perk to living without a refrigerator. Not that she wanted to be super thin. She liked her body, her curves, and she was strong, had meat on her bones, enjoyed food. So unlike the woman she'd met earlier, outside of Mags', Lorna Doyle, who probably ran to burn off her morning celery juice. Lorna calling Mags paranoid was such crap. Mags was so not paranoid. Mags was alert, intelligent, open, friendly, and most of all transparent. Not some old biddy peering out of the blinds every time a car door slammed. She pictured Mags on her red cruiser pedaling along the riverside bike path, the handlebar-basket woven through with plastic flowers, and realized she was smiling.

She mopped up a bit of spilled cleaner with a rag. Thought about the footprints in the office carpet. Should she be worried? No. The trailer belonged to someone else now. Why wouldn't they do a walkthrough? And why was she even being drawn into the trailer park drama? She was just the housecleaner! In point of fact, she wasn't even that anymore. But that was housecleaning for you: a practice in civil inattention. You pretended you didn't hear the whispered phone calls, or see the evidence of binge-eating at the bottom of the trash, or the hidden coffee can of cigarette butts in the garage. Then one day the job was over, and the lives you'd vicariously come to know were out of your life. For good.

Still. Something about the footprints bothered her.

As she loaded up her caddy, furniture oil dribbled onto her sneaker. She hastily tried to wipe it off, but it was too late, the oil had left an ugly stain right by one of Olive's lightning bolts. Shit! Blinking back tears, she leaned against the Camaro. Took a few centering breaths. Just because it felt like everything was going wrong didn't mean it was. There was still that rustic, charming apartment to look at. Maybe that would bring some good news. She took the black and white kerchief from her caddy and tied it around her head, Rosie the Riveter–style. The kerchief didn't anchor under her ponytail like it used to, but she was glad she'd cut her hair. It had turned out surprisingly well considering she'd just tipped her head upside down and had Olive lop the ponytail off. It had even gotten curlier and seemed somehow bluer. Looked good with the flamingo rubber gloves too. Hard luck, she felt, was no excuse for lack of style.

Her phone buzzed. Now what? She checked the readout. Another unidentified number. Thankfully, not the lawyer's. She let it go to voicemail. *Hello. My name is Ida. I'm a friend of Mags'. Please call me*. It was probably about cleaning. Mags recommended her a lot. Or had. She hit call back, then realized that this Ida might not know Mags was dead. Damn.

"Hello?"

"Um. Hello. You just called me? You said you're a friend of Mags'?"

"Yes." Ida sounded old. "Thank you for calling me back so quickly."

"Sure…um…I'm not sure if you know this or not, but Mags died yesterday."

There was a long silence before the old woman responded. "I'm well aware, thank you. It's actually the reason for my call. It's my understanding that you're the one who found her?"

"Yes, I am."

"I have a few questions about *how* you found her."

Zeddi glanced at the time. "Of course."

"I am…we were…close," Ida sputtered, followed by the sound of her blowing her nose. "I'm sorry. I just can't get used to…it's just so…I'm sorry. Let me pull myself togeth—Claude! Please! Not now!"

"I'm sorry, what?"

"I apologize. I was talking to my brother, he was…never mind. It's not important, it—Claude! Did you hear me?"

Zeddi waited a few seconds before saying tentatively, "I'm really sorry for your loss, Mags was a—"

Ida cut her off. "My questions have to do with how you found her, if she—Claude! Please. Stop! The raven has had plenty to eat today. Oh, this is hopeless. Is there any chance we could speak in person? Say, later today? Or tomorrow? It's important."

Raven? "I'm pretty busy today."

Papa Glen was calling. She shot him a text saying she'd call him back. He shot back that it was important.

"Tomorrow then?" Ida asked.

"Are you in town?"

"Whalers Point."

Zeddi had only been to Whalers Point once before when she and Olive had driven up the coast to check out a possible rental. *No children! No pets!* the ad had read, but she'd tried anyway. The drive alone had been worth it, ten miles of oceanside fields filled with pumpkins. She'd promised Olive they'd return closer to Halloween to get a jack-o'-lantern. Maybe she could kill two birds with one stone. "I won't be able to get there until late afternoon."

"Three o'clock?"

"We'll shoot for that. I'll have my daughter with me."

"Olive. Yes, of course. That's fine. I'll put us together a snack."

She knew Olive?

Ida gave her the address.

"By the way, my name is Zeddi."

"Yes, I know. Mags spoke of you and Olive often."

A lump settled in Zeddi's throat. "Okay. See you tomorrow."

"Oh, and if for some reason Claude answers the door, don't be put off. He's big but he's harmless."

"Good to know." It didn't occur to Zeddi until after she'd hung up that Turtle might not even make it to Whalers Point, but she'd cross that hurdle when she got there, just like she'd cross the hurdle of big and harmless Claude, and a hungry raven, and this inquisitive woman, Ida. Trust. She had to trust. She took a deep breath.

Next up, Papa Glen's call.

She prayed it wasn't anything urgent, that Papa Alan hadn't taken another fall. Papa Alan insisted the falls had nothing to do with his Parkinson's, but of course they did. Papa Alan wasn't a falling kind of guy. Thankfully, he hadn't broken anything. Yet. She wished that they hadn't moved so far away, but Yucca Valley's desert climate was supposedly good for Papa Alan's health, and Papa Glen was having a blast with his gay gardening club and Stonewall Golfers.

"That was quick," Papa Glen said when she called back.

"You said it was important. What's up? Is Papa Alan okay?"

"He's fine. Well, he's not happy with the medication they've got him on. Says it makes his mush-mouth worse. And he keeps getting these dizzy spells—though he denies it. But he hasn't fallen again, thank God. We've got an appointment this afternoon. Everything okay with you, kiddo?"

It sounded like he was cooking. Now that he finally had the open kitchen and granite countertops he'd dreamed of for years, he was constantly trying out new recipes. She pictured him in his blue denim Men at Work apron.

"Um. Yeah," she said, guardedly. "We're pretty good. I was just about to head off to work. Olive's at school."

"Is the new school working out better?"

"Yeah. The school is great, a much better fit." *If only.* "Of course, she's still finding her way." Before he had a chance to ask about the housing situation, which she'd led them to believe was a bit more legit, she added, "And her teacher is great. So, tell me. What's up?"

"We got a call I thought you should know about."

"Oh yeah?"

"A lawyer. He's trying to reach you."

Papa Alan shouted, "Tell Olive the condo pool is up and working again!" It sounded like he was just passing through. He'd never been big on phone calls, but since being diagnosed, he'd gotten even worse. He'd gone into overdrive with his projects, especially the weaving. In the past year he'd made Zeddi four shawls. She didn't even wear shawls.

"What did this lawyer say he wanted?"

"He wouldn't say. Just that he needed to get ahold of you. And that it was important. Is everything okay?"

"Yeah, um…he called me too. I was just about to call him back when I got your text. I'm not sure what he wants."

"Will you keep us posted? We're here for you, you know that."

"Sure. It's probably just a mix-up. But I'll let you know."

"Okay, well, we love you, kiddo. Call if you need anything. And call when you know something. Really, Zeddi."

Did he know they were homeless? Had he somehow figured it out? Had Olive let it slip?

"Stop badgering our daughter!" Papa Alan piped in.

"Okay, okay!" Papa Glen said. "Kiss, kiss, Zed. Love you!"

"Love you!" Papa Alan called.

Now she really *had* to call the lawyer. Papa Glen wouldn't rest until she did. But what could he possibly want? Did child protective services send out lawyers? She shook out her shoulders, jumped up and down a couple of times, dropped back onto the paint bucket, went to recent calls, hit call back.

A perky female voice greeted her. "Ari Miller, attorney at law. How may I help you?"

"My name is Zeddi Osborne. I'm returning your call."

"Hmm. Okay. Let me just see if Ari is available."

Zeddi pressed down on her knee to keep it from bouncing.

"This is Ari Miller," a man said.

And? Zeddi made herself speak. "Hi, I'm—"

"Zeddi Osborne. Yes, I know. And you're calling in regard to Margaret McKenzie's recent death."

Margaret McKenzie? Who...? "Oh, you mean Mags?"

"Yes, Mags. Condolences, by the way. I understand that you two were close."

"Kind of. I mean, you know I'm just her cleaning lady, right?"

"Well, I'd say you're more than that because you're also the beneficiary of the bulk of her estate."

CHAPTER SEVEN

From the looks of it, Ari Miller had scored the best real estate in the converted Victorian. Second floor with a stellar view of downtown, his office was airy, light, and oh-so-tasteful. Zeddi, feeling a churned-up cocktail of relief and shock, took it all in from one of two sling-back leather guest chairs facing the desk. To her left was a blown-up photo of a younger Ari mountain biking through a gorgeous red-rock canyon, to her right a wall of diplomas and awards. The man himself sat before her behind a glass-topped desk, his copper hair showing signs of gray, his skin not as ruddy. He was clearly enjoying himself. His chinstrap beard, fully gray, stretched into an expansive grin, his two bottom front teeth slightly overlapped. "You seem surprised."

Zeddi peeled off her hoodie. Was the place warm or was it the sudden adrenaline rush? "Could you just say it one more time, please?"

"Mags left her trailer and everything in it to you."

She wadded up the hoodie "Wow." Set it in her lap. "Not that I'm complaining. I just don't understand. I mean, I'm just her housecleaner. I mean, we were friends too, but I haven't known her that long. I mean…well, I don't know what I mean. And don't get me wrong, I'm thrilled, this comes at a really good time. I'm just shocked."

He cocked his head. Drew his eyebrows together. "She must have felt you deserved it." The crow's feet put him at least ten years older than her, but the guy radiated youth, health. He wore his shirt sleeves rolled up, his graying reddish hair gelled back, pricey watch on his tan wrist. "This really comes as a total shock?"

"Total."

"Interesting. It was my understanding that she was going to tell you in person."

"Well, she did try to talk to me, but I...I...canceled on her. I...uh...my daughter was sick and I...uh..." Why why why hadn't she gone over anyway? But at the same time, she was getting a house! A place to live. A home. Her home. That she *owned*. It was unbelievable. Bizarre. Fantastic. If only she could thank the person responsible. Or ask her why. She rested her hands on her chest to slow her heart. Wiped at her eyes.

Ari handed her a tissue. "I understand that your daughter and Mags were close."

Zeddi blew her nose. "They were. Olive got mixed up one day after school and went to Mags' instead of meeting me at the corner. She thought it was my day to clean there. By the time I figured out where she was, the two were dissecting owl pellets." She daubed her eyes. "They shared an appreciation for that kind of thing."

"Sounds like Mags."

"You knew her? I mean, of course you knew her. But besides being her lawyer?"

Her mind was whirring so fast, it was a miracle she could catch any single thought, let alone turn it into words. The El Rio was such a cool trailer park: resident owned, a nonprofit. And there was this anything goes feel to it. People squeezed tiny vegetable gardens into every available dirt plot, painted their trailers in wild colors, installed creative add-ons—and there was art everywhere: sculptures, murals, tacky yard art. She loved all of it. Had from the first time she'd driven in. And now it was going to be her home, her and Olive's home, their neighborhood. It was unbelievable! Unbelievably good. It was such a great location. Butted up to the river levee, the park was an easy walk to downtown *and* to Olive's school. And they wouldn't be renting. No one could ever kick them out—unless she didn't make payments. Were there payments? No, Ari had said, it was paid off. She'd just be responsible for upkeep and yearly taxes. But why had Mags left it to them? Why? She couldn't wait to tell Olive. And Dan. Her dads. They were going to be thrilled. And Sylvie. Maybe she could invite her down? Maybe they could pick up where they left off. Maybe...but wait, Ari was talking. She should be listening.

"...so yeah," he said, coming to the end of whatever it was he was saying. "I guess you could say I knew her. And yeah, her giving you this house is just like her. But then, you know how impulsive she is. *Was*."

Did she? Not really. But then, she knew so little about Mags—besides her being incredibly generous. But if Ari said Mags was impulsive, so be it. It was certainly an impulsiveness that worked in her favor.

"My mom always said Mags was like a tornado," he said. "You never knew where she was going to land."

"Wait. Your mom knew her too?"

"I just said that."

"Right. Don't mind me. I'm just kind of..." Zeddi twirled her fingers at her temples.

"I'm sure. But I think you know my mom too. Roni Miller?"

Zeddi forced her brain to think. "You're Roni's son?"

"Guilty as charged." He laughed.

She gave him a closer look. Sure enough, he was an older version of the boy in the photo she dusted on Thursdays. "Small world," she said. There was a dad in the photo too. Jace? Was that his name? She'd never met him. Just knew his bedside stack of science fiction novels, the shaving cream and soap scum in his sink. But why was she even thinking about soap scum? She could move out of the driveway! Out of the van! She shoved the crumpled tissue into her jeans pocket. "So, how does this work? There must be papers I need to sign..."

"For now, I'll take care of all that."

"Okay. Thank you. And um..." How to ask? "How long will it all take? I don't mean to sound pushy. It's just..."

He held up a hand. "Mags told me a little about your situation. I feel confident she'd want you to move in as soon as is convenient. It will take a while longer to get all the paperwork in order. But as her lawyer, and friend, I say the place is yours. It seems highly unlikely anyone will contest the will. There was only one other beneficiary, and she won't be a problem. She received a good sum of money."

"Are you sure?"

"Trust me. I know all the parties involved. Mags was like a second mother to me."

"Wow...this is just...I can't..."

"Do you have a key?"

"I do."

"Well, there's another one in here." He handed her a manila envelope. "Go through it at your leisure. You'll find her car registration, some insurance papers, and some other stuff."

"I get her car too?"

He leaned back in his chair, cradled his head in his hands. "Yup. Free and clear."

"So, um, there's no next of kin?" No one who might be leaving footprints in Mags' office?

"There was her sister…"

"Right, but she died recently?"

"Exactly."

"So no one else? I mean, I guess I'm just wondering…I mean, did she tell you why she was leaving it to me?"

"As I said, she was very taken with you and your daughter."

"Well, we loved her. She was good to us. It's just…" Whose were those footprints? Did someone else have a key? Maybe she should get the locks changed. She *should* get the locks changed. She glanced at her phone. Ten forty-five. Still two houses to clean. No. She'd reschedule. Inheriting a home was reason to take a day off. But wait, he was looking at her, waiting for her to finish her sentence. Only what was it? What had she been saying? "Sorry. I'm just feeling a little overwhelmed. So that's it? We're done? I can move in today?"

"Pretty much. At least for now."

"Wow." She stood. "I guess you never really know."

❖

Back in the van, Zeddi sank into the seat, stunned. "Thank you, Mags," she said out loud. "I don't exactly understand how we deserved this. But thank you."

It took a few tries to get the van to start, but once it did, she headed straight for the trailer, her mind loop-de-looping with the logistics of it suddenly being moving day. She and Olive would have to share Mags' bedroom at first, and Mags' bed. She'd look for a fresh pair of sheets. It would be too weird to sleep in sheets that Mags had slept in. She could bring their sheets in from the van if need be. That would work. Or she could swing by Ross and buy a new pair. That would work too—now that she didn't need to put away every cent for first, last, and deposit. Now that she had a cushion of money. Hell, they were rich! Were going to get their own rooms! Not right away, of course. They'd have to clear out Mags' office. But once that was finished, they could take a day trip to Sacramento and get their stuff out of storage. She'd have to rent a U-Haul. Maybe she'd keep Mags' cool sleigh bed. Leave her old crappy bed in Sacramento.

She jammed on the brakes. Stop sign. Must stop. Must calm down. Stay focused. But there was no calming down. Her emotions were slamming around inside her like a team of roller derby girls.

Turning into the trailer park, she experienced a moment of panic. What if there'd been a mistake? What if the trailer wasn't really hers? What if— She cut the thought short. The trailer was theirs. The lawyer said so.

She blocked Mags' ancient orange Audi in the carport. Only now it was *her* ancient orange Audi. Was it manual or automatic? She had no idea. But it couldn't have come at a better time. Approaching the trailer door, she flashed on soldiers she'd seen in movies: so desperate they'd annex the boots of the dead. But this was *given* to them. They were *not* scavengers.

She used the key the lawyer had given her. Like the mermaid key, she had to wiggle it before the tumblers engaged, then *click.* She took a breath, sent out another silent thank you to Mags, then opened the door to her new home.

Barnaby welcomed her with one long yowl. Whatever had spooked the fat orange cat earlier was obviously forgotten. His mind was on Greenies, the crack-like dental pellets Mags gave him every time she got home. He was a Greenie addict, expecting to be rewarded with each accomplishment—including getting up off the couch to stretch, purring, and greeting Mags at the door. Zeddi bent down to give him a few pats, stroked his fluffy tail. "Hey, buddy, you okay? You missing Mags?" She hadn't thought about inheriting him too, but here he was. Olive would be thrilled.

He circled her ankles, purred. She got him a Greenie from the Greenie jar. "I know, I know," she said. "I miss her too. But we'll take good care of you." She shrugged off her hoodie. Made herself set the hoodie on the green chair where she'd found Mags. If she was going to live in this trailer, she was going to have to make peace with the fact that Mags had died in it. She headed straightaway down the hall to the office, to the footprints. A part of her hoped they wouldn't be there, that she'd imagined them. But there they were. Heading from the hall to the desk, then back out to the hall. They were intentional steps. Someone knew just what they were looking for. *Ari?* He had a key and might have had reason to get something from Mags' desk. She should have asked him. Or looked at his feet.

She scanned the room. Was anything missing? How would she know? She opened the top desk drawer. Pencils, pens, some old sunglasses, Post-its, the usual. The contents of the other two drawers were equally mundane. But whoever it was could have gone through the whole house. The older, worn carpet would never tell. She walked slowly down the hall, looking for another sign that someone had been there.

Mags' hemp backpack purse on the dresser looked undisturbed. Was it? There was no way to know without looking inside. It felt like such a violation. Then again, technically, Mags' hemp backpack purse was now her hemp backpack purse. Right. She unzipped it, pulled out Mags' wallet. Credit cards, ID, eighty-six dollars cash, a small, crinkled headshot of a woman. *Who?* She studied the two-by-three. *Her sister? A friend? A lover?* Mags never talked much about her personal life. Her cell phone was there too. Probably not a robbery, then. There was no sign of a break-in. Whoever it was had a key and probably had reason to be there. She returned to the office and scuffed out the footprints. Weeks of living in the van had made her jumpy, that was all.

She called Dan. He answered with a gruff, "Yeah?"

"Hey," she said. "I have a favor."

"Zeddi, do you know what time it is?"

"I do." Dan never rose before noon, except for Dance Church on Sunday mornings. "It's just...I've inherited this trailer..."

"Wait. What?"

"I know, right? But I've just come from the lawyer's, and apparently I've inherited the trailer of the woman who died yesterday. The one we told you about. Anyway, I want to sleep here tonight but I think someone else has the key. Do you know a good locksmith?"

"Well, hell. That's crazy."

"I know. I'm in total shock."

"And you knew nothing about this?"

"Nothing."

"Wow. This is big news. Where is this trailer, if I may ask?"

"The El Rio Mobile Home Park."

"Seriously? You scored a trailer at the Rio?"

"I guess. I mean, yes, I did. I'm here now. I—"

"I'm coming over," he said. "This, I gotta see. And I'll bring my tools and change out those locks."

"Thank you! Dinner's on me tonight. I'll cook—in our new home!" Now she *had* to reschedule her clients. Good. Who could focus on cleaning when they'd just inherited a home? She opened a kitchen cabinet: lentils, rice, tomato sauce, pasta. On the counter: a loaf of bakery-baked bread. In the fridge: eggs, broccoli, almond milk. Pawing through Mags' life felt so wrong. At the same time, what a blessing. Not only did she have a new home, she had a kitchen full of food.

"Give me thirty minutes," he said.

"Coffee upon your arrival," she said.

After hanging up, she did another walk-through, Barnaby trailing behind. Something just didn't feel right. Was it that Mags had died so suddenly? Or was something else stirring up the energy? The long-legged spider by the wood burning stove was back, the one that Olive said spun when you touched it.

She touched it. Sure enough, it spun.

CHAPTER EIGHT

Nice place." Dan stood in the doorway, tool bucket in hand, signature amber-lensed aviator sunglasses shielding his eyes from the sun that had finally broken through and was now flooding the living room.

"You need me to close the blinds?" Would the ancient blinds on the sliding glass door even close?

"It's cool. I'll keep my shades on." He set his tool bucket next to Mags' overcrowded hat rack. "You said there'd be coffee?"

"Just made a pot."

He wandered into the center of the living room, did a three-sixty. "Man, you didn't just inherit a trailer, you inherited a *life*."

"I know, right?"

"You really scored, Zed."

"You make it sound like I did something to get this."

"You must have. People don't just give people trailers."

"I'm as surprised as anyone."

She picked out one of Mags' hand-thrown pottery mugs from the shelf, filled it with coffee she'd made in Mags' Chemex, joined him in Mags' living room.

"Am I drinking the coffee of a dead woman?"

"Dan!"

"Just asking."

"Not that it should matter, but no, it's mine. I brought it in from the van."

He took a sip. "Italian?"

"You know your coffee."

He strolled over to Mags' crows. "She's the artist, I take it. The one you've talked about."

"Yeah."

"I like. Her color choices are psychedelic." He stepped in for a closer look, stepped back for the long view. "She sure doesn't skimp on paint. Looks like she trowels it on." He did an about-face and looked out at the garden. "Also, a grower of herbs, I see."

"Not the kind you like."

"Hey, I like *all* herbs. Just some a little more than others."

"I suppose you know what all these are?"

"I do as a matter of fact. That's sage. Over there is oregano. And that is some kind of…thyme, I think. Looks like she has some lemon balm too."

"Your knowledge never fails to astonish."

"Thank you. I make a point of astonishing people. So, you going to give me the tour?"

"It'll take about three seconds."

"How many bedrooms?"

"Two. She used one as an office-slash-art studio. Ultimately, it will be Olive's room."

"Speaking of the little sprite, does she know of this sudden windfall?"

"Not yet. She's in school."

"School? Zeddi! You need to bust her out. This is a big day for you two."

"I thought about it, but she's got that oral report today."

"Oh, yeah. Harriet Tubman. She practiced it on me. It was a little fact-centric. I told her to add a few jokes."

"What possible jokes are there to be made about Harriet Tubman?"

He scanned the books on Mags' bookshelf. "I was trying to get her to think of her report as more than just spewing facts."

Zeddi checked the Kit Cat clock. If she left soon, she could hit recess. "You're right. I should get her. But let me show you the place first."

She stopped at each point of interest. Stacked washer and dryer complete with laundry basket and almost-full bottle of detergent. Small bathroom with herbal bar soaps and fancy shower nozzle. Office with ancient computer, bookshelf of art supplies, easel, and closet full of mystery boxes. Master bedroom with antique double sleigh bed and yet another bathroom with yet another basket of delicious smelling herbal soaps, plus a full closet of clean towels—and a *bathtub*. All of it, curiously, now hers. Back in the living room, she said, "I keep waiting for the other shoe to drop."

He settled onto a barstool at the counter separating the kitchen from the living room. "It's gravy for sure." He drained his coffee. Set his cup on the counter. "So, tell me about this lock sitch."

She told him about the footprints too, and about her phone call with Ida.

He picked up the small brass Chinese Fu dog sitting by the salt and pepper shakers. Turned it around in his callused hand. "You want someone to come with you tomorrow when you talk to this Ida and her *harmless* brother Claude?"

"No...she sounded all right. But the locks—"

"Not to worry. I'll check the windows too."

"Thanks. Okay then, I'm going to go get Olive, or at least pull her out of class long enough to tell her. Make yourself at home. There's more coffee if you want it."

"You know," he said, placing the Fu dog back on the counter, "I'm going to miss you two."

What? Dan never said stuff like that. "No, you're not."

"I am." He shrugged. "I'd gotten kind of used to having you around."

She set her hands on his shoulders. Looked him in the eye. "We're not going to give you a chance to miss us. Now that Mags is...gone, you're the only real friend we have in Tres Ojos."

The corner of his mouth raised slightly.

❖

Zeddi peered through the partially open classroom door. It was excruciating to watch. Olive spat out her oral report on Harriet Tubman like a machine gun unloading bullets: fact after fact after fact with barely a breath between. The kids looked completely bored. "In conclusion," Olive said, fingering the single three-by-five card she was allowed,

"Harriet Tubman was a real heroine. The kind you could really get addicted to!" Only one person got the joke and she laughed hysterically, which prompted Miss Marks to look up from sorting papers and clap. "Thank you, Olive! That was wonderful!" The bell rang, and the kids shot from their seats. "We'll do the rest of the reports after recess."

Zeddi searched for Olive in the gaggle of recently freed children swarming out the door. Spotted her. "Olive!"

Olive spun around. "What are you doing here?"

Momentarily tongue-tied by the realization that she'd interrupted her daughter in the middle of a seemingly successful conversation with another little girl—*a friend? Was it possible Olive had actually made a friend?*—she asked, "How did your report go, sweetie?" But she could not take her eyes off the girl next to Olive. Each of her nails was painted a different neon color, while her vest was decorated in buttons and rick rack and peace signs. She was adorable.

"It went great!" the girl said. "Especially that part about a heroine you could get addicted to!"

The girls high fived.

Zeddi thrust out a hand. "Hi. I'm Olive's mom. What's your name?"

The girl was small for her age but had a confident handshake and made direct eye contact. "My name is Isabella Grrraciela Mendez." She excessively rolled her *r*. "Daughter of Luciana Camila Mendez, a physician's assistant with an eagle eye, and Santiago Alejandrrro Mendez, a man who can get you the best car loan ever!"

"She's an aspiring actress," Olive explained. "But until she's discovered—"

"—she'll write her own parts!" the girls chimed together, then broke into giggles.

"Nice to meet you, Isabella Grrraciela Mendez. My name is Zeddi Claire Osborrrne, mother of Olive Arrriana Osborrrne, as well as being…" And then, she couldn't help herself, she drummed her hands on her thighs. "Wait for it…Wait for it…" She flung her arms wide. "Recent HOMEOWNER!"

Olive stepped back. "What?"

"Big news, Olive. Can I talk to you for a sec?"

Olive glanced at Isabella.

"It's cool," Isabella said. "I need to get my snack out of my cubby."

"Healthful apples and delicious cheese sticks!" the girls chimed together, prompting another round of giggles.

Once Isabella was out of earshot, Zeddi broke the news.

"You mean, it's *ours* ours?" Olive asked. "Like, forever ours?"

"*Ours* ours for as long as we want it. I was going to spring you out of school early so we could celebrate. Dan's already over there, helping to fix a few things up. But if you want to stay…"

Olive adjusted her glasses while deciding. "Just more oral reports, and Isabella already did hers. I'll come. But I need to get my books out of my cubby. And I have to tell Isabella something. We were going to…" But she was already bouncing out of earshot.

A friend. Olive had a friend!

❖

On the ride back to the trailer, Zeddi couldn't help herself. "So, Isabella seems nice."

Olive leaned against the van window. "She is." Typical Olive, acting like it was no big deal. Zeddi waited. There'd be more. "She gets me," Olive said finally. "And I get her."

"That's good. Because you're worth getting."

Olive glared at her. "Well, duh."

Zeddi swallowed a smile. One thing she never had to worry about: Olive's self-esteem. If someone didn't get her, she always figured it was on them.

Olive rested her feet on the dashboard and sighed. "It makes me kind of sad that we get Mags' house. I mean, the only reason we're getting it is because she's dead."

The light turned green. The car behind them beeped. *Seriously?* He wanted her to run over the woman with the stroller? "I know what you mean about the house," Zeddi said. "It makes me sad too. But at the same time, it makes me happy she wanted us to have it, and it's a lot because of you."

"I know. She liked me a lot."

"And you liked her."

"True. But I'm not leaving her a house, am I?"

Zeddi eased into the intersection. "Hey, I have an idea. What do you say we pick up some bagels on our way home? For you, me, and Dan?"

Olive waggled her Converse sneaks. "Cool. I can't wait to tell him how good my joke went over."

❖

"So, dude, what do you think about your new home?" Dan asked, setting down his bag from the hardware store.

Olive flopped down onto the couch. "Great great *grrreat*! And a little weird. I mean, the place looks different now that it's ours."

Zeddi looked up from the contacts on her phone. "Take your coat off the floor, please."

"How so?" Dan asked.

"Just different."

"We're going to have to decide what to keep and what to let go of," Zeddi said.

Olive leapt off the couch. "We have to keep it all!"

Zeddi caught Dan's eye. They exchanged smiles. "We still have all our stuff in Sacramento—"

"I know, but—"

"And we for *sure* need to make room for your bed in the office, so we're going to have to get rid of *some* stuff."

"Wait. I'm going to get my own bedroom?"

"You are."

"Yes!" Olive pumped her fist. "But let's keep *most* of her stuff."

"We'll see. Now, coat please."

"Where should I put it?"

Good question. Where to put any of their stuff? "How about the bed?"

Olive dragged herself dramatically to the coat, picked it up as if it weighed a million tons, then shifted into overdrive and tore down the hallway to the bedroom. "I get my own room! I get my own room!"

"My kingdom for that kind of energy," Dan said.

Zeddi laughed. "No kidding."

Olive tore back into the room. "Hey! Now that we have a home, can Poppi and Gramps come for Christmas?"

Would Papa Alan be up for the drive? Zeddi would have to ask.

"We'll see. Now, why don't you find us some plates while I see if I can reschedule my afternoon jobs?"

"Bagels! Bagels! Bagels!" Olive belted out.

Two phone calls later, she joined Olive and Dan at the wrought iron table in the tiny backyard. "Success," she said. "I have the whole day off."

Dan and Olive were already well into their bagels. "How much do I owe you?" Dan said.

"How much do I owe you for the new locks?"

"How about we call it even?"

Olive looked up from her bagel with hummus and tomatoes. "How come we're changing the locks?"

Zeddi shot Dan a look. Olive didn't know about the footprints, and she wanted to keep it that way. "It just seemed like a good idea now that the trailer is ours."

Olive frowned. "O-kaaay." She could always tell when Zeddi was keeping something from her.

"Not to change the subject," Dan said, helpfully. "But what's in the shed?"

Zeddi looked over her shoulder at the tall wooden vine-covered shed tucked into the corner of the yard. It would be a good place to store her cleaning solutions. "Gardening stuff, I assume. I guess we'll have to saw off the padlock. Unless you know another trick."

Mouth full, Olive shouted something unintelligible.

"Excuse me?" Zeddi said.

Olive made a big production of chewing and swallowing. "Three, thirty-two, sixteen. The combination to the medicine shed. It has to be."

Zeddi set down her bagel. "Her what?"

"Those numbers on the piece of paper that Mags gave you? Combination? Duh."

"But what's this about a medicine shed?"

"That's what she calls it."

Zeddi wiped a smear of hummus off Olive's nose. "What kind of medicine?"

Olive huffed impatiently. "I don't know. A couple of times when I was doing my homework, people came over to pick up their medicine."

Dan raised an eyebrow.

"Not Mags," Zeddi said.

"Not Mags what?" Olive said.

"Nothing."

Olive squinted at her.

"What?" Zeddi said acting innocent.

Olive took another bite, chewed for a while, then said, "She was going to show me next time I was here, only now..."

"So you haven't been out there."

Olive shook her head.

Zeddi twisted around to get a better look at the shed. It was a pretty good size. Bigger than most gardening sheds. It even had its own little outdoor light. "I guess once we're done with our bagels, we better check it out. See if you're right about the combination."

❖

Sure enough, the combination did the trick, and the door swung open.

"Whoa," Zeddi said when she caught sight of what was inside. "This is amazing."

Olive pushed past her to look inside the wooden shed. "Cool!"

Dan peered over Zeddi's shoulder. "Holy shit."

Zeddi jammed her hands into her hips. "I knew she was into herbs. But this is more than herbs."

"Way more," Olive said. "Waaay waaay more."

Faded jewel-colored fabrics draped from the rafters. A cobwebby white paper lantern hung skewed on a single hanging bulb. A mandala featuring the four directions adorned the warped plywood floor, at its center a pentagram. But it was the altar along the back wall that captivated. From a small skylight, a shaft of celestial dust motes illuminated its scatter of occult-ish items. Mesmerized, Olive advanced toward the waist-high, rectangular table covered in dusty purple silk. "It's one of the thirteen..." she whispered reverently.

Zeddi raised an eyebrow. "Huh?"

Dan laughed. "*Kingdom of the Crystal Skull.*"

Of course. Olive had spotted the child-size quartz skull sitting on a stand crafted from antlers. "Indiana Jones, I should have figured."

Olive loved Indiana Jones. More than loved him. She wanted to *be* Indiana Jones. Had already announced her plans to dress like him on Halloween a little over a week away.

Olive lurched forward.

Zeddi grabbed her by the waistband of her jeans. "Whoa! Whoa! Whoa! Not so fast!"

"But Mom! Why not? It's *ours* now!"

"Out of respect to Mags. At least until we learn a little more about what all this is, what it meant to her." And because Olive was the original bull in a china shop. "We know it's here. We can come back. For now, though, let's leave it be. There's plenty in the trailer to explore."

"But Mom!"

"I mean it, Olive."

Olive squirmed out of her grip. "But how are we going to find out about it when she's dead?"

"We'll ask Ida tomorrow when we go see her."

Olive spun around. "We're going to see Ida?"

"You know her?"

"I met her once."

"And?"

"She's nice."

"Yes, well, apparently, she wants to meet us, so we're going tomorrow after school. Until then, hands off. Deal?"

Olive slumped. "O-*kay*. But can I just *look*?" She bugged out her eyes.

Dan shook his head and chuckled. "Didn't fall too far from the tree, that one."

Zeddi whacked him in the stomach. "Shush, you." Then to Olive, "Yes. You may look. But no touching."

"You think the old lady was some kind of witch?" Dan asked.

"Her name was Mags, and I have no idea." But now that she thought about it, Mags had once considered the moon cycle when deciding whether to throw out a stack of papers she hadn't read yet. *Aw heck, the moon is waning*, she'd said, *just go ahead and toss 'em*. There were other indications too. One time, she'd given Zeddi a piece of tigereye for courage and protection. And whenever they were leaving, she said, *Surrounding you in white light!* Zeddi had just thought she was an old hippie.

She followed Olive into the shed and immediately felt...what? *Warmer? Mildly electrified? More alert?* She couldn't put her finger on it, but she felt *something*. There was a strong smell too. Earthy. Sweet. No doubt coming from the tall bookshelf of jarred herbs adjacent to the altar. Angelica root, bloodroot, wormwood, the labels read. There were tons of them. Mags' medicine. There were coffee cans stuffed with colored candles and incense too. But what was the strange feeling? She closed her eyes. Tried to identify it. Then did. It felt as if the room was watching her. Her eyes flew open. She glanced over her shoulder. But it was just Dan, arms above his head, hands gripping the door sash.

"You okay?" he asked.

"Fine. Why?"

"You looked a little spooked."

"I just feel Mags is all. This shed is like walking into her heart." Olive cringed. "Ew!"

Zeddi joined her at the altar. "Why ew? I loved her heart."

Olive shrugged, her fingers just shy of touching a spiral of black and white seeds circling the skull on the antler stand. It looked more like a cheap trinket you'd pick up in Tijuana than anything Indiana Jones would be interested in. The quartz was murky, the cuts jagged. What had Mags seen in it? The skull was so different from the rest of the stuff on the cluttered altar, which was all hand-crafted and gorgeous. There was a crystal-tipped wand wrapped in fringy leather and beads, a silver double-edged dagger, a hand-blown pentagram paperweight, a Native American peace pipe. There were Celtic runes, a white-sage smudge stick, a toss of Chinese coins, a scatter of small bones, and lots and lots of feathers. There were figurines too: Aztec, Greek, Hindu. And various small musical instruments: Tibetan bells, rattles, flutes, a thumb harp, finger cymbals. So much, it was hard to take it all in.

"An omnist," Dan said from the doorway. "Interesting."

Olive whirled around, bonking the edge of the altar. "What's an omnist?" A white tapered candle attempted a suicidal leap to the floor.

Zeddi saved the candle midair. "Olive!"

"What?"

"Just...Be careful, please."

"An omnist," Dan said, "is someone who believes in all religions."

Olive considered this, then concluded, "Me too. I'm an omnist too." And then went back to studying the altar.

Zeddi placed the candle back in its holder, then asked Dan, "And you know this, because…?"

Dan shrugged. "I read."

A worried look crossed Olive's face. "Wait. Isn't this cultural appropriation?"

Right. Time to parent. "Yes and no," Zeddi said carefully.

Olive knit her brows. "What does that mean?"

"What do I always say?"

Olive huffed a sigh. "Few things are black and white."

"And?"

Another huffed sigh. "Context, context, context." Olive glanced at Dan to get his take on the context thing. She was always trying to impress Dan. But he, unhelpfully, threw his hands up as if to say, *Don't look at me*, so she turned back to Zeddi. "Okay, what context?"

"Mags was old, and from the looks of it she collected these things at a time when most people in this country believed Christianity was the only true religion."

"Many still do," Dan interjected.

"True, but it used to be that way even more. Lots of people had no idea there were other ways to worship. So in a way, Mags was a revolutionary. She was acknowledging that the world was a big place full of all kinds of ways to worship, and I'll just bet you the different cultures represented here in all of her things had her full respect."

"Because she was an omnist," Olive concluded, "like me."

"Exactly."

Seemingly satisfied, Olive moved on. "So if you want to see Ida, she's here." She slipped a yellowing photo from the altar. Held it out for Zeddi.

Zeddi almost laughed. She knew this game. Olive was testing her. How hard was the no touching rule? She took the five-by-seven black-and-white from her. Looked at it.

Olive turned back to the altar. Picked up a bean.

"Olive," she said, without looking up from the photo.

"Okay!" Olive shot back and returned the bean to the altar, which Dan took as his cue to leave the two alone.

Five young women and a single man posed by a redwood. They wore bellbottoms, halter tops, miniskirts, and fringy vests. One was Mags, another Roni Miller. Tons younger. But who were the others? On closer inspection, one of the unknown women had clearly been ripped out of the photo then taped back in.

"Which one is Ida?" She hoped it wasn't the ripped-out woman. It spoke of a very complicated relationship.

Olive pointed to the dwarf next to Mags. "That's her."

Zeddi took a moment to examine the photo before returning it to the altar. "Okay, well, how about we—" Turning, she noticed a small wooden desk to the right of the altar. It was straddled by two straight back chairs. Suspended from the ceiling above it hung a dusty pair of owl wings. On the desktop was a spread of three tarot cards.

High Priestess. Pan. Death.

An uneasy feeling crept up her spine. Had Mags known she was going to die? She spun around, clapped her hands together, tried to keep her tone light. "How about we go unload our stuff from the van? We can ask Ida all about this stuff tomorrow."

"But I'm not done looking!" Olive whined.

She took Olive by the shoulders and herded her out the door. "We're going to have plenty of time to look later."

Outside, Dan was removing the new lock from its packaging. "All good?"

Zeddi could only hope so.

CHAPTER NINE

Zeddi jolted awake, her heart slamming in her chest. She scanned the room. Where was she? Right. Mags' bed. Mags' bedroom. Olive next to her sleeping, peacefully. It was just a nightmare, nothing real. But it had seemed so real. She'd been back in Sacramento cleaning the small charter middle school she'd hoped to get Olive into—only for some reason she was doing it at night. Going from empty room to empty room, straightening desks, wiping down blackboards, scraping squashed gum out of the carpet. But just out of sight someone was following her. Someone who wanted something from her. "What do you want?" she shouted into the dark hallway, but there was no answer, just an ominous buzzing. She picked up a spray bottle of ammonia. Grabbed her utility knife. Approached the door. Stepped through it. Mags! Sitting in the middle of the hallway in her green chair, surrounded by flies, her eyes glassy, vacant.

Zeddi flopped onto her back, damp with sweat, and stared at the ceiling. She was safe. Olive was safe. So why was her heart still racing? She took a deep breath. Another. Not only safe but comfortable. The bed wasn't too soft or too hard, it was just right. She chuckled. *Goldilocks my way back to the present. There's a strategy.* She breathed in the fresh smell of the sheets she'd found in the back of Mags' linen closet, pulled them up around her neck. The sheets were at that worn-thin, super-soft stage.

A shell nightlight in the hall cast a dim amber glow in the room. Each time she'd cleaned, she'd removed cobwebs from the nightlight, but could never catch the spider weaving them—never even saw the little beast. Was the spider asleep now or busy spinning her tiny web?

The bulb had a flicker meant to replicate a burning flame. The shadowy doorframe, Mags' robe hanging by the closet, the tall brass lamp next to the dresser all trembled to life with the light's undulations. She rolled onto her side. On the nightstand, Mags' half-moon glasses balanced precariously on top of a splayed-open paperback. Mags had not been ready to die. Not at all. The whole room whispered it.

A light rain began tap-tap-tapping against the metal roof. It was such a relief to be out of the van. And soon she and Olive would have their own rooms, even their own bathrooms. It was more than she could have hoped for. She'd let Olive decorate her room however she wanted. They could do one room at a time: clear it, take stuff to Goodwill, paint, get new curtains. It would help the place feel more like home.

Tonight, it felt anything but.

She rolled over to watch Olive sleep. She loved watching Olive sleep, loved the way she gave herself over to the activity. She lay on her stomach, arms and legs splayed, a slumbering starfish—with one large, snoring barnacle stuck to her head, his little white paws waggling as if chasing a dream mouse. Barnaby. He was part of the family now.

The vision of the glassy-eyed, fly-infested Mags wouldn't go away. She rolled onto her back again, cradled her head in her hands and listened to the thermostat clicking, the ice maker clunking. The windows rattled in the wind. Something feral screeched outside. She'd have to get used to these noises. The rain came faster, hitting harder. Mags' wind chimes clanged instead of chimed. Would she hear someone in the backyard if they were sneaking around? Or in the shed? But why would they be? She massaged her jaw. Thought about the tarot cards. She'd had a reading at a psychic fair once. She and her friends had gone just for fun. The spread of her cards was more elaborate than the three-card spread in the shed. It was circular. When the Death Card showed up in her Wealth House, the heavily eyelinered fortune teller had assured her that the card was metaphoric, that she needed to shed some of her beliefs about money.

But Mags really was dead. No metaphor there.

Barnaby growled in his sleep.

"Who tossed you out?" she whispered to him.

His fat paws began to rapidly jerk, like he was running through some dreamscape.

She peeled off the blankets. There was no point in fighting it. She wasn't going to sleep. She quietly rolled out of bed, slipped on leggings and a sweater, found her socks, and tiptoed into the kitchen, where she flicked on the light and rummaged through the cabinets in search of some calming tea. Mags had usually blended her own, and steeped each cup of mixed herbs in a small bamboo strainer perched on the lip of the mug. But Zeddi didn't have the patience to search through all the labeled jars, instead choosing a dusty box of chamomile tea bags way in the back. *Score.*

It was a relief to be able to get up. Sleepless nights in the van had been tough. She'd lie there reading on her iPad or bundle up and sit out in the driveway. Standing in a kitchen making tea was such luxury. She watched the tea steep, then laced it with honey and settled onto the couch. She pulled the crocheted afghan over her legs. Thought about turning up the heat. Wondered who was paying the utilities now that Mags was dead. Was there a grace period? Tomorrow she'd figure out how to transfer the bills into her name.

Outside in the herb garden, the string of draping solar lights was almost out. It made the hour, half past three, seem that much later. Tick-tock, tick-tock went the Kit Cat clock with the wandering eyes and wagging tail.

A light from the neighbor's backyard suddenly, aggressively, angled across Mags' raised garden bed and lit up the corner of the shed. Apparently, there was another insomniac in the 'hood. Lorna Doyle? Her son Jeff Dante? What had Lorna said? That she was helping him to get back on track? What did that mean? What track had he fallen from?

The light went out, and the shed disappeared. So did the raised herb bed. Just the faint glow from the solar lights now. Zeddi blew on her cup of tea. The rain turned to a drizzle. She listened for a while. Sipped her tea. The neighbor's light flashed on again. Motion detector? She waited to see if it stayed on for the same amount of time. It did. Something was setting it off. No big deal. No need to catastrophize.

She carried her tea over to the bookshelf and stared at the eclectic collection. Maya Angelou, Susan Sontag, Susan Griffin, Audre Lorde, Adrienne Rich were intermittently tucked in between mysteries, best sellers, and nature and travel guides. She returned to the couch, too keyed up to read, and looked around at her new home. The neighbor's light shot on again. Was someone out there? Should she check? She eyeballed Mags' rubber garden clogs by the sliding glass doors. How easy it would be to just slip them on over her socks. She wouldn't even have to get wet. From what she could hear, the rain had drizzled itself out. But going out into the night was spooky. The thought pissed her off. She hated to be ruled by fear. Didn't want to be one of those women scared of everything. She set her tea on the coffee table, slipped on Mags' green rubber gardening clogs, kissed the trust tattoo on her inner wrist, and headed into the dark.

It was drippy outside. She pulled her oversized cardigan tighter around her. Flicked on her phone flashlight and sidestepped a trickle coming off the roof, making a mental note that the gutters needed cleaning. Tall redwood fences, too tall to climb, surrounded the small yard. If a person wanted to sneak back there, they would have to come around the trailer from the front. Good to know. She walked over to where the light had been coming from, peered through a crack in the fence. Sure enough, there was a fixture secured high enough that it would spill light into her yard. Also good to know. But what was setting it off? She shone her phone light onto the fence separating her backyard from the bike trail along the river levee and listened. Although she couldn't see the river, she could hear it. It was louder at night. Strange to be so close to the river and not be able to see it. But the fence offered a nice privacy. During the day, the bike path on the other side was a thoroughfare for commuters and sightseers.

In the silence of the night, she could hear a couple of drunk guys arguing, a distant car with a bad muffler, even the seals barking out on the bay. Nothing that would set off the light. She turned to head inside but spun around at the sound of a low growl and a scratching noise. The fence rattled. More growling. A raccoon topped the fence. Then another. And another. The neighbor's light flicked on. Okay then, nothing to fear.

But now that she was out there…

She tucked the phone flashlight under her chin. Three, thirty-two, sixteen. The combination came to her easily, which surprised her. She rarely remembered numbers of any sort. The lock released with a satisfying click. She propped the shed door open with a heavy potted herb and pulled the cord for the white paper lantern. A moth fluttered in.

The soft amber glow from the light was warm, inviting, and cast a truly magical aura over everything. No doubt if something bad should happen, the shed would protect her by Harry Pottering itself to life.

The owl wings would flap, the double-edged knife would fly about, the crystal skull smack its jaws. The thought made her laugh. Made her miss Mags.

There were books on the bookshelf she hadn't noticed before: herbal dictionaries, books about healing, diet, some Joseph Campbell titles too, the I Ching, a couple of pamphlets on ceremonial magic, and a book on voodoo magick. "An omnist indeed," she said aloud, liking the sound of the new word, liking the idea of it. She pulled down a book that looked like a diary, its cover a collage. In the center, a photo of a young Mags, only the artist had given her wings and set her floating in a magical wood, where fishes swam through the trees and a small pond was studded with stars. It was beautiful, dreamlike.

She debated opening it. Mags hadn't been dead forty-eight hours and here she was wearing her shoes, standing in her magic place, pawing through her private life. Still, something around her death just didn't sit right. Maybe it was nothing. But maybe it was something. And if it was, and if this was going to be home, she had to figure out what, why. Home had to feel safe. Period. She cracked the first page and was met by Mags' back-slanting handwriting. The first entry was dated April 28, 1972.

> *It's getting too expensive to drive down to Venice Beach all the time so I have decided to start my own coven here in Tres Ojos. The work Zsuzsanna Budapest is doing is too important not to do. We need to wake the Goddess in ourselves! In the world! Put an end to this war, to all the suffering!!*
> *I will continue my activist work as well, but adding this spiritual element feels vital. I have invited some of my women friends over to see if they'll join me, and tonight I will cast my first circle. The Goddess is Alive! Blessed Be.*

Zeddi flipped through the rest of the spiral-bound book, pausing here and there. It was filled with other short journal entries, many of which read like the minutes of a nonprofit. Who was there, and the purpose of the circle: heal the earth, put an end to the war, help Ida's mother go in peace. She was surprised to see her client Roni Miller among the attendees. She didn't seem the witchy type. Then again, the meetings had taken place over forty years ago. People changed.

There were spells in the book too, recorded like recipes in a cookbook. Each spell began with a purpose—love spell, binding spell, protection spell—followed by a list of what was needed: candles, herbs, bowls of water, incense, string. There were incantations to be spoken, actions to be taken, things were to be cut in two, burned, buried, frozen.

So that answered that question. Mags was definitely a witch—or had witch tendencies. At least she had from the years 1972–1974. After that the sporadic entries stopped. Zeddi could relate. She'd never had much success journaling either. Apparently, Mags had the same problem.

> *I have to get better about recording our meetings! Tried to get someone else to act as secretary, to keep our coven's Grimoire, but they all say as High Priestess it's my job, which is complete phooey. I don't even know how I became High Priestess, but I suspect it was for the sole purpose of making me take notes. I will get better though. This work we are doing is too important.*

Zeddi laughed at this final entry. Or was it the final one? She flipped through the blank pages in the rest of the book. Found another entry toward the back.

> *Summer Solstice, 1989*
> *Last night I told Constance she was no longer welcome at our gatherings. I will continue, privately, to weave protection around her, to keep her safe. But how difficult to protect someone from themselves. I waited too long. I know this. Her presence in our circles has been so disruptive—and she keeps pushing. But she is my sister, and now I have banished her. I feel terrible. I feel justified, but I feel terrible!!! She screamed such horrible things at me. But it was not her screaming. I know this too. A darkness has taken over her soul. What have I done??????*

Zeddi stared at the entry.

Outside a night bird screeched.

The neighbor Lorna had mentioned something about Mags' sister. What was it? Zeddi racked her brain. Something about her death seeming fishy to Mags. Zeddi clutched the journal—grimoire—to her chest, whispered, "Mags, is there something I need to know?"

Of course, there was no answer. The dead took their secrets with them. She waited anyway, and a thought drifted through her mind. High Priestess. Mags. She took a step backward. Made herself look at the tarot spread. *High Priestess. Pan. Death.* Had Mags placed the cards intentionally as a message—or was it just her last reading?

Regardless, Zeddi owed it to Mags to find out what she could. She laid a palm on the High Priestess card. "I'll be back," she said, though she didn't know who exactly she was talking to—*Mags' ghost? Some evil person?*—but someone was listening. She could feel it.

Buzzing with adrenaline, she strode back to the trailer. Once locked safely inside, she stood at the kitchen counter and googled Zsuzsanna Budapest on her laptop.

Barnaby rubbed against her leg.

She bent down and gave him a pat. "What are you doing up?"

He yowled.

She grabbed him a Greenie.

The Wikipedia page loaded.

In the seventies, Zsuzsanna Budapest had founded something called Dianic Wicca, a form of Wicca that worshiped the Goddess. She clicked the Wicca hyperlink and nosed her way down the rabbit hole. There were all kinds of witches: sea witches, kitchen witches, green witches, hedge witches, Correllian witches, Alexandrian witches; witches in Chile, Mexico, South Africa; witches practicing everything from voodoo to Native American rituals. There were witches who considered themselves shamans, witches who said shamans had nothing to do with witchcraft; witches who belonged to covens, witches who practiced alone; witches who practiced white magic, posting spells about healing, love, and prosperity, and witches who practiced black magic and posted YouTube videos with names like *How to Curse or Hex Someone You Hate.* There were witches who spelled magic with a *k*, witches who didn't. There were high school witches, supermodel witches, even Christian witches. She shook her head. No wonder the world was in such sorry shape! With all these witches shooting spells at each other, they probably canceled each other out all the time.

She yawned. It was time to sleep. She'd be no good to anyone if she didn't sleep. She shut the laptop. Flicked out the light. Ambled down the flickering shell-lit hallway to the bedroom where Olive managed somehow to take up the entire queen bed.

Just as she was drifting off, she had a realization. The woman in the photo Olive had shown her was the same woman in the portrait shot in Mags' wallet.

Ida.

CHAPTER TEN

In the morning, Turtle's engine wouldn't even try to turn over. Dazed from lack of sleep and bizarre dreams, Zeddi grabbed the keys to Mags' Audi. It rumbled to life. She ran Olive to school, enjoying a stick shift for a change, then returned to the trailer and called AAA. Forty minutes before they could come. She only had two apartments to clean in the same complex, turnovers for a property management company. Easy. Just clean and get out. If Turtle was truly dead, she'd load the Audi's trunk with her cleaning supplies. In the meantime, she brewed a second cup of coffee, settled onto the couch, and dialed her dads. She couldn't wait to tell them the news. Such a relief to be able to tell the truth about their living situation. She set the phone on the arm of the couch, set it to speaker, and took a sip of the delicious freshly brewed coffee. Papa Glen picked up on the third ring.

"You're not going to believe my news."

"Good or bad?"

"Good."

"Hang on. I'm going to put you on speaker. Hon? Hon? It's Zeddi! She has some good news."

She told them about the trailer. Left out her growing suspicions regarding Mags' death.

"Fantastic!" Papa Glen said.

"W-wonderful," Papa Alan said. The slurring of his speech was getting worse.

"I know. I still can't even believe it."

"You're going to need a bunch of death certificates," Papa Glen said. "To be able to put everything into your name."

"Do you need help? D-do you need us to come?" Papa Alan asked.

Much worse. "No. We're fine." How could this be happening to her gorgeous father, a man who always seemed indestructible to her? "This lawyer? Mags' executor?" she continued. "He's offered his help, so we're good. But Olive did mention that maybe you'd come for Christmas?"

"Count on it!" Papa Alan asserted.

"We'll see," Papa Glen said. "We're still trying to get his medication right."

"I'm right here," Papa Alan said. "And I'm fine and will be fine at Christmas."

"You fell the other night."

"I t-t-tripped. It had nothing to do with this…di…sease."

Zeddi stared at a small gathering of brown birds pecking around in the garden. "Well, Christmas is a long way off. We can talk about this later. In the meantime, we're still coming down for Thanksgiving."

"That's great," Papa Glen said.

"And we *are* coming at Chr-ristmas!"

Papa Glen laughed. "I'm telling you, Zeddi, there's no controlling this man of mine."

"No c-controlling *me*?" Papa Alan shot back. "He's got me on this health r-regimen that's going to kill me. You know how I feel about vegetables!"

Zeddi reached for her coffee. Took a sip to keep from crying. "Love you."

"All right then," Papa Glen said. "Kiss kiss."

Papa Alan made a kissing sound. "Bye, Zed."

"Let us know if you need anything."

Once she'd hung up, she let the tears flow. Of all people to get Parkinson's, why did it have to be Papa Alan? He hated not being able to do for himself; he had to be driving Papa Glen crazy. She wiped her eyes with a tissue. Stared at her phone. Dialed the attorney. Miss Perky Pants patched her through.

"I was wondering about death certificates," Zeddi said when he came on the line. "Do I have to order those? Or…"

"Nope. I'll get you some. It generally takes ten to twelve days."

"Okay. Thank you." Zeddi tossed the tissue. "One more thing. I was wondering, is anyone in charge of putting together a service for Mags?"

"Ah. Yes. That would be Ida."

"Okay, I'll ask her."

"You know her?"

"We're getting together later this afternoon." The silence that followed prompted her to ask, "Is there something I should know?"

"Just that Ida can be a tad unreliable when it comes to…anything. It's not intentional. I don't mean that. She's just—how can I put this?—eccentric in her view of the world."

"I'll keep that in mind when I meet her, thanks. You've been a great help."

"Any more questions, I'm here."

Zeddi set the phone face down on the coffee table. Stared at its faux-wood case. There was still some time left before the tow truck would come. She *could* call Sylvie. Invite her down. But would it be too forward? Had the night meant as much to Sylvie as it had to her? She checked the time. Early, but not too early. But had Sylvie moved on? That was the question. It had been ten weeks, and they'd only had the one night, and so far, it was always her doing the calling. But that wasn't true. Sylvie had called a couple of times right after the move, wanting to come down, and Zeddi had kind of put her off. *Had* put her off. It was too complicated in the van.

Sylvie picked up on the third ring. She'd clearly just woken up.

"I'm sorry," Zeddi blabbered. "I didn't realize how early it was."

"It's fine." Sylvie yawned. "Great. I just"—another yawn—"I need to be up anyway. I had a rough night is all. Work stuff. Things I should have said and didn't circling around like vultures in my head." Her voice had a husky timbre, even when fully awake.

Zeddi wondered what her bedroom looked like. She'd seen glimpses when they'd FaceTimed. A bookshelf. A bunch of folded paper birds hanging from the ceiling. But the bed, she hadn't seen the bed. "Do you feel like talking about it?"

"I'd rather hear about you, Ms. Zeddi. How's Tres Ojos treating you?"

Zeddi felt herself blush. "Pretty good. We finally have a place to live." She told her about the trailer.

"Wow. That's wild. So I guess you won't be moving back any time soon."

The night of kissing hung silently between them. It had been so spontaneous. So impulsive.

Zeddi and she stood in the alley after the show, the performers all gone to pack up their costumes after smoking a celebratory joint. Zeddi hadn't smoked pot in so long that she got really high and had trouble understanding what Sylvie was saying—something about a dimmer malfunction? But being high wasn't the only obstacle to listening. Sylvie's adorable heart-shaped lips, and her eyes that were picking up light from somewhere, and the neat short nails on her hands all made it hard to focus. And before she knew it, a now or never feeling rose up inside her, that feeling of standing at the edge of the swimming pool and forgoing the timid-toe temperature check, and instead deciding to plunge right in. Maybe it was because she was moving in a couple of days. Or because it was her first night out with adults in ages. Or because she was high. Or maybe it was because Sylvie was just so damn cute in her vintage plaid pantsuit. Whatever the reason, she lurched forward and pressed her lips to Sylvie's, knocking Sylvie back into a brick wall behind her. It was shocking. Thrilling. Quick. And so unlike her. And for a moment, they just stared at one another and Zeddi was sure she'd made a terrible mistake. But then Sylvie took Zeddi's face in her hands and kissed her back. A huge tongue kiss. And then the two of them laughed and laughed, then kissed some more, then laughed then kissed. Then there was no more laughing. Just kissing. Touching. That wall propping them up.

Then Daria had popped her head out the door and said, *Hey girl, I promised I'd get you back by eleven.* And Zeddi had pulled out of the kiss, gasped, *Sorry. I have to get home to my kid.* And Sylvie had gasped, *You have a kid?* And she'd gasped, *Yeah. Olive. She's nine.* And then there had been that awkward moment and Zeddi'd felt herself closing off, readying herself for rejection. But Sylvie had said, *Cool. I'd love to meet this Olive of yours.* And then reality had reared its ugly head and she'd had to say, *Oh yeah, and I should tell you, too, that I'm...um...we're leaving town in two days. Moving, actually* and

Sylvie had stepped back. *Moving, where?* And Zeddi had glanced at the door Daria had left open. *Tres Ojos*, she'd managed to say over the din of her heart shattering into a million zillion pieces, because here, finally, had been the kiss she'd been waiting for, the happily-ever-after kiss she'd stopped believing in. And she'd prattled on and on about the housesitting she had all lined up and the spot at the school for Olive and a cleaning business she was taking over. And Sylvie had looked so crestfallen, so sad. *Well...you better go then*, she'd said, and emitted this dejected little laugh. Somehow phone numbers had been exchanged, and there had been promises to keep in touch, but—

"You still there?" Sylvie asked.

But Zeddi wasn't still there, she was a hundred and fifty miles away. "Yeah," she said quietly.

"You must have made some kind of impression."

"Huh?"

"To get the trailer."

"Right. I—" And just then the stupid tow truck pulled up out front. "Hang on," Zeddi said, and flew outside to wave down the driver, but realistically she couldn't keep Sylvie on the line while she dealt with the van, so she said, "Sorry, but I've got to go. Long story involving a tow truck. I'll call you back. Promise."

A jumped battery later, her heart was still doing loop-the-loops in her chest, as she thanked the driver and listened to him tell her, "You should get that alternator looked at. That battery was not old. It could die on you again."

She signed the paperwork. Took the keys from him. There were so many things she should do.

CHAPTER ELEVEN

The drive up the coast was ridiculously gorgeous. The dark cottony clouds of an incoming storm hovered over the bay, while along the snaking highway it was crisp and sunny. To the left, strings of pelicans wheeled over the sparkling water. To the right, crows hopped around fields blazing orange with pumpkins. "Another murder!" Olive yelled each time they passed a group of crows challenging a scarecrow. Farm stands boasted Fresh Pies! and Corn Maze This Way!

They'd taken the Audi. Getting pulled over for a registration check seemed less likely than Turtle crapping out again. Besides, the Audi was fun to drive. It felt like a golf cart. Sunroof cranked open, heat blasting, so decadent, so exactly what they needed.

"Can we bring Isabella to the corn maze?" Olive asked, her hands gathering wind out the sunroof.

Zeddi's heart did a little happy dance. "Sure. Maybe this weekend? Sunday?"

"Yesss!" Olive shrieked into the wind. "Sundaaay!"

Whatever other screwed up things she'd done as a mother, Tres Ojos she'd gotten right. Olive was thriving.

"You promise on the way home we can stop and buy a pumpkin?" It was about the hundredth time Olive had asked this.

"Like I said, we'll see. Looks like a gnarly storm is moving in." The waves were getting bigger and choppier by the minute, the wind combing through the tall grasses.

"If we can't, we have to come back tomorrow. Or the next day. Or the next! And we have to get two pumpkins so we each get one. Or three! We can invite Dan over! Or maybe—"

"We'll make sure you have a pumpkin before Halloween. We have over a week."

"Not *any* pumpkin. Not a *supermarket* pumpkin. We need one from *here*."

Zeddi chuckled. The girl knew what she wanted, that was for sure. "Okay. We'll make it happen. Promise."

Whalers Point. Perched on cypress-dotted cliffs, the tiny seaside town was home to abalone farmers, surfers, artists, and recluses; there were no fast-food joints, no grocery stores, no gas stations, just a small cluster of sea-battered homes, a few businesses aimed at those traveling the scenic highway, and one large, abandoned cement plant around which the town was built in 1906. She and Olive had learned about the cement plant on their last visit when they'd checked out the historic two-cell jail that now served as a tiny museum. *The two-minute museum*, Olive had called it.

Dora the Explorer (Olive's name for Zeddi's GPS) directed them to a short dirt road leading to a constellation of homes overlooking the bluff. *You have arrived*, the electronic guide announced in front of a light blue clapboard cottage surrounded by a fenced-in vegetable garden. Zeddi pulled up alongside the white fence, closed the sunroof, and shut off the engine. A strong gust of wind blew the door back when she tried to open it.

Olive muscled out the passenger side, her hair dancing in the wind. "Mom! Look!" She pointed at a huge fringy purple flower growing next to the stone path that led to the front door. "An artichoke! It's what they turn into if you don't harvest them." The flower, waving in the wind, sat atop a rangy plant like a crown.

"Wow." Zeddi buttoned up her sweater. "I had no idea." Where did Olive learn these things?

From behind a spire of kale, came the words "I always leave one to flower." A second later, Ida stepped out. A dwarf, yes, but that clearly was no disability. She wore a holster for garden shears and trowel buckled around her waist, a light blue cotton dress over blue jeans, a cardigan over that, and child-sized red rubber boots. "I feel it's only right to allow the plant to experience its full potential," she said, shoving her blown-free gray hair back into a tortoiseshell claw clip. Her eyes were rimmed in red, and bloodshot. She'd obviously been crying.

"You must be Ida." Zeddi reached out a hand. "I'm Zeddi."

Ida's handshake was strong and callused. "It's a pleasure to finally meet you. Mags spoke of you often."

Zeddi fought the urge to ask what exactly Mags had said about her. Knowing might explain why Mags had left her the trailer. But the question could so easily be construed as fishing for compliments. "It's nice to meet you too," she said. "I'm sorry the circumstances are such sad ones."

Olive stepped around the artichoke. "Remember me?"

"Of course I do. You're Olive." Ida squeezed Olive's hand. "You're just getting off school, is that right?"

"Yep. And I could sure use a snack."

"Excuse me?" Zeddi said.

"What? You told me she was going to have snacks!"

"It's fine," Ida said, laughing. "I did promise snacks."

"Well, thank you." Zeddi turned to Olive. "But some manners would be appreciated."

"Sor-*ry*," Olive huffed.

A sudden gust turned a pile of leaves into a mini tornado.

Ida picked up her harvest of beets. "What do you say we head inside—out of this wind?"

❖

Ida's home was the definition of cozy. A fire crackled in a brick fireplace. Copious pillows covered an old sofa. The floor was carpeted in a faded Oriental rug. Tchotchkes everywhere. But the most noticeable thing was the tall dapper man in the ivory cable knit sweater sitting by the window, hands the size of dinner plates folded neatly in his lap.

"This is my brother, Claude," Ida said, as she exchanged her boots for a pair of worn sheepskin slippers. "Claude, this is Zeddi, the one I told you moved into Mags' trailer. And of course, you've already met Olive."

"Hey, Claude," Olive said.

"Nice to meet you," Zeddi said.

Claude responded in a high, childlike voice. "How you?"

"Fine, thank you," Zeddi said.

Claude stretched his mouth into a practiced smile, then went back to staring out the window.

"He doesn't miss much," Ida remarked. "He was surprised to see you getting out of Mags' Audi."

Zeddi shrugged off her sweater. Was Ida casting judgment about her using Mags' car? She didn't seem to be, but it had to be a little strange for her.

"Just throw your coats anywhere," Ida said. "We don't have a proper coat closet."

"Should we take off our shoes?"

"No need. But thanks for asking."

Olive stripped off her purple puffy jacket and dropped it on the floor.

Zeddi picked it up and, along with her own wool sweater, laid it on the back of the sofa. You had to pick your battles.

"Make yourselves at home," Ida said, indicating the sofa facing the fire. "I'll just get us those snacks."

As she settled onto the worn couch, Zeddi made a mental note to get firewood for Mags' wood burner. Or maybe there was some tucked outside somewhere? She'd have to look. A fire in the fireplace was so comforting. Above the mantel hung what was obviously one of Mags' paintings: a pod of dolphins arcing up out of a silver moonlit sea. It was beautiful. You could almost hear the waves. She glanced around the rest of the room.

Various alterations had been made for someone with dwarfism. A thin plexiglass rod hung off the light switch to make it reachable, step stools were set in strategic spots. There was a small green overstuffed chair with an accompanying table and reading lamp next to Claude's large one by the window. Another short table was by the door with a heap of mail. There was a low row of pegs where several coats hung, and a small lap harp and stool in the corner. All very nice, but what did this Ida want from them? Why were they here?

Ida returned with a tray of nuts and dried fruit. "You'll have to excuse Claude's woolgathering. We don't get many visitors. Do we, Claude?"

Again the practiced if slightly vacant smile. "No visitors. No." Again a return to his woolgathering.

"Woolgathering?" Olive asked. "What's that?"

"I guess it's an old-fashioned phrase. It means daydreaming. Claude is an all-star daydreamer. He's been living with me for eight years now. My parents had him in a group home in Santa Barbara, but once they died, I brought him here to live with me. I couldn't stand to think of him in that home. And he's able to care for himself, mostly, he can shave and shower, and he has his chores: taking out the trash, vacuuming. He's even learned how to make himself a cup of hot chocolate. Isn't that right, Claude?"

This got his attention. His eyes brightened. His fingers drummed on his lap. "Chocolate?"

Amused, Ida shook her head. "Not yet. You just finished a cup. You can have one with supper."

Clearly disappointed, Claude turned back to gazing out the window.

What kindness Ida showed him. Caring for him couldn't have been easy, and yet she did it with such grace—and love.

"You play the harp," Zeddi noted.

Ida set the tray on the redwood burl coffee table where a dragon-decorated teapot and cups were already laid out. "Not formally trained, but I like to see what it can do." She sat on a zafu meditation cushion across the table from Zeddi and Olive. "Tea?" She lifted the teapot. "It's herbal. My autumn blend. Cinnamon, cardamom, cloves, ginger, and a few other goodies."

"Sounds great," Zeddi said.

"Whoaaa…" Olive said. "The tea pours out the dragon's nose."

"It's Chinese, and very old. Like me," Ida said.

Olive used both hands to pick up the smooth teacup, sniffed its contents, took a sip, then set the cup back down. "So, are you a witch too?"

"Olive!" Zeddi scolded.

"What?" Olive pointed to the hearth where a large river rock was painted with a pentagram. "Look!"

"I'm sorry," Zeddi said. "We just came across Mags' shed and it's…we have a lot of questions is all."

"I bet you do," Ida said, and smiled. "But rest assured, my philosophy is the only bad question is the question not asked. I have some questions myself, which is why I asked you here. So, to answer yours, Olive, as simply as I can, yes, I suppose you could call me a witch. Artemis knows we used to call ourselves that. And we still call our little group a coven, though we meet so rarely anymore." She drifted for a moment, and Zeddi remembered Ari saying she could be a bit fuzzy. Was that the word he'd used?

"I like the feel of the word witch," she continued. "It carries quite a kick. But, as with most labels, I fear it's misleading. That said, I do cast the odd spell here and there. Honestly, my hands are so full with Claude, I haven't been practicing much of anything these days— besides making sure he gets fed and stays out of trouble. Does that answer your question?"

Olive's eyes grew wide as planets. "You know how to cast spells?"

"I do. But anyone can cast a spell. It's simply a matter of knowing how."

"Could Mags cast spells?"

Ida's eyes filled with tears.

Zeddi rested a hand on Olive's thigh. "Maybe that's enough questions for now, sweetie."

Olive picked up a dried pear and stuffed it into her mouth.

Outside, the wind blew, rattling the windows, thrashing the trees. Inside, the loss of Mags hung in the air, static and heavy. Ida covered her face with her hands. Olive gave Zeddi an apologetic look. Zeddi ruffled her hair—*it's okay*—and pulled her close. Somewhere in the back of the house a window whistled.

Ida took a tissue from her sleeve, blew her nose, dabbed her eyes. "Yes, in the same respect that I am a witch, Mags was a witch. She was part of our coven. And yes, she cast the occasional spell too."

"I thought so," Olive said.

"You thought right," Ida said.

"Snack!" Claude interjected.

"Claude," Ida said. "If you want some snacks, go get yourself a bowl. You know where they are."

He heaved himself up from the chair and strolled primly off to the kitchen.

"If I don't make him get up sometimes, he never will," Ida explained.

Zeddi nodded. It was the same with Olive.

The fire popped a glowing ember onto the stone hearth. Ida rose from her cushion, took the poker from the stand, and shoved the logs back, wielding the regular-sized fire tools with the ease and freedom of a person years younger. "I wish I'd taken her seriously," she said softly. "She was so sure there was something fishy about her sister Constance's death. And now…well, something just isn't sitting right."

So that was it. Ida felt something was off about Mags' death.

Olive swallowed a mouthful of dried apple. "Are you talking about Connie?"

"Yes, Connie," Ida said. "But only Mags called her that."

"I met her once. I didn't know she was Mags' sister, though. We were making sand candles after school and she came over. They went outside to talk about something."

Ida studied her. "Did Mags mention what they talked about?"

Olive shook her head. "Nuh-uh."

Claude came back with his bowl, picked through the snacks, taking mostly dried pears and Brazil nuts, and returned to his chair by the window. Ida poked at the fire. Zeddi cradled the warm teacup in her hands. She wanted to pursue Ida's comment about something not sitting right about Mags' death, since she felt the same, but suddenly her lack of sleep was ambushed by the warmth from the crackling fire, by the lazy late-afternoon light slanting through the window, by the hypnotic whistling of the window. It was trancelike. One by one she felt her muscles loosen, even the tiny ones holding her eyelids open. They'd grown so heavy. She tried to keep them aloft, focusing on Mags' painting over the mantel where Mags' dolphins leapt from the water and twisted in the air, then on the fireplace where the flames shapeshifted into a stormy sea of blues and greens, and Ida into a miniature female Poseidon wielding a trident—

A violent shaking jolted her awake. Instinctively, she threw an arm in front of Olive. "Was that an earthquake?"

Ida turned to face her. "That? No. Just a wave. Sometimes the big ones shake the house. Especially at high tide. And with this storm coming…"

Olive squirmed out from under her arm. "That's so cool! Like we're in a boat."

Zeddi blinked a few times. Reached for a cashew. "So, um, anyway, what you were saying about something not feeling right?" She blinked a few times. *Wake up. Wake up.* "The neighbor said the same thing about Mags thinking there was something fishy about her sister's death, and…um…" Should she tell her about the footprints? No. Not with Olive there.

"Someone let Barnaby out," Olive said. "Because he was out when we found Mags."

"Really?" Ida hung the poker on the wrought iron stand. "That *is* strange. I have never known Barnaby to show even the remotest interest in going outside." She turned to Zeddi. "May I ask how you found Mags?"

"She was sitting in her chair," Olive said. "And Barnaby was outside in the rain."

"She looked peaceful, her hands in her lap," Zeddi added. "Still, something just didn't feel right to me. Still doesn't. The coroner said she died of natural causes, though."

"Yes, I know. Is there anything else that you noticed? Anything unusual?"

Zeddi shifted on the couch. How much of this did she want Olive to hear? "There were two teacups in the sink. So maybe someone visited her?"

Ida's hand flew to her chest. "Oh, dear!"

"What?"

"That's exactly the way Mags found Constance. Two teacups, hands in her lap."

"Wait." Olive lurched forward on the couch. "Mags was in the same exact same position as her sister?"

"From what you've just told me, yes."

"So they were probably murdered by the same person!"

Murdered? Okay, that was it. Time to cut back on the scary movies. "That's enough, Olive," Zeddi said. "No one was murdered."

Ida studied Olive for a moment. "Mags always said she appreciated your candor."

Olive grinned. "She did?"

"Yup."

"Cool!" Olive did a thumbs up. "Wait. What's candor?"

"Speaking your mind," Zeddi said.

"Oh, yeah," Olive said. "Like candid."

"Exactly." Zeddi turned to Ida. "So"—*if she wasn't suggesting murder*—"what exactly *are* you saying, Ida?"

"Honestly, I'm still so in shock I don't know what I'm saying. But, well, something seems *very* off. And I—" Ida's jaw trembled.

Zeddi prompted gently, "What?"

"I just feel it my duty to let you know what you and Olive are getting into. Mags would want me to."

"By inheriting the trailer?"

"In part."

In part? Zeddi sat up a little straighter.

"Is this about the crystal skull?" Olive blurted. "It's one of the thirteen from Indiana Jones, isn't it? I knew it! I knew it!"

"Honey…"

"It's all right," Ida said.

"Olive loves all things Indiana Jones," Zeddi explained.

"Of course. What's not to like about Indiana Jones? But I don't believe our skull is one of the thirteen," Ida said to Olive. "I believe all Indiana's skulls wound up with the aliens."

"Oh yeah," Olive said, and drummed her fingers on her upper lip as she considered the logic of Ida's statement.

"But our skull may be involved," Ida said in all seriousness.

Zeddi popped a dried apricot in her mouth to keep from laughing out loud. In danger because of a crystal skull anyone with a brain could buy on Amazon? It was outright ridiculous. Ari the lawyer was right. Ida was more than eccentric. She was full on—

Whap! Whap! Whap!

Whap! Whap! Whap!

Zeddi spun around. *What now?*

A large black bird perched on the outside sill, its long-pointed wings rising and falling to stay balanced in the wind, struck its beak against the window again.

Whap! Whap! Whap!

"Wow!" Olive trumpeted. "There's a huge bird trying to get in!"

"A raven," Ida said. "Claude, would you please go feed Bird."

"Your pet?" Zeddi asked. The thing could poke your eye out.

"I'm afraid it's the other way around. It started out innocently enough, us occasionally putting out cracked corn. Now a day doesn't go by that Bird doesn't show up and demand to be fed."

"Can I go?" Olive pleaded.

"Be my guest," Ida said. "But keep your fingers away from that beak. It's sharp as a steak knife. Trust me. I know." She held up her left pinkie. The tip was gone.

Zeddi swallowed back her horror. "Um…how long have you been feeding him?"

"Years. Claude loves her and cares for her, and though I hate to admit it, I've grown to like our scrappy old friend. She's a survivor, that one."

Zeddi waited until Olive and Claude were gone, then got straight to the point. "Okay. What did you mean by 'what we've gotten ourselves into'? What *have* we gotten ourselves into?"

"What was it *you* didn't say earlier?" Ida countered. "I saw it on your face. There's something."

For a moment, they just stared at each other, waiting, daring the other to speak. Then Zeddi broke. "All right. I agree with you. I can't put my finger on it, but there's an unsettled feeling inside the trailer. And after Mags died? That night? Someone came in. And it was locked, I know, because I'm the one who locked it when I finished cleaning. But the next morning, when we went back to feed Barnaby, because we weren't sure anyone would, there were fresh footprints in the carpet in her office, leading straight to the desk and back. Do you know who that might have been? Does someone else have a key?"

"To be completely transparent, I have a key. She had one for my place as well. But I can assure you it wasn't me. I can give you the key if you like."

"That's okay. We've had the locks changed."

"Good move."

"Because?"

Ida sighed. "I'm just not sure where to begin."

"How about with who else might have had reason to come into the trailer after she died."

"First, there's something I need to tell you."

"Okay…"

Ida picked up a small purple pillow from the floor by the fireplace and held it to her heart. Her lower lip trembled. "Mags was the love of my life."

Zeddi's heart turned to mush. How could she not have realized this? Why hadn't Mags told her? "I wondered...I found your photo in her wallet."

"Oh! I had no idea she still kept that in there." Ida sniffed back tears. "We had our ins and outs over the years. Goddess yes! Other lovers too. So many! Back in the day, we were an incestuous bunch. But in the end, she was the one, and I was her one, even though we could go months at a time without seeing each other. We're both awfully stubborn—which is why we could never live together. We've tried, believe me. But lately—" She buried her head in the pillow and sobbed.

Zeddi waited. Dan was right. She hadn't just inherited a trailer. She'd inherited a life. A complicated one, it seemed.

Ida finally came up for air, wiped her eyes. "The whole Constance thing! Mags was obsessed! It was all she'd talk about. I couldn't stand it. Told her she was getting paranoid in her old age. She didn't like that. Anyway, we were taking some space. Not unusual. But now she's..."

"You didn't get to say goodbye," Zeddi said gently.

"I just can't believe she's gone. I can't—" She gave the pillow one last hug, then carefully set it back in its place by the fire. "To return to your question about the key, Mags was always misplacing hers, then having new ones made, so it's anybody's guess who could've gotten their hands on one. That's why she put a combination on the shed, so she wouldn't lose that one too. Did her trailer seem ransacked in any way?"

"Not that I could see. Just those footprints."

A wind chime clanged, the raven croaked. Ida walked over to her side of the coffee table. "I'm frankly surprised she didn't tell you about Constance."

Zeddi glanced out the window wishing she could see Olive, praying her fingers were intact.

"I didn't actually know Mags that well. She and Olive were much closer. She looked after her in the afternoons sometimes, after school." But why had Mags never mentioned Ida? "She did try to connect. Said she had something important to say, but I had to cancel on her." Damn. Now *she* was tearing up. "The thing is, Olive was sick," she blubbered, "so I really had no choice. But Mags was upset, I could tell. I should have—"

"Oh sweet pea…" Ida circled the coffee table. "You had no way of knowing." She climbed onto the couch and handed Zeddi a tissue plucked from the mouth of a fish-shaped box. "I can't imagine what this must seem like for you, falling in with this pack of old witches."

Zeddi wiped her eyes. "Things are just moving so fast, and this all seems so—" She stopped short of saying *crazy*.

Ida got the implication. "I understand."

"I mean, last night I found her diary thingy—grimoire, I guess it's called—and I was like, *what?* I saw your name in the book too. And Roni Miller's. I just…I don't…I mean…I don't get it. Do you think the whole witch thing has anything to do with Mags' death?"

"I suspect it does, yes."

So she'd inherited the trailer because Mags was murdered—by a witch? Was that really what Ida was saying? She wished she weren't working on half a brain cell. Wished she'd gotten a better night's sleep. Wished she could keep from crying. But there was something she wanted to get off her chest before this conversation went any further. "Mags leaving us the trailer was a total surprise. I want you to know that. We had no idea."

"I know."

"I just don't want you to think—"

"I don't. I'm glad she left it to you, though I admit I was surprised."

"So you didn't know."

"I didn't."

"Do you have any idea why? I mean, I'm grateful and all—"

"I suspect she felt she could be of help. And she was very taken with Olive."

Zeddi nodded. "Well, if there's anything you want, just say the word."

"That's very kind of you, dear, but as you can see"—Ida indicated the room with a sweep of her hand—"we have plenty of stuff. In fact, I should send you home with some. Fifty years of accumulated junk."

Zeddi blew her nose. Ida's belongings were far from junk. Native American rugs, Hawaiian tiki masks, a collection of Mexican tree of life candelabras, tons of shells, a lampshade made from sea glass, all in need of a dusting, but nice. "That's okay. I don't even know what I own yet. Not really."

"Of course you don't. How could you?" Ida pulled a couple more tissues from the mouth of the fish. They both blew their noses.

Zeddi tucked a leg beneath her. "So, what do you want me to do? About Constance. About Mags. Because if you think they were murdered…that's what you're saying, right?"

"I'm afraid so," Ida said.

Zeddi took a sip of the spiced tea. "Then it seems like we should call the police."

"I have."

"And?"

"They treated me like a delusional old woman, just as they did when Mags contacted them about Constance's death. And why wouldn't they? Neither of us had a shred of evidence."

"Huh. So that avenue is out. The only evidence I have are footprints and a rain-soaked cat. I don't suppose they'll take that seriously."

"So you want to help?"

"I suppose it wouldn't hurt to poke around a little. Ask the neighbors if they noticed any unusual visitors. Maybe as I go through Mags' stuff, I might find something useful." What could it hurt? She owed it to Mags, didn't she, to see what she could find out? Mags had given her a home. And if she'd been murdered, as Ida was suggesting, then she had to do something. "I'll help as much as I can," she said finally. "I mean, if there's a murderer out there—"

Ida finished her thought. "We need to put a stop to them."

A strong gust arced down the chimney, causing the fire to briefly flare up.

"So what do I need to know?"

"How about I give you a little coven history."

❖

"Where to begin?" Ida mused. "I believe we have a little time. If I know Claude, he's taken Olive out to see his precious chickens." She tugged gently on the loose skin under her chin while deciding. "The early seventies. Yes. I think it best we go back to the beginning, when we were just a group of friends full of ideas about remaking the world. Some of us were starting families, some were entering into the work world. But we all wanted to believe there was more to life than jobs and parenting or being somebody's wife. Then Mags took the fated trip to Venice Beach and met Zsuzsanna Budapest. That changed everything.

"Zsuzsanna Budapest was a remarkable woman with a remarkable vision. A world where women had power—where the Goddess ruled," she said. And it was this Zsuzsanna Budapest, or Z, as Ida called her, who opened their klatch of friends up to the world of Wicca. "Z was revolutionary," she explained, "even within the world of Wicca. 'No longer would we worship the male God, the horned God. Enough with him,' Z said, 'he's done enough damage.' Instead we would worship the Goddess Diana, the Goddess Artemis, Kali, Isis. Mags returned again and again, each time coming back with thrilling stories of their gatherings."

She paused to take a sip of tea, then continued.

"The Susan B. Anthony Coven was what Z called her coven. Didn't we just eat that up! And didn't we just eat it up when Zsuzsanna got arrested and charged for an illegal tarot card reading in '73. Can you believe it?" At the time, Ida clarified, fortune telling was considered illegal in the state, still was in some states, and Zsuzsanna had called it a witch hunt. Ida's eyes twinkled as she recalled how they protested in the streets when the case went before the California Supreme Court. "And we won!" Ida said, clapping her hands together. "The laws against fortune telling were struck down in the state. Oh, those were lively times!"

"I bet," Zeddi said, remembering the photo of them on the altar. But what did any of this have to do with murder? She took a sip of tea.

"Ultimately, we got tired of all the travel, though. It was just too much to keep up with. So we formed our own coven with Mags as high priestess. We cast spells to end the Vietnam War, spells to help members get impregnated, spells for safe travels, prosperity, success, protection, you name it, we were Dianic witches to the core. That is until Roni fell in love with Jace, and we all loved Jace, and so we shifted from the women-only thing and invited him into our coven. But we still worshipped the Goddess, and he was fine with that. He liked being our one male, and we liked it too. Then Shakineh—only she was

Nora then—had a fling with this Harley guy and gave birth to Dahlia, our first daughter. Then Roni had Ari, our first son—"

"Mags' executor, the attorney."

"Yes."

"I just met him."

"Of course. I spoke to him earlier today too, about Mags' burial wishes. She told me she'd like to be cremated and planted under a tree, but she never told me where or what kind of tree."

Zeddi smiled. Ida really did love Mags, that much was evident. "If you don't mind me saying, it's hard for me to imagine Roni as a part of all of this. She doesn't seem the type."

"The type?"

"She seems kind of…conservative. I mean, I just know her from cleaning her place, but she—"

"Well, this was the seventies. We were all quite different then."

"Right. So I didn't mean to get you off track." If there was one. "You mentioned earlier that skull might be involved?"

"Are you too warm? We can crack a window—"

"I'm fine. So, the skull—"

"—was given to us by the high priestess of another very powerful coven—a coven this high priestess felt had turned against her. She was sure someone among them was practicing siphoning."

"I'm sorry, practicing what?"

"Siphoning. It's low-class, nasty magic used by desperate, greedy witches. It's basically stealing the power of another witch." She said this as though she were talking about roasting potatoes, like *of course* there were witches who siphoned other witches' powers.

"You can do that?"

"Sadly, yes. But it's frowned upon. And can be dangerous. It may well have been why Hecate was dying. That was the old witch's name, Hecate. Someone in her coven may have been feeding off her power. It's not unheard of. Anyway, we met Hecate in Big Sur on a new moon, on a cliffside laced with sacred hot springs.

"It was quite the scene," she said wistfully. "The Milky Way blanketed the sky, the ocean roiled below. It was the last night of a weekend gathering of witches and pagans from all over. Hecate was honored in several of the circles. We thought her ancient!" Ida laughed.

"But we also thought her wonderful, powerful. She was British, which made her all the more exotic to us. But she was also very ill, and everyone understood it was to be her last gathering. Oh, didn't we feel special when she bade her young companion to come find the five of us! We'd been singing and dancing around the bonfire. But you can bet when she called, we went. The young woman led us to a yurt overlooking the cliff where Hecate lay shivering and weak on a cot under a heap of blankets. She didn't have long to live, she told us, but she'd been watching our little group all weekend, and had had a vision. We were next in line for the crystal skull!"

A painful memory crossed Ida's face. She picked up her tea, then set it back down without taking a sip. "Well, more than just the skull was passed on to us that night."

Zeddi waited, but Ida seemed lost in the past. "More?" Zeddi prompted.

"Excuse me?"

"You said more was passed on to you that night."

"Yes. Of course. When she died."

"So she did die?"

Ida nodded. "I'm just not sure how much to tell you. What Mags would want me to tell you."

"Tell me whatever you think might help me understand. Because right now, I'm not sure how all this applies?"

"Right. Okay. The skull." Ida cleared her throat. Rubbed the knuckles of one hand with the other. "We each tried scrying with it, some with more success than others."

"Okay. I'm sorry to keep asking. Scrying?"

"Predicting the future. You know, like with crystal balls? Tea leaves?"

"Ah."

"The skull has been passed down for centuries. It's very powerful. I'm sure you felt its aura."

"Sort of," Zeddi lied. No point in hurting Ida's feelings.

"Constance, Mags' sister, was particularly drawn to it, but then she started practicing in ways that made us uncomfortable, using the skull to gain personal power, or so we thought. Artemis! We were so self-righteous! Called her a charlatan! Anyway, we did a vote, decided the high priestess, Mags, should be keeper of the skull, and she could decide who had access. Our decision made Constance so angry she quit the coven, or we made it impossible for her to be a part of it, I don't remember. Maybe Mags asked her to leave. It was an emotional time. Constance was not easy to get along with."

"Mags mentioned it in her grimoire. Said she'd asked her to leave."

"Well, there you have it, then." Ida cocked her head. "You know, come to think of it, I wouldn't mind having that."

"The skull?"

"The grimoire."

"It's yours. I hope it's okay I already read it a little. You're also more than welcome to the skull."

"I think you should read it all. Goddess knows we need some objectivity right now. I'm much too entrenched."

Outside, Olive shouted, "Here, birdie! Here, birdie! Have another!"

Worried for Olive's fingers, Zeddi was about to suggest it was time for them to be on their way.

But Ida wasn't done yet.

"That crystal skull," she said, sliding off the couch to tend to the fire. "It remained a thorn in Constance's and Mags' relationship for years. Or, I should say, *one* of the thorns. They had so many. Mags began to feel strongly that the future was best left alone, that mucking around with it only led to heartbreak, which drove Constance crazy. 'Hecate gave it to *all* of us,' she'd scream, 'Not just you! And if you don't want it, you should let one of us have it!' Even I could see her point. But Mags would not be swayed. As I said, she could be stubborn."

"I didn't really know that side of her."

"For her, the skull was a burden. Still, she took caring for it seriously, and so long as Constance practiced the dark arts, and ran her *fortune-telling business*, which even I have to say was very shifty, she refused her access, which I have to think was a good thing. Constance was unstable. As for Mags, she was much more comfortable working with herbs, doing her healing arts, and only got more that way as she grew older. But in these past six months or so, Constance seemed to be getting her act together, and she and Mags had come to some kind of truce. When I asked Mags about it, she just said, 'We're both learning to forgive.'"

"Did this truce have to do with the skull?"

"I thought so, though I never asked. Mags was very touchy about that skull. I figured she'd given it to Constance at last, or given her access. Something. But if you say the skull is still in the shed, well, I guess I was mistaken. Oh, Mags was beside herself when Constance died! She bitterly regretted that the two of them hadn't gotten closer sooner, that she hadn't been a better advocate for her. She blamed herself for their estrangement, thought it was all her fault. Then she came up with this notion that Constance had been murdered. Said, 'My sister was not a peaceful woman. She would not have sat peacefully sipping tea if she felt death circling.' As I said, I thought she was being paranoid, and we had this terrible fight. Now I feel the same about Mags' sudden death. Death would not, *could* not have caught her unawares. She was too good a witch for that. And she was healthy as a horse! No, I'm afraid, her death has the smell of witches' work."

"You mean a spell?"

"Along with a potion of some kind. A little belladonna, white snakeroot, oleander...there are many possibilities. Tricking the taste buds of a witch is difficult, but it's not impossible. And there are other ways."

"But who would do that?"

Ida looked directly into her eyes. "That's the question, isn't it?"

"Mom!" The kitchen door slammed open, and Olive came rushing in with a basket full of eggs. "Mom! Did you tell her about the tarot cards?"

Ida looked at Zeddi. "Tarot cards?"

Olive, winded and gasping for breath because, apparently, the need to remind Zeddi about the tarot cards was so strong she'd run all the way from the backyard to where she now stood, chest heaving, in the doorway. "There were three on her table in the shed!"

"Dare I ask which three?"

"High Priestess." *Gasp!* "Pan." *Gasp!* "And death." *Gasp!*

"In that order," Zeddi added.

Ida shook her head. "Oh, dear."

Olive set the eggs on the table and kneeled on Ida's meditation cushion. "They have to be clues."

Another thunderous wave shook the house.

"Poor Mags," Ida said, shaking her head. "She must have felt so alone. Oh, why didn't I take her more seriously? Why didn't I..." She pressed her fingers to her lips.

"How could you have known?" Zeddi comforted. "Even now, you telling me about it, it's pretty hard to believe." *Very* hard to believe.

Olive shoved a dried pear into her mouth. "What did I miss?"

"Talking with your mouth full," Zeddi said. "Not pretty."

"But Mom…"

"You should talk to Roni," Ida said. "Get her take on all this."

"Will do. I clean for her Monday."

"We should talk to the neighbors too," Olive said. "See if they saw anything suspicious."

Right. We'll just stroll the trailer park saying, Hi! We're your new neighbors. Oh, and by the way, have you happened to notice anyone suspicious slinking around with a cheap crystal skull, or brewing caldrons of poison?

Still, something had to be done. She couldn't feel at home in the trailer until it was.

CHAPTER TWELVE

The storm hit while Zeddi was plating up chicken-cheese-green-chile quesadillas and thinking about how the lawyer had called Ida unreliable. She hadn't seemed unreliable. A little spacy maybe. Mostly just sad. The tale she'd told was another story. So outlandish! Especially the part about the crystal skull. Wanting to believe her, Zeddi had gone out earlier to give the skull one more chance to prove its supposed powers. She'd taken it in her hands. Tried to feel its aura. The exercise didn't do much for Ida's credibility. Still, as she weighed the blond coroner's mundane assessment of natural causes against Ida's fantastical one of witchcraft murder, her gut told her to believe Ida. Or at least open her mind to the possibility.

Rain pelted the sliding glass doors. A sudden gust rattled them. "You want dinner at the kitchen counter, or shall we eat on the couch and watch the rain?" she called out to Olive while throwing tortilla chips and cherry tomatoes on each plate. "Olive? Did you hear me?"

Freshly showered, favorite dinosaur slippers propped up on the coffee table, Olive was snuggled onto the couch next to Barnaby, humming to herself as she often did while reading. Little tuneless melodies that Zeddi loved.

"Earth to Olive. Earth to Olive."

Olive looked up. "Mom, did you *read* this?"

"What's that, honey?"

"What Mags wrote right before she was murdered!"

Damn! She'd meant to put Mags' grimoire away.

"'How can I convince Ida we're in danger when she won't talk to me?'" Olive read from the grimoire. "'Is she even listening to my voicemails? Tomorrow, I'm going to make the drive out there. Make her listen. If something should happen to her, I would never forgive myself.'"

Zeddi carried in the plates from the kitchen, nudged Olive's feet from the coffee table, set their dinner down. "Olive, we don't know for sure she was—"

"And then she says, 'I wish I knew who to trust. I have never felt so alone.'"

Zeddi took the grimoire from her. "Okay. That's enough." But damn! What else had she missed when flipping through the book?

"Mom..." Olive said.

"Eat," Zeddi said. Not that she had much appetite now.

Outside, the wind howled.

After dinner, it took a few episodes of *Glee* for Zeddi to finally get Olive to take her current book to bed. Steeped in *Harry Potter* books and *Sabrina* episodes, Olive considered herself an expert in all things magic, and therefore the perfect person to figure out who might have murdered Mags, what spell they might have used—and she would not stop speculating. Fortunately, when it finally came time to tuck her in, Zeddi found her, novel in hand, eyelids at half-mast. And the rain had finally let up, leaving a peaceful quiet in its wake.

"Hey, kiddo. Time to put the book down."

"But I'm at a really good part."

Gently, Zeddi slipped the paperback from her limp grip. She was grateful Olive appeared to have moved on from Mags' death, she just wished she could. "Something to look forward to tomorrow," she said and set the book on the nightstand. Olive yawned. Zeddi pulled the covers up. Kissed her forehead. "I'll be in in a bit. There's a phone call I need to make first."

Olive yawned a second time. "About work?"

"Uh-huh," Zeddi lied.

"Okay. Oh yeah, and I forgot to tell you. I volunteered to take care of Creep, the class rat, next weekend. I mean, now that we have a home—"

"A rat?"

"Don't worry. He has a cage, and a hammock. It's cool." She yawned again, her eyelids fluttering. "Three stories."

"The cage?"

"Uh-huh."

Zeddi stroked her head. "I wonder how Barnaby is going to like that?" Secretly, though, she was thrilled. Olive was engaging with her new school.

"I bet they'll get along," Olive said, before rolling over and dropping off.

Just before ten, dishes washed, laundry folded, more stuff transferred out of the van, she got up the nerve to text Sylvie and ask if she'd be up for a FaceTime. Her timing was perfect, Sylvie replied. She was on a short break between shows.

Right. It was a Friday night. When people without kids actually did things like go to burlesque shows. Her phone buzzed. She hit accept and Sylvie's face lit up the screen.

A herringbone beret sat flipped adorably backward on Sylvie's head. "I haven't got a lot of time. We added a late-night show tonight. Some dancers down from Portland. But we haven't opened the house yet, so I'm good for a few." She was calling from the tech booth. Was wearing red overalls. Could she be any cuter?

"Zed, you gotta see these costumes!" She flipped the phone's vantage to give Zeddi a look at the stage.

Great. Sylvie in a theater full of gorgeous, voluptuous, glittery women. "That sounds so fun," she said, and slipped into the backyard so as not to wake Olive. "Wish I could be there." Overhead, three bats whirled about in the darkness, preying on tiny unsuspecting insects. She could hear the river running.

"Everything good with you?" Sylvie asked.

Zeddi blew air through her lips. Ran a hand through her hair. "Mostly. But it's gotten a little..." She searched for the word. "Things are just..."

Sylvie's expression shifted to one of concern. "I'm listening."

Zeddi took a deep breath. "This is going to sound wacko, but the woman whose trailer I inherited? She was high priestess to a coven of witches who think she was murdered. Or that's what her girlfriend says. She's also a witch, and old—same coven. I met her earlier today. Her name is Ida. She's very nice and wants my help figuring out who murdered Mags."

Sylvie raised her eyebrows. "Whoa."

"Right?"

"And here I thought you were going to give me news about the van."

"Oh that. Yeah. All I need is a new alternator."

"Simple."

"Yeah. Compared to—"

"The murder of a witch. I'd say so. Do you believe her? Trust her?"

"Weirdly, I do. But I'm pretty sure there's stuff she's not telling me."

"Like what?"

"I don't know. But I aim to find out. I don't think I can feel safe in the trailer until I do."

"That makes sense. So you're going to help her?"

"I'm going to ask around a little, yeah. I clean for one of the other witches in the coven. I'll talk to her. See what she has to say. The whole witch thing is—"

"A twist for sure. You know what kind of witch?"

Zeddi thought for a moment. "Dianic, she said."

"Ah." Sylvie took a sip from a blue travel mug. "Goddess worshippers. Got into a bit of a scandal a while back for being transphobic."

"Really?"

"Yeah. They wouldn't let trans women into their ritual circles. *Very* women centric. Lots of dykes."

"That's not good. The transphobia I mean."

"Yeah. Pretty closeminded. But my understanding is, some of her followers broke with her over this."

"I can't imagine Ida being transphobic. She's a total sweetie."

"There you go then."

"But how do you know all this?"

"I'm a librarian, remember?"

"Which means what? You know everything about everything?"

Sylvie laughed. "Hardly. But I do know a little about a lot of things. I helped this woman who was writing a paper on how practicing witchcraft can help women deal with past abuse and domestic violence. It gives them agency. It was an interesting thesis."

Was there anything about Sylvie she didn't like? Every time they talked, she gave Zeddi one more reason to want to spend more time with her—as if that night of kissing wasn't enough. Zeddi breathed into the ache of wanting her. Wanting more.

Sylvie cocked her adorable head. "What?"

"Nothing. Just thinking."

"Hang on." Another face appeared next to Sylvie's on the screen. A woman with teased hair, huge lips, and massive fake eyelashes. There was some kind of crisis involving a spotlight. "Gotta go," Sylvie said after a few seconds. "But keep me posted, okay?"

"Sure. Have a great show!"

After hanging up, Zeddi sat in the backyard awhile, listening to the river, trying to fight the feeling that when she'd left Sacramento, she'd left behind her one chance at true love.

CHAPTER THIRTEEN

With Halloween only a week away, Olive was of the strong opinion that they were already running late putting her costume together. "A week! Just one week!" she wailed. She was also pissed at Zeddi for not allowing her to carry the crystal skull as a part of her costume.

"Why not?" she whined. "It's *perfect* for Indiana Jones."

"Because I don't feel right about it, that's why." God, could she sound any more parenty? But telling Olive that Ida claimed the skull had magic fortune-telling powers would make Olive want it even more. And who knew? Maybe the skull did have powers. Maybe she just couldn't feel it. Lately, it seemed like anything was possible. "I just don't think we should mess with anything in the shed until—"

"Until what?"

"Until I say it's okay. How's that for being a mean mom?"

"Mean," Olive sulked. "Besides, you touched her grimoire."

"Olive, you're giving me a headache."

"Well, you're giving me one."

They were on their third thrift store and still hadn't found a suitable jacket or sturdy, child-sized leather belt. They'd found the hat right off. It was perfect: felt fedora, slightly beat up, and best of all, it fit. Some guy had had a really small head. The whip and holster were another issue. Maybe a drugstore's Halloween display?

Zeddi riffled through a rack of jackets. "Anyway, you're going to be holding the whip, and you'll need a hand for your candy sack. The skull would just get in your way."

"The whip goes on my belt."

"The answer is still no. I'm sorry, Olive."

Olive squinted at her.

Zeddi ignored her.

"I just don't think it's fair. Mags would—"

"Olive, stop."

"I'm just saying—"

"Stop. I mean it."

Olive squinted harder.

Zeddi pawed through a few more jackets. Spotted the perfect one. Faux leather. Worn. Lots of pockets. "What do you say we focus on finding you a jacket? What do you say we find one like"—with a flourish, she pulled the jacket from the rack—"like this!"

Olive brightened immediately. "OMG! It's perfect!" She grabbed the jacket and hastily threw it on. It hung off her like a tent.

"We'll shorten the sleeves," Zeddi said.

Olive maneuvered around the too-long sleeves, oblivious. "It even has an inside pocket where I can put a compass! Thank you, thank you, thank you!"

Next up: belt, whip, and holster.

❖

Sunday morning, Zeddi chose her best jeans, a cozy blue wool sweater, and Ugg boots; Olive, her favorite puffy jacket and new Indiana Jones hat. Armed with a canvas tote filled with sandwich bags of homemade cookies, they set out to meet the neighbors.

"You play good cop, I'll play bad," Olive said.

"Olive, we are not going to grill people."

"Why? Someone might have seen something suspicious."

"We ask *nicely* if *perhaps* they saw someone unusual coming and going. That's it. We want them to like us. These are our new neighbors. Remember what Gramps always says."

Olive groaned. "You catch more bees with honey. But what if somebody saw something?"

"If they saw something, they're going to want to tell us. Okay?"

"O-*kay*. Cookies and small talk it is."

That's pretty much what they got too. Throughout the park, people had heard about Mags' death. Apparently, she'd had a big presence in the community. People were going to miss her riding around on her bike, miss her herbal remedies, and if not miss her political petitions, notice the lack of them. They even met a few nice-seeming kids, though Olive eyed them skeptically. But no one reported anything even remotely suspicious. *Strangers were always on Mags' doorstep*, they said. *They came for the remedies.*

Strolling back to the trailer, they passed the clubhouse where a senior Tai Chi class was underway. *Slow-motion kung fu*, Olive called it. As they made the turn onto their lane, they spotted Lorna Doyle doing her cool-off walk after a run.

"Hey!" Zeddi called out before Lorna could disappear inside. "We missed you earlier. We're delivering cookies to the neighbors."

Lorna held the trailer door ajar and blotted her cheeks with her sleeve. "Oh, hi. You're the cleaning lady, right? Zinnia, was it?"

Olive snickered.

"Actually, it's Zeddi. And this is my daughter, Olive. As it turns out, Mags willed us the trailer. We're your new neighbors." So there.

"My *son's* neighbors," Lorna clarified.

"Right. You're visiting."

Olive held up a baggy of cookies. "Want some? They're homemade."

"I don't do sugar," Lorna said, "but I'm sure my son will appreciate them. Thank you."

A gruff voice from inside yelled, "Mom! You're letting in the cold!"

"I'm just talking to your new neighbors," she singsonged back.

"What do they want?"

"They brought us cookies!" She turned back to Zeddi and Olive. "You'll have to excuse him. Jeff, er, Dante has a sleep disorder which keeps him up much of the night."

"Is it Dante or Jeff?" Olive asked, going into detective mode.

"His given name is Jeff, but he…um…goes by Dante now." She rolled her eyes. "Anyway"—she thrust out a pale hand—"welcome to the neighborhood." The sweaty handshake was clearly meant to end the conversation, and just to seal the deal, she shook Olive's hand too. But Zeddi wasn't done with her. Not yet.

"One more thing," she said.

Lorna glanced worriedly over her shoulder. "Yes?"

"The other day you mentioned that Mags had some concerns about her sister's death?"

"Has something surfaced?"

"Just some things I'm trying to follow up on. Is there anything else she might have mentioned?"

"Only that she seemed very upset, and—"

"Did you notice any suspicious activity?" Olive cut in. "Anyone hanging around who seemed un-*usual*?"

Lorna fiddled nervously with her collar. "I'm not quite sure what you're suggesting."

"On the day of the—"

"Olive!" Zeddi barked. "That's enough."

"Mom!" Dante yelled. "Shut the door!"

"I'm sorry." Lorna peeled off her sweaty headband. "This simply isn't a good time. I'm sorry if I—"

"It's fine," Zeddi said. "Just wanted you to know we're here. And if you ever need to borrow a cup of sugar while you're *visiting*…"

"Thank you. But as mentioned, I don't do sugar. And now…" She stretched her lips into what she obviously thought was a smile. "I'm sure you understand." She didn't wait for an answer.

"I'm putting her at the top of my suspect list," Olive grumbled as they walked away.

"Olive. Just because someone is rude doesn't make them a suspect."

"How about the mysterious Jeff Dante? What's going on there? He didn't come to the door when we knocked before. Maybe he knows we're on to him."

Zeddi pulled out her keys. "I really don't think we should be spreading the rumor that Mags was murdered."

"I didn't."

"You were about to."

"It was my strategy."

"Whatever. Just don't do it again. Please. Now how about some lunch?"

❖

Keep. Toss. Donate. Zeddi made three separate piles in the office. She couldn't wait to give Olive her own room. Even in Sacramento, Olive hadn't had a real room. Only a curtained-off alcove.

Already, getting space from each other had been wonderful. At the moment, she didn't even know what Olive was doing in the front room. Well, she probably *did* know. Playing on the laptop. She'd let her go another fifteen minutes. Olive was adjusting. They both were.

Next up: a large plastic tub of art supplies. Pipe cleaners, glitter, a whole jar of googly eyes, a sack of dyed chicken feathers. Zeddi set the box in the keep pile. She and Olive both loved art days. Next a box full of file folders labeled with people's names. She randomly pulled a file. Tom Arns. Opened it. Kidney stones. Mags had prescribed lemon juice, basil juice, apple cider vinegar, and something called kidney bean broth. *Success!* was written at the bottom of the page. *Stone is passed. Surgery averted.* Zeddi smiled. Returned the folder to the box. Set the box on the recycle pile. Noticed a partial footprint indentation still in the carpet by the desk. She examined it closely—a boot perhaps, and large. She snapped a picture before aggressively rubbing the print out with her toe.

Now, what to do with a box full of old bank statements and tax records? She created a new pile: Ask Ari Miller, then tackled a box full of old photos. Real photos. The kind printed on glossy paper, that someone had to buy film for, then pay to get a look at. She loved old photos, there was such a deliberateness about them, a specialness. She could spend hours perusing the bins of photos in antique stores—before Olive, that is. She'd make collages from them. Someday she'd get back to it.

She settled onto the floor with the box. Pulled out a small, creased, square black-and-white of two curly-haired girls sharing a pinwheel lollypop. *The Girls, County Fair, 1941* was scrawled on the back. Mags and Constance? The next photo was of a couple in wedding garb. They stood ramrod straight and vaguely scowled at the camera the way people used to do when being photographed. In another photo a priest lay a hand on the head of a teenage girl in a white dress. Below it— score!—an actual tintype of—

A loud buzzing made her hiccup in surprise. What the hell?

"Got it!" Olive yelled.

Ah. The doorbell, *her* doorbell, and Olive was going to—but wait. If someone was coming to pick up herbs, Olive would have to inform them that Mags was dead. *Murdered!* Zeddi could imagine her saying. She hopped up and vaulted over a milk crate of small blank canvasses to cut Olive off at the pass, but wasn't fast enough. Olive was already facing off with Ari Miller.

"You must be the girl I've heard so much about," he said.

Olive shrugged.

Zeddi peeled a piece of trailing Scotch Tape off her sneaker. What was he doing here? "Olive, this is Mags' lawyer," she said, praying like hell that he wasn't there to tell them about some mix-up, that the trailer wasn't really theirs.

"Ari," Ari said to Olive.

"Olive," Olive said to Ari. "How did you hear about me?"

"Mags was very fond of you."

Olive shoved her hands into her pockets self-consciously.

"What can I do for you?" Zeddi asked, nearly elbowing Olive in the head. Why was she so out of her body?

"Mom!"

"Sorry, sweetie. Um…could you take my laptop in the bedroom, please?"

Olive squinted a few seconds.

Zeddi squinted back.

Bested, Olive huffed off. She hated being treated like a child. Especially in front of adults.

"Would you like to come in?" Zeddi asked.

"Sure. Thanks." Burnt-orange Patagonia jacket, crisp jeans, Allbirds, Ari had skipped the hair product too. So different from his lawyer persona. Was this a social call?

"Sorry," Zeddi said, quietly. "All these changes are a lot for a nine-year-old."

"I can imagine."

"Um, can I get you something to drink? Oh, and while I have you, do I need to keep Mags' tax forms and stuff like that? I'm just sorting through some of her stuff."

"Nope. I've got what I need. After Constance died, Mags made a big point to get her affairs in order. Constance left an effing mess, if you'll excuse my language. And no thanks on the drink. I was just in the neighborhood and thought I'd drop by to see how things are going."

Zeddi let out a sigh of relief. "Thanks. So far so good. There is one thing. I've come across a box of photos. Maybe some your mom would be interested in? Or you? I just started going through them, so I'm not really sure what's…you know, important."

"Want me to take a look?"

Did she? Not really. He seemed nice enough, but she'd been so enjoying the time alone. Still, looking through photos might offer an opportunity to segue into the circumstances around Mags' death. See if he thought there was anything suspicious. "Sure," she said, beckoning him down the hallway. Truth was, the further she got from her conversation with Ida, the more far-fetched all of it seemed.

He stopped at the office door, raised an eyebrow at all the boxes. "Wow. You don't mess around."

She returned to her spot on the floor. "I'm going to turn this into Olive's room."

"Nice." He surprised her by ignoring the chair and plopping down next to her. Barnaby sniffed his knee. He waved the cat off—"Git!"—and shook his head. "Why do cats always gravitate to people who are allergic?"

It wasn't spoken like a real question, so she didn't answer, but Barnaby got the message and slunk off.

He took a photo from the box, then after the fact asked, "Do you mind?"

"No. Go ahead." She pushed the box toward him. "Take all you want. I'm going to show them to Ida too."

"You had a good visit with her?"

"Yeah. I like Whalers Point. And Olive got to feed their raven."

He chuckled derisively and picked up another photo. Stared at it for a couple of seconds. Pinched the bridge of his nose. Coughed. Tossed the photo back in the box.

"Someone you know?" Zeddi asked.

"Mags' sister, Constance." He pulled a hanky from his pocket. Blew his nose. "Darn allergies."

Allergies? Really? Or doing that man thing of covering up

emotion? Zeddi retrieved the photo from the box. Studied it. Face a map of wrinkles and wearing a seventies-style blouse with billowing sleeves and fraying jeans, Constance sat on a ratty orange plaid couch, a cigarette cocked between her fingers, and stared defiantly at whoever was taking the photo. Her roots were showing. "Her big sister?"

"Younger." He leaned in for a second look. "She led a hard life."

"Were they close?"

He shrugged. "Sometimes. Constance was not what you'd call easy to get along with. She had issues. But she was…"

She waited for him to finish.

He picked up another photo.

"Oh my God. It's little me and the coven."

Zeddi took the photo from him. Young Mags, Ida, his mom Roni Miller, and some other people stood proudly around a wooden cradle with a baby in it. "You know about the whole witch thing?"

He leaned in to look at the photo. "Know about it? I lived it. The coven was everything growing up. We didn't do parties like normal families, we did *rituals*: full moon, new moon, harvest, Beltane, first day of school; you name it, we had a ritual for it. Mom cast spells to help rid me of acne, spells to help me get a girlfriend."

"And yet you turned out so normal."

He took the photo back, set it in his keep pile. "I like to think so."

The way he talked about the coven, it was like he was discussing a book at a book club—a book club he had issues with. But what kid wants their mom casting spells to rid them of acne?

"So, Ari—"

The doorbell buzzed.

"Olive! Would you get that?"

"I'm in the bathroom!"

"Never mind then. I'll get it!" She pushed the box aside. "Be right back."

She opened the door to find Dan, work gloves in one hand, a cup of coffee in the other.

"Thought you might have another project I could lose myself in."

"Actually—"

Right then Ari stuck his head out of the office. "If you don't mind, I think I'll take you up on that glass of water."

Clearly taken aback by Ari's presence, Dan tucked his work gloves into his armpit. Adjusted his sunglasses. "I didn't mean to interrupt or anything."

"You didn't. We were…um…" She gestured to Ari, who was now standing in the hallway. "Meet Ari Miller, Mags' lawyer. We were just going through some of her photos. He was friends with Mags and I thought he might want some. His mom was too."

"I see," Dan said coolly.

What was with him? "Ari, this is Dan. Our friend."

Ari extended a hand. "Nice to meet you."

The handshake that followed was more the sizing up between two rival primates than a how-do-you-do: Dan, the younger of the two by a good fifteen years in his black faded bomber jacket and engineer boots; Ari, mid-forties in his white-soled Allbirds and pale chinstrap. Zeddi almost laughed. Men could be so ridiculous. Then again, had she given Dan the wrong idea about their relationship? She thought she'd been clear.

Dan ran the back of his thumb across his bottom lip. "Since you're obviously busy, I can come back."

"Actually, *I* should go," Ari said. "I still have errands to run."

"No. I'll go," Dan countered.

"There's no need to rush off," Zeddi said. "Either of you."

"Really," Ari said. "I'll just get my jacket. You don't mind me taking a few photos?"

"Take all you want."

He disappeared into the office.

Zeddi turned to Dan. "So?"

He pulled Olive's knitted dinosaur hat from his back pocket. "Thought I should return this. Olive left it at the house."

She took the hat. "Thanks. But you can give it to her yourself. She's in the bedroom."

"Nah. I got other stuff to do."

Stuff. Right. Two seconds ago, he was offering his help.

Ari had to angle around Dan to get out, but once he'd made it outside, he said, "I'll give you a call when those death certificates come in."

"Thanks."

Dan waited until he'd driven off in his Miata. "I guess I should call next time?"

"Dan, you are welcome here anytime." *As long as you're not acting like a bonehead.*

"Just give Olive the hat, okay?"

Zeddi shut the door behind him. Time for a talk with Dan. Definitely.

CHAPTER FOURTEEN

Zeddi let herself in through the Millers' back door, then stopped in her tracks. There, sitting at the immense buttery granite island of the oh-so-chic contemporary kitchen with its spectacular view of the canyon, was Roni Miller, mother of Ari Miller, the attorney. Roni was never there when Zeddi showed up to clean. Not since the initial meeting when she'd walked her through the enormous split-level house pointing out areas of importance had Roni Miller deigned to be in the same room with Zeddi. Occasionally, she'd come dashing in between hair appointments, nail appointments, theater guild appointments, but she never stuck around. But here it was eleven o'clock, and Roni, dressed in a very un-witch-like gray velour tracksuit, was parked on a barstool, cup of coffee to her left, neglected crossword to her right, and looking like hell. From the looks of it, she hadn't even combed her hair.

"I guess I should have knocked," Zeddi said.

Roni continued to stare blankly out the window. "Why?"

Because you make a point of not being here when I clean? Even told me once that you can't stand to watch someone touch your things. But Roni's question was rhetorical. Obviously.

Zeddi set her caddy on the floor. "I'm so sorry about your friend."

"Thank you," Roni said without feeling.

Do you think she might have been murdered? was an awkward question to ask, especially of someone you barely knew, who was probably grieving, no less, so Zeddi tried to think of an appropriate segue. One that didn't sound too ludicrous. But her mind was sluggish from a night of so little sleep. It didn't help that Roni always made her feel insecure. Suddenly, all she could think about were her fading blue highlights, her slightly stained jeans, the oil smear on her sneakers. She peeled off her jacket. Laid it on a bench by the door. There was no shame in being a housecleaner—even though women like Roni made her feel otherwise.

Roni stared out the window where a dense fog drifted between cypress trees, making them appear and disappear. Zeddi waited for her to at least look at her or address whatever it was that was hanging in the air.

Roni finally removed her large, bulky-framed glasses and rubbed her eyes, and said, "I apologize for not warning you that I'd be here, but I'm having one of those days when I just can't deal. I'm in no mood."

"Would you like me to come back another time?" Zeddi asked the back of Roni's head. Hopefully not. The next two weeks were booked solid from all the juggling she'd had to do after moving.

Again, Roni made her wait. No surprise there. Even when she wasn't grieving, Roni was the type who acted like the world owed her. Ironic, given the woman was drowning in money. Her husband, Jace, an early tech pioneer, *was one of the lucky ones*, Roni had once said, and got out before the tech giants were revealed to be what they were: evil miners of people's personal data. *He could still feel good about himself*, she'd said, laughing.

Zeddi leaned against the pantry door.

Roni took a deep breath.

Zeddi straightened. The whole silent interaction made her feel like a dog waiting on its owner's command. She returned to leaning against the door. She was no dog.

Roni ran her fingers through her messy shoulder-length salt-and-pepper hair. "No. Stay. But I'd like you to do something different today, that is if you don't mind."

Zeddi kept her mouth shut. The simple word yes could add on hours of work.

"I have some silver that needs polishing," Roni said. "I thought maybe we could do that instead of the guest bathroom, which hasn't been touched since you last cleaned it. We could even skip the guest room. We're not expecting anyone. We can catch it next week. You good with that?"

There was no way to gauge the request. *Some silver* could mean anything from a couple of vases to place settings for twelve. "So long as I can get out of here by two. I have to pick Olive up from school."

"Ah yes, Olive, of course. Well, that should be no problem."

Zeddi picked up her caddy and headed for the sink. "Oh, and I met your son, Ari."

"Well, goodie for you," Roni said, before swiping up her crossword puzzle and coffee and heading upstairs.

"Where do I find the silver?" Zeddi called after her.

"I'll have it out by the time you're done with the house," Roni's disembodied voice called back.

❖

As promised, the silver was laid out on the maple dining room table when Zeddi finished cleaning. No sign of Roni, though, which meant no chance to question her. So much for making good on her offer to Ida about talking to Roni. She picked up a rag, chose a storytelling podcast, and stuck in her earbuds. *Fine.* She only had an hour left anyway, and there was quite a bit of silver.

Briefly, she let her eyes rest on Mags' painting hanging by the picture window. A phoenix rising from the fire. It was beautiful, powerful, all reds and golds. What kind of friendship had the two women had? They seemed cut from such different cloth. "Sorry, Mags," she mouthed to the painting, "but she doesn't like me."

Midway through a *Moth* podcast about a pastor being mugged, Roni strolled into the dining room and plopped down on one of the eight white high-backed leather chairs—a glass of red wine in one hand, a pack of Gauloises and crystal ashtray in the other. Under her arm, she carried what was left of the wine bottle. She set it and the ashtray on the table before pulling out a second chair and propping up her stockinged feet. She was surprisingly agile for her age.

"I hope you don't mind," she said.

Zeddi paused her podcast. Tugged out her earbuds. *Don't mind what? You joining me? You smoking? You interrupting my podcast? You drinking without sharing?* Not that it mattered. Roni didn't care one way or the other if she minded. It was her house, she could sit wherever she damn well pleased.

"Nope," Zeddi said, attempting to sound like she, too, could care less. She glanced at her phone. There was still time. But how to broach the subject? She picked up a CD-sized silver bowl. Squeezed out a bloop of polish. Rubbed the polish into the bowl. There were eight bowls, each made of super-thin silver with exotic etched decorations. They looked handmade, old, and a perfect topic to prime the pump. "What are these, anyway?"

"Finger bowls. I never use them. I never use any of this stuff," Roni said, indicating the silver. "Would take it all down to Goodwill if Jace would let me. But he's attached. His mother's legacy. From Burma, or I suppose we call it Myanmar now. His great-greats were medical missionaries. Baptist. Came home with all these treasures to be passed down again and again until…who knows? Someone finally has the guts to get rid of it. I'm sure his ancestors were lovely people. Whatever. They spawned a wretched woman who begrudgingly bestowed the eight precious little bowls and one hideous candelabra upon her only darling son, along with a lifetime's worth of guilt should he ever sell them, or, God forbid, melt them down. I send her little thank-yous every time I have to polish the things myself, thank her for dying so young. I polish them as a way of keeping my eye on her. Keep your enemies close, as they say."

Roni was buzzed. Definitely.

"So, am I supposed to be casting a spell?" Zeddi asked. Hint hint. Prod prod.

Roni didn't take the bait. Just laughed a throaty laugh. "I've just been feeling her stirring things up lately, and I want *her* to know *I* know what she's up to."

Another bloop of polish. Something was clearly bothering her. Or was getting sauced in the middle of the day how she grieved? "I'm sure you're shook up about Mags."

Roni stared into the remaining splash of red wine in her glass. Knocked it back. Poured herself more. Continued to stare at the glass. "*Shook up* are not the words *I* would use. Devastated. Terrified. Angry. Lost. Those are some of the words *I* would use. First Constance, now Mags. Something is wrong. Very wrong. Surely you know that. You've talked to Ida. No sense playing dim." She shook a smoke partway from the pack. Lit it with what looked like a solid gold lighter. Took a long drag. Her slender hands were trembling. "And please don't give me that cigarettes-give-you-cancer look. Everything gives you cancer these days. Even the sun, for Christ's sake."

Zeddi realized she'd stopped polishing and started up again.

Roni took a quick hit off her cigarette and immediately blew out the smoke, taking no time to enjoy it. "It's no coincidence. I'll tell you that."

"That's what Ida thought."

"I know," she snapped. "Believe me, we've talked." Suddenly distrustful, she locked eyes on Zeddi. "She was very taken by you, Mags was—and by that daughter of yours. God! To hear her speak of Olive…"

Zeddi nodded, but she didn't like how Roni sneered Olive's name.

"According to Mags," Roni continued on, oblivious, "Olive was the thing that was going to protect her. Look how well *that* turned out. She's dead."

Zeddi stopped polishing. *What?*

Roni sucked down another shot of nicotine. "The trailer was originally to go to Constance. Did you know that? Mags felt she'd *wronged* Constance, blamed herself for Constance's *inability* to get her life together. Then Constance died—or was murdered, according to Mags, though she never used that word, but she wouldn't stop harping on how her death didn't *feel right.* I thought she'd gone completely off the deep end, but now she doesn't seem so crazy, does she? Now that she's dead too. *I'll* say something doesn't feel right. Both of them sitting peacefully in their chairs…"

"What did you mean when you said Mags thought Olive would protect her?" Zeddi asked as casually as she could.

"Oh, just that Mags became obsessed with your daughter. If she wasn't talking about Constance's death not *feeling right,* she was talking about Olive. How she had so much white light around her, how she was like a living amulet. Said she was perfect. That's why you got the trailer."

Okay. That was it. No more pretending. Zeddi slapped down the rag. Looked Roni right in the eye. "Hold on, *what?*"

"Ida didn't tell you? Of course she didn't." This time Roni took a long, satisfied drag on her smoke, savoring the exhale.

"Tell me what exactly?"

"She was priming Olive."

"Priming her? For what?"

Roni stubbed out her smoke, slid down in the chair, and closed her eyes. "Do you always ask so many questions?"

Was she nodding off? Hell no! Not if Zeddi could help it.

But Roni continued on with her eyes shut.

"Back in the day, Jace used to be a part of our monthly gatherings. He loved being the only man, the special man. A real feminist. He even used to jokingly call himself a lesbian. I called him that too. We thought we were so unorthodox. So edgy."

Why was she telling her this? And what did she mean about priming Olive? Zeddi picked the rag back up and began rubbing the dried polish from the first of the eight bowls. There was nothing to do but sit back and listen, hope Roni looped back around.

"Well, that didn't last!" Roni said after a short, jagged laugh. "After a few years, he started accusing us of ganging up on him. Said he was tired of hearing about our menstrual cycles. But to be truthful, all his spells were answered when his tech company went public. Suddenly we were richer than God."

"Must be nice."

Roni returned from whatever vision she'd been watching on the back of her eyelids and stretched her lean arms above her head and rolled her wrists, her ginormous diamond ring riding sidesaddle on her slender finger. She lit another cigarette. "It has its perks. Would you like some wine?"

"No thanks. I still have to pick up Olive, who you said—"

"Oh, that's right. You're in the early phase of parenting—before your child grows to hate you."

"Ari hates you?"

"I'm probably exaggerating. Excuse me. I have a tendency." She wiggled her fingers in front of her face. "Pay no attention to the man behind the curtain. Seriously, I do exaggerate. Ask Jace. He'll tell you all about it. Ari doesn't hate me; he just doesn't enjoy being around me. That's what Jace says. Splitting hairs, I say."

"I didn't get that feeling from him."

"And you're an expert on my son, because…" She was slurring now.

"I'm not saying I'm an expert. But he did come over to the house when I was going through Mags' photos, and he picked some out for you. Ones he thought you'd like."

"Did he?" she asked bitterly.

"He did."

"Huh. We'll see if I ever see them."

Zeddi picked up another bowl. Tried to make her next question sound casual. "So back to what you said about Mags priming Olive."

"Forget I ever said it."

"Not sure I can."

"Try."

Okay. Another tactic, then. "How about the coven. What is it you guys do exactly?"

Roni hugged her glass to her chest. "Good question. You should talk to Shakineh. She's very witchy. Years ago, when she lost Dahlia, her daughter, to a drunk driver she really embraced the Wicca Way. It brought her comfort, I suppose, thinking she had some power. She also grew very needy after Dahlia's death. Insisted we gather once a month. And so we did. We do. Or try to. As for Mags and Ida, they've gone a little native, if you catch my meaning. Sage and peace pipes, medicine bundles, prayer blankets. It's all the four directions with them, all focusing your energy. Sand paintings. Oh, and they're always talking herbs. God, the two of them could put you to sleep with all their tincture talk. I'm sure by now you've seen Mags' shed. All those jars of God knows what. Shakineh, though, pure Wicca. Very traditional: tarot, scrying, necromancy, you name it. If you're looking for a witch, she's your gal." She took another slug of wine.

"And you?"

"Me?" She inhaled through her nose. Gazed at the sun breaking through the fog hovering in the canyon. "I don't know what I am anymore." She flicked the long ash of her cigarette at the ashtray and missed. She was definitely unraveling.

Outside, a red-tailed hawk circled.

Zeddi picked up the last of the bowls and began rubbing off the polish. How to keep the conversation going? She looked to Mags' painting for strength. "Let me ask you again—"

"Don't," Roni snapped.

"But if Mags was—"

"Mags would never hurt your precious girl. Satisfied?"

Not at all, but clearly she wasn't getting any more out of Roni. She'd have to ask Ida about the priming thing. "So, Ida thought Mags' death might have had to do with the crystal skull."

"Uh!" Roni slapped the table. "That damn skull! The only one interested in that skull was Constance—and she's dead." She held up a finger. "Actually, not true. Lately, Shakineh's been on about it—again. Apparently, her crystal ball is out of commission. It's not *responding*. I swear, the woman needs a twelve-step for scryers, she scries to find out the damned weather. Get a fucking weather app, I tell her, they're more predictable. But like I said, ever since Dahlia was killed..." Roni ran her fingers around the collar of her sweater. "Is it hot in here or is it me?"

"I think it's you."

"Can you believe, I still get hot flashes? Mags was always on me to take this herb or that, but I'm no good with that kind of regimen. I don't have the patience to measure out all those ingredients. And I can't stand the taste. One brew she foisted on me, I swear, it tasted like something nasty scraped from the gutter. It was hideous."

"Ida said Mags and Constance had recently started getting along. That is before—"

"So it seemed. I never expected the truce to last. The two were like oil and water. You'd think they'd worked it out and then they'd be at it again."

Roni shook another smoke from the pack even though she already had one lit in the ashtray.

"Do you even consider yourself a witch?" Zeddi asked. "Because, honestly, you don't really fit the profile."

Roni tapped the unlit cigarette on her lips. "It's not the kind of thing you can just shake off. Trust me, I've tried."

A key rattled in the front door. Roni quickly slipped the empty wine bottle onto the floor beneath the table. Gave Zeddi a warning smile.

"Babe?" a deep voice called out.

"In here with the cleaning lady!" she called back.

❖

Jace Miller entered the dining room as Zeddi was wiping the polish from the candelabra. He was a good-looking man. In shape. Tall, gray hair pulled back into a man bun, big smile, gold cashmere sweater. "What's up, babe?"

Roni shrugged. "Just two girls gabbing away."

"I'm polishing," Zeddi said.

"I see. Thank you. Zeddi, right?"

She nodded. "And you're Jace?"

"Guilty as charged." He gestured toward the silver. "That was my mother's."

"So I'm told. Burmese." She watched him glance at the floor by Roni's foot. Watched him see the empty wine bottle. Watched him make the choice not to mention it.

"I stopped by the nail salon," he said to Roni, who still had her back to him. "I was going to surprise you."

"Really?" Roni winked at Zeddi, then glanced over her shoulder to him. "How so?"

Zeddi focused on the polish wedged in the candelabra's filigree.

"Yeah. I thought we could do sunset on the boat. The fog finally burned off and it's beautiful out there. Calm. Lots of pelicans. There may even be some sooty shearwaters left. They were out there this morning on my run."

"I don't really feel like it."

"Babe. You've got to get over this funk. Why don't we get you showered up? And then I'll take you to dinner on the boat. We can pick something up. Italian. Fish tacos. Your call."

She shrugged his hand off her shoulder. "You don't have to treat me like a child."

"Really?"

Roni leaned toward Zeddi, whispered loudly, "He doesn't believe me."

"Is this about the witch killings?" Jace said wearily to Zeddi. "If so, I apologize." He walked over and sat in the chair next to Roni's. "Babe, nobody's coming for you. And if they are, I'll protect you." He held out his arms, and shock of shocks, Roni, the ice queen, melted into them, a scared little girl. "Come on now," he said, patting her back as if she were a newborn. "It's going to be okay. I promise. I'll protect you."

CHAPTER FIFTEEN

Zeddi wished she could settle. She needed to get through her emails. Her brain, though, would not stop chewing on her afternoon with Roni. Socked feet propped up on the coffee table, laptop on her lap, she stared at the green chair where she'd found Mags, dead. Her gaze drifted to Olive, alive, bathed and dressed in her glow-in-the-dark skeleton pajamas, and lying dreamily on her stomach in front of the fire, math homework momentarily forgotten. Mags priming Olive: What did that even mean? Was it the ramblings of a bitter, drunk, paranoid woman, or were she and Olive in deeper than she realized? And what did it have to do with the trailer? Roni had seemed so angry about her and Olive inheriting it. Was there something about the trailer? Something in it?

Barnaby rolled onto his back and stretched. Olive absentmindedly patted his tummy. She was usually so driven when it came to schoolwork. It was nice to see her spacing out for a change. If only Zeddi could find it in herself to be so chill. She created a sticky on her desktop—*Call Ida. Ask about Mags and Olive. About priming.* She looked up from her laptop, worried that she and Olive might somehow have become targets of whoever had killed Mags and her sister. If that's what had even happened. If. If. If. It all seemed so unlikely. So absurd. Yet...

She googled *Witch Priming*, found nothing even remotely useful. She broadened her search to just *Witchcraft*. There were so many kinds of witches! If Madam Google was to be believed, at that very moment witches all over the world were lighting candles to attract new jobs, chanting chants to attract love, sticking needles into poppet dolls to torture ex-lovers, casting spells to sway elections. There were spells and hexes speeding through the air like Wi-Fi signals. There were even witches who cast their magic through technology. Technopaganism it was called. She closed her laptop. It was too much! She stared at Olive, who was out cold and spooning Barnaby by the fire. She picked up her phone, snapped a photo, and texted it to her dads.

Papa Glen texted back a heart emoji.

She texted one back. Maybe she should call. No. She'd wind up telling them about the witch stuff. They'd worry.

She yawned. Not even seven o'clock and she felt like joining Olive and Barnaby's cozy cuddle puddle. But she did not want to go to sleep. After Olive went to bed, the night was hers. She could do some blind contour drawings, a practice Daria had turned her on to, or play the ukulele, or write in her diary. Anything. Having a house gave her such freedom. She set down her laptop. Rubbed her face awake. Fresh air, that would wake her up. She slipped into the backyard, leaving the sliding glass doors cracked open in case Olive called for her.

It felt yummy to be outside. The sweet maritime stink of the night. The sound of the river rushing past. It was chilly, but clear. Nice.

And then there was the shed.

Just sitting there.

And inside the shed, the crystal skull that either was or wasn't the reason that Mags either was or wasn't murdered. Could it really be what all this was about?

She used the phone's flashlight to open the lock. Cracked the door. Flicked on the light. Eyeballed the tacky quartz skull. *Seriously? You have magic powers?* She walked over to it. Picked it up. Again. It wasn't much bigger than a grapefruit and had about the same allure. Still, she stared into it, trying to feel something. But there was nothing to feel. Just high-end curio. Roni had acted like it couldn't possibly have had anything to do with the sisters' deaths, and Zeddi was inclined to agree. But Roni could have been lying. Maybe *she* wanted it. Or wait. No. Roni had said the witchy witch—what was her name?—Shakineh wanted it. She'd run the idea by Ida, see what she thought. But could she even trust Ida?

She turned the skull in her hands. "What has Mags gotten us into?" she asked aloud to the skull. "Are Olive and I safe? Tell me, oh magic skull." But the skull had nothing to say. She set it back on the altar, looked for other items that might be worth killing for. Saw nothing on the altar. Pulled back the velvet and looked under it. Nothing but cobwebs and a few rusty gardening tools. She turned to the small desk. Nothing but the tarot cards, a small blank spiral bound notebook, and a jar of pens. She walked over to the shelf of herbs. Noticed a notebook she hadn't seen before. Opened it. Same as the files in the office: people and their health problems. Everything from something called leaky gut syndrome to the side effects of chemotherapy. A number of pages were dedicated to helping women with menopause. Who would possibly want to hurt this woman who so obviously just wanted to help others?

Her phone buzzed in her pocket. She checked the readout.

"Hey, Ida. What's up?"

"I just had this feeling I should call you."

"A feeling, huh?" She poked her head out the door to make sure Olive was still sleeping, then settled onto one of the two wooden stools by Mags' desk. "Well, I just happened to be out in Mags' shed."

"Really? I was sitting here reading when all of a sudden I thought, call Zeddi. I get these notions sometimes. Perhaps it's because you were in the shed, among Mags' things."

"I'm just trying to see if there's anything out here that might help me understand Mags, and who might have wanted to hurt her. Anyway, I'm glad you called. I was going to call you tomorrow."

"Oh?"

"Yeah. I saw Roni today. She's pretty messed up about Mags' death."

"Yes. I talked to her as well."

Suddenly, the sliding glass door blasted open. "Mom! Mom!"

Zeddi shot from the stool. "In here! In the shed!"

Olive charged out into the yard. "Where?"

"Hang on," Zeddi said to Ida before stepping out into the night. "What's up?"

"I was looking for you everywhere!" Olive gasped.

"Sorry. You were sleeping and I didn't want to wake you. You okay?"

"We got a really, really weird phone call."

"We?"

"The *landline*. I didn't pick up because I thought it would be for Mags. But then they left a message, a really scary one."

"Who left it?"

"How should *I* know? They didn't leave a name, and the phone just says private caller."

Zeddi returned to Ida. "Can I call you back?"

"Please do," Ida said. "I don't like the sound of this."

Inside the house, Olive hit replay. A robotic, sexless, ageless voice said, "And so it shall come to pass. What is yours will be mine. What was given will be taken away. It is the sacred order and must be upheld."

Zeddi willed the muscles in her face to remain neutral. Demanded her hands not to pick up her own phone and dial 9-1-1. It was just a phone call. Phone calls couldn't hurt you. But how creepy! She was dying to play the message again to dissect it, but made herself say, "You're right, Olive, it is scary sounding." She intentionally kept her tone steady, or as steady as possible. "But you know what I think? I think whoever left that message is a big scaredy cat. Anyone with any guts would have used their real voice. And we really don't even know if the message was meant for us." Like that mattered.

Clearly unconvinced, Olive walked over to the fire, hefted Barnaby into her arms, and pulled him close. The orange and white cat was almost as big as she was. Zeddi joined them by the fire. Tossed in a log. "I think we should call Ida. Tell her why I had to hang up on her so quickly."

"You did?"

"Uh-huh. When I heard you call, I told her I had to go. Now, I bet *she's* worried. I think we should let her know everything's okay, so she's not scared."

Olive peered out from behind Barnaby. "Good idea."

Zeddi moved Olive's homework to the coffee table, sat down cross-legged in front of the fire next to her, and pulled out her phone. Cuddled up next to her, the ever-patient Barnaby nearly squeezed to death in her arms, Olive hit redial. Was Zeddi right to play this down? Should she be calling the police instead of Ida? But what was it really? A prank call? Weirder still, a witch call?

"It's us," Zeddi said. "Me and Olive. We're on speakerphone."

"Hi, Ida!" Olive called out.

"We just wanted to tell you why I had to hang up. Someone left a strange message on Mags' landline."

"They disguised the voice, made it sound AI," Olive added.

"Probably used Audacity or Garage Band," Zeddi clarified. "Or a voice bot."

"Said what is ours will be taken away," Olive reported, still breathless. "But we think they're scaredy cats, since they had to disguise their voice."

"I think that's a very good assessment of the situation," Ida said. "But you know what I also think? I think there's something we can do to really put that scaredy cat in his place."

"Or her place," Olive pointed out.

"Right you are. Or her place."

"What's that?" Zeddi asked.

"Is it too late for me to come by? I think we should cast a circle of protection around the house."

"Cool!" Olive said, leaving Zeddi no option but to agree.

❖

"I don't get why she's not here yet," Olive whined.

"Honey, Whalers Point is a good thirty minutes away."

"It's been longer than that."

"Maybe she had things to do before she left."

Olive wasn't the only one who was impatient. Waiting for Ida to arrive, Zeddi's mood had changed from scared to pissed. How dare someone try to threaten them? Or threaten Mags! How *dare* they? Meanwhile, Olive had grown more nervous with each passing minute. *Why was Ida taking so long?* she wanted to know. *What if the bad person came by before they'd cast the circle of protection around the house? What if something bad had happened to Ida? What if that was why she was taking so long?* Her questions were nonstop, which just made Zeddi that much angrier. That anyone would go out of their way to terrify a child. Even now, as Zeddi cleared Mags' clothing from a dresser drawer, she could feel Olive's anxiety as she sat there on the double bed, knees drawn up to her chest, assembling and disassembling her puzzle ring, over and over. It was heartbreaking. Why had she agreed to Ida coming? What good would it do? And what did she even really know about Ida?

She held up a blue cashmere sweater. "What do you think? Keep or give away?" It was a perfectly good sweater. Something she'd never be able to afford.

Olive didn't even look up. "I wish she'd get here."

Zeddi dropped the sweater back in the drawer. So much for that diversion technique. "How about this? How about I get the baseball bat from the van? Would that make you feel better? We can put it by the door. Better yet, by the bed. That way, we'll be able to protect ourselves if need be."

Olive looked up from the puzzle ring. "The skull crusher?"

"Yep."

"Our weapon of mass destruction?"

"That's what I'm talking about," Zeddi said.

"That's a great idea! I mean, just in case."

They high fived.

Zeddi closed the dresser drawer. "I'll go get it."

"I'll come."

But the doorbell buzzed.

Olive raced for the door.

"Hello, hello!" Ida said, breathlessly. "I'm sorry it took me so long. I simply couldn't find my rattles." She was dressed in a beautiful woven sage and blue serape, and her unruly gray hair poked out from beneath an old felt fedora with a colorful hatband. A hemp cloth sack hung off her shoulder.

Olive frowned. "Where's Claude?"

"I left him at home. He's okay by himself now and then. He knows to go to the neighbors if something unusual happens."

"What's in the bag?"

Zeddi closed the door behind Ida. "Give her a chance to get here, Olive."

"It's fine. Let me just...let me..." Ida's eyes suddenly brimmed tears. "Oh! I told myself I wouldn't do this." She pressed her fingers against her eyelids as if it were possible to push back the gush of tears. "It's just to be here"—she sniffed—"without her..."

"Of course," Zeddi said. "Take your time. And thank you for coming down." She handed Ida a tissue.

"I'm sorry," Olive said. "I didn't mean to—"

"No need to be sorry," Ida gestured with her hand. "Just being here..."

Olive gave her a hug.

Zeddi wanted to join in but felt embarrassingly tall. Instead, she absentmindedly fiddled with the hem of her cardigan, realizing that until this moment she'd actually harbored some doubts as to the nature of Ida and Mags' relationship, if it was as loving as Ida had claimed, but not now. No one could fake the kind of emotion Ida was exhibiting. Ida was hurting. Bad. The kind of hurt that only the loss of a deep love could cause. And Olive's response, this warm, heartfelt hug, made her so proud of her daughter.

She handed Ida another tissue.

Ida blew her nose, dabbed at her eyes, said to Olive, "So enough of this weeping, we have some important conjuring to do tonight, some magic that's going to keep you and your mama safe." With that, she clunked the hemp-cloth bag down by the coffee table and began emptying its contents—four empty jars, three leather-wrapped bundles, an abalone shell, a handful of cloves, a carton of milk, three persimmons.

"What *is* all this stuff?" Olive asked.

Exactly. How could empty jars keep them safe?

"We're going to cast such a strong circle of protection that nobody will dare mess with you."

"FYI," Zeddi said, "it's a school night, so we can't stay up too late."

"Mo-*om!*" Olive complained.

"Got it," Ida said, and nudged one of the leather-wrapped bundles toward Olive. "Shall we see what's inside?"

Zeddi settled onto the couch across from where they stood together at the coffee table.

Olive made quick work of opening the bundle. "Wow! Can I take it out of its holder?"

"Careful!" Zeddi cautioned.

"It's called an athame," Ida said. "And it's very sharp."

Olive pulled the dagger from its sheath. "Are we going to kill somebody?"

"Of course not," Zeddi said. Then looked to Ida. *Right?*

Ida took the dagger from Olive. "Athames are not generally used for killing people. They're used for casting spells. Though, in a pinch, I suppose—"

"But we would *never* do that," Zeddi said pointedly. "Ever."

"The athame is magic?" Olive asked. "It has powers?"

"Only the power we give it," Ida said, and held the knife up to the light. "But I've had this one a long time, so I've given it a lot of power. Like so many things, it's become an old friend. But tools are not the magic, they are just tools, always good to keep that in mind." She turned to Olive. "Shall we?"

Olive glanced at the two unopened parcels. "But what are—"

"We'll get to those. First, let's hear that scaredy cat's message."

Olive shuddered. "Oh yeah."

Really? Ida was going to make Olive listen to it again? Hadn't it already spooked her enough? But Ida strode over to the answering machine.

"And so it shall come to pass. What is yours will be mine. What was given will be taken away. It is the sacred order and must be upheld."

The voicemail wasn't nearly as scary this time. More like a bad prank call.

"I couldn't agree more, Olive," Ida said. "That's one big scaredy cat, and not a very smart one either, leaving their voice with us—even if it has been doctored. It gives us a handle on who we're banishing from our circle." She hit playback again, and this time Olive made fun of the recording, mimicking the robotic words.

As far as Zeddi was concerned, Ida had already performed pure magic by lessening Olive's fear. But Ida wasn't through yet. "What do you say we banish this scaredy cat all the way?"

"Cast the circle?"

"Exactly!"

Olive shot her two thumbs up.

Ida grabbed the athame and cloves and headed for the sliding glass door.

"Jacket," Zeddi reminded Olive.

Olive grabbed it from the couch and took off.

In the backyard, Ida took a moment to gaze up at the moon. "My goodness. A beautiful gibbous moon. Waxing." She said it as if she'd only just now noticed it. Which was unlikely. The drive down the coast would have provided plenty of time to notice the moon. Ida wanted Olive to see the moon. That was Zeddi's guess.

"Gibbous?" Olive said.

"It comes from the root word that means humpbacked."

"It looks humpbacked."

A sliver of cloud sliced through the hump. The river burbled. Someone in the distance whistled a bright tune. But out there, somewhere, was another someone who'd left a creepy message on their machine.

"We start with the west," Ida said, and swept back her shawl to pull out a compass on a watch chain. She held the compass out to Olive. "You want to show us which way that is?"

"Thataway!" Olive said, pointing to the shed.

"Impressive," Ida said.

It was. "How did you know that?" Zeddi asked.

"Mags and me did the four directions before making art. Especially when we were painting dreams."

Ida studied her for a second. "She had you painting dreams?"

"Just once," Olive said offhandedly.

Chilled, Zeddi gathered her sweater up around her neck, buttoned up all the buttons. *Priming.* Mags had been practicing magic with Olive. How could she not have known this? Why hadn't Olive mentioned it? Or maybe she had? Ever since reading the Harry Potter books, Olive was always talking about magic. Maybe Zeddi just hadn't taken her seriously enough. But why should she? There was nothing evil about Mags. Still, Roni's toxic words were poisoning her feelings about their friend, she could feel it—and she didn't like it. Nor was she sure she liked this whole circle casting thing. What good would it do?

She made an effort to catch Ida's eye, but Ida was busy maneuvering around two galvanized compost bins squeezed into the narrow corridor between the back of the shed and the tall fence that separated them from the as-yet-unmet neighbors. Neighbors Zeddi was hoping to get along with—provided they weren't too alarmed by them skulking around in the dark.

"Can you hear our scaredy cat's voice in your head?" Ida asked Olive.

"Yup," Olive said.

"Good, that's who we're talking to." She lifted the athame into the air. Waved it around. Whispered. "Go! Go!"

"Are you drawing a pentagram?" Olive asked.

Zeddi gripped her daughter's hand. There had to be a way to put a stop to this without upsetting her too much.

"I am," Ida said. "We need to send out the message that this is *your* home now. And that evil is not welcome."

It took Ida's *your home now* for Zeddi to realize that Ida wasn't just casting a circle of protection around the trailer for Zeddi and Olive, she was also using the ritual to let go of her own attachment to the trailer, a place she'd no doubt spent many hours with Mags. Zeddi's heart softened. Ida was family, and one thing her dads had taught her, you stood up for family, helped family. She released her grip on Olive's hand. If casting this circle helped Ida let go, so be it.

Ida began to chant a short incantation, encouraging them to repeat after her. Together, they called on the waters of the earth to protect the house and all those who lived in it. They cast out negativity, anger, and fear, and it felt good, surprisingly powerful. Then, once this had been completed, Ida handed Olive some cloves.

"What do I do with them?" Olive asked.

"Sprinkle a few on the ground."

"Should I say something?"

"You can."

"Okay. I'm going to."

"All right."

Olive thought for a minute, then instead of sprinkling the cloves on the ground, she pitched them like a baseball. "Go *away*!"

"Wow!" Ida said. "That was some powerful magic!"

Olive smiled. "Cool."

"Okay now, which way is south?"

Olive pointed to the street. "Widdershins!"

"Exactly! Always widdershins when casting a banishing spell."

"Widdershins?" Zeddi asked.

"Counterclockwise," Olive explained.

Zeddi trailed behind them to the small wooden side gate leading to the street where they went through the same routine, only this time calling on the fires of the earth to protect them. When it came time to dispense with the cloves again, Olive added, "And don't come back!" Apparently, the magic was already working. Olive seemed much calmer, much more like herself.

They circled around to the east, where a tall fence separated them from Lorna Doyle and Jeff Dante's backyard. Zeddi noticed a knothole and thought, *why not?* She peered through it while doing her part to call on the earth beneath their feet; and there, in a dimly lit, sadly undecorated room, sat a pasty, skeletal, mid-thirties man wearing a black sleeveless T-shirt. His feet were propped on a metal desk, his baby-fuzz skull tipped back, his ears ear-budded and his eyes closed so he could focus on the air guitar he clearly believed he was shredding. Poor Lorna. To have your sweet baby turn into *that*, to a Jeff Dante. And then she remembered something. Mags had once mentioned a next-door neighbor fellow who fed Barnaby when she was out of town. Could this possibly be him? No way. Jeff Dante looked more like the kind of guy who tortured cats than fed them.

"Mom! Mom!" Olive tugged her sleeve. "It's time for the north!"

In the herb garden, they faced the fence that rose between them and the river and called upon the air. Once Olive had pitched her cloves, Ida instructed them to turn inward to the center of the circle they'd made around the trailer. "Now," she said, "we need the rattles."

"The other bundles," Olive said, her voice full of awe.

"Exactly," Ida said. "Be a dear, would you? Run back inside and get them for us?"

Zeddi waited until Olive was out of earshot before asking the question that had been nagging at her. "The phone message, do you think it was for us? Me and Olive?"

"It's possible," Ida said slowly. "But I think there's another possibility. One that makes more sense."

"Which is? I mean, I need to know if we're in danger. So be honest with me. Because I'm a breath away from calling the police."

"And what would you tell them?"

Zeddi exhaled loudly. "Point taken." Anything she'd say would sound like the ravings of a seriously disturbed house cleaner. "Just tell me what you know. Everything. Please."

"Right. Well, there's another coven. Constance's. They're an eccentric bunch. A couple of them live out by the river now in tents."

"Last Stop Camp?"

Ida nodded. "There may be drugs involved. Some mental illness too. And now, with Constance gone, I'm sure they're at loose ends. Perhaps one of them didn't know Mags had died."

"And so left her a creepy message?"

"It's not the first time they've pestered Mags. As I said, they're an odd bunch—very loyal to Constance. One of them goes around dressed like a pirate. You may have seen him around. I know for sure *he* wanted that skull on behalf of Constance. He felt it was her right to have it. And now that she's gone…"

The skull. Again. "It's just—" But she was interrupted by Olive charging through the glass doors with the rattles.

"Mom! Look how cool these are! They're made from real tortoise shells!"

Zeddi forced a smile. "Wow. Pretty magical."

"They were a gift from a dear old friend, she was Iroquois," Ida said, switching gears effortlessly. "Turtles are sacred to the Iroquois. Their myths describe the earth resting on the back of a turtle, so I felt very honored when she gave them to me." She took one of the two rattles from Olive and handed it to Zeddi. "But now comes the fun part. Make as much of a racket as you can. Just rattle, rattle, rattle. Fill the whole circle with your own special energy. Let everyone know this is your house now. And you can't be messed with."

So they rattled and rattled, chanting, "Be gone! Be gone! We banish you!" while Ida traced one last large pentagram above her head, the athame's blade glinting in the moonlight. It actually felt good, cathartic even. She just prayed the neighbors wouldn't mind. Then Ida said, "For this next part, we're going to need to get some things from the shed."

Zeddi nearly tripped over a potted succulent. Next part?

❖

Zeddi held a flashlight as Ida dialed in the combination on the shed's lock. "You know the combination," she commented.

"Oh yes. I've spent hours in here with Mags putting together remedies. We created this one cleanse that was popular back in the eighties. Everyone wanted in on it." Ida nudged the door open, flicked on the light. "Here we are." She turned to Olive, who'd slipped in behind her. "Now, what I need you to do is find a few herbs for me. You can use my stool if they're too high up."

My stool, Zeddi noted.

Olive strode over to the shelves. "Okay. What first?"

Once again, though, Ida was fighting tears. Zeddi laid a hand on her shoulder. "You okay?"

"I'm sorry...I guess...It's just..." She sniffed. Wiped back the tears. "It's just...being back here..."

"There are a ton of jars up here," Olive said. Oblivious. "I hope I can find the ones we need."

Ida took a long deep inhale, exhaled it slowly, then stopped short when she saw the three tarot cards on the desk.

"What?" Zeddi said.

Ida glanced pointedly at Olive. Mouthed, *Not now*.

"What's skullcap?" Olive asked impatiently.

"It's good for many things," Ida replied. "Insomnia, anxiety, inflammation—but we won't be needing it tonight. If you're interested, I can teach you about all these herbs. I'm not as knowledgeable as Mags, but I know a thing or two. For now, though, why don't you find us lavender and black salt. I suspect we can find rice and basil in the house."

"Lavender! Got it!" Olive handed Zeddi the jar.

"I know for sure there's rice," Zeddi said. "We brought some with us. I'm not sure about basil."

"Here's some basil," Olive said.

"Okay," Ida said. "Grab that. And do you see any black salt? We can use regular table salt in a pinch."

"Found it!" Olive said, and held the jar up like a hard-won trophy.

"Good job. Now, back to the house."

Inside, Ida's carton of milk still sat on the coffee table. "Should I have put the milk in the fridge?" Zeddi asked as she threw another log on the fire. "Or does it matter? I mean, if we're using it to do magic..."

Ida laughed. "Actually, I brought it to drink. I thought we could warm it up, sprinkle it with a little cinnamon, maybe add some honey."

"And the persimmons?"

"A gift for you. My tree is loaded this year."

"What about these empty jars?" Olive persisted. "What are *they* for?"

"That," Ida said, "is what you're about to find out."

"I'll put the milk on the stove," Zeddi said.

Over the next half hour, while sipping warm milk with cinnamon and honey, Ida instructed Olive to fill each of the empty jars with a handful of lavender for purification, basil to banish negative energy, black salt for protection, and brown rice to bring good fortune. These they placed around the house, once again correlating with the four directions. This time Ida let Olive make up her own incantation, which conveniently got longer and longer the closer it got to her bedtime.

"Okay, Olive," Zeddi said, as she waved Ida's smudge stick of white sage and cedar, "I think the east is good and protected, as is the west, north, and south. What do you say you finish up, then go brush your teeth?"

"One more thing," Olive said, and continued her improvised incantation. "We're not scared of you one little itty bit. Not scared of you Mr. Scaredy Cat, not at all. Because we have the"—she made muscle arms—"Pow-waaah!"

"Olive…"

"I said"—Olive crouched low, weightlifter-style—"the Pow-waaah!"

"Olive…"

Olive raised her arms in the air. "THE POOOW-WAAAAAAH!"

Ida clapped her hands and whooped. "Well done! I think that's the best spell I've ever seen!"

Olive gave Zeddi a self-satisfied look.

Zeddi couldn't keep from smiling. It was such a relief to see Olive back to her old self. "All right, Ms. I-Got-the-Pow-wah. Now go brush your teeth and get ready for bed. It's already past your bedtime."

"But Mom—"

"Olive."

Huffing, Olive marched off toward the bedroom, stopping midway down the hall. "Here's one thing I don't get. We made the circle and *then* we cleared the energy in the house. How could any bad energy get out if it's already in the circle? It seems like it would be trapped."

"Good question," Ida said. "Let's see if I can explain it. Part of the way a circle protects you is you can work magic through it, but others can't. Whatever it is you want to keep out, the circle will keep it out. But *you're* in charge of the circle, and *you* get to say what's inside it, and anything you don't want in there, *you* have the power, and the right, to make it leave. Does that make sense?"

"Totally," Olive said, clicking her fingers into two little pistols.

"It's like the one-way mirrors in detective shows. Power goes only one way, baby, *my* way, cuz I got the pow-waaah!" Finger pistols drawn, she pirouetted once, then headed down the hall only to stop one more time. "Oh, and did I tell you? I'm going to bring home the class rat this weekend! His name is Creep. He's really cool. He's—"

"That's enough, Olive," Zeddi said. "Call when you're ready for me to tuck you in."

"Whatever!" Olive said, and slunk off, making it sound like it didn't matter to her one bit if she got a good-night kiss, which they both knew was not true. Olive always wanted to be tucked in. Then again, she was getting more independent by the minute. No slowing down that train. Zeddi dreaded the day when the nightly ritual was no longer wanted.

"I can see why Mags was so taken with her," Ida mused. "She's really quite a spirit."

"She's a spirit all right."

"Mags mentioned that Olive's father isn't in the picture."

Zeddi noticed her mug was empty. "Um…can I get you something else to drink?"

Ida reached into her bag. "Actually…" She pulled out a small half-filled bottle of brandy. "That is, if you're interested."

"*So* interested," Zeddi said. "I'll get us a couple of glasses."

"And I didn't mean to make you uncomfortable asking about Olive's father. It's really none of my business."

Zeddi searched the cabinets for something worthy of brandy, found a couple of wine glasses. "No. It's fine. It's just…" She plopped down next to Ida on the couch. Glanced down the hall to make sure Olive was out of earshot. Whispered, "He's not someone I wanted to include in my life, in our lives. It's a choice I made, and sometimes it's been hard, doing this alone, especially financially, and sometimes Olive asks about him, and I've told her the truth. 'He gave me you,' I tell her. That's enough. So far, she's been satisfied with that. But…" She shrugged.

Ida held up her glass. "Well, good for you. I'm sure you know what you're doing."

"One can only hope." They clinked glasses.

"Mom!" Olive shouted from the bedroom. "If you want to kiss me good night…"

"Okay! Just a minute!" Zeddi took a sip of brandy. "Yum. I don't know why I don't ever think of brandy."

"It's good on these chilly nights."

"Apparently." Zeddi set her glass down. "Can you entertain yourself for a few minutes while I say good night to her? Also, I need to get something out of the van for her."

Ida stroked Barnaby's tail. "Don't worry about me, I've got my old friend here for company."

"Okay then, back in a flash."

Zeddi returned with the skull crusher. "Just in case," she said heading back to the bedroom with the bat.

"There's some good magic for you," Ida said. "Very proactive."

Olive's eyes were already at half-mast when Zeddi got there, the book in her hands sagging.

"One chapter, then lights out," Zeddi said, sitting beside her.

"But I'm at a really good part," Olive whined. "Frodo is about to—"

"Frodo will be there tomorrow." She showed her the bat. "And I brought this. Not that we're going to need it with all this protection."

Olive yawned. "Cuz we got the pow-wah."

Zeddi set the bat by the bed. Ran her fingers through Olive's hair. "Love you."

"Love you too," Olive barely managed to mumble.

Zeddi stroked her head until Olive fell asleep, then gently tugged the book from her hands and peeled off her glasses. Setting both on the nightstand, she kissed Olive's forehead, whispered, "Love you, bug," and flicked out the light.

Back in the living room, Ida was standing by the sliding glass doors humming an odd tuneless tune while looking out onto the dark night. She'd taken one of Mags' wool hats from the hat rack and held it tenderly to her cheek. Zeddi watched her for a bit, her heart going all soft, then flopped noisily down on the couch to alert Ida to her presence. "Okay. What did you see when you looked at those tarot cards?"

CHAPTER SIXTEEN

Ida topped off her brandy and scooted back until her boots dangled off the edge of the couch. "I noticed two worrisome things, but I didn't want to say anything in front of Olive." She glanced down the hall.

Zeddi followed her gaze. "Not to worry. She sleeps like the dead."

"Those tarot cards," Ida said, "the three on the desk, is that how you found them?"

"I haven't touched them. Why?"

"The card in the middle, the Devil, it wasn't from the same deck as the other two. It was from the Rider-Waite deck."

"I'm not sure what you're saying."

Barnaby leapt off the couch, stretched, and headed for the warmth of the fire.

"When you first mentioned the spread of cards, I thought it was strange. Mags wasn't big into tarot, not in years anyway, but when I saw the spread, I understood. It was the deck she'd recently discovered, an herbal deck. One of her favorite clients gave it to her. She got a big kick out of it. Right up her alley. Said the creators of the cards really knew their stuff, that the herb they chose for each card was spot on."

"And?"

"I'm sorry. The light distracted me."

Jeff Dante's motion-detector light. "Yeah. I've got to talk to him about that. I'm not sure how Mags put up with it."

"He's kind of an odd duck, that one," Ida said.

"You know him?"

"Met him. But he and Constance were thick as thieves. Or so Mags said."

Zeddi slipped off her boots, tucked her legs up under her. "You think he is—*was*—part of Constance's coven? You said she had her own, right?"

"I believe he was, yes."

"So do you think he might have something to do with…?"

"As far as I know, he and Mags got along. She hired him from time to time to help out in the garden. But then, Mags wasn't always the best judge of character. She was too trusting. People took advantage."

"I'll talk to him—if I can. His mother is staying with him. She kind of runs interference."

Ida nodded.

"So. You were saying…"

"Yes." Ida busied herself with a piece of lint she'd picked off her shawl. "Before the herbal deck, if Mags ever pulled a card, which was rare, it would have been from the Motherpeace deck, a feminist deck with round cards. The moment the Motherpeace deck came out, she burned her Rider-Waite deck. I burned mine too. Actually, we all did at a new moon ritual. Our little coven was giving up the patriarchal horned God for the many faces of the Goddess. It was years ago, but it was powerful magic. Changed all of our lives."

"So, the middle card, the Rider-Waite card?"

"Mags wouldn't have used it—under *any* circumstances. And that center card, that Devil card was Rider-Waite, no question."

"Wait. The Devil? That wasn't the center card. It was Pan."

"That's what you'd told me, but that's not what I saw out there."

"But it has to be. Unless…" Zeddi uncrossed her legs. Reached for her boots. "Who else knows the combination?"

"Who doesn't?" Ida scooched off the couch. "I don't know how many times I told Mags she should be more careful about who she gave the combination to. But you know Mags, she was trusting. She let clients pick up their remedies when she couldn't be there to meet them. She'd tell them to use the side gate, the one we used tonight, and come around into the backyard. She'd give them the combination, leave their mix of herbs on the shelf in a little bag with their name on it. She had a drop box for their payments. The honor system."

Zeddi headed for the door. "Screw that. I'm switching out the shed lock with Olive's bike lock." She opened the front door. "Her bike is out front. I'll meet you out there."

By the time Zeddi got to the shed, Ida was standing by the small desk. She was right. The middle card was no sweet little half-human-half-goat Pan. Not even. The middle card had been replaced by a hideous centaur with bat wings and a grotesque scowl and a man and woman chained at his feet—the Devil himself. "Someone's been out here since we moved in," she uttered softly as she reached for the card.

But Ida blocked her. "Wait! Roni and Shakineh need to see this." She pulled out her phone and snapped a photo. "Now get a pitcher of water from the kitchen—that green one Mags keeps on top of the fridge."

"Because?"

Ida snatched up the card and headed for the altar.

Okay then.

Zeddi went for the pitcher. When she returned, Ida was standing on the small red stool and facing the altar, devil card in hand, a black candle burning before her. "Ready?"

"I guess."

Ida ripped the devil card in two and dropped it into an emptied-out jar. "Fill it with water, please." Zeddi did as she was told while Ida incanted, "With this water, we extinguish the fire of your power." Once the jar was full, Ida screwed the top on and tied a black ribbon around it. "With this cord," she continued, "we bind the wings of your power that it may fly no more." She rotated the jar three times. Widdershins, Zeddi noted. "Your power is now unwound. It has no force, it has no momentum, it is nothing to us." Then, with one sharp breath, she blew out the candle.

Zeddi waited a few seconds. "So that's it?"

Ida picked up the jar. "Once I get home, I'll stick the jar in my freezer. Of course, it would be stronger if we knew exactly who we were aiming our spell at."

Zeddi took the jar from Ida who climbed off the stool. "And the freezing is because?" She set the jar by the door.

"It binds their power."

"Ah." *Of course it does.* "So…you said there were two things. What's the other thing?"

Ida pointed to the altar. "That's not the skull."

Finally! Something that made sense. The tacky Tijuana skull

really *was* a tacky Tijuana skull. "But that skull *is* the skull that's been here since the get-go. I'm sure of it. Whoever switched out the tarot card didn't switch out skulls. This is definitely the one that's been here all along. Maybe whoever broke in has it already?"

"It's possible."

"But that makes no sense. Why come back again?"

Ida shook her head. "I wish I knew."

"So, just to narrow it down—or can we? You said a lot of people would have had access to the shed?"

"I'm afraid so. This used to be our clubhouse. Jace built it shortly after Mags moved in. We performed our rituals here when it rained. There weren't all the herbs then, just the altar." She gestured to the floor. "It was my idea to paint the mandala and the pentagram, but Mags designed it. Roni came up with the fabric for the ceiling. And, of course, many of Mags' clients had access."

Zeddi pointed out Mags' client notebook and suggested that it might give them an idea about who had access to the shed.

"One would hope. Mags wasn't the best record keeper."

"Right, well, you want to take it with you? See if anything jumps out?"

"Sure."

"What are you thinking?"

"Nothing."

"You saw something."

"No. I just…"

"Just?"

"It's nothing."

But it was something. Zeddi hoped silence would draw it out.

It didn't.

"Well, I appreciate you coming down here," she said finally. "The ritual really helped Olive." She wished it had helped *her* a little more. She took the High Priestess card from the desk and placed it at the center of the altar, then put some feathers around it.

"I think we can assume the intruder's intent with the tarot card was to scare you," Ida said adding a bundle of sage to Zeddi's impromptu offering. A quartz crystal too. "Fear, you see, makes people extra susceptible to dark magic."

Fear makes people susceptible to just about everything.

"Would you like me to stay the night?" Ida asked. "I'd have to get Claude, of course. But if it would make you feel safer…"

Zeddi settled onto one of the stools by the desk. "Do you think all this is aimed at me and Olive? Is that why you're asking? Because earlier you said that this was all probably aimed at Mags, that a member of Constance's coven didn't know she was dead, and that the creepy phone call was aimed at her."

Avoiding eye contact, Ida, now back on her stool, fiddled with a spread of shells on the altar. "I said it was *possible* that the phone message was meant for Mags. Possible implies other possibilities, right? You understand that? Because this *could* be aimed at you. We just don't know at this point, really, do we? But I will tell you this, if this dark magic is aimed at you—*if*—it will follow you wherever you go, whether you're here or somewhere else."

That was comforting. Zeddi picked up a small fossil from the desk. Ran her fingers around the spiral of some long-ago creature. In less than a week she'd gone from a simple single-mom housecleaner to a possible target of a witch war. It was hard to wrap her head around. "We'll be okay, but thanks for the offer. But one more thing: Do you really believe spells can change the outcomes of things? I mean, do you really think that circle we cast tonight will protect us? Or that stuff you did tonight with the card? Because…" Zeddi stopped short of saying, it seemed idiotic. It didn't matter. Ida wasn't even listening. Or didn't appear to be as she straightened a feather on a bundle of feathers wrapped in leather and beads.

"I made this for her many years ago," she said finally. "We found the feathers on one of our beach walks. It was a wonderful day. We'd packed a lunch and combed the surf all day."

"Do you want it?"

Ida set the feathers down. "No. I have enough things to remind me of her. But to answer your question—I did hear you, dear. It's just being in this shed without her, it's really…Whoever did this to her…" She dropped her head into trembling hands.

"We'll find them," Zeddi said, gently.

Ida pulled a tissue from her sleeve. Blew her nose. Dabbed at her eyes. Laughed a sad little laugh. "Take two: Yes, I do believe in spells." She took a deep breath. "I owe my life to them. But I'm not narcissistic enough to believe that witches are the only ones working them. I believe people are casting spells all the time and don't even realize it. They're convinced something's going to happen, they make it happen. They're convinced it won't, they make sure it doesn't. And people sabotage their magic all the time. Surely, you've seen this. People going through life blind, wielding their magic like some brute club, swinging it willy-nilly, hoping to Artemis they hit something. The only thing separating those of us who call ourselves witches—or shamans, or pagans, or what have you—from the rest of the world is that we've learned to direct our magic in a conscious way. Casting spells sets intention. Just as meditation does. As prayer does. It forces us to be clear about what we want and to focus our energies on getting it—and by energies, I include action. I believe for spells to work they need to be supported with *action*. For instance: if you cast a banishing spell on, say, an ex, and you want them out of your life, but then—and I've seen this many times—you keep checking up on them through friends or social media, you're nulling out the spell. Does that make sense?"

"Totally."

"Every action we take is a kind of magic," Ida continued. "Like that baseball bat you brought in."

"The skull crusher?"

"Is that what you call it?"

"Olive named it that."

Ida laughed. "That is some great magic. The circle was cast, but the bat is there to back up the spell. The trick is to pay attention. To be conscious. Always."

"Then what happened to Mags? How could someone have…"

"I suspect she let her guard down. Trusted someone she shouldn't. It was always her Achilles heel. I keep trying to dream on it…"

"And by *dream on it* you mean…? Because you mentioned dreaming before, at your house."

Ida pulled her shawl tighter around her. "It's cold out here. Shall we go inside?"

"What are you not telling me, Ida?"

Ida smiled dolefully. "So much. But tonight is not the night. I'm beyond exhausted."

Much as she wanted to pry, Zeddi didn't. The old woman had already done so much—and she *looked* exhausted, the creases in her face shadowed and deep—and she still had a good thirty-minute drive ahead of her. Let it rest, Zeddi told herself as she switched out the padlocks, popping the one from the shed into her pocket along with a mental note to remember to put it on Olive's bike, then remember to tell Olive she'd done it.

On her way out the door, Ida poked at a piece of steel wool shoved into a hole by the floorboard. "You might keep an eye on this. Keep it filled with steel wool, or better yet, fix it. Lots of rats out here by the levee, and they're always on the lookout for cozy nesting sites." That said, she took the jar with the soggy, ripped-up devil card, and stepped into the night.

Zeddi clicked the lock shut. "You up for another sip of brandy?"

Ida had her phone out. "I should head home, make sure Claude hasn't gotten into any trouble." The phone cast an eerie shadow on her face.

"Checking in on him?"

"No, I'm calling a meeting of the coven. And I'd like you and Olive to be there. There have been some suspicions around Mags' relationship to Olive, and I think meeting her, and you, would put them to rest. What's your day like tomorrow?"

Suspicions? "Roni said something about Mags priming Olive for something. Is that what you're talking about? Because if Mags was doing that—"

Ida hesitated before saying, "Mags was clean with her magic. Always."

"That didn't really answer my question."

"You didn't really ask one. Or not the one you want to ask."

True. "So, was Mags priming Olive?"

"No. Absolutely not. Sounds like she was teaching her about casting circles, though. But priming, no."

Zeddi studied Ida. So far, she'd proved to be a straight shooter. If she said Mags wasn't priming Olive—whatever priming even was—it was probably true. Then again, Mags and Ida had been estranged. Would she even know? And was a coven meeting with a bunch of strangers something she really wanted to subject Olive to?

"What do you say?" Ida said.

They stepped inside.

"I don't know."

"I understand your reluctance, Zeddi, but as a coven we will be able to cast a much stronger circle of protection around the two of you. I think it's important."

Zeddi stared down the hallway to where Olive was sleeping. A stronger circle of protection, what harm could there be in that? It would probably put them both at ease. And if it was just Ida and Roni and this Shakineh woman…no problem there. Besides, Olive would love getting to go to a coven meeting. She was actually a little curious herself.

"One question. Do you still consider yourself to be Dianic?"

"Why?"

"Because I just learned that this Budapest woman is—"

"Ah. Transphobic. Yes. I'm afraid that's the case. And the answer is no. Dianic was just the gateway for me, as it was for Mags. It's a shame, though, about Z being so close-minded. There are many Dianic witches who have broken from her for that very reason. I stepped away long before. The older I get, the harder it is for me to subscribe to any organized religious group. There are always so many dos and don'ts, which seem counterproductive, you know?"

"I do."

"So what do you say? Are you up for meeting the coven?"

"I guess," Zeddi said finally. "Yeah. We'll come. I work until three, when I pick Olive up."

"Good, I'll see if we can meet shortly after. I'll text as to where. Likely it will be at Shakineh's. There will be a sick cat that needs nursing."

"You can scry through your phone?"

"Not at all." Ida chuckled. "I'm being informed by the past. Shakineh *always* has a sick cat. But then, she has so many."

Inside, Zeddi threw another log on the wood burner and downed the last drops of her brandy.

Barnaby, still by the fire, stretched a long cat stretch, then strolled over to where Ida was packing up and rubbed against her leg. She gave him a few loving pats. "I know, I know, I miss her too." She hefted the canvas bag onto her shoulder. "I'll let you know about the meeting."

Zeddi was taken aback when, mid-hug, Ida took her by the shoulders and looked her in the eyes. "I don't know exactly what's going on, Zeddi, but I will do everything in my power to keep you and Olive safe. That's a promise. It's what Mags would want. Me too."

Zeddi opened the door for her, then realized she had another pressing question. "So how do you drive? I mean, how do you reach the gas and brakes and stuff."

Ida wiggled her fingers in the air. "Oh, I have my ways." But after stowing her bag in the trunk and settling into the car, she lowered the window. "Truth be told, they make wonderful pedal extenders for little people. Now, have a good night. And don't hesitate to call if you need something. Anything."

❖

Zeddi checked on Olive. She was out cold. A force of nature when awake, the girl completely gave it up each night. But what were her dreams? Olive claimed not to remember them, but sometimes she whimpered in her sleep. Zeddi hated that some unseen monster might be chasing her sweet daughter, but there was no way to protect her from everything. Zeddi knew this, as every parent did. Still, she did what she did most nights: imagined a halo of white light surrounding Olive. She'd never thought of it as a spell before. Now she couldn't *not* think of it that way.

Barnaby hopped up on the bed, curled up next to Olive, and engaged in a short kitty bath.

"Good kitty," Zeddi whispered. "Keep her safe." She returned to the living room to clean up. An itchy mix of tired and wired, she collapsed onto the couch. Seven days since she'd found Mags. Seven days since she'd been saved by the bell from homelessness. It was inconceivable.

She picked up her phone. Read a text from Papa Alan. He thought the place looked nice. Wanted photos. Papa Glen had sent one too. He wanted the address so he could send a care package.

She checked the time. Nearly ten thirty. Too late to text back, but Sylvie would still be up.

Sylvie picked up on the first ring. "Zeddi."

"Hey."

"You okay? You sound kind of...small."

Zeddi laughed. "Yeah, well, things are getting a little weird around here."

"Do tell."

Zeddi told her about the phone message, the cards, the skull, everything. It poured out of her like water. And Sylvie listened. When Zeddi was finally finished, Sylvie said, simply, "Do you need me to come down there? If you feel like you're in danger, I'll drive all night. Call in sick tomorrow. Just say the word and I'm there."

Zeddi felt herself starting to choke up—Sylvie was willing to call in sick for her!—and she wanted to say, *Yes, please!* but knew she'd be saying it for the wrong reason. She wanted to be near Sylvie so she could kiss her, not because Sylvie thought she needed protection. It felt manipulative to make her come down for that. "No. It's okay," she said finally. "We'll be fine." Talking about it all had already helped so much. "Tell me about your life," she said, walking over to the stove to make some tea. "A distraction would be nice."

Sylvie told her about the library, about having to cover for a sick librarian, and about her brother who'd been rushed to the hospital after an overdose. It put Zeddi's issues into perspective. What had really happened after all? A prank call? A switched-out tarot card? They talked until they were both yawning, then said goodbye a bunch of times then finally hung up, Sylvie sleepily offering one last time to make the two-and-a-half-hour drive.

After hanging up, Zeddi settled further onto the couch, pulled the blankets over her legs, and told herself to relax. She was not in mortal danger. She'd just fallen into a nest of trippy old women. It was nothing. She believed this.

Until she hung up.

Until the silence of the trailer started seeping in around her.

Until she felt that haunting feeling that Mags was watching her, expecting something of her.

She tossed the blankets off her legs. Went to check on Olive again. Still out cold. Of course she was. She returned to her spot on the couch, willed herself not to call Dan. Then did.

"What now?" he answered.

"Has it ever occurred to you I might just call because we're friends?"

"Not really, no."

Was he hurt or multitasking? Hard to tell with Dan.

"Well, too bad for you then, because that's the reason I'm calling."

"To be my friend?"

"No. To talk to you because you *are* my friend. That's what people do with friends, in case you're wondering. *Normal* people anyway."

"Well, I'm definitely not normal. But you know that."

"I do."

"So, what's up, *friend*? What do you want to talk about?"

"I thought you'd never ask."

"I'm asking."

Zeddi's throat constricted. "Things have gotten really strange over here."

"Strange how?"

She told him everything.

"Well, damn," he said, after she'd finished. "As usual, you're having all the fun. Do you have any theories yet? Any suspects?"

Jeff Dante's motion detector light flashed on in the backyard.

"Not really. No."

"You need me to come over?"

Yes. No. She was not a damsel in distress. Would not be. She would be the hero of her own story. More importantly, to be Olive's hero. "No. We're good. I just wanted someone else to know what's going on. Someone nearby." She picked at a cuticle. Made herself stop. "But I was thinking, I know at night you turn the ringer on your phone off. I was wondering if tonight you might make an exception."

"Of course. Anything else?"

"No. I've changed out the padlock on the shed and you did all the other locks. I think we're good. We *are* good."

"How about I stop by tomorrow and take a look at the lock on the shed?"

"That would be a real friend-y thing to do."

"Okay then," he said. "I'll do it. Expect me around noon. If you feel like making lunch, I won't squabble."

After hanging up, Zeddi sat for a few moments trying to figure out how she was going to make lunch at noon work. She'd have to get through her first client quickly. It was doable.

The long-legged spider by the wood-burning stove had returned. She got up, secured Olive's homework into her owl backpack, and whispered to the spider, "Keep an eye out," before flicking off the lights and heading to bed. She took her phone with her. Left it on the sink while she brushed her teeth. Put it on the dresser while she put her sleep shirt on. Left it on the nightstand when she slipped into bed.

Lying on her back next to a sprawling Olive, she listened to Barnaby scratch at the kitty litter in the bathroom. When he returned, he jumped onto the bed and settled onto her chest, little claws kneading the blanket. She tried not to think about where those feet had just been. Ran a hand down his back. He continued kneading. She rubbed him behind the ears. He had to miss Mags. Who knew what rituals they'd shared? After a few more rubs, he yawned and dropped his heavy head onto her neck. It was nice. Like a hot water bottle, only better because he purred. But she'd never be able to sleep with him there. He had to weigh over ten pounds, and his whiskers kept tickling her chin. After a few minutes of snoring, he started his nightly chasing of dream mice, little paws twitching. She rolled onto her side, evicting him. Incensed, he jumped off the bed and began sharpening his claws on the cat scratcher by the dresser. She dropped off to the sound of the scratching, then woke to him kneading her chest again. It was going to be a long night.

CHAPTER SEVENTEEN

No need to clean, Evie Walker's text said. The family was down with COVID. Since it was such short notice she promised to leave Zeddi's check in the mailbox.

Coffee in hand, Zeddi stared at the text from her first client of the day. Only now it wasn't. Now she had the morning to herself—and she was going to get paid for it. She took a self-satisfied swig of the milky coffee. Texted Evie Walker back that she hoped they felt better soon and that she'd leave some chicken soup on their doorstep when she swung by to get the check. Customer service. It kept them coming back.

"Olive!" she yelled, as she wrangled the twist tie on the bread sack. "You want peanut butter and jelly or cheese?"

"Bat wings and lizards please! And no sprouts! Just bat wings, lizards, and mayo!"

Zeddi chuckled. The upcoming coven meeting was all Olive could talk about. Unlike Zeddi, she hadn't been kept up all night by Barnaby hopping on and off the bed, or the heater kicking on with its *click click click*, or the wind rattling the windows, or the bizarre dreams she'd had after she finally did manage to drop off. Houses with secret rooms, shadows with piercing eyes, a path of human skulls. At one point she'd actually gasped awake. She didn't remember the dream exactly, only the teacups of blood.

"Are we going straight to the coven meeting after school?" Olive yelled. "Or are we coming home first? I don't want to wear my coven outfit to school!"

Coven outfit? "Coming home first! Ida's going to meet us here."

She spread peanut butter on a slice of whole grain bread, sprinkled it with raisins—bat turds, oh yeah—then tossed a few mini carrots and an apple in along with the sandwich. Her jaws ached from a night of clenching. Her shoulders too. She rolled them to release the knots. Had half a mind to go back to bed after dropping Olive off at school. But by the time she got home, she was in no mood to nap.

A free morning was too valuable to waste. She made herself another cup of coffee, fried an egg, tossed it onto a piece of thickly buttered toast. Sitting at the kitchen counter, she bit into her egg toast and thought back to the day she'd found Mags. Two teacups in the sink. Mags had hosted someone on the day she died. Someone she trusted. Who?

Outside, a blue jay was frantically pecking dirt from a large blue ceramic pot—making a mess. She reached over to the answering machine. Hit play. It was pointless. The robotic voice was too doctored. Another bite of toast and egg. Jeff Dante knew Constance and Mags. Maybe he could offer some insight. But would he talk to her?

The blue jay plucked something from the pot. A peanut in the shell. A squirrel on the fence chittered at the jay. *My peanut! My peanut!*

A final swig of coffee.

A final bite of egg toast.

Maybe another walk-through of the trailer would reveal something. Wandering slowly down the central hallway, she stopped in the office, the bathroom. There had to be something. In the bedroom, she rifled through Mags' backpack purse, her drawers, went through the master bathroom cabinets. Nothing. She returned to the cluttered office, angled around her toss-keep-donate piles. Stared at the desk. Someone had wanted something in the desk. She picked up a stack of unopened mail. Junk mostly. Some bills. A day planner dropped to the floor. She set the mail aside, picked up the planner, flipped it open to Wednesday, October twenty-first, the day she'd found Mags. There were two entries. One for two thirty: *Zeddi coming to clean.* Another before that. Noon: *The Talk.* Capital T, capital T. The teacup person, it had to be! Mags was gearing up for an unpleasant conversation. You didn't call something The Talk unless you were dreading it. Didn't capitalize unless it was important. It wasn't much, but it was something. It confirmed that Mags had spent her final hours with someone she expected. It wasn't for certain that the person had *killed* her. But it wasn't for certain they hadn't either. She set the planner down. Pulled up the sleeve of her sweatshirt, kissed the wrist tattoo and grabbed a jacket. She would not be scared off by some Tarot Card Burglar.

The morning was chilly. She rubbed her hands together before entering the combination into the lock on the shed. Clicked open the shackle. Opened the door. Flicked on the light. Everything looked just as she and Ida had left it the night before. Olive's little padlock had held. She checked the time. Nine fifteen. Too early to knock on Jeff Dante's door? Probably. She locked up the shed. Went back inside. Made the bed. Washed the sink-load of dishes. It felt good to clean up, but strange. Mags was everywhere. She could feel her, almost as if Mags was waiting. She tossed the sheets from the van into the washing machine. Their own bedding might help the trailer feel more like home. She brought in other random items from the van too: the ukulele, Olive's markers, her yoga mat. Taking out the recycling, she spotted Lorna heading out for a run and waited for her to round the corner before trotting over and ringing Jeff Dante's bell.

She rang it again.

And again.

If no one was home, it didn't matter. But if Jeff Dante was home—

The door flew open. Dressed in rumpled black sweats and muscle tee, wiping crusties from his eyes, Jeff Dante looked like Gollum facing the light of day. She half expected him to start spewing a spittled *Me wants it. Me needs it. Must have Precious.* Instead, he pointed a chalk-white finger at a small, skewed sign by the door, and hissed, "It says no soliciting." He was taller than she'd expected. Still, because of his crap posture, she was able to see an intricate tattoo peeking out beneath a new fuzz of hair.

"I'm not soliciting. I'm your new neighbor." She made an effort to smile innocently. "I just wanted to say hi! Sorry if I rang a lot. I wasn't sure the bell worked." Another smile.

Steely eyed, thin lips pursed, he spat, "Hi," but didn't let go of the doorknob. "Is that it?"

She took a step backward. Hated herself for it. "So, you knew Mags? Were friends with her?"

"Yeah, I did. But I wouldn't say we were friends."

"I thought you fed her cat sometimes."

"When she was *away*, okay? It's not like I saw her much."

"Right. But she obviously trusted you." *Likely gave you a key.*

He gripped the top of the doorframe with the hand that wasn't gripping the knob. An inked python coiled up his arm ending at his shoulder. He had an amazing amount of armpit hair. "Is there something you want? Because I'm kind of busy."

Busy sleeping? Busy making creepy phone messages? Another smile. Not that they were doing much good. "Nothing in particular. Just wanted to say hi and offer my condolences. I mean, I thought you two were close. Guess I was mistaken. It was her sister who was your friend, right? Constance?"

Now, *he* stepped back. "Who the hell are you? And what do you want?"

"Like I said—"

He held up his hands. "Look. I'm not interested, okay? If you need a cup of sugar or whatever, go somewhere else. Got it? Now, we are done." He slammed the door shut.

Stunned, she stood for a couple of seconds staring at the faux wood door inches from her face, then threw back her shoulders and said loudly, "Oh, and by the way, my name is Zeddi, and we need to talk about your motion detector light." Striding back to her trailer, she tried to hide the fact that her knees were all wobbly—just in case he was looking—then once inside, she collapsed onto the couch and took a couple of shaky breaths. The guy was lying. He had to be. Mags wouldn't have given him a key and trusted him with Barnaby if they hadn't had *some* kind of friendship. So why get so hostile at the mention of Constance? What was that about?

She checked the Kit Cat. Dan would be over soon. Time to come up with lunch.

❖

"Stop, before you stick your foot *all* the way down your throat," Dan said.

But Zeddi couldn't stop. Her train of thought had pulled out of the station fifteen minutes ago when she'd met him at the door, him with his tools in hand ready to come to her rescue once again. She was full-speed-ahead barreling down the track now. She hadn't planned to assault him with her concerns the moment he'd stepped through the door, but no sooner had he set down his tool bucket than she'd said, "Come on, take a walk with me, out by the river, there's something I need to get off my chest."

Now here she was spewing at him as they walked the bike path. But she needed to come clean. Needed to make sure she wasn't using him. "I just mean, if I've led you on in any way—"

His engineer boots came to an abrupt halt. "Zeddi. I mean it. Stop."

She crossed her arms. Made herself shut up. This conversation was never easy. Guys could be so clueless when it came to lesbians, especially ones who wore dresses like she did, thinking all it took was the *right* man to get under their skirts. Dan didn't seem like that type, but you never knew, he'd been so obnoxious with the lawyer.

She gazed out at the river. It was a whole other world *on the other side of the fence*, as Olive called the river levee. During commute hours the path was a highway of bikes. Now there were just a few walkers, the occasional bike. The sun glistened on the slow-moving water. But she wasn't here for the view. She needed to be clear with Dan.

"It's just—"

"Stop."

He picked up a plastic six-pack ring sitting under a bush. Took a knife from his pocket, sliced open each of the rings. "People are pigs," he said.

"You're changing the subject."

A mangy dog barreled in front of them and into the water, scattering the ducks. "Apollo! Apollo!" The guy doing the yelling rode slowly past on a tricked-out bike with banana handlebars. He wore a long filthy coat with silver buttons and a tattered tricorn hat. Hooked onto his bike: a small tarp-covered trailer with a sleeping roll and other belongings. A small flag with a skull and crossbones was fixed to the back fender and fluttered in the slight breeze. The homeless pirate! The one Ida had mentioned, one of Constance's disciples, it had to be. She'd said he lived at Last Stop Camp by the river, and that was just a mile off.

"Sorry about my dog," the pirate grumbled. But he wasn't sorry. You could tell. He just wanted to avoid confrontation.

"No problem," Dan said, and watched until the pirate and his rig set sail down the pathway.

"I think he might have known Mags' sister," Zeddi whispered.

Dan strolled over to the curbside trash can and tossed the cut-up plastic. "Now who's changing the subject?"

"I'm just saying—."

"Not going to let you do it, Zed. You got this started, now you have to listen to what I'm going to say. You're a beautiful woman, yes, and I like you, yes, but I would never try to start something up with you. I'm way too messed up for that. Besides, you're gay."

"Well, yeah. But some guys—"

"I'm not some guy."

Zeddi took this in. He was right. He wasn't just some guy. In the weeks she'd known him, he'd become a real friend. She stared back out at the river. A raft of ducks wallowed in one of the eddies, their green heads disappearing in the murky water for seconds at a time before popping back up again into the daylight. Sometimes she felt like she spent half her life with her head in the muck too.

"You are *not* messed up, Dan."

"Yes. I am. Every night I wake up thrashing and punching, heart slamming so hard in my chest I'm sure I'm having a heart attack. Every day I have to steer clear of anyone who might offer me oxy. And believe me, the list goes on. I. Am. Messed. Up. I wouldn't wish me on anybody. I'm no different from your pirate there. I've got screws loose you've never even heard of."

A duck skidded into the water and paddled back to the eddy. Another followed.

"Then what was up the other day when the lawyer was over? You were acting all hostile."

He laughed. "Is that what brought this on?"

"Well?"

He shrugged. "Just because I'm not interested doesn't mean I don't care about you."

"And by caring about me, you mean…"

"I just didn't get a good hit off him, that's all."

She kicked at a pebble in the path. Watched it skitter into the grass. "You never get a good hit off anyone."

He feigned hurt. "Ouch."

"It's true."

"Like I said, messed up."

"Not messed up. Picky."

He stepped aside as a woman on a bike sailed past. "Zeddi, even if you weren't gay, even if you were interested in that lawyer, which I'm not saying you are, your life is yours to live. But FYI: anybody messes with you two is gonna get his eyebrows blown off by a full-on blast of PTSD rage. Just warning you."

She smiled. No doubt they would. "Okay. Well. I just needed to check."

He sank his hands into the baggy pockets of his low-slung jeans and continued walking. "Nah. We're good."

"Yeah, we are," she said.

They strolled in a comfortable silence for a while longer, watching the waterfowl and passersby. Then he said, "Besides, there's that girl back in Sacramento. What's her name?"

The mere thought of her caused Zeddi to double over. "Sylvie," she moaned.

"Wow," he said. "You've got it bad."

"So bad," she said. "How did you know about her?"

"Olive."

Right. Olive, who never missed a beat. "It's just, everything about the move to Tres Ojos has been so good, I mean, besides the whole witch thing, which, granted, is disturbing. But Olive is thriving, my business is thriving, we just inherited a home. Still, I can't stop thinking that I made the mistake of my life by leaving Sylvie. I've never felt that way about anyone."

He nodded. "And the problem?"

"She lives in Sacramento."

"So?"

"It's hours away!"

He stopped walking. Turned to face her. "Zeddi. What did we learn from the pandemic?"

"That it sucked?"

"That we really have no idea what's around the corner. Right? I mean, just because you don't understand how it can work doesn't mean it can't work. Have a little faith, woman."

She rolled her eyes, and they started walking again. But really, what he was saying wasn't all that different from what Ida had said about people casting unconscious spells, *Convinced something will happen, you make it happen. Convinced it won't, it won't.* It was all about setting intention, she'd said. Maybe she should leave the door open? Not be so quick to think things with Sylvie could never work out. "You know," she said, picking up a cool broken bit of rhinestone jewelry and pocketing it. "You sound kind of like this witch I know."

"Aw," he said. "Now you're just flattering me."

She gave him a playful punch in the arm.

He gave her one back. "So, can we eat lunch now? Because I'm starved."

She felt a ridiculous grin spread across her face. So good to have a friend—a real one.

❖

Olive slung her backpack onto the van floorboard before climbing in. "I thought we weren't using Turtle for a while."

"Dan replaced the alternator." He'd also put a sturdier lock on the shed and done yet another security check on the trailer, but Zeddi didn't mention it. No need to scare her. "How was school?"

"Great! Isabella asked if I could trick or treat with her! They start downtown, they go right after school before the businesses run out of candy, then hit the neighborhoods that give out the good stuff, regular-sized candy bars, not those stupid *fun-sized* ones." She air-quoted fun-sized to show her total disdain. "Her whole family goes, she has a bunch of brothers and sisters, their mom drives them, there's this one neighborhood you have to hit early because this lady owns a candy store and she gives out *really* good candy only she runs out, so can I go? Can I?"

Zeddi realized she was tightening her grip on the steering wheel, and made herself stop. This was no time to be overly protective. Olive was making friends. Friends were good. "Sure," she said, doing her best to sound carefree. "I'd like to talk with her mom, though—or dad—before then, just to work out the details."

Olive wrestled with the seat belt. Got it to click. "Her mom said to call her. Gave me her number." After rooting around in the side pockets of her owl backpack, she came up with a rumpled slip of paper. "Here."

"Great." Zeddi merged into the swarm of SUVs picking up kids. As usual, it was a nightmare. Clueless parents swerving in and out. Clueless children charging into the street. Bicycles swerving every which way. "I was thinking, it's probably best if we don't tell anyone about all this witch stuff."

"I already told Isabella. But it's okay. Her grandmother is a curandera, and that's kind of like a witch, only Mexican. I told her about going to the coven meeting and everything. I told her I'd give her details tomorrow at lunch." Olive bounced in her seat, legs pumping. "I! Can! Not! Wait! What do you think we're going to do at the coven meeting? I know we're going to cast a circle. Witches always cast circles. But *then* what?"

A blue Prius veered in front of them. Zeddi hit the brakes. "Okay. Keep it to just her, though. For now."

"What time are we going again?"

"Ida's going to pick us up around five. Someone named Shakineh is going to cook us all dinner, so you have to do your homework before we go."

"Maybe it will be like in the *Temple of Doom* when they served Indiana Jones monkey brains and eels and eyeballs."

"Did you hear what I said about your homework?"

"I heard! I will! But when do I get to get a pumpkin? I want to get a pumpkin! Pumpkin! Pumpkin! Pumpkin! Pumpkin!"

"We can get one at Safeway right now."

"Nooo! I want one from the farmers! Out in the fields! We have to do a corn maze! You promised!"

"Halloween isn't until Saturday. It's Tuesday, we have time. We'll go one day after school." Zeddi flicked on her blinker. What was she going to do without Olive on Halloween? Stay home and give out candy? By herself? It sounded so pathetic. Maybe Dan would want company.

"Oh! I almost forgot!" Olive said and thrust at her another slip of paper. "You have to sign a permission slip for Creep."

"Who?"

"The class rat. I *told* you. I volunteered to take him home for the weekend."

"Oh, right. I'll do it when we get home."

Great. She'd get to spend Halloween with a rat.

❖

Ida showing up with Claude was a surprise. Zeddi had assumed she'd leave him at home.

"Oh, he always comes with," Ida said as she bent over to tighten the lace on her leather shoe. "He loves coven meetings. The girls all make such a fuss over him."

Wearing a snappy trench coat and huge galoshes, Claude stood priggishly under the carport.

Zeddi waved and smiled. "Looking good, Claude!"

He waved back and smiled his gorgeous smile.

"You two want to come in? Olive's not quite ready, she's still dressing." Or she believed Olive was dressing. She really had no idea what she was up to in there as she'd locked Zeddi out of the bedroom over an hour ago. "Olive? Are you almost done there?" she called down the hallway.

"Almost!"

"We are early," Ida said as she crossed the threshold. "It's always hard to judge the traffic."

"Especially at this hour," Zeddi said. She adjusted a clip in her hair. "I swear, commuter traffic starts at three around here."

"Earlier," Ida groused. She turned to her brother. "Claude, either come inside or stay outside. But we're going to close the door, so make up your mind."

Claude didn't budge.

"I don't think he fully understands that Mags is dead," Ida said. "I think you being here is confusing him." She turned to Claude. "So that's your decision, is it? To stay outside? All right then. But no complaining about it being cold." She shut the door. " 'Stubborn as a warped window,' our mother used to say."

Zeddi laughed. "Talk about stubborn. Olive! You coming?"

"One more minute!"

Zeddi grabbed her pea coat from the coat rack. "We need to go! The coven is waiting!"

"I said I'm *coming*!"

"It's really all right," Ida said. "Shakineh always runs late. But while I have you alone, let me ask you this: Was Roni drinking when you saw her?"

"Oh yeah. Hard."

Ida furrowed her brow. "I was afraid of that."

"Does she have a problem?"

Before Ida could answer, Olive shouted, "Are? You? Readyyy?"

Ida joined Zeddi in yelling, "Ready!"

From behind the closed door, Olive began singing the *Star Wars* theme song. "Dohhhn dohhhn, don-don-don-don, don…" At the first crescendo she flung open the door. Her outfit consisted of red rain boots, black leggings, black T-shirt, black sequined shawl, and a black beret set at a jaunty angle. Still singing, she slowly promenaded down the hall.

Incredulous, Zeddi asked, "Where did you find all that?" Her own simple terra-cotta sweater, black skirt, and knee-high boots now seemed horribly inadequate.

"In Mags' closet." Olive struck a pose. "Don't I look *fab*-ulous?"

"You do!" Ida said. "And I'm sure Mags would love it."

Zeddi had to admit, she loved it too. "Shall we?"

CHAPTER EIGHTEEN

"Wow!" Olive exclaimed as she frantically struggled to release her seat belt. "This place is awesome!"

Zeddi helped her with the latch then undid her own. Shakineh's house really was impressive, what you could see of it from the street anyway. Like the rest of the opulent houses along the stately boulevard (painted ladies, she'd heard them called), it was an old Victorian embellished with tons of gingerbread and stick-and-ball detailing. Unlike the rest of the houses, it was a jungle of broken trellises, old fruit trees, and overgrown creeping vines. The neighbors had to hate her.

Zeddi shut the car door. "She lives here by herself?"

"No." Ida locked the car. *Beep!* "She has renters."

As they picked their way down the uneven stone pathway, the closer they got to the house, the shabbier the place looked. The railing leading up to the front porch was broken, bits of gingerbread were missing, one of the upstairs windows was covered in cardboard and duct tape, and the whole three stories of it (four if you counted the widow's walk) needed a serious paint job. And there were cats everywhere: two on the front porch and another perched over a gopher mound in the weedy front yard, a couple of kittens tumbled by the pathway that spooked and ran off when Olive tried to pet them.

"Not to worry," Ida said. "There will be plenty of house cats to pet. Trust me."

A pair of crows in a persimmon tree were busy eviscerating one of the orange fruits. A chilly gust lifted a pile of dead leaves and sent them spiraling across the yard. Zeddi flipped up the collar of her pea coat.

Now *this* was what you called witchy. The porch cats scattered when they climbed the steps.

"These are mostly feral," Ida said to console Olive. "They only come around to be fed. You'll find some friendlier ones inside." She gestured to the goblin head knocker on the heavy purple door. "Would you do the honors?"

Affronted, Claude stated, "My job."

Ida patted his arm. "It's okay, Claude. Remember how good it makes us feel to share."

Olive had to stand on her tiptoes to reach it. Three sharp raps.

Clutching the potted-marigold hostess gift to her chest, Zeddi wondered what she'd gotten them into as a shuffling sound approached. It was like some low-budget horror flick. She imagined being greeted by a dead-faced, stooped-over butler in tails, or an Igor-like laboratory assistant with bulging eyes. The woman who greeted them was even better. Ancient, with a heap of unnaturally jet-black hair bundled atop her head, she had a powdery, geisha-white face interrupted only by a slash of blood-red lipstick wicking into the rays of her wrinkled lips, and two violet hawklike eyes outlined in heavy black eyeliner. Predictably, she was dressed head to toe in black, the sleeves of her lacy dress draping to her knees. Around her sinewy neck hung a huge medallion of a full moon flanked by two crescent ones. Now this was a witch.

Yellowed teeth smudged with lipstick greeted them as the slash of red split into a wide grin. "You made it!" Shakineh crowed and bent forward to get a good look at Olive. Clasping together her bony hands, which were half-gloved in black lace, she continued, "And you must be Olive! Oh, I've heard so much about you! And look how wonderfully you're dressed. Perfect for tonight! I gave Mags that shawl you're wearing. I purchased it in Morocco. I went for the sole purpose of finding myself. Of course, I didn't. One rarely finds oneself when searching. Ha!" She slapped her thigh. "Isn't that the truth! But I did come home with some wonderful treasures, and that shawl was one of them, though I'm not sure Mags ever fully appreciated it."

Taken aback, Olive said simply, "You have lots of cats!"

"Oh my Goddess, yes, too many, but I love them all. Do you like cats?"

Olive nodded, her hand reaching for Zeddi's skirt.

"Oh good. If there's one you want to take home, just let me know." Resuming her upright posture, the old witch grimaced and grabbed her lower back. "Oof! Not as nimble as I used to be." She forced a smile. "And you must be Zeddi."

"I am."

"But come in, come in! Roni and Jace are already here." She swept the purple door open further. "It's chilly out, and I've a fire blazing in the fireplace."

"Smells good in here," Ida said, then, "Come along, Claude."

Noting the long dark curtains, the gothic furniture and wallpaper, Zeddi realized she'd missed the mark on her hostess gift. The potted marigold was way too perky. She handed it over anyway. "Thank you for inviting us into your home."

Shakineh took the plant, her thick crimson fingernails biting into the green plastic-wrapped pot. "How sweet of you! I simply love marigolds." She pinched one of the orange flowers off the stem and popped it into her mouth. "Yum. Peppery. I'll add some to the salad. They'll give the greens the perfect kick." She turned her attention to Claude. "Now be a dear, would you? Take everyone's coats, hmm? You know where they go, in the den."

She ate a flower, Olive mouthed to Zeddi.

Zeddi wiggled her eyebrows, mouthed, *I saw*. Though in her opinion, Shakineh's flower munching was more for effect than anything. She was clearly one of those people who loved shocking other people. One thing was for certain though, tonight was not going to disappoint. Zeddi helped Olive off with her shawl and gave it, along with her own pea coat, to Claude, who trundled dutifully down the long hall with the armful of coats. Shakineh took off in the opposite direction, beckoning them to follow her down another long dim hallway with flickering sconces. A whispered argument floated toward them from the living room. Jace and Roni. Shakineh began to hum loudly, as if to cover the sound, or warn them that company was coming. Olive's grip on Zeddi's skirt intensified, stretching the elastic waistband of the skirt down around her hip. Zeddi yanked it back up, gave Olive's shoulder a squeeze. If anything got scary, they were leaving. Period.

Standing next to a tall, ornate molded-plaster fireplace, Jace smiled broadly when they entered the living room. Roni's smile was much less convincing. Perched on an adjacent burgundy Victorian sofa, she looked as though she'd just swallowed a mouthful of vinegar. They'd obviously been caught mid-disagreement, and couldn't have looked more out of place among the dusty portraits and gloomy tapestries that hung off the walls: Roni, in her simple lavender cashmere sweater and white tailored slacks; Jace, in his man-bun, crisp jeans and a long-sleeved microbrewery T-shirt. A long-haired gray cat eyed Roni's lap. She obviously wanted nothing to do with it. The fire spit and crackled.

"Jace," Ida said. "This is a surprise."

Shakineh joined him by the fire, took his arm in two of hers. "Isn't it wonderful? Even I didn't know he was coming!"

He artfully extracted his arm from Shakineh's grasp and held up his hands in mock surrender. "Hey. I'm here for the food."

"I made him come," Roni said, scowling at the cat. "Told him he didn't need to stay for the rites."

Shakineh singsonged, "But you never kno-*ow*, he might change his mi-*ind*."

"I wouldn't count on it," Roni said. She tossed the cat before it could climb onto her lap. Picked some cat hairs off her slacks. Smiled at Ida. "Thank you for setting this up. I appreciate it, as you know."

Ida walked over to the couch and gave her a hug. "What's a coven for?"

"What indeed?" Roni said tepidly.

"So, what's it been?" Jace squatted to hug Ida. "Six months? More?" *Very athletic.*

"Too long," she said. "But it's nice to see you now. Even if it's just for dinner."

Olive tugged at Zeddi's skirt again, and whispered, "Mom, look!" She pointed to a large aquarium on a low Oriental cabinet. "A snake!"

Zeddi yanked up her waistband again. Sure enough, in the aquarium, a snake was slithering off a piece of dead branch into the duff below. It was the second snake she'd seen that day, the other the tat on the arm of her creepy neighbor, Jeff Dante. A two-snake day, she mused.

"Hello, Zeddi," Roni said, finally acknowledging her. "Thank you for coming." Her tone made it clear that despite the gathering, Zeddi was still, and always would be, her housecleaner. Roni shifted her gaze to Olive. "And you must be Olive. We've all heard *so* much about you. It's nice to finally lay eyes on you."

Olive made only the slightest effort to turn away from the snake. "Um, thanks. Nice to meet you too."

"You like snakes?" Jace asked.

"Yes, do you?" Shakineh echoed.

"I guess," Olive answered shyly.

Zeddi gave her ponytail a tug. "Are you kidding? You love snakes. It's something she and Mags had in common. A love of reptiles and spiders."

"And birds," Olive added.

Zeddi caught Jace's eye. They shared a smile. Like Ari, his bottom two teeth overlapped slightly. They were handsome men, the Millers, and they knew it.

Behind him, above the fireplace, hung another of Mags' paintings: a spider on a single thread blowing across an abstract purple and blue sky. Like her other paintings, the paint was so thick it had to have been applied with a palette knife. It was also very Shakineh, just as the painting for Ida was very Ida, and Roni's very Roni. It also needed a good dusting.

Claude returned from his coat excursion and plunked down on a large throne-like chair by the door. He looked proud of himself.

"But please," Shakineh said, sweeping wide her arms with the draping sleeves to indicate the rest of the seating to their small entourage, "make yourselves comfortable."

Zeddi chose a Morris chair opposite the couch. Ida grabbed a stool by the fire. Olive went straight for the aquarium.

Shakineh laughed. "I can see someone needs to meet Evanora. But first…" From a crystal decanter, she poured them each a glass of syrupy-looking red juice, then took the balled-up snake out of the aquarium and brought it to a simple straight-backed chair where she sat with it on her lap. Olive kneeled next to her while Zeddi couldn't take her eyes off Shakineh's bare feet. Her crimson toenails curled downward over the tips of her gnarled toes like claws, one of her toes crossing completely over another of them on the hard wood floor. *Not toes, talons.* "She's a ball python," Shakineh explained to Olive. "And you can see why. She balls up as a defense mechanism."

"Like an ostrich," Olive said, "sticking its head in the sand when it gets scared."

"Exactly. Not very effective."

"The medicine of denial," Ida chimed in. "I wouldn't underestimate it."

Roni shot a look at her husband. "So true."

"What?" Jace said defensively.

Roni picked up her glass of pomegranate juice. Sniffed it. Grimaced. And returned it to the glass coaster, untouched.

Jace coughed pointedly into his hand.

She pointedly ignored him.

Ida had instructed Zeddi not to drink any alcohol, smoke any pot, or engage in any other kind of mind-altering practices before coming. *Our minds need to be clear for what we're going to do*, she'd said. Zeddi wondered if Roni had followed the rules. She glanced at Ida, but Ida was too busy poking at the fire to notice.

Then Ida hooked the poker onto the stand, and addressed the group. "With everyone here, we should talk about Mags' end-of-life wishes."

Roni nervously jiggled one of her ankle boots. Shakineh picked up a delicate wooden fan and began fanning herself. Jace cleared his throat.

"I believe Mags and my son already went over all this," Roni said.

"I'm not talking about her things, Roni."

"I know. I know." Roni rocked forward and wrapped her arms around her waist in what looked like a self-inflicted straitjacket. "God, I hate this!"

Jace set his juice on the mantel and settled onto the arm of the couch next to Roni. He began massaging her shoulders. "It's been hard on all of us, Ron, but she led a good long life."

"Oh, for God's sake! What does that even mean? And why do you keep saying it?"

After a few squeezes, he gave up. Zeddi didn't blame him. Roni was not appreciative.

Meanwhile, Shakineh's fanning had become so vigorous that poor Evanora balled up even tighter—if that were possible. "First Constance and now Mags. We're dwindling at a terrible rate."

Roni reached for her glass again. "Who's next? That's what I want to know. And who…" Again, she set the glass down, untouched.

"Can we not go there, hon? Please? Can the five of us, or seven"—Jace tossed an apologetic smile to Zeddi—"just have a simple dinner together? Like old times? Is that too much to ask?" He looked to Ida and Shakineh for support. Zeddi glanced at Olive, assessing if it was time to leave or not. Olive was still zeroed in on the snake.

"Of course we can," Shakineh conceded, and set down her fan. "No pressure. Just dinner."

"I've already set up the cremation," Ida continued. "But she wants her ashes buried under a tree—though she didn't specify which tree—or where."

"Typical," Jace muttered.

Roni slapped his leg. "Jace!"

"What? I'm just speaking the truth. We all know it. We loved her anyway. But she was impulsive. You yourself always said she was like a tornado. How you didn't know—"

"I know what I said, thank you."

"I was thinking," Ida interrupted, "it would be appropriate to bury her ashes on the Day of the Dead." The fire behind her flared up.

Shakineh's hands flew to her chest. "She's here."

Olive looked up from petting the snake. "She is?" She echoed Zeddi's thoughts exactly.

"Possibly," Ida said. "But it could also be the cedar kindling I just threw on. Now, if we can get back to what I was saying. I'm talking about this Sunday. I think she'd like us all there. Would that work?"

"Where were you thinking?" Roni asked.

"The coast? Up by me? She loved the cypress grove. We'd have to be discreet about it, though. It is illegal."

"Which is ridiculous," Roni said.

"But true nonetheless."

"Works for me," Jace said.

"Me as well," Shakineh said, and absentmindedly handed the balled-up Evanora to Olive, who held the snake in front of her like a birthday cake, her own eyes wide as dinner plates. "But I say we confirm with her during tonight's séance."

Olive and Zeddi met eyes. *Séance?*

Ida nodded. "Goes without saying."

Zeddi set her glass down on the arm of the wooden chair a bit too forcefully. "Séance?"

"Are we going to get to talk to Mags?" Olive asked, excitedly. "Because if we do, I have something I want to ask her."

"I expect we all have questions for her," Ida said kindly.

"I'm not sure about this," Zeddi said. "This is the first I'm—"

"Nooo," Olive said. "We have to do the séance!"

"Of course you're welcome to leave at any time," Ida said. "But I really encourage you to stay. If at any time, you feel uncomfortable, we'll stop."

"Regardless, you simply *must* stay for dinner," Shakineh said.

"I thought you said we were going to be casting a circle of protection," Zeddi said softly to Ida.

"And we are."

It was hard to think with Roni's ankle boot waggling so much.

"Pul-leeease?" Olive pleaded.

Zeddi closed her eyes. Took a breath. Why was she resisting? It wasn't like they were really going to call up the dead, that was impossible. She looked to Olive, whose hands were clasped around the snake as if in prayer, her mouth silently pleading *please please please*. Looked to Ida, who gave a small reassuring nod. "All right," she said at last. Then clarified to Olive, "But if I say it's time to leave, we leave."

"Okay. I promise."

Shakineh rose from her chair. "Wonderful! Then it's time to put Evanora back. Time to eat. Because I hear it's a school night for somebody," she said in a tone she obviously reserved for children, "so we can't be keeping her out too late."

Olive squinted hard at Zeddi, like it was her fault it was a school night.

Zeddi walked her over to the aquarium. Lifted the lid so Olive could return Evanora to her happy place behind the glass. Said quietly, "Hey, a snake and a séance in one night, no complaining."

On the way to the dining room, Zeddi was so focused on the way that Shakineh laid her hand on Jace's lower back—as though he were her man, not Roni's—she nearly tripped over a cliche: a green-eyed black cat crossing her path.

❖

Shakineh's braised chicken stew lolled, red and soupy, in a silver tureen at the center of the long mahogany table. Served with slabs of butter-slathered crusty white bread and a salad spiced with Zeddi's marigolds, the stew looked feral as the outdoor cats, the chicken bones sticking up out of the cloudy broth, unknown vegetables bobbing up beside them. "Say when," Shakineh said as she hovered behind each person ladling their bowl full of her creation.

Zeddi stared at the soup. How to eat it? The vegetables could be spooned up easily enough, the thick, reddish broth too, but the chicken posed a problem. Thighs and legs were still on the bone. Fingers? Knife and fork? It didn't help that the room was so dimly lit. Ida, next to her on a thick foam booster she'd brought from home, spread her black cloth napkin neatly across her lap. "You are one special guest, Olive. Shakineh made you her specialty."

Olive, sitting to Zeddi's right, peered cautiously at the concoction before her. She looked horrified. Zeddi prayed whatever she was thinking, she'd keep to herself. Above them, electricity from a droopy crystal chandelier emitted a slight buzz. At the head of the table, Shakineh filled her own bowl, then slowly, delicately removed each black-lace half glove and set them to the side of her plate. Her movements were precise, intentional: the tilt of the ladle, the angle at which she set the gloves.

A cat brushed up against Zeddi's leg.

"It's been so long since we were all together," Shakineh began. "Or *almost* all together." She rested her gaze on two empty place settings at the other end of the table. Her eyes filled with tears. One setting was for Mags, obviously. But the other? Zeddi remembered the daughter. Lost in a car wreck. Suddenly, Shakineh's eccentric behavior made sense. To lose a child that way, how could you not go barking mad? Zeddi blinked back some tears of her own.

The cat circled her other leg.

Shakineh, still standing at the head of the table, made the rounds with her eyes, holding each person's gaze a few seconds until moving on to the next. That is, until she got to Olive, who was staring at her bowl of bony stew, oblivious it was her turn for *the look*.

Zeddi nudged her.

"What?"

Zeddi nodded toward Shakineh.

Olive looked up. Saw everyone was waiting on her. "Sorry. Am I supposed to do something?"

Shakineh hooted with laughter. "Oh, it's good to have a child around! A reminder of the future." Wiping the tears from her eyes, she swept her dress beneath her and ceremoniously lowered into her chair. "Shall we?"

"Definitely," Ida voted. "I'm starved."

"Me too!" Claude seconded.

Zeddi was just about to pick up her spoon and test the waters when the four witches clapped their hands together, flicked their palms up to the sky, and chanted, "Blessed be! Grateful we!" accompanied by some joyful murmurings from Claude. This completed, they plunged their fingers into the deep bowls and attacked their chicken stew like hungry raccoons.

Olive blinked aggressively at Zeddi. She hated anything that even remotely resembled what she referred to as *mushy food*, which could include anything from certain sushi to the bits of soggy lettuce left in the sink strainer. Said it hurt her fingers to touch it.

Zeddi laser-eyed her, *Just try it.*

Mercifully, Olive did, and mercifully, after a few tentative bites of chicken, concluded aloud, "This is what I call real finger food!"

Even Roni laughed.

"Seriously, it is delicious," Zeddi said. And it was. Tender, flavorful, and falling off the bone.

Midway through the smacking of lips and licking of fingertips, Shakineh, who was particularly predatory as she snapped apart chicken bones and sucked the marrow, gestured with the stab of a drumstick. "I saw something today. A dark energy—"

Ida silenced her with the wag of a finger. "Nuh-uh. Not until we're done eating."

"Agreed," Roni said.

"It goes against the codes," Ida said.

Olive grabbed a piece of bread and slathered it with butter. "What codes?"

"The codes of the coven," Jace said in a mocking tone. Not unkindly. More like he was in on the joke.

"We have hundreds of them," Ida said. "Most we don't even remember because they get made up on the spot."

"As situations arise," Jace clarified.

"And get forgotten as quickly as we make them," Roni added. "But this one we *never* forget, do we? Not after a few Beltanes ago."

"Never mix business and eating!" Ida and Roni said together.

"It's not exactly business," Shakineh protested, and blotted her lips with a black napkin, as if preparing to say more.

"But it is," Roni said. "And you know it."

"What happened a few Beltanes ago?" Zeddi asked.

"Shall we just say," Ida began, her eyes twinkling, "that when you get older your digestion changes, and talking about difficult subjects while eating can bring on disastrous results."

"Hideous results," Roni said.

"And on that particular Beltane…" Ida said.

"Between the subject matter and those damn green peppers…" Roni coaxed.

"Oh, my Goddess!" Shakineh asserted. "Is this really something we need to share?"

"I wasn't there but I've heard *all* about it," Jace said, chuckling.

"And heard and heard…" Roni said, now also laughing. "All that night."

"I really think it was the green peppers," Shakineh said, but she'd been swept into the laughing too.

"Wait." Olive looked up from her heavily buttered piece of bread. "Are you talking about farting?"

"Are we ever!" Jace said.

Olive burst into giggles. Roni snorted she was laughing so hard.

Ida wiped her eyes with her napkin. "And so it was added to the codes: No talking business while we eat."

"And no green peppers!" Roni said.

Shakineh shrugged. "I did used to put them in everything."

"Until we made her stop," Ida said.

"Pee-ew!" Claude said, waving his meaty hands in front of his face. "Pee-ew!"

Which made them all burst into a second round of laughing.

"See what I have to put up with?" Jace said to Olive and Zeddi. "It's not easy."

Roni slapped his arm. "Oh hush."

It was nice to see that Roni and Jace got along sometimes. Nice to feel the family energy of the entire group. They obviously had a lot of history together. As Jace leaned over to give Roni's shoulder a squeeze, Zeddi's eyes drifted to the china cabinet behind him. It was crammed with oddities. A stuffed bird, several very large eggs—*ostrich? emu? dinosaur?*—a silver cast of a hand, a few straw dolls, some random bones, something hidden under a hump of black velvet. The skull? Surely not. Surely if she'd had the smarts to steal it, she'd have the smarts to hide it better. Or maybe she wanted them to see it?

The room fell into silence. All except for Shakineh's cracking of chicken bones, and the occasional slurp of broth. Olive went for another piece of bread. Since her proclamation about the stew being *real finger food* she'd pretty much steered clear of it. But that was okay, she'd tried it, which was all Zeddi ever asked of her.

"So," Olive said, after swallowing her lump of buttery bread, "are you guys omnists or are you just plain witches?"

"What the hell is an omnist?" Roni asked.

"An omnist believes in all religions. My friend Dan said Mags was an omnist because of her shed."

Thigh bone in hand, Ida cocked her head. "That's a very interesting question, Olive. What made you think of it just now?"

Olive pointed to the china cabinet where below the mysterious lump that might or might not be the crystal skull, there was also a shelf full of unusual menorahs: one with nine small silver skulls, another of copper-wired bones. "Because menorahs aren't witch things. They're Jewish. Plus, there was a mezuzah by your front door."

There was? Zeddi hadn't even noticed.

"Do omnists need to believe everything every religion prescribes?" Ida asked.

Olive thought for a moment. "I'm not sure."

Jace pulled out his phone, googled omnist. "Says here: recognition and respect of all religions. More recently it's come to mean an acceptance of the legitimacy of all religions."

Ida set her thigh bone on the silver charger beneath her bowl. Licked her fingers clean. "That sounds about right. I pick and choose what I like from different religions. I think they all have things to offer."

"And I'm cynical about *all* religions," Roni one-upped. "So I suppose I'm a kind of omnist too, in that I'm wary of all of them—equally."

"Surely you don't mean that," Shakineh said.

Roni blotted her lips. Dropped the napkin in her lap. "Sorry to disappoint, Shakineh, but I do. I really don't know what to believe anymore. Except that organized religion pits people against each other."

"Well, yes," Shakineh said, snapping a bone in two. "That goes without saying. But you *do* believe. I know you do." She sucked the marrow from the bone and tossed it back in the bowl.

Roni stared into the glass of water cupped between her hands. She looked defeated and sad. Another silence fell over the group. Something obviously wasn't being said. But what? Zeddi placed a hand on Olive's thigh. She didn't want her thinking it was her fault that the room had gone all somber. Whatever was going on between these people, this coven, it wasn't because she'd asked if they were omnists, that's for sure.

"I'm probably more influenced by Wicca than anything else," Shakineh finally said to Olive. "But I'm also Jewish. And a little Buddhist: a Jubu."

"We've all been influenced by Wicca," Ida said. "It's what brought us together."

"And Wicca is witches?" Olive asked.

"That's a loaded question," Ida said. "I think it's safe to say all Wiccans are witches, but not all witches are Wiccan. Wicca is more a belief system while witchcraft is more nuts and bolts."

"Prayer with props, as Mags used to say," Shakineh interjected.

"Exactly."

"I guess I understand," Olive said.

"How about you, Jace?" Ida challenged. "Are you an omnist?"

Jace looked up from his phone. "You know me. I'm not big on labels. Now, can I help clear dishes?"

"No, you may not," Shakineh said, standing. "But there is something you could do for me." She was back to singsonging, as she rounded the table, came up behind him, and lay her veiny hands on his shoulders.

"What's that?"

"You could stay for the—"

"No way." He attempted to push back his chair, but couldn't without ramming into her. "I was clear about this when I got here."

Shakineh didn't budge. "But we need you. Mags needs you."

He rested his forearms on the table, said patiently, firmly, "There is nothing the dead need from the living."

"Mags would have agreed with you about that," Ida said. "But sometimes the living need things from the dead."

"And by that you mean?"

"Just what I said. You have to admit, there have been some peculiarities around Constance's and Mags' deaths."

"No, Ida, I don't have to admit that. I'm sorry, but I don't."

"The missing skull?" Shakineh prodded. "Don't you think that's a little strange? That it should go missing right when she died?"

Zeddi shot a look at Ida. *They know about the missing skull? I thought that was just between us.* But all eyes went to Jace when he thundered, "You women and that damn skull! No one cares about that skull besides you! In fact, I seem to remember, love," he said to Roni, "you saying something along the lines of, if anyone had a motive for stealing the skull it would be Shakineh because…what? She couldn't scry due to her ball being on strike."

"I said no such thing," Roni snapped.

"Real-*ly.*"

Again, Zeddi tried to connect with Ida, but Ida was focused on Shakineh, whose chalk-white fingers were fluttering frantically around her face. "Why would you say such a thing, Roni? Mags was my friend! I would never—"

"If you say so," Jace said, taking the opportunity to push his chair back a few inches. "But I seem to remember you and Constance ganging up on Mags about that crystal skull."

"That was a long time ago. And I would hardly call it ganging up."

"Really? Because that's *exactly* what I'd call it, the two of you nagging her about it all the time, accusing her of monopolizing it—"

"Jace," Roni said. "This is not the time—"

"I think it's *exactly* the time. You three are so sure someone murdered her—" He threw up his hands in disgust.

"Jace, what's this about?" Ida said. "Surely you're not suggesting Shakineh killed Mags."

"Of course not! I don't think anyone killed her! Or killed Constance, for that matter. I'm trying to show you how ridiculous you're all acting. The sisters were old, as we all are, and they died. Period. End of story. People die. Oh wait. Not end of story. Constance was a drug addict too. That might have been what killed her. She was a drug addict *and* she was old. That's probably what killed her. As for

Mags, it was just her time. What's wrong with that? This case you're building, and dragging Zeddi and…and—"

"Olive," Zeddi supplied.

"Yes. Olive—dragging Zeddi and Olive into—it's pure hogwash!"

The silence that fell over the room this time was charged, electric. Ida was the one to finally have the courage or wherewithal to break it. "Surely you know there's more at stake than the skull."

Zeddi shifted in her chair. *What? What besides the skull?*

Jace ran his fingers from his forehead to his graying man bun. "Here is what I know, Ida. Ever since Constance's death, my wife has been walking on eggshells. And since Mags' death, it's like she's walking through a minefield. Even Ari says so."

"Leave Ari out of this," Roni said coldly.

"Why? He's your son—*our* son."

"And wants nothing to do with me."

"Why would he? You jump at the sound of the doorbell. You drink yourself into a stupor every night."

"His dislike of me isn't recent, and you know it. In fact, sometimes I think you've been turning him against me."

"No, hon, you've been doing that all by yourself. You've turned into someone even I don't know. You lock the door behind me when I take out the trash."

"I never did that."

"Yes, you did, love. More than once."

"Did not."

"Jace," Ida cut in, but she didn't follow it up with anything. What was there to say? It appeared a marriage was breaking apart in front of their eyes. Claude began to rock and quietly moan. Zeddi glanced at Olive. The green-eyed black cat had jumped onto her lap; she was petting it aggressively. Good. The cat would keep her occupied. But she was listening. Olive was always listening.

Jace dropped his napkin on the table and sighed loudly. "I shouldn't have come. I knew it, and then I came anyway. That's on me. But this…" He shook his head vigorously from side to side. Took another deep breath. "I'll just grab my bike out of the back of the car and ride home. Leave you ladies to your conspiracies and hocus pocus."

Shakineh stepped out of his way as he leaned down to kiss Roni, only Roni turned her cheek away from him.

Claude's rocking and moaning got more intense.

Jace let Roni's snub sink in, then faced the rest of the table. "Shakineh, lovely dinner—really, as always. You do know how to throw a dinner party. And I'm sorry if I hurt your feelings, but someone had to at least *try* to get you ladies to see the light. Ida, great to see you too. It's been too long." He turned to Zeddi and Olive. "And it's been a pleasure to get to know you two a little, and I'd encourage you to take all this conspiracy talk with a grain of salt, but then, what do I know? I'm just a guy. I can't read tea leaves or talk to the dead. All I know how to do is write code and pay a bill now and then."

"Really?" Roni said. "That's all you know?"

He wanted to say more, you could tell, but he just strode out without even saying goodbye to poor Claude.

CHAPTER NINETEEN

You could hear the door slam all the way from the dining room. Time to go? Maybe. It wouldn't be unreasonable, not under the circumstances. But if she and Olive left now, they'd miss out on whatever was going to happen next—and something was definitely about to happen. You could feel it in the room, see it in the women's expressions. Ida was laser-eyeing Roni, her brow furrowed and full of concern. Roni was glaring at the bowl of bones in front of her like maybe if she glared at them long enough they might turn back into a chicken. Meanwhile, Shakineh stood by the kitchen door wringing a cloth napkin to death. Zeddi didn't need to look at Olive to know what she was up to. She was trying to appear invisible. She knew Zeddi was close to pulling the plug and she wanted her séance and was doing everything possible to avoid making eye contact—the green-eyed cat in her lap getting treated to a full body massage. Zeddi folded her napkin, once, twice, briefly weighing the pros and cons of staying or leaving, then made a decision: time to get to the bottom of this witch stuff. She tossed the napkin onto the table. Bring it on.

Ida had clearly come to some kind of decision herself. "What's going on with Jace?" she asked Roni, her tone terse, confrontational. "And more importantly, what's going on with *you*?"

"Yes, what *is* going on with him?" Shakineh echoed, adeptly skirting the second half of Ida's question. "He was acting so strangely. Accusing me of stealing the skull! Implying I might have...have... killed Mags! What a thing to say! So utterly cruel!"

The poor-me monologue that followed was unbelievable. Shakineh spoke as if her pain over Jace's behavior outweighed Roni's. Roni was his *wife*—and he'd been a total ass to her, in front of her friends no less. How could Shakineh's pain have been worse? How could she think it was?

"Are we still going to do the séance?" Olive asked, when Shakineh took a moment to catch her breath. "Because if we don't, I want to hold the snake again."

"Olive—"

"What? I was just asking."

"That's fine that you asked," Ida said. "I was wondering the same thing myself."

"We have to do the séance!" Shakineh demanded through a gush of tears. "I've been preparing for it all day!"

Roni sniffed into the back of her hand. "Agreed." The bulky diamond riding side-saddle on her finger. "And I apologize. I shouldn't have pressured him to come. And I shouldn't have made you suffer through our marital issues. I'm sorry."

Shakineh began to aggressively clear dishes. "You push him, Ron."

"Don't," Roni said.

"You do."

"Don't. I mean it."

"Shakineh!" Ida said sharply. "Why are you doing this?"

"Doing what?" A fork toppled off the stack of plates and clattered to the floor.

"Offering unwanted marital advice to Roni."

"Really," Roni said. "He's *my* husband!"

Shakineh dropped the plates down onto the table and spoke in a controlled voice. "But surely he belongs to all of us."

It took some effort on Zeddi's part not to spit her mouthful of water onto Jace's abandoned place setting. *He belongs to all of them? What?* Next to her, Olive began to fidget. Zeddi willed her to stay quiet. Shakineh was a loose wire, Roni was spitting mad. With emotions riding this high, who knew what bits of information might accidentally get spilled?

"Obviously, we have some work to do before this séance," Ida said calmly, and slid off her cushion. "Our energy needs to be clear. Claude, would you please give Zeddi and Olive a tour of the house?

Maybe show them the room where, *if* we do the séance, we're going to do it? Would you please? I think we three need a moment to clear our energy. We can't risk attracting some dark soul into the circle. We've had enough of that lately."

"I'm happy to clear the table," Zeddi blurted.

"Best not," Ida said, ushering Roni and Shakineh into the kitchen.

Ida's dismissal of her from the coven's inner circle did not sit well. How was she supposed to give an informed, objective assessment, as Ida herself had asked her to do, if Ida shut her out? As for eavesdropping, impossible. The octagonal séance parlor below the house's turret was a long hallway away, totally out of earshot. Still, it was worth standing in the doorway, ear to the corridor, just in case. She felt bad for Claude, but she was only half listening to him as he tried to direct their attention to the various aspects of the séance parlor. He'd taken the responsibility of showing them the house *so* seriously, toured them through each gloomy room, stopped at the various points of interest, especially the taxidermies: rearing reptiles, birds hung in stasis between flight and death, an arching cat. Evidence of the dead daughter was everywhere: little altars in the corners, table-top photos, a cushion with her face embroidered on it. It was like walking through a mausoleum. The whole house felt like it was sobbing. It didn't help that during the tour Olive had bounced off the walls the whole way, chased after cats, asked questions, then not listened to the answers. By the time they reached the parlor, where they were now, poor Claude was in a total swivet.

"Olive," she said. "Let's listen to what Claude has to say before we go touching things. Even then, we probably shouldn't touch."

"But Mom, it's a crystal ball! I want to see my future."

"I don't think it's wise to mess with a witch's crystal ball. Right, Claude?"

Massive tabby slung over her shoulder, Olive huffed an exasperated breath, then turned her back to the massive ball on the pedestal.

"So, this is where the séances take place?" Zeddi asked politely, gesturing to the low round table covered in purple velvet. It was surrounded by cushions instead of chairs, Japanese style.

"Yuh," Claude said, dismissively. He wanted them to look at the multiple shelves of cut crystals and candles, not the table. He pointed to the candles, then to himself. Several times. "My job. Me."

"Excuse me?"

"I light candles. Me."

"You light the candles? It's your job to light them?"

"Yuh."

He caressed the velvet-damask wallpaper with his elegant hand. Pointed to a mahogany armchair with threadbare gold padding by the window. "My chair." He said it a second time, this time directed at Olive. "*My* chair!"

"Got it," Zeddi said. "We won't sit in your chair."

Satisfied, he went on to haltingly explain that he didn't actually participate in the séance, but sat in this chair while the witches went about their business. "I quiet," he insisted. "Must be very quiet."

"Gotcha." Zeddi patted his large arm. "You stay quiet. That's good. I expect we will too."

"What are all the mirrors for?" Olive asked. Every wall was covered in them: big ones, little ones, haphazardly hung like paintings in a pack rat art collector's home gallery.

"Spirits, they come."

"Ah. Little doorways to the other world."

"Wait," Olive said. "You mean ghosts come in through the mirrors? What do they look like?" At some point, Zeddi noticed, she'd lost her beret.

Claude either didn't understand the question or was just tired of Olive asking and then not listening, because he just stood there, mute, blinking his brown eyes.

"I guess we'll see," Zeddi said to Olive. "You still okay with this? You want to go home? It's okay if you do."

"No way! If Indiana Jones can face the Angels of Death in *Raiders of the Lost Ark*, I can face the ghost of Mags in a séance. She'll be a nice ghost."

"Okay. But if you change your mind, say the word."

"I won't."

"Com'ere. Give your mama a hug."

Olive obliged, though she was too keyed up to give much of a hug and she refused to put the cat down. Still, the hug was sweet, if cut short due to Claude accidentally knocking over a candle, which startled the tabby and sent it springing from Olive's shoulder and onto the floor, where it then dug its claws into the faded Oriental carpet and executed an impressive hairpin turn into the hallway, Olive hot on its heels. Claude, meanwhile, displayed a surprising burst of speed and agility and caught the candle midair. Zeddi offered him an apologetic smile, but he refused to even look at her.

What was taking the witches so long? She walked over to the shelf of crystals. It made her uneasy knowing that anything she told Ida was being relayed directly to the other witches. Could she trust Ida? She wanted to. She truly liked Ida. But what did she really know about her? What did she really know about Mags? She shook the tension from her shoulders. Glanced down the hallway. If only she could come up with some pretense for getting closer to the kitchen and the witches' conclave. *Mags' paintbrushes, yes!* The perfect excuse to wander back into the living room and possibly, quite innocently, overhear what was going on in the kitchen. She'd been asked to bring something meaningful to Mags, and what, she'd reasoned, could be more meaningful than Mags' leather pouch of brushes, which were currently in the living room, which was right by the kitchen. The perfect alibi. "Um, be right back," she said to Claude, and took off before he could object. In the hallway, she nearly tripped over Olive, who was on her hands and knees in a lock-down stare with the fat tabby.

She paused in her mission. Crouched next to Olive. "What do you think about all this?" she whispered. It was always good to get Olive's take on things.

"I don't like Roni. She's weird."

Really? Zeddi almost laughed. Here they were in this truly eccentric woman's house, surrounded by way too many taxidermies and cobwebs, and Olive thought *Roni* was weird? But there was no point in asking Olive to be more specific, to perhaps question *why* she thought Roni was weird. Olive experienced the world in broad strokes. Weird was just that, weird. Still, it was worth noting. "Okay, well, let's keep an eye on her."

"Will do," Olive said, her eyes never leaving the cat.

Zeddi made it to the living room just in time to see the kitchen door swing open. "Claude!" Ida shouted as the three witches spilled out of the kitchen. "Light the candles! The séance is on!"

Damn. Whatever energy had needed clearing had obviously been cleared. Ida looked determined, Shakineh delighted, and Roni...well, she looked miserable, but then, she always looked miserable. Zeddi tried to catch Ida's eye, to see if she could glean anything that had taken place inside the kitchen, but Ida went straight for her backpack and started rummaging through it, ignoring her completely. Hmm. There were any number of reasons Ida might not have wanted to talk just then. Still, it grated. But the séance was on, so things were moving. Zeddi kissed the tattoo on her wrist, grabbed the bundle of paintbrushes, and headed back to the parlor, where she and Olive once again found themselves waiting in the hallway while each of the witches, who now all had to pee, took turns using the one working bathroom in the house.

"Do you really think we're going to see Mags' ghost?" Olive asked quietly while Claude lit the candles.

"I don't know. I've never done this. But in my experience, the dead usually stay dead."

Olive fiddled nervously with her glasses.

"What do you think?" Zeddi probed. "Do you think Mags is going to show up?"

"I think she's already here."

❖

"Before we start—"

"We have to turn off our cell phones," Roni said, interrupting Ida.

Shakineh's hands flew to her face. "Blessed Goddess! The wireless hub too!"

Olive huffed impatiently. Zeddi could have. Here they'd finally gotten everyone's bladders empty, finally gotten all the candles lit, finally settled around the low table, and now they were all going to have to get back up and search out their phones, because apparently none of the old women kept their phones with them. "Senior moment!" Ida apologized to Zeddi and Olive. "But we do this all the time: get here and *then* remember." So off they went to locate their phones, only Shakineh couldn't find hers, so of course they had to help her look. "Try calling her," Zeddi suggested. So Roni, who'd already powered down her phone, had to power it back up, then she had to find her cheaters so she could read her contacts, because none of them actually knew Shakineh's phone number, including Shakineh. Ultimately, the phone was discovered under a couch cushion in the living room.

Once seated back in the parlor, Ida chuckled. "Take two," she said, and resumed her spot at the head of the table with her hands rested upon it. She looked beautiful, the candles on the shelf behind her casting a halo around her wispy gray hair, the low table a perfect fit for her short stature. "But before we start, there are a few things you need to know." She directed this to Zeddi and Olive. "One, it's important that you want to participate. Do you want to participate?"

"Yes!" Olive said.

"Ditto," Zeddi said.

"It's also important that you stay open to the possibility that we *can* connect with the dead. Can you do that?"

"Yes!" Olive said.

"Ditto," Zeddi said. She would try.

"And one last thing..." This time, Ida included everyone. "If anyone should become frightened, or have reservations of any kind, we stop. Plain and simple. Understood? If you're scared, we stop. Period."

"Understood," Zeddi said.

"Okay," Olive said. "But I won't get scared."

"No, I don't suppose you will. But if you do, if anyone does, just say the word *enough*. Got that?"

Everyone nodded.

"All right then. Shakineh, would you cast the circle?"

Clearly surprised to be given this honor, Shakineh began nervously fluttering her hands around her chest and face. "Me? Oh, my Goddess, yes. I just hope I can do it justice. Mags always cast such a beautiful circle." She pressed her palms together at her heart, took a long, slow, centering breath. "But I will do my best."

"You've got this," Ida said.

"Agreed," Roni said, though she was obviously growing impatient, which only worsened when Shakineh had to dance around working out a foot cramp before beginning.

"Damn old bones!" Shakineh grumbled as she rocked back and forth from one foot to the other.

Roni wasn't the only one growing impatient. Olive looked like she was about to pull her eyebrows out. Finally, though, Shakineh began.

The circle she cast was similar to the one Ida had performed at the trailer, only more elaborate. When she called on the west, she passed around a crystal bowl of water. Roni, the first to receive it, held it perfunctorily to her face, smelled it, dipped her fingers in it, flicked some drops into the air, then handed it over to Zeddi, who followed suit. Why not? It was just water. As the bowl circled the table, Shakineh invoked various goddesses to help in parting the veil. She added planetary references too, and spoke in what sounded like an ancient tongue. For the south, a long fireplace match was lit. This too was passed around, giving each person a chance to light one of the unlit white pillar candles on the table. For the east, a carved wooden bowl of dirt was treated much like the water: They each breathed it in and ran their fingers through it; Ida even rubbed some up and down her arms, streaking them with the rich soil. The north they honored in unison, blowing big lungfuls of air into the room.

Once the circle was cast, Shakineh returned to her cushion and laid her hands on the table. "Shall I go first?"

"Might as well," Roni said.

Shakineh pulled a colorful silk scarf from the neckline of her dress. "Mags," she said. "I've brought the silk scarf you painted for me after Dahlia died. You always wanted me to give it back to you. There was something on it you wanted to fix. But I wouldn't give it to you. I love the scarf as it is." She set the scarf on the table, and the women began to hum, each one a seemingly random different note. The effect was discordant, jarring, and only got more so as they began to modulate pitches and tones. They passed through humming to oohing and aahing, to making strange guttural throat-clearing noises, then came back to pleasing harmonies, then on to clashing ones. Were she and Olive supposed to join in? If so, how? Just start making noises? She looked around at the witches for a clue. Heads tipped back, eyes closed, they were like a pack of howling wolves, swaying from side to side. Olive gave her a questioning look. She shrugged. And then, as abruptly as the humming began, it stopped, and Roni set an oil-spotted three-by-five card on the table.

"Mags. I've brought your recipe for white chili. It's in your handwriting. You even drew a little bowl of chili in the corner with the word *Yum*. Anyway, the ink has faded, and I can't quite make out the last two ingredients."

"I loved that chili," Shakineh said, and smacked her lips as though tasting it.

"Me too," Ida said.

The three took a quiet moment to remember the chili, then started up humming again. Zeddi closed her eyes. Best just to listen, she decided. Their collective sounds were profound, wild, powerful, like taking an acoustic bath. Then, just when she was sure the walls and the ceiling were about to dissolve, it grew silent, and Ida placed a dried sprig on the table.

"I've brought you a dandelion from my yard. It's my concession to you, my darling Mags." She soldiered on despite her voice catching in her throat. "After all these years of me cursing the darn things in my vegetable bed, and you telling me, *But Ida, it's so much more than a weed. But Ida, the bees need them.* Well, I'm here to tell you I finally took your advice and brewed some up for my arthritis, and it's worked wonders. I haven't taken an aspirin in a week. It's helping with my digestion too. Therefore, no more sticking dandelions in my compost. From now on, I will harvest them for sacred, healing use, or let them be."

Roni arched an appreciative eyebrow.

"I'm pulling out all the stops tonight," Ida said, her eyes swelling with tears. "She won't be able to resist holding the dandelions over my head."

Ah. So the point of the offerings was to bait Mags with things she'd want to return for. Interesting.

Again, the women began to howl and hum, the intensity of the song (if you could call it that) swelled into what sounded to Zeddi like a final crescendo, and then, again, they stopped on a dime, and all eyes were on her, including Olive's. Olive was worried because she didn't know Zeddi had brought the paintbrushes.

Zeddi gave Olive a look, *I got this,* then set the holster on the table. "Olive and I have brought your paintbrushes."

"Brava!" Ida said.

"Because you loved to paint."

"And you were real good at it," Olive improvised, "especially when you painted animals."

"Exactly," Zeddi said. "And the brushes miss you."

"Yeah," Olive said. "And so do I."

The witches nodded their approval—a relief—before they closed their eyes, and this time took up hands to make their odd sounds. Zeddi grasped Olive's hand on one side, and Roni's on the other, and suddenly, with just the touch of their hands, the energy in the room turned electric—as if the atoms had begun to spin faster. Involuntarily, Zeddi gasped. It actually seemed suddenly possible that Mags might spring forth from the ether. Unnerving as hell, yes; challenging everything she believed about the dead, yes; but possible. Maybe the dead weren't totally gone. Maybe they were hovering around, just waiting to be called upon. She was dying to open her eyes, and at the same time, terrified to.

A loud ripping sound—or was it a feeling?—slapped the back of her eyelids as they exploded in a swash of dazzling gold, so bright she had to squint her closed eyes.

"Welcome," Ida said.

"Mags!" Shakineh cried.

Roni's grip on Zeddi's hand tightened.

Zeddi's grip on Olive's hand tightened.

What she was seeing, feeling, was breathtaking, kaleidoscopic, the colors folding and revealing, folding and revealing, a living origami of light, only the light, the colors, were sentient, hypnotic—alive! And despite her previous reservations about totally succumbing to this ritual, she couldn't help but travel toward the sensuous skyrocketing light show, if travel was even the right word. She could feel the cushion beneath her, could still feel Olive's and Roni's hands in hers. At the same time, she was flying! Careening! Spiraling and twisting with the light! And then the cushion was gone. And Olive's and Roni's hands were gone. Her own hands gone. But it was okay. It was wonderful! Like bathing in contentment and profound belonging—in fathomless love.

*My dear friend...*floated into her mind. It was Ida, only it wasn't Ida, and there were no words. It was the essence of Ida, the essence of communication. Pure. Transparent. Without the constraints of language. *As you well know, we don't have much time. Our bodies are not as strong as they once were. But it is so good to join with you. We miss you here on Earth.*

Zeddi realized she'd begun humming at some point, she could feel the vibration in her chest, in her mouth, on her lips, but she had no idea when she'd begun, or how she knew the right note to hum. She just knew it. Was part of it.

There are some matters, Ida imparted, *earthly matters, that we must discuss with you. We want to bury your remains by the cypress grove up by my place, on the cliffs. Does this suit you?*

Vivid golds and oranges exploded into pure joy. Mags was happy.

Good, Ida imparted. *We thought you'd like that.*

The colors morphed into what Zeddi knew was an abstract dandelion, and she could feel Ida laughing. *I know I know. You told me so. Now, as you can see, we have some visitors with us, Zeddi and Olive.*

A banner of starry-night swirls shot across the back of Zeddi's eyelids. Should she say something? Had she said something? But words were impossible. Unnecessary. Humming was all that was needed. Zeddi felt herself fragmenting, becoming everything and nothing all at once, and it was magnificent. Delicious. She—

Mags, what happened to you? Who murdered you?

The strident thought cut through the starry-night swirls like a comet, desperate and harsh. It was Olive, she was sick of waiting, she wanted answers. Of course she did. That's why they'd come. But not yet. *Not yet.* Zeddi wanted to hum some more. Wanted to dance with the colors some more. But now there was this thudding, this pounding. Her heart? No. Not her heart. What then? Zeddi tried to focus on the colors, the love, but the thudding was getting louder and louder. Da dum. Da dum. It *was* a heartbeat. Just not hers. Meanwhile, a hideous inky blackness was bleeding into the beautiful colors. *No!* It spread like veiny arteries on a wet watercolor, stealing all the colors. Eating them. *No! No!* Zeddi screamed silently. *Get away! Get away!* But she was no match for the thudding, the blackness. The dream was slipping away, away, becoming a memory, then a memory of a memory, then a memory of a memory of a memory. Her hands returned. The pillow beneath her returned. Someone had let go, had broken the circle. *Olive!* No. Olive's hand was still in hers. Warm and small, and clutching hers fiercely. It was Roni's hand that was gone, that had let go. She fought to return to the place of colors and love, to Mags, but all she could find were her own lungs gasping, her own heart pounding, her own mouth dry as dust.

"Roni!" She heard Ida's voice, her real voice, cry. She sounded frantic, scared, and it hurt Zeddi's ears. "Are you all right?"

Through a fringe of eyelashes, Zeddi saw Roni slumped over the table, Ida shaking her. "A glass of water," Ida barked.

Shakineh flew from the room.

"Roni! Roni!" Ida shook her some more.

It was like watching a movie. Detached. Zeddi was a witness to the scene, not a part of it. Only Olive's hand was real, the small fingernails pressing crescents into her palm. Olive was scared, and it was her job to protect her, comfort her. She fought her way back to the room, to life. She had to protect Olive. She turned toward her.

"Are you okay?"

Olive eyes were wide—wild. "What *was* that?"

Wrapping her arms around the person she loved more than anyone in the world, Zeddi stammered, "I...I don't know, honey." What had she been thinking including Olive in something like this? She'd thought the séance was bogus, that was it. She'd never really believed they'd be summoning the dead. Was that what had even happened? She grasped for a memory of what had just passed, but it slipped further away.

Behind them, Claude paced in circles, moaning. *Shut up!* Zeddi felt like screaming. But she also understood how he felt. It's how she felt on the inside, as though she'd been ripped wide open, then left that way, gaping, empty. But his moaning was driving her crazy. "Is Roni all right?" she finally thought to ask.

"I don't know," Ida said. "She's still breathing. Her heart is still pumping." She shook Roni again, a little more vigorously this time. "Roni. Roni!"

Shakineh charged into the room, glass in hand. "Water."

Ida took the glass from her. Flung the water in Roni's face.

For a second there was no response. Then Roni sucked in a tremendous lungful of air.

"Thank Goddess," Shakineh said.

Clearly in pain, Roni massaged her temples. "What happened?"

"You passed out," Ida answered. "What do you remember?"

Roni pulled at her hair like she was trying to yank out a headache by the follicles.

"I passed out?"

"You did. Now what do you remember? Before it's all wiped away."

"Uh…"

"What?"

"Casting the circle…the offerings…Mags…and then…and then…" She shuddered. Pulled at her hair some more. "Nothing."

"Think."

"I can't!" Roni began to sob.

Ida rubbed circles on her back. "It's all right. It's all right. The séance was too much. We're getting too old for this work. It's too draining."

Shakineh flicked on the overhead light. It was blinding, like staring at the sun through dilated pupils. Olive shielded her eyes.

"It's this damn autoimmune thing," Roni bawled. "It's made me so weak." Trembling, she picked up her phone and shakily powered it up.

Autoimmune? Zeddi watched Shakineh pinching out the candle flames with her fingertips, watched the smoke spiraling off the dead wicks. She felt so bleary. So hung over. So stupid. She realized she was standing. When had that happened? Shakineh brushed by her to get to the candles by the window. She seemed to be moving at high speed, everyone was.

"I cast a strong circle," Shakineh said. "Right? So how did they get in? I don't understand. And who on earth was it?"

"Jace?" Roni said into her phone. She was in the hallway now. Had left the room.

Olive leaned her full weight against Zeddi, almost toppling them both. "I want to go home." She whimpered. "I'm really tired."

Zeddi squeezed her tight. "Okay, honey. We'll get you home." She was tired herself, exhausted. Just staying upright seemed hard. She was also frightened.

Ida came over and took hold of Olive's shoulders. "Are you okay?"

Olive nodded.

"Follow my finger with your eyes."

Olive did.

"Are you sure you feel okay?"

"Yeah, but…"

"But?" Zeddi and Ida said together.

Olive shrank into herself. "But I think something really bad happened to Mags."

"I think you're right," Ida said. "And I think we need to get to the bottom of it."

CHAPTER TWENTY

Zeddi gazed out the back seat car window to the rain-slicked street. Olive, belted in next to her, was conked out. Ida was driving, Claude riding shotgun. It was just past eight, but it felt like midnight. The world outside looked bizarrely vivid. It was like the séance had somehow sharpened her vision—all her senses really. Streetlights haloed in fog appeared to breathe; reflections of traffic lights on the wet blacktop undulated green and red—like when she'd done mushrooms, only more intense. And the sounds! The sticky swish of the tires on the wet road, the whiny squeak of Claude's seat as he rocked forward and back, forward and back. It was distracting to say the least. Her emotions felt vivid too. Fear, awe, anger all stormed inside her, but mostly she was worried about Olive. Walking to the car, Olive had been so drained she could barely pick up her feet. She was exhausted herself, but not like that. What had happened in that circle? The dark energy was still crawling beneath her skin. It was like a million creepy caterpillars wriggling around. That it was probably crawling around inside Olive too made her sick. Why hadn't she asked more questions about what they were getting into? And why hadn't Ida warned her?

Olive whimpered in her sleep, kicked out a foot as if fighting something off. Zeddi rested a hand on her thigh. Olive settled.

A part of her wanted to give in to the exhaustion, to lay her head in Olive's lap, slip into sleep. If she did, maybe she could find her way back to that beautiful place of swirling magic colors. Maybe she could...

No.

If she slept, she might forget. Somehow she knew this. She rubbed her eyes, opened them wide, squeezed them shut, opened them wide again. Regardless, the events of the night were receding, just like dreams did when you woke up. But what had happened was not a dream. It was real. She was as sure of this as she was of the paintbrushes in her lap, and now that she'd had a taste of it, she wanted more, she *craved* more. The feeling was not a comfortable one, this acute *want* that had awakened in her. She rubbed her face, pinched her cheeks, tried to move past the yearning, but its grip was strong.

Think! Think! she demanded of her addled brain. *Make sense of what has just happened.* Only it made no sense. If the dead could be contacted, it meant there was life after death. Only it wouldn't be life because death was the opposite of life. So what *was* it? And wouldn't she know about it? Surely, that little secret, that the dead weren't really dead, would have been leaked to the public by now, some *20/20* episode, somebody's YouTube channel. It was too big a thing for anyone to keep under wraps. It just was.

In front of her, Claude continued rocking, a human metronome. *Squeak squeak squeak.* He was probably bouncing off Ida's mood. Ida hadn't said two words since they'd loaded into the car. She was driving like a maniac; she barely stopped at stop signs, gunned it in between intersections—as if the night hadn't been stressful enough! *I should offer to drive.* Then she remembered the pedal extenders. She was trapped. She hated being trapped. Anger surged up, eclipsing the other emotions inside her. She leaned forward, grabbed onto the back of Ida's seat. "What the hell just happened, Ida? Is that usual for a séance? Do the dead usually just pop in for a visit then get squashed by some horrible, vile evilness? Is that how these things usually go?" Her heart was pounding in her chest, she was shaking, her eyes stinging.

Claude's rocking got more aggressive. *Squeak squeak squeak.*

Zeddi made herself breathe. "Say something. Please."

Ida finally did. "That's a difficult question to answer." Her voice was hoarse, tight, as though her vocal cords were knotted up. She sounded exhausted too. Zeddi tried to care, she did, but the look on Olive's face after the séance, it was a look no mother ever wanted to see on her child's face: eyes teeming with fear, little chin trembling, as though her whole world had just been ripped from beneath her, which it had. Zeddi's own too. That the dead were just a séance away was unimaginable, impossible, paradigm-shifting. But that was nothing compared to the evilness that had infected the circle. It was pure, vile, chilling. She'd had no idea something so heinous was even possible. And that that evil had entered Olive's body, had slipped in through her sweet little pores and wrapped around her tender heart made Zeddi so angry she wanted to hurt someone. Bad. But who? What? "Well?" she prodded. "I mean, if you're not going to break it down for me, could we just do the Cliff Notes? Because, I don't know, I feel a little freaked out at the moment. You invited us to this thing, this séance, me and Olive—"

"Is she asleep?"

"Out cold."

"Good."

"Why good? Why don't we start with that? Why is it *good* she's sleeping?"

Zeddi glanced back at Olive just to make sure. Her seat belt was cutting into her neck. She attempted to adjust it, but Olive wouldn't budge. "I get that you don't feel like talking, Ida, but you owe me something. You do. That was crazy what just happened. I mean, it seems like we really contacted Mags…"

"I believe I told you that that was a possibility."

"I know, but—"

"But what?" Ida swerved into the turn lane, slammed on the brakes. "You didn't think we would? You thought this was all some little game?"

"No. I just…" Zeddi fell back into her seat. She was shattering, splintering, exploding.

Jolted awake by the sudden stop, Olive murmured, "Mom? Where are we? What's going on?"

Zeddi fixed her seat belt. Stroked her head. "Just heading home, honey. Are you—" But Olive had already dropped back to sleep.

The light turned green. A river of oncoming cars prevented Ida from making the left turn.

A couple of guys stood at the corner, waiting to cross. Even through the fog, Zeddi could see the long coat and tricorn hat. The pirate! It had to be. How many urban pirates could there be in Tres

Ojos? The bike with the banana handlebars and attached trailer was there too, and the dog, Apollo. She focused on the other guy. He was either upset or excited, it was hard to tell, his back was to the car, but he was gesturing emphatically. Then he turned, abruptly, and cast his gaze directly at the car, at Zeddi. She froze. Jeff Dante! Or could he even see her in the car? Probably not. But she couldn't trust her brain. It was too fuzzy. But seeing him and the pirate had to mean something. Didn't it? Ida had said the pirate was one of Constance's disciples, and Jeff Dante, he'd acted so squirrelly when she'd mentioned Constance. Was he a disciple too? What was she not getting?

The car behind them honked. Ida was crying. Damn. Zeddi unbuckled her seat belt. Scooted forward in her seat. "Ida. I'm so sorry. I just—"

Ida wiped her eyes and made the turn, then pulled into a small free parking lot at the edge of downtown and cut the engine. "Claude, get me a tissue from the glovebox, please," she said, sniffing.

Claude stopped rocking and popped the glovebox.

"Ida, I…"

Ida waved her off and continued to quietly weep.

Chastised, Zeddi retreated to her place in the back seat. Stared out the moonroof to a patch of backlit clouds. She liked to do her crying in private too. Still. What the hell was going on? Ida's suppressed sobs, the *squeak squeak squeak* of Claude's seat, Olive's sleep-snuffles all sounded so loud. Like the sounds were bypassing her ears and entering through her skin. Would she be this way forever? Would Olive? It was unbearable! She covered her ears, not that it helped, and gave into her own tears, let them flood her face. She couldn't remember ever being this scared.

"I'm sorry," Ida said after a while. "I don't mean to be short with you." She blew her nose. "But tonight scared me. I have no idea who entered our circle, or what, but whatever, whoever, it was…well…I just don't know, that's the thing, and it was strong magic, very strong. I'm quite sure it's what's responsible for Mags'…" Her words caught in her throat. She powered on. "I just don't understand. Shakineh cast a strong circle. We were specific in our toning." She blew her nose again, blotted her eyes. "If only Mags were here. She would know what to do."

Zeddi scooted forward in the seat. "I just don't get *what* happened, or who or what we contacted, or who or what contacted us. This is all new to me. But I can't imagine what you're experiencing, I mean, Mags was your love, it's just—"

"Why didn't I listen to her? Why didn't I believe her?" Ida sobbed. "There's so much I haven't told you, Zeddi, but tonight I'm just so exhausted. I'm sure you are too. Entering dreamtime takes its toll, and we're all getting too old for these crossings. Well, you're not, you and Olive are young, but the rest of us, especially Roni, she's fragile, very fragile, she wasn't up to this tonight. We shouldn't have put her through it." Another sob. "Oh, Mags! Who got to you?" She reached for the tissue again. Cried some more.

Zeddi waited an appropriate amount of time before saying, "Dreamtime?"

"Yes. I told you."

"Uh…no, you didn't," Zeddi said gently. "You just invited us to a coven meeting. We didn't even hear about the séance until tonight. And this dreamtime is brand new."

"Really?"

"Really."

Ida blotted her eyes. "That's terrible. I've been so scattered lately. I—"

"I get it, you must really be hurting, but yeah, tonight kind of blew me away."

"Kind of! I imagine it was more than *kind of*. To enter dreamtime with no warning. I'm very sorry. I really thought—"

Claude groaned and continued his rocking. He was clearly shaken up too.

"Hush, Claude. We'll be home soon enough. Or…actually…" Ida drummed her fingers on the steering wheel. "Do you have any ice cream at the house?"

"I saw some in the freezer. A gallon of vanilla."

"Perfect. Claude? Would you like some ice cream?"

Claude stopped rocking. "Ice cream!"

"All right then." Ida fired up the Honda Accord. "Let's put Olive to bed, get Claude a big bowl of ice cream, and you and I talk. Sound like a plan?"

❖

"Olive will be fine," Ida reassured Zeddi after Zeddi's third trip down the hallway to check on her. Or was it her fourth time? She was feeling so disoriented. Extreme fatigue, terror, and a troublesome itchy craving to return to the place of beautiful colors swirled inside her, making it hard to focus. Her hearing, thankfully, had returned to normal, or almost normal—sound was still weirdly distracting, but it wasn't as loud. Her muscles, though, begged for sleep, her mind to shut down. Still, she would not give in to her drooping eyelids until she had some answers.

She unzipped her boots, slipped them off, lowered herself slowly onto the couch, and forced herself to focus on the cup of microwaved leftover coffee cradled in her hands, forced herself to focus on Ida— who'd settled onto Mags' green chair, which she tried to convince herself was no cause for worry. The chair hadn't killed Mags. Still, just seeing her sitting there, looking so old, so dog-tired, so small. Would Ida be next? Not if she could help it. But could she? She was so out of her depth.

Ida glanced around the room nervously. Claude, seemingly content at the kitchen bar, was busy sculpting his ice cream into a little vanilla mound. *Scrape scrape scrape* went the spoon again the bowl. *Scrape scrape scrape.*

Ida popped the top on her reusable turquoise water bottle. "Fortunately, it's not within the dead's power to hurt us physically, but that's not to say Olive won't be upset or confused. You may need to share with her some of what I've shared with you. She may also forget all about what happened tonight. People often do. Just like with dreams, they remember parts of it or just forget it entirely. Keep an eye on her. Wait for her to bring it up, and if she does, treat it as you would a dream. That's essentially what dreamtime is."

"Dreamtime?"

"How we reach past the veil," Ida said. "Once in dreamtime, we can call in the dead—or recently dead. And it isn't really the dead per se. It's not like spirits maintain a personality. No, nothing could be farther from the truth. It's more like…when a person dies, they get folded back into the Divine Resonance. Do you see?"

Maybe if Claude would stop playing with his ice cream she could. "Um. No?"

Ida took a long pull off her water bottle. "Sorry. Entering dreamtime always makes me so thirsty." She took a slow jittery breath, centered herself, then continued in a hushed tone. "Let me try this again, backtrack a little. When we're born, we are each of us an infinitesimal bit of energy released from the Divine Resonance, and we each have our own particular frequency, our own particular tonality, and this frequency is as unique as a thumbprint or snowflake, but inaudible to our human ears. Much like Wi-Fi, or a dog whistle, what the scientists call *ultrasonic*. The same goes for everything on the planet, animal, mineral, or vegetable, everything, everyone, has this sonic thumbprint. You with me so far?"

"Yup. We all have a God-given sound that we can't hear."

"More like, we are all *made* of sound. Everything is. Sound is what binds matter together. We are both *made* of sound, and *swimming* in sound. It's a big concept, I know, and I don't fully understand it myself."

Zeddi held up her hands in mock surrender. "Hey, after tonight, I'm willing to believe anything. So does that explain why my hearing—"

"Yes. I'm sure your sensitivity to sound has been awakened. It will return to normal if it hasn't already."

"It's getting there."

"Good. Now, this next bit is more complicated. You ready?"

Zeddi slid her feet beneath her skirt. "We can only hope." In retrospect, her choice of clothing was so off. Sure that the whole coven thing was bogus, she'd dressed for a simple night out with friends. Then again, how did one dress for a crash course in otherworldly realms? The answer was quick to come. Like Olive, of course.

"The Divine Resonance," Ida began, "this sea of sound, is extremely curious, and It learns through all that It creates, and It changes in response to what It learns. So, besides each of us having our own particular sonic thumbprint, we also have, each of us, been created for a particular purpose…"

"Okay? And that is?"

"To answer one of the Divine's zillions of questions, act as one of its experiments, if you will."

Zeddi took a swig of coffee. It tasted like what it was: lukewarm stale coffee. "I just don't get how all this applies to tonight." She got up to add some sugar, re-nuke it. Maybe that would help. "You sure you don't want some coffee? I'd make you a fresh cup."

Ida held up her water bottle. "I'm fine. Thank you." But she trailed after Zeddi into the kitchen and continued to speak quietly, as if the evil presence they'd encountered in the séance might still be hanging around, eavesdropping. "Let me see if I can explain. The trick to calling in the dead is finding the exact frequency of the person you're seeking to contact. When we're toning, as we were in tonight's séance, well, it's a bit like archery. We're aiming for a bullseye—only it's a bullseye we can't see or hear. It's more like…oh…trying to find, say, a tube of lip balm in the bottom of your purse, without looking. You know how you fumble around hoping you can feel it? Well, in our case, we're feeling around using sound. If we're lucky, as we were tonight, we'll hit that perfect combination of sounds that creates a greater sound, an inaudible one, the sonic thumbprint of whomever we're trying to reach, in this case Mags, and the Divine will be tricked into thinking there's something more to be learned from that particular experiment. If we do our job right, the Divine will release that bit of consciousness back to us, briefly. It's a bit like teasing a cat with a peacock feather. And it's tricky: too many voices and you dilute the frequency; too few and, well, you saw tonight, it's horribly draining. Dangerously draining. Tonight with one woman down, we were…well…"

The microwave dinged loudly. Too loudly. Zeddi removed her coffee. "And the bribes?"

Ida leaned against the refrigerator and stared at the ceiling. "They may only serve the living, that's what Roni says. They certainly help us focus, and we definitely have better luck when using them."

"How about the mirrors? Claude said—"

"I know what Claude says. He loves the mirrors." She glanced at him briefly. "Don't you, Claude?"

He mumbled something, then shaved a curl of ice cream off his perfectly sculpted mound.

"And Shakineh is convinced they help, says the Divine, like a crow, appreciates shiny objects. I'm not convinced, but the mirrors do no harm, and heaven knows, we need all the help we can get these days."

They returned to the living room: Ida to the sliding doors where she pressed her palms against the cold glass and stared out into the dark; Zeddi to the cozy, warmly lit corner of the couch. Resting her socked feet on the coffee table, she asked, "And anyone can do this? Do a little singing, enter dreamtime, and visit the dead? Because what I saw, what I *felt*, really seemed like Mags to me. All those colors."

"Is that what you saw?"

"Until the scary part, yeah. It was like watching Mags paint."

Ida turned to her, a pained look on her face. "That's lovely you saw that."

"It's not what you saw?"

"No. Rarely do we see the same thing."

"But—"

"What you saw, Mags painting, was your brain trying to make sense of what it couldn't understand. That's why interpretation is so very important to what we do, and where things can get a bit thorny. That's what we Keepers—"

"I'm sorry, Keepers?"

Another long sigh. "I really didn't tell you any of this?"

"Nope."

"Oh Goddess, I've just been so scatterbrained since Mags left us." She tucked a stray gray curl back into the beaded clip holding her hair. "So. The Keepers of the Sacred Song is the order we were drafted into all those years ago in Big Sur. I did tell you about Big Sur, didn't I?"

"Some."

Ida retrieved her water bottle from where she'd left it on the chair, fingered it nervously, glanced over her shoulder like there was someone outside she needed to confer with, then said, "Okay," and turned to Zeddi. "I guess after tonight, you deserve to know."

On the couch, the two of them facing one another, their backs against the couch's arms, Ida's pale blue eyes blazed as though lit from within. She explained that Keepers were a dying breed, and that parting the veil, intentionally as they'd done that night, was just one aspect of their work and required at least two Keepers to be effective. Parting the veil took skill, she said, a skill that could be taught, but she explained that the majority of Keepers had been given a major leg up through transmission. She herself had attained the Gift that way, though she'd struggled more than Roni and Mags, who'd taken to it immediately. "I'm naturally a bit absentminded," she confessed. "Even after receiving transmission, I had to develop my focus, learn to listen in that way that's deeper than hearing. Transmission didn't take at all with Shakineh. I've got to hand it to her, she earned the Gift the hard way, through years of disciplined practice. Even after transmission, it takes continuous practice to keep the Gift alive. And there are some, who no matter how much they want it—"

"Never get it," Zeddi surmised.

Ida gave her a thumbs up. "Exactly. So you see how crucial accurate interpretation is to our work. If our energy isn't completely clean, if our circle is not completely clear, if we allow our desires to color the outcome in *any* way, we are doing a great injustice to our gift, to the world, and it can get messy, believe me."

"Is that what happened tonight?"

Ida bit her lip. "I really don't see how it could have."

And yet it obviously had, because whatever had happened in the séance was definitely messy. Zeddi sipped her sweetened nuked coffee. Not much better. "So, you have to be a Keeper to enter dreamtime, is that right?"

"Yes and no. Occasionally, the Divine can be accessed through regular sleep dreams. And, just as a point of interest, we are not the only ones who dream. Plants dream, rocks dream, rivers dream."

"Okay, but—"

"But I'm getting off topic. Right. The point is, sometimes the Divine slips in and steers a particular dream in a particular direction. I'm sure you've experienced this, that dream that just seemed so real it took your breath away, or actually changed you somehow? That was the Divine Resonance trying to realign you in some way, to your purpose—"

"Of being one of its guinea pigs."

Ida laughed uneasily. "I guess you could put it that way." She took another long swig from her bottle. "I'll probably have to pee all night."

Zeddi held up her mug. "Me too."

Barnaby scratched noisily in his cat box. Zeddi tried to blot out the sound by staring at the woodburning stove. Maybe she should make a fire. It was chilly. Or maybe she was just scared.

Claude started rocking again.

"Should I get him more ice cream?"

Ida shook her head. "We won't be much longer."

"Can I just ask one more question?"

Ida's shoulders drooped with fatigue. "Of course."

"Transmission?"

"I'll see if I can make this quick. You remember the old woman I told you about? In Big Sur? Hecate? The one who gave us the crystal skull?"

Zeddi nodded.

"That weekend she gave us more than the skull. She gave us the Gift. That's transmission, when a Keeper, at death, passes the Gift on to another—or in our case, quite remarkably, passes it on to several others. Numbers were down, you see—still are—so she did the extraordinary and passed it on to four of us at once. She was a very powerful Keeper. She actually tried for five, but as I said, it didn't take with Shakineh."

Barnaby strolled into the room and yowled to be fed.

"So, you, Mags, Roni, Shakineh, and…?"

"Mags' sister, Constance. Like Mags, it came easily to Constance—too easily, and she grew drunk with the power. That's a lot of what pulled her and Mags apart. Mags accused Constance of abusing the Gift, of engaging with Keepers of questionable ethics and profiting financially off the Gift, which, if not strictly forbidden, is frowned upon. Honestly, none of us knew what we were getting into that night when Hecate called us to her deathbed. I certainly didn't. We'd just met her at a gathering. I think I told you all this. Z Budapest was holding a big Wicca gathering; Hecate, a revered high priestess, was very ill, dying in fact, and she called us to her bedside."

Barnaby yowled again.

"And that's when she gave you the Gift?"

"Not right away, no, she explained to us her intentions, said she was quite sure she was going to die that night, then asked us to cast a circle and sit by her as she went about it. Well, she didn't die that night. Or the next. We had to recast the circle a number of times for bathroom breaks, to eat, but the promise of what she was offering kept us in that little yurt perched on the cliffs. Our youth too. I could never sustain a circle that long now."

Another yowl.

Zeddi got up to fetch Barnaby a Greenie.

"Anyway…" Ida followed Zeddi with her eyes. "The witches of her own coven circled like vultures, but she wouldn't allow them near her. Called them a bunch of Siphons. Said she would curse them from beyond if they disobeyed her.

"I personally thought Hecate nuts. Thought all of them were. But Mags was smitten with the whole scene, and since I was smitten with Mags—we all were—we stayed. But the moment Hecate returned to the Divine—"

"You mean died?"

"Yes. Any doubts I had about her promise evaporated. Transmission is like…" Ida searched for the words to describe it. "Being hit by a tsunami of sound. You're assaulted by what the stones hear, the birds, the whales, the trees, the spiders; you can hear atoms humming, cells replicating, the galaxies spiraling—all at once. It's cacophonous!"

Zeddi closed her eyes, trying to imagine what that must have been like. Just the bump in sound she was experiencing since the séance was disquieting. But to hear atoms spinning! What did they even sound like?

"But in that moment of transmission," Ida went on, "the swirl of the universe cleaved open inside me and zillions of frequencies imprinted on me. *That* is transmission, *that* is what made me a Keeper. And transmission only happens if you're lucky. Or," she mused, "unlucky. I sometimes have my doubts. At the time, I was sure I was dying, but I also had no fear of death, I welcomed it. Because for a split second I understood myself to be a part of the Divine, and it was magnificent. Oh, I chased that feeling for years. Still do. It can be quite addictive, as I'm sure you can imagine after your small taste tonight. But over the years, I've come to accept my limitations. Yes, I was fortunate to have transmission take; yes, these frequencies all imprinted on me; but that doesn't mean I know where to find them, or even know what they mean. Imagine trying to tune into a single radio station when you're being bombarded by them."

Zeddi gave Barnaby a pat and returned to the couch. "So was that transmission I experienced tonight?"

"Goddess no!" Ida chuckled sadly. "You were brought along as our guest, into our collective trance. Believe me, if it were transmission, you would know. What you got was a tiny tiny taste." Barnaby jumped onto Ida's lap and began headbutting her for a pat. "Such a pill," she said, rubbing him lovingly.

"I was just thinking, could someone have killed Mags to gain her power?"

"That's the million-dollar question, isn't it? As I said, a Keeper passing on the Gift at death is not the only way to attain it, but it is surely the most powerful way. A crash course, if you will."

"Does it have to be given willingly?"

"It does."

"So if someone murdered Mags for it…"

"They would have had to convince her to hand it over first."

"If that's the case, our killer was probably someone she knew."

"I hate to think it."

Ida had to be terrified she was next. If Mags knew the person, she probably did too. "You did say numbers were down."

"There's another possibility. Our culprit could be one of the letters."

"Letters?"

Ida explained that when a Keeper got to a certain age, or received some terminal diagnosis, they began to receive letters from other Keepers who had candidates for transmission. It was a common practice. Traditionally, requests were made in the form of letters, paper letters with envelopes. "Though it's not unheard of these days to get an email request," she said. "They come from all over the world."

"Was Mags getting these?" Zeddi asked.

"Oh yes. We all do. Though most of us just toss them. *Junk mail*, Roni calls them. She doesn't plan to pass the Gift on to anyone. Mags felt a Keeper should seek out her own candidates. But Shakineh, now, she keeps every single letter she gets. I'm afraid we've led her to believe she gets more than the rest of us. They mean so much to her. I usually at least read mine, then into the compost they go. I expect when the time comes, I'll know what to do. Or I hope so." She shuddered. "For reasons none of us understand, transmissions haven't been taking like they used to, and people just don't want to train themselves in the art of listening anymore. As I mentioned, it's grueling and often futile. And with so few Keepers left to train them."

"We should look through some of Shakineh's letters. Maybe one of them will stand out as being particularly desperate."

"Agreed. I'll ask her."

"How many Keepers would you say are around here?"

Ida's cat-patting grew absentminded as she considered the question. "Hard to say."

Tres Ojos was a hotspot, she said. Or had been. She admitted that she'd lost touch. So many Keepers she knew had died off, and she hadn't kept up with the recent transmissions. "Mags was always after me to find a replacement, but I've come to a place in my life where I'm not even sure I *want* to pass it on. The Gift is such a burden. Mags and I argued about this many times: whether our sacred singing makes the world a better place. As I said, it all comes down to interpretation, and interpretation can so easily go astray."

Claude's rocking was growing more aggressive. The poor man was obviously ready to go. Ida had to be too. It had been such a long night. But there was still so much Zeddi didn't know, and if she didn't ask now, the window of opportunity might slam shut. "So how come I've never heard of you Keepers?"

Ida arched an eyebrow. "Would you have believed someone if they'd told you?"

Point taken. "So what's the deal with Jace? Is he a Keeper?"

Ida sighed, then set Barnaby to the side and stood. "He was. He's one of the few who took the time to learn it. It's how he won Roni's heart. But I have no idea whether he still has the Gift. As I said, it takes constant practice, especially for those who had to learn it the way he did, and it's been so long since he's even tried, at least as far as I know. But Roni and Jace's relationship is too complicated for us to untangle tonight." She gathered up her wrap and threw it over her shoulder. "And now, I really have to get my brother home. I'm sure tonight was scary for him. For you too. I'm so sorry I didn't warn you. Claude, put your coat on. It's time to go."

Claude did as he was told. He even returned his bowl to the sink.

"And you, dear," Ida said taking Zeddi's hand. "I can't even imagine how you're still standing."

After watching them drive off, Zeddi checked on Olive again. Confident she was sleeping peacefully, she let herself collapse on the couch. It wasn't even ten o'clock and she was near comatose. But she made herself stay awake, made her brain sort through all she'd learned. Three things were abundantly clear. One: these witches were the real deal. Two: Mags had not died from natural causes. And three: until they figured out what was going on, none of them were safe.

She reached for the laptop on the coffee table, typed up some notes in a file labeled DON'T FORGET. Having completed that, she set the computer aside and stretched out on the couch to rest her eyes. But there was no rest for her ears. The Kit Cat clock ticked, the refrigerator whirred, the heater clicked, Barnaby's nails caught on the carpet as he padded his way across the room to her. Even the river rushing to the sea, she could hear that too.

CHAPTER TWENTY-ONE

Zeddi's eyes shot open. Another nightmare. What this time? She closed her eyes, tried to return to the dream. It had been super scary. She'd been in Turtle, she remembered that, and was gripping the steering wheel, she remembered that too, but somehow she'd been behind the empty driver's seat, not sitting in it, and the seat dug into her chest as she stretched over it to steer. There was no getting to the gas and the brake, her feet were stuck to the back floorboard, still, somehow, she managed to keep the van speeding up a twisting redwood-lined highway in the mountains. But why? She rubbed her face. Oh yeah, she was chasing Mags! That was it. And Mags was in the Audi—and Mags had Olive. She remembered beeping the horn repeatedly, screaming, She's my daughter! Mine! But Mags just wouldn't stop.

She stared at the ceiling. Massaged her jaws. It was just a dream. A stress dream. Or was it one of those special dreams that Ida had talked about? No. It didn't feel like that. Pure stress. She tried to turn onto her side, but something wouldn't let her. Barnaby. He was on her chest, staring at her. When had he climbed up there? For that matter, where was she? What time was it? The couch. Late. She'd conked out after Ida left—after the séance. The séance. *Shit!* Just the thought of it set her heart racing again. She closed her eyes. Listened. Breathed. Her ears were back to normal. That was a relief. She stroked Barnaby from head to tail, let his purring calm her. More details from the dream began to surface. There had been a snake somewhere in the van. She never saw it but knew it was there. "Tell me the truth," she whispered to Barnaby. "Was Mags trying to recruit Olive?" Barnaby's response came in the form of a headbutt to the neck. More pats please. She set him aside, rolled off the couch, and strode down the hallway. Olive was sound asleep in bed. Phew.

❖

On her lunch break, Zeddi swung by Last Stop Camp in search of the pirate, hoping he might offer some insight into who Mags' sister, Constance, was. Green smoothie in hand, she strolled through the maze of tents and tarps and bicycles and wagons, she maneuvered around shopping carts filled with people's earthly goods, overflowing trash bags, and random junked-out furniture. It was muddy and smelled of urine, but the day itself was dry, the residents out and about. Everyone, it seemed, was grateful for the appearance of the sun. The camp was bigger than it looked from the street. Sadder too. Sopping wet clothes hung on a filthy bungee-cord laundry line that was strung between two tents, a man and woman were making a platform from shipping pallets, another woman, cursing at someone only she could see, sat on a milk crate in front of a tent filled with what looked like trash. Further along, a bike tire was locked to a fence, the rest of the bike gone. How did people wind up at Last Stop Camp? Had they burned all their bridges? Was there no one left to love them?

She checked her phone to see if Ida had returned her earlier text. Ida had, and texted back that she was at the dentist with Claude and would be free for a phone call by two o'clock.

She slid the phone back in her pocket and strolled down another row of tents where a woman was passing out waxed-paper-wrapped sandwiches from a baby stroller equipped with a cooler. She offered Zeddi a turkey sandwich. "No thanks. I don't live here," Zeddi said, sounding way more defensive than she'd intended. "I'm just looking for someone."

The woman smiled, knowingly, like she heard this all the time, and carried on. Zeddi stepped over a used syringe, and sucked on her smoothie.

Then she spotted him. He was draping a sleeping bag over a grimy yellow tent, Apollo the dog at his side. She resisted her impulse to shout *Ahoy Matey!* Said instead, "Excuse me, sir, could I talk to you for a minute?"

The pirate eyed her suspiciously, or one of his eyes did. The other drifted up to the right. "Me?"

"Yeah. You were friends with Constance, right? Constance McKenzie?"

He scratched at his arm. Shifted his weight from one mud-caked pirate boot to the other. Glanced nervously over his shoulder. Scratched his arm some more. She recognized the signs of addiction, and it made her sad.

"Who wants to know?" he grumbled.

"I do. I'm—was—a friend of her sister's? Mags McKenzie?"

"So? What's that got to do with me?" More scratching. More shifting around. The guy was jonesing for sure.

"I don't know if you know this, but she just died."

"Of course I know, man. That was weeks ago." Another look over the shoulder.

"I'm talking about Mags."

He was having trouble focusing. "Wait. Who?"

"Constance's sister, Mags."

He removed the tricorn hat. Ran his fingers through his greasy hair. Returned the hat to his head. "Holy hell."

"You knew her?"

"About her, man, *about* her. She and Constance…" He shook his head.

"She and Constance what?"

"Nothing. Just that…I don't know. Argh! She's dead?"

Zeddi nodded.

He yanked the sleeping bag back off the tent and started muttering to himself. "Time to batten down the hatches. Pull up the ladders. Set sail. It's not safe in these waters. No way. No how."

Some mental illness in the mix too?

"What about Mags and Constance, what were you going to say?"

"Nothin'. I wasn't gonna say nothin'! Now leave me—"

Zeddi stepped forward. "One more question, if you don't mind, then I'll leave. Do you know a guy named Dante?"

He froze.

"I take that as a yes?"

He began rolling up his sleeping bag. Apollo whined.

"I only ask because—"

"I'm done talking!" he snapped, his hands trembling, his breathing uneven gusts.

"Is he—"

"I said done! I'm *done*." He drew even further into himself, his muttering indecipherable.

Clearly, there was no point in pushing him. She pulled a five-dollar bill from her pocket. "Thank you for your time."

He snatched up the money. Shoved it in his pocket. "Watch your back, man," he said out of the corner of his mouth.

"Why?"

But he was done with her. Just like he said.

❖

A double shot of espresso got Zeddi through her final house of the day. Now she had an hour to kill before she had to pick up Olive. She texted to see if Roni had found her sunglasses on the deck. She was pretty sure she'd left them there when she'd cleaned. Roni texted back no, but she was welcome to drop by and look, to use the back gate.

Damn. She'd hoped to get some time alone with Roni. Ask her what she'd made of the séance. She drummed her fingers on the steering wheel. Seemed like it was all dead ends today. She'd make the drive anyway. They *were* a favorite pair of sunglasses. She called Ida on the way over.

"Zeddi," Ida answered. "What's up?" She sounded annoyed.

"Is this a bad time? I thought you said—"

"It's fine. I'm just off the phone with Roni. She's at the doctor. I'm worried about her—on top of which I'm trying to figure out what to do with Claude's dental work. They say two teeth have to be pulled, two more need fillings. They're suggesting implants because he won't wear his partial. It's just been one of those days. Now, how can I help you?"

Zeddi took the on-ramp, merged into the flow of traffic. "Roni has an autoimmune disorder?"

"That's what we think. Lyme disease hasn't been ruled out, though. It's been tricky to diagnose. The doctors are stumped. Mags was working with her. I feel terrible we put her through that last night. She's just not strong enough to enter dreamtime anymore. Last night made that crystal clear. Shakineh and I are going to try again on Samhain. Just the two of us. We'll see if we can get in, but—"

"Samhain?"

"Halloween. How's Olive?"

"So far so good. Like you said, she seems to have forgotten a lot. She talked about the snake and the cats and the dinner, a little about the singing, that's about it. I keep thinking about what you said, though, about Mags saying numbers were down. Be straight with me, Ida, was Mags trying to recruit Olive? Or prime her, or whatever?"

There was a long pause.

"Are you still there?"

"I'm trying to decide how to answer your question."

Zeddi cranked open the van window. She needed air. Fresh air. She unbuttoned the top button on her jeans too. Loosened her collar. "It seems like a pretty simple yes or no, Ida."

"It does seem like it, doesn't it?"

"Well, was she?"

"First of all, nothing is ever done without full consent. And in the case of a child, parental consent. That said, she did feel Olive had potential. She thought she might be a natural."

"A natural?"

"A natural Keeper. They do exist. They're generally women who, without transmission, without being taught, are born with the Gift and just have to be shown how to use it."

Zeddi flicked on her blinker. The cement truck in front of her was spitting gravel. "Why didn't you tell me this before?"

"I wasn't sure about you yet. And to be honest, I may be overstating Mags' interest in Olive. She just felt Olive was special, that's all—and she *is* special. She's a wonderful girl. Has Olive said something to you that made you feel Mags was overstepping in some way? Is that it?"

The blue Prius poking along in the fast lane wouldn't let her in. "No. Olive has nothing but good things to say about Mags."

"There you have it then."

"But she's a kid. She'd like anyone who offered her cookies and milk."

"I understand."

"But..."

"Yes?"

Finally the Prius caught on. Zeddi pulled out from behind the cement truck. "If she *were* a natural…"

"If she were a natural, Mags would have approached you about mentoring her."

Zeddi whacked the steering wheel. The phone call! *There's something I need to talk to you about. Something best talked about in person.* That had to be it. "What do you think? Do *you* think Olive is a natural?"

"She could be. She made direct contact with Mags during the séance. That's unusual. Many naturals go their whole lives without truly understanding their gift. They usually become artists of some kind, writers or painters. It's speculated that Virginia Woolf was a natural. Frida Kahlo as well. It's nothing to worry about."

Except that Woolf took her life and Kahlo spent hers painting tortured self-portraits. But this wasn't the time to discern whether or not Olive had the Gift. In the light of day, she wasn't even sure if she believed in the Gift, or any of this witchy stuff. Though Olive did have super graphic dreams. She shook her head—*stop, just stop*—and flicked on her blinker to exit. Still, *something* had happened in that séance, something she couldn't explain away. "Another question. Last night, did another soul slip in? Is that what happened? An evil one? Is that why it got so dark?"

"It wouldn't be the first time. Back in the day, before we refined our talents, we used to call in all kinds of straggling souls, but it hasn't happened in eons. Somehow there was a breach. I'm just not sure how. Which brings me to something I feel I should mention. When we were out in Mags' shed the other day, I noticed that Hecate's grimoire wasn't there. You didn't take it by any chance?"

"Hecate?"

"The old woman I told you about, in Big Sur."

"Oh yeah. Uh, no. The only grimoire I've seen is Mags' and I told you about that."

"Would Olive have taken it?"

"No. I haven't allowed her to touch anything back there. Why?"

"I'm just wondering if Shakineh—"

"You think she might have been the one who broke in?"

"She wouldn't have viewed it as breaking in. She would have

viewed it as taking what was rightfully hers. The grimoire is pretty much a step-by-step guide to the work we do. It was her primer when she was studying for transmission. She was always after Mags to give it to her. I'll ask her if she took it."

"And if she took it?"

"It's fine. It's if she *didn't* that worries me."

"Because?"

"Because that would mean someone else took it. I'll get back to you."

"Would you ask her about the letters too? If we can look at them?"

"Will do. Is there anything else? Because I really need to call the dentist. I don't think Claude would be up for implants. He's terrified of dentists. Will barely open his mouth, let alone let them drill. But something has to be done. He keeps losing his partial."

"One last thing," Zeddi said.

"Yes?"

Zeddi told her about stopping by the homeless camp and the pirate's reaction to her mentioning Dante. "I'm going to try and talk to Dante again. There's something going on there."

"Sounds good. Bring a piece of hematite when you see him. For protection."

❖

Zeddi parked on the street and walked around the back through the short gate that led to the Millers' generous deck overlooking the canyon. Woodpeckers chattered and swooped from live oak to live oak, but besides that, it was so, so quiet. The tranquility of the one percent. Rather jarring after the chaos of the homeless camp. But it was a gorgeous day. Why not allow herself to enjoy the peacefulness of the rich? She could hang on the sunny deck for a few—

But wait, the sliding glass door on the deck was wide open. That was odd. Roni was always on her about making sure the house was locked up when she left. Maybe Roni was back from the doctor? No. Ida had just spoken with her, and she was at the doctor's. Zeddi was about to call out when Jace and a very attractive, very young woman sauntered from the direction of the master bedroom, laughing. Hand on her lower back, he guided her along as if the poor, pretty little decades-younger thing in tall yellow pumps couldn't possibly find her own way to the door. Zeddi squatted behind a potted tree fern to wait them out. Meanwhile, her sunglasses remained balanced precariously on the railing just out of reach. Within seconds, her thighs began to complain. Maybe she should just woman up and announce herself. She wasn't doing anything wrong. She had Roni's okay to be there, but since they appeared to be engaging in their final goodbyes, she stayed put. Then, damn it, the goodbye started turning into more of an encore. She rocked back onto her heels. Sighed. She'd never be able to get her sunglasses now; she'd made the drive out for nothing. But it wasn't nothing. Something had been learned. Mr. Nice Guy, Mr. I-Just-Swung-By-To-Take-My-Beautiful-Wife-Out-To-A-Sunset-Dinner-On-The-Bay couldn't be trusted. Mr. Man Bun was a big fat liar.

CHAPTER TWENTY-TWO

The crisp air blowing off the bay felt so refreshing. If only it could blow away her worries. Zeddi loved being outside, did her best thinking outside, and Olive was right: getting their pumpkin at the farmer's pumpkin patch was way better than picking one up at a grocery store. If only she could quit thinking about the stupid voicemail she'd left for Sylvie, inviting her down for Halloween. She'd prattled on and on about how great Tres Ojos was, when all she'd really wanted to say was *I've got the trailer to myself that night. Want to come down and try kissing again? Maybe naked this time?* Then she'd left a stupid text apologizing for her stupid voicemail. Why wasn't Sylvie responding?

Sitting on a hay bale, she rested back into the pyramid of bales behind her and watched Olive and Isabella race up and down the rows. They were having a great time checking out the variety of pumpkins, stopping abruptly at particular ones, turning them this way then that, then running on again, laughing and screaming the way only nine-year-old girls can do.

It was a fluke that Isabella was even with them—a great one. Earlier, when Zeddi was waiting for Olive to get out of school, she'd struck up a conversation with a cool mom in jeans, red cowboy boots, and a vintage bolero jacket with embroidered flowers. She'd had no idea the cool mom was the mother of Olive's new friend, Isabella, until the girls skipped over together. But it was perfect. Zeddi and Luciana got to work out the details about Olive spending Halloween with them. Better yet, she liked Luciana. Could even imagine her being a friend. Then Olive asked if Isabella could come with them to the pumpkin patch, and now here they were, the late-afternoon winter sun casting long shadows across the farm, Olive with her cool friend who had a cool mom.

If only her mind would quit chewing on the damn voicemail. Better that than thinking about the séance. It hurt her brain to think about the séance. All that stuff Ida had told her about sound, dreamtime, had made so much sense the night before. But here, now, under the big sky, surrounded by happy pumpkins and laughing children, everything just seemed so...regular.

A flock of blackbirds exploded into the blue sky. They spiraled and twisted, then landed in a nearby artichoke field. She stretched out her legs, pulled her knit cap down over her ears. Ida had warned her that the memory of the night might fade, and it had. Her rational mind kept hacking away at it, telling her what she'd experienced was impossible. But it wasn't just that. A big part of her *wanted* to simply stick her head in the sand, pretend Mags had died a natural death, pretend she'd never experienced dreamtime. The denial wouldn't last, though, that was for sure. The second she unlocked the door to the trailer, the urgency would return: She'd get that feeling that someone was watching her, waiting for her. No, until this prickly feeling was resolved, she'd never be able to feel completely safe in the trailer, never feel like it was home. If only there was someone she could talk to, who could offer her some insight.

"Mom!" Olive called. "Can we get some of these little gourds too? They're so cute!"

"Sure! A few!"

Then it came to her: Who to call. She pulled out her phone. A single bar. It was worth a try.

"Hello? Hello?"

"Can I speak with Ari Miller, please?"

"Hello? Is anyone there?"

She walked a few feet to the right. "Can I speak with Ari, please?"

After a bit more back and forth she was finally patched through. "Hey Ari. I'm in a field of pumpkins and service is a little sketchy, but do you have a minute?"

"Sure. Everything going okay?"

How to even explain? "Actually, things have gotten a little strange."

"Zeddi? Zeddi?"

A few steps to the left. "Better?"

"Gotcha."

"I was just saying…um…well…could you and I maybe talk sometime soon? Some weird stuff has been going down, and I just…"

"Uh-oh. You're breaking up again. Want to call me back? Or, better yet, come into the office tomorrow, say, late afternoon? I think I have an opening. Or Friday?"

A text came through from Sylvie. She'd gotten Zeddi's text and wished she could come down but had a burlesque show to light that night. She also apologized for not texting sooner. Said a shitshow was coming down at work. A homeless activist had accused her coworker of turning away the unsheltered. She said she'd call later.

"Zeddi? Are you there?"

"Um…" Damn. No Sylvie on Halloween. But she hadn't scared her off, either, that was something. "Um. Maybe Friday? I'm pretty slammed with work tomorrow, and I've got to help Olive with her costume. She's going as Indiana Jones. She loves Indiana Jones."

"Totally get it," he said. "I'm a fan too."

"Actually, now that I think about it, Friday is out too. I have a triple-header. Maybe sometime next week?" She replied to Sylvie's text with a thumbs up, then texted her a line of rainbow hearts.

"I'm not going to be around," he said. "I'm leaving Sunday for a short trip down to Death Valley. Is it something you can talk about now? I have a few minutes."

"I could try. I don't know if you know this but—"

"Zeddi? Zeddi?"

Nope. This wasn't going to work. "Now can you hear me?"

"Yup. And I just had an idea. You got any plans for Saturday evening? I mean, I know it's Halloween, and this might sound nuts, but just seconds ago my other plans fell through. We could do an early dinner on the strip, watch the Halloweeners pass by. The thing is, I'm feeling…responsible. There are things I should have told you, warned you about. If you're up for it, we could do it over dinner. Just a thought. Olive could come too."

Zeddi kicked the dried mud off her boot. "Actually, Olive has other plans. But uh, yeah, that could work. An early dinner would be great. I mean, we have to eat, right? I just have some questions."

"I bet you do. Pick you up at, say, five thirty?"

"Or I could meet you there."

"How about I park at your place and we walk over together. Parking will be a bitch downtown. Halloween in Tres Ojos is serious business: adults in costume, kids in costume, dogs."

She realized she was nodding. "Cool. I need to see what time Olive is meeting up with her friends."

"Great."

"And just so you know, I might dress up. Just because."

"The thrown gauntlet has been noted," he said. "And just so *you* know, this is a big relief for me. I've been feeling guilty I didn't prep you better. I'm glad we found a time."

"I'll text if anything changes. And thank you for making time for me."

She regretted the plan the moment she hung up. Spend Halloween with someone she barely knew, a guy with a chinstrap no less. It was bound to be awkward. How many hours did a man have to spend maintaining such a beard? It seemed excessive. Vain. But she didn't have to like him. And if he could answer even half of her questions, it would be worth it. Probably best for her not to mention that she'd seen his dad humping Miss Yellow Pumps in the hallway earlier in the day, though. Yeah, probably best not to mention that.

She climbed to the top of the hay-bale pyramid, looked out over the pumpkin patch to the sun sinking behind the ocean. So maybe she wasn't going to get to be naked with Sylvie on Halloween, but at least she wasn't going to be stuck spending it with the school rat. Maybe things were looking up.

"Mom!" Olive yelled. "I found the perfect one for Dan! It's the shape of that ugly picture he has in his bathroom."

The Edvard Munch print, *The Scream.* "Great! He'll love it!" She shot him a text telling him they were up the coast, had picked him up a pumpkin, and invited him to carve it with them on Friday afternoon. If he wasn't available, she typed, she'd leave the pumpkin on his porch on the way home.

Home. It was her first time since moving into the trailer to write that word. It didn't feel quite real, she thought, as she watched the three little incoming dots pulse on her screen. *Friday is good* finally popped up, plus he warned that a storm was blowing in on Halloween—and a lunar eclipse. He asked if she wanted to hang together. Said they could walk downtown.

She responded that she and Olive had plans. But she had more than just plans. She had *a* plan. She was going to sit the geeky lawyer down and find out what was up with these witches.

CHAPTER TWENTY-THREE

It was amazing Olive could breathe. She was out cold on her tummy with her face smashed into the pillow. Zeddi checked the clock. Eight minutes until the alarm. She had a long day in front of her. Three cleaning jobs. She had to put together a costume too, and carve pumpkins with Dan, and go by the Boys and Girls Club to sign up Olive because now that Olive knew Isabella went to the Boys and Girls Club she wanted to go to the Boys and Girls Club, which ultimately was great, but at the moment felt like just one more thing there wasn't time for.

The window by the dresser rattled with the wind. A cold front had moved in overnight. She listened to the wind chimes clanging in the backyard and tried to remember her dreams, but they'd gone wherever it was dreams went. She flicked the alarm off seconds before it rang, rolled out of bed, padded barefoot to the hall thermostat, and turned it on. A low rumbling followed by the sound of air pushing through ducts. Heat. Such luxury.

Two cleaning jobs under her belt and one to go, she and Olive were in the van headed for the Boys and Girls Club. Olive was in a mood. They both were.

"*Why* can't I do my homework at the trailer?" Olive whined for the third time. "I'm old enough to be there by myself."

"You just can't. I'm sorry. It doesn't feel right. Not yet. But the Glynns' condo is a quickie. I promise."

"But I hate doing homework in the van."

"You can do it in the condo if you like, while I clean."

"I hate that too!"

Zeddi reached across the seats and gave Olive's shoulder an affectionate squeeze. "Hey, we're about to sign you up at the Boys and Girls Club. That's good, right? Pretty soon you'll be able to hang out there while I work. You and Isabella."

Olive stared at her flip phone.

"Olive, what's up?"

"Nothing."

Zeddi waited. Not one to suffer silently, Olive would cough it up sooner or later.

It turned out to be sooner. "I don't get to go with Isabella on Halloween," she moaned.

"What?" Oh no. Zeddi raced through the tail end of a yellow light. "Why not?"

"Her grandma's sick. They have to go to Gilroy."

"The whole family?"

"Uh-huh."

Damn. Since being invited, it was all Olive had talked about. Zeddi patted her leg. "Oh honey, I'm so sorry."

Olive stared forlornly out the window. "It's okay."

"We'll come up with something fun. I hear downtown gives out candy."

"Yeah. I'm the one who told you that."

"Right. But we can go down together. We'll make it fun. I promise. We can…go out to dinner on the strip." Like she was going to do with Ari. "Do the 'hood later."

Olive took off her puzzle ring. Started messing with it. "I guess."

"We can hit a couple of neighborhoods. Indiana Jones and…" What what what? "Day of the Dead Woman."

Olive rolled her eyes. "Day of the Dead Woman?"

"Yeah," she improvised. "I'll go through Mags' closet. I think I saw a colorful kimono in there. I'll pair it with some leggings, Frida Kahlo my hair with flowers. Do some cool Day of the Dead makeup."

"Great. Halloween with my mother who can't decide if she's La Catrina or Madame Butterfly."

Zeddi had to laugh. Where did she get this stuff? She flicked on the blinker. Of course, if she followed through with this plan, she was losing her chance to grill Ari Miller. "On the other hand…"

Olive didn't even look up from her puzzle ring. "On the other hand, what?"

"I have an idea."

"That's always dangerous."

"Just hear me out. What if Isabella could spend the night with us? Or a few nights if need be. You guys could go out with Ari and me."

"You're going out with that lawyer guy?"

"I told you this morning over breakfast. We're having dinner. I want to see what he has to say about all this coven stuff."

Olive looked momentarily interested, then sighed dramatically. "She probably can't."

"You don't know that." Zeddi scanned the street for a parking spot. "And unless you ask…"

"I know, I know," Olive said, jadedly. "The answer is always no."

"But if you ask…"

"You have a fifty-fifty chance of it being *yes*. I know!"

"So?"

Another dramatic sigh. But Olive pulled out her phone and shot Isabella a text.

Zeddi spied a spot on the other side of the street. With any luck it would still be there by the time she'd made the block. She made the turn.

Olive looked up from her phone. "She thinks she probably can!"

Hallelujah.

CHAPTER TWENTY-FOUR

F riday's after-school quest for an Indiana Jones whip had turned into a nightmare. They'd tried every thrift store, every costume shop, every drugstore Halloween display in a fifty-mile radius. Not a whip to be found. Even Amazon, which she hated to resort to (she was a stickler for shopping local) couldn't get them one on time—or one that she could afford. "I have one more idea," Zeddi said.

"Which is?" Olive sulked.

"One second."

They were sitting in the van outside the latest failed attempt, Creep the rat on the van floor, his cage steadied by a bungee cord. She texted Dan. Asked if they could switch pumpkin carving from that afternoon to the next day, Halloween, in the morning. He texted back, *How early?* She texted ten and that she'd provide the doughnuts. He responded that if he made it eleven and included a couple of maple glazed, he'd be there.

"What's your idea?" Olive asked.

"There's a grown-up store that might carry whips."

"Why would *they* carry whips?"

"Trust me, would you?"

But it too was a no go. "I just sold the last one fifteen minutes ago," the gorgeously androgynous salesclerk said. "Have you tried the party shop?"

Loading out of the van at the trailer, Olive wailed, "But Indiana Jones has to have a whip!"

By now, Zeddi had a raging headache. Besides the failed whip search, and her lack of sleep, she'd cleaned three houses—one with an old dog that had what the owners politely referred to as *a dribble problem*—and had only one thing on her mind: Tylenol. But she was the adult here. "We still have tomorrow."

"But we've already checked *everywhere*!"

Zeddi tightened her hold on the trailer's doorknob. "Maybe Dan will have some ideas."

"He WON'T!" Olive howled. "EVERYONE IS ALL OUT!"

"Keep your voice down, please. The neighbors will think I'm torturing you."

Olive tumbled past her into the house. "You ARE!"

Zeddi peeled off her coat, tossed it on the couch. "How about we try and make a whip?" she said, calmly.

"How?"

"Rope? Electrical tape?"

Which wound up looking exactly like what it was, a knot of taped-up rope. From there, the night devolved into a thrown-together dinner of avocado toast and eggs, a shower each, and the two of them falling asleep to a stupid Netflix neither of them had the energy to change.

Zeddi woke a little later to the sound of her phone. *Sylvie!* She texted she'd call right back, put Olive to bed, then video called her back.

Sylvie was sitting on her bed, her back against the wall, her blanketed knees pulled up to her chest. She looked smaller than usual. Exhausted. "Sorry I didn't call back yesterday. After we texted, I got a call from my mom. My brother found her stash of cash and stole it."

Her pain made Zeddi's heart hurt. "I'm so sorry."

"Yeah. I keep telling myself it's the addict who did it, not my brother, but you know, it's getting hard."

They looked at each other for a few seconds, then Zeddi asked if there was anything she could do to help, and Sylvie said sometimes she wished she could get the hell out of Dodge, that her mother and her brother were too enmeshed, that even though he stole from her, she welcomed him back into her home, cooked for him, let him use the car, while Sylvie was left to clean up his mess. "I need to just remove myself from the dynamic," she said. "Let them do their thing."

Watching her, Zeddi wished so much she could hold Sylvie in her arms, comfort her. "Sounds like you're all give out," she said, using a Papa Alan term.

Sylvie nodded. "And you want to hear something strange? I keep dreaming about you. I'll be in the middle of some boring dream that has nothing to do with you, maybe a stress dream, or just some random dream, then suddenly there you are, behind me, or doing a walk-through, or just…there, and it always makes me so happy. And the dreams seem so real once I've woken up. It's just that…" Sylvie shook her head of curls, stared across the miles into Zeddi's eyes.

"I know," Zeddi said softly. "I was there." Because she knew that Sylvie was talking about the kiss.

"Do you ever…?" Sylvie said.

"Yes," Zeddi said, because yes she too thought about the two of them together all the time.

A charged silence followed the exchange, and Zeddi was sure Sylvie could hear her heart pounding. She held the phone to her chest to see if indeed Sylvie could, and they both laughed. Then they spoke a while longer, Zeddi curled on the couch under the afghan, Sylvie, tucked into her bed. After a while, they could barely get a word out between yawns, so decided to try to fall asleep together, each cuddling a pillow, pretending, only Zeddi couldn't fall to sleep, so she watched Sylvie sleep for a while, then reluctantly ended the call, and texted: *See you in dreamtime.*

CHAPTER TWENTY-FIVE

Halloween morning, Zeddi sat bundled in a blanket in the small backyard, a half a cup of coffee cradled in her sweater-covered hands while Olive and Dan scooped pumpkin innards onto a piece of newspaper by her slippered feet. Rain was predicted for later in the day. An eclipse too. Isabella, arriving that afternoon, would spend two nights with them. She'd let the girls have the big bed, take the couch for herself. She took a small sip of coffee. She wanted it to last.

"Did you ask Dan about the whip?"

"No. I forgot," Olive sulked.

Right. She forgot. Which meant *Mom, you deal with it. And if you don't, I'm going to have another meltdown.*

Dan squinted pointedly at the dull morning light, a reminder that he was not a morning guy. "What about a whip?"

"We don't have one," Zeddi said. "And there isn't one to be found in all of Tres Ojos."

"I see," he said. "And Indiana Jones *has* to have a whip."

Zeddi nodded.

Olive, wearing her coat over her pajamas, pretended the conversation had nothing to do with her. But she was listening. Hell yeah, she was.

"Hmm." Dan stroked his beard. "That's a problem for sure."

"Yes, it is," Zeddi said. "We tried to make one, but it didn't work out."

Olive looked up from her pumpkin. "It looked like crap!"

"Olive."

"What? It did!"

Dan set his ice cream scoop next to his Munch pumpkin. "I wonder why it was so hard to find one?"

Olive shrugged.

"Do you suppose other people are going as Indiana Jones?"

Olive looked up, horrified. "*Other* Indiana Joneses?"

He mimicked her shrug. "Someone's buying all those whips."

"But…"

"Maybe you should put your own spin on the costume."

"Like *how*?"

"I don't know. Come up with some other cool kind of weapon. Something that's unique to your *interpretation* of Indiana Jones. You could do like an…Indiana Olive."

Olive pushed her glasses up her nose. Blinked nervously. "What are you talking about?"

"I don't know. I was just thinking, what if you did something a little different? You know, come up with your own unique spin. Did something no one else would do."

"Like *what*?"

"Well, maybe you already have what you need. Maybe there's some other kind of weapon."

Olive shook her head. "Nope. Me and mom don't have weapons. We don't believe in violence."

He shook his head. "That's too bad." He went back to scooping. "Because I think it would be really cool to be Indiana Olive. No one else would do that."

Zeddi watched as the wheels turned in Olive's head. Whatever angle Dan was working, she prayed it would work.

Olive dropped her ice cream scoop. "Wait! I know the perfect thing!" She shot up and charged into the house.

Zeddi chugged the final sip of her coffee. "If this works, I owe you big time."

Dan laughed. "No, you don't."

She pointed to his cup. "Refill?"

"That would be great."

She took his cup from the short brick garden border. "Oh, and thanks for not bringing the chain saw."

"I'm telling you, they work great on pumpkins."

"Just not on my nerves."

He studied her a moment. "You okay?"

"Yeah. Why?"

"You seem a little distracted."

"I'm fine."

But she wasn't fine. She hadn't had a good night's sleep since the séance. How could she? She was trying to sleep in Mags' bed. Mags who wasn't really dead, only sort of dead, because apparently people didn't die, they turned back into sound, sound you couldn't hear but somehow was the glue of the universe. One night when she couldn't sleep, she'd visited with Madam Google. Come across a NASA recording of each planet's unique sound. It was mind blowing, beautiful, and kept her awake for hours fretting about how many other things she didn't know. Which beat the night she'd spent berating herself for being furious at Mags for involving them in all this witch stuff. Sweet Mags, who'd given her a home, who'd given so much to Olive, who she now *for sure* believed was murdered. It scared the hell out of her, and in the middle of the night, made her want to pack up and move back to Sacramento, in with Sylvie. Even though she'd have to oust Sylvie's roommates first. And even though she wasn't sure Sylvie would want her to move in. And even though all her old friends were still childless and partying so they had nothing in common. And even though Olive had been so unhappy in Sacramento. But in the middle of the night, it all made perfect sense. Happily ever after was just a simple move away.

"Seriously," she repeated. "I'm fine. I just need some more coffee."

Olive charged past her with the baseball bat. "Here's my interpretation! The skull crusher!"

"Wow," Dan said. "Now *that* we can work with. Throw a strap over that bad boy, sling it over your shoulder. You could wear it like a quiver, you know, for arrows, only it would be for bludgeoning the bad guys."

"I know what a quiver is," Olive said.

"You're encouraging my daughter to bludgeon people?"

"You bet. If she's going to be Indiana Olive, she's got to have her thing."

"Mom! Can I decorate it? Paint Skull Crusher on it? Please please please?"

Zeddi glared at Dan.

He smiled innocently.

"Okay," she said finally. What else could she say?

"But if you're going to wear it," he said, "you've got to know how to use it."

Zeddi shook her head incredulously. "If you don't mind, I think I'll skip this part." But she watched them through the glass doors. "Go for the kneecaps first," she heard him tell Olive. "It's your best bet."

Inside, Creep the rat nestled into the soft fleece at the bottom of his cage.

❖

"She's here!" Olive shouted and slammed out of the trailer.

Equally pumped, Isabella popped out of the SUV and, trailing Olive, charged past Zeddi into the trailer. Luciana hopped out of the passenger side. She looked frazzled, her long dark hair in a messy ponytail. "Thank you so much. She was so disappointed about not spending Halloween with Olive."

"It's no problem. Really. In fact, it's great." Zeddi peered into the SUV. "Hey, I'm Zeddi."

"Tiago," the lanky man behind the wheel said. "Thanks for taking her." He smiled a patient smile. Behind him, a toddler in a car seat was crying. A boy, seat-belted in next to the toddler and playing on his tablet, looked to be about six. Tiago's phone rang. "Excuse me," he said. "But I have to take this."

"Understood." Zeddi left him and met Luciana at the back of the SUV.

"This should be everything," Luciana said, pulling a daisy-covered roller bag from the trunk. "If I've forgotten anything, my apologies. It's been a crazy morning. I just can't get Xavier to settle." She handed Zeddi a large black trash bag. "Her costume. It's very elaborate. She made it herself."

"Is it your mom who's sick?"

"No. It's my granny-in-law, and she's not sick. She fell and broke her hip. She's ninety-two. We're going to see about bringing her home with us. She's very stubborn. Doesn't want to leave her garden. My poor husband is out of his mind with worry."

"Good luck with that."

"And I hate to drop off Isabella and run, but…"

"It's fine. We'll take good care of her."

"Thank you. And you have my number."

"Yup. And you have mine. But really, no need to worry."

"Okay, thank you. I mean it."

When they hugged, Zeddi was once again struck with the feeling that Olive wasn't the only one who'd made a friend. Santiago seemed nice too.

Inside the trailer, Olive was showing off her costume.

"Indiana Olive!" Isabella squealed. "I love it!"

Zeddi felt like hugging her. It was just the affirmation Olive needed to feel confident about her costume. She set the roller bag and trash bag on the floor. The trash bag was light for its size. "And what are you going as, Isabella?"

"An ah-le-bree-hey," Olive said. She glanced at Isabella to make sure she'd pronounced it correctly.

"I'm sorry, a what?"

"An alebrije," Isabella repeated.

Now that she knew she'd said it correctly, Olive acted like she was an expert. "You know, like in *Coco*? The dog? The panther?"

Zeddi thought back to the Disney Day of the Dead movie and remembered the brightly colored animals with magic powers.

"Only they're not always animals," Isabella clarified. "They're spirit creatures."

"Yeah," Olive said. "Magical."

"I see. And that's what you're dressing as? An…"

"Alebrije," Olive said, exasperated.

Isabella pulled several large colorful foam costume pieces from the trash bag. "I'm going to wear my leotard underneath. This one goes on my head, these on my arms, and this is my tail. It comes off in case we have to sit down. I'm going to paint my face too." The pieces of layered cut-foam feathers had Velcro fastenings and easily doubled Isabella's size. They were going to be a challenge in a crowded restaurant.

"Well, we're going to leave in about an hour, so make sure you leave plenty of time to dress. In the meantime, Olive, why don't you bring this stuff back to the bedroom?"

"Oh, and I have to show you Creep," Olive said. "He's back here in the office, which is going to be my bedroom as soon as we get my stuff moved in."

"Creep!" Isabella shrieked happily, and the two girls took off for the office, Isabella's suitcase and costume pieces left behind.

But who cared? Olive had a friend!

❖

Ari Miller wasn't there yet. He'd texted he'd arrive shortly. Zeddi hoped so. Costumed and ready to go, the girls were jumping off the walls.

"All the candy will be gone by the time we get there!" Olive complained.

The plan was to stroll the downtown strip, get as much candy from shop owners as possible, then Ari had made a reservation at a burger place where they could watch the costumes go by. After that, Ari said he had a surprise. Zeddi hoped it wasn't an outdoor surprise. Rain was predicted.

She was doing a final check of her Day of the Dead makeup in a small mirror by the bookshelf and re-bobby-pinning a silk flower in her hair when the doorbell buzzed.

"I'll get it!" Olive whooped, and ran for the door, the skull crusher on its leather sling bouncing on her back. But it wasn't Ari, it was Jeff Dante, risen from the swamp.

Zeddi came up behind Olive. Wrapped a protective arm around her. "Can I help you?"

"Can I have a word?"

Now? But he'd clearly put some time into his appearance. Porkpie hat pulled low over his shaved skull, clean shirt—and he seemed nervous. "It'll only take a minute," he said, his hands dug deep into the pockets of his low-slung jeans. "It's kind of important."

She gave him a long slow look. Something was up. Obviously. Whatever it was, the girls didn't need to hear it. She gave Olive's shoulder a squeeze, said, "I'm going to step outside a minute."

Olive shrugged and returned to Isabella and Creep.

Zeddi closed the door behind her. "We need to keep this quick.

I'm expecting someone." Someone that could kick your ass, she tried to project.

"You got it," he said. "But let's get out of this wind."

And go where? No way was she going into his trailer or following him someplace they couldn't be seen. His cleaned-up appearance wasn't *that* nice. "Okay." She led him around to the side of the trailer by the fence. And while the lace-up pair of heels would suck if she needed to run, they'd be perfect for smashing down on the arch of a foot—if needed. "What's up?"

He reached into his pocket, pulled out a fist full of cash.

What the hell?

"I stole it," he said, "from Mags." He shifted weight from one foot to the other. "After she died."

"You what?"

"When I worked for her, she'd pay me out of this cash envelope in her desk. This isn't all of it, but some of it—*most* of it. I'll get you the rest. It was two hundred and fifty total. I'm short seventy-five."

"Let me get this straight, you let yourself in with your key?"

"Right."

"And stole the envelope?"

"Right."

So *his* were the footprints in the office carpet. "Why didn't you tell me this before?"

"Why do you think?" He kicked the toe of one taped-up sneaker into the heel of the other. Did a self-conscious shrug. "Anyway, Mags was good to me. She didn't deserve me stealing from her. The thing is, I'm back on the wagon now." He thrust the money at her. "So just take it."

She didn't. The money didn't feel like hers. It was Mags'. "Is that why your mom is here? To help you...?"

He nodded. "Yeah. She still believes in me. I don't know why sometimes."

Because she's a mother, that's why. Still, something wasn't sitting right. "How come you got so defensive when I mentioned Constance?"

He stared at his sneakers.

"How did you know her?" she persisted.

He began to squirm. "I can't tell you that."

"Tell me or I won't take the money and your karma will be fucked forever."

He frowned. Wiped the back of his hand across his five o'clock shadow. "I guess technically, now that she's dead—"

"Yeah?"

He took a deep breath. Let it out. "She was my NA sponsor. It freaked me pretty bad when she died. Kinda pushed me over the edge, you know? Sent me on a bender."

"So you weren't part of her coven?"

He took off his hat. Ran his hand over his skull. "You know about that."

"I do."

"I was, then I wasn't, then I was. I didn't have the discipline, you know? That shit takes work. She always said I had potential, though. Paid me to sit in on her sessions."

"Her sessions?"

"Yeah. There were a few of us. She'd line up these people who wanted to connect with the dead. We'd sit around some candles, do some chanting. I never felt anything, though. But you know, grieving people, they're willing to believe anything, pay anything. She had all the bells and whistles, put on a really good show. But that was back when she was using. When she wasn't using, she was a force, you know? The real deal. She was *connected*."

So she was a charlatan. No wonder Mags had issues with her.

Again, he thrust the wad of bills at her. "Just take the money, okay? I'll give you the rest when I have it. I'm sorry about Mags. She was a good woman. I didn't even know she and Constance were sisters until a couple of months ago when Constance came by my trailer to check on me. It sucks that they're both dead, you know? One right after the other like that. It sucks."

She took the money with the intention of donating it to Narcotics Anonymous. "It took guts coming over here."

He nodded. "I guess. And I'll get you the rest, I promise. I just got a job on a fishing boat."

"Okay. I'll hold you to it."

"Well, that's it. That's all I have to say."

She spotted Ari's red Miata making the turn onto her block. "And my ride's here. So, we good?"

He nodded. "I hope so."

"Me too," she said, and waved down Ari. "And if you ever need a cup of sugar, *neighbor*..."

He held up his hands in mock surrender. "All right, all right. Enough with the sugar."

CHAPTER TWENTY-SIX

A ri Miller slid out of his midlife-crisis, cherry red Miata and threw his arms open wide to show off his costume. "Get it?"

"You dressed as a nerd?" It was the best she could come up with. Brown tweed suit, round wire-rim glasses, dorky bow tie, gelled hair parted on the side. So *not* otherworldly, which she hoped reflected the conversation to come.

He shook his head and laughed. "Olive will get it. You, by the way, look very pretty."

Slightly condescending, but okay...she *had* killed it on the costume. In the back of Mags' closet she'd found a pair of batiked harem pants that went perfectly with the kimono. Made herself a silk-flower crown. Painted her face into a gorgeous skeleton. "Let me just get the girls." But there was no need. They were already stampeding out of the trailer, their plastic pumpkins ready for candy.

"Aren't you going to say hi to Ari?"

"Oh. Hi, Ari," Olive said. "*Now* can we go?"

Isabella showed a bit more manners and held out her hand. "Isabella Graciella Mendez at your service, but today you can just call me Alebrije Extraordinaire!"

Ari took her hand. "Nice to meet you, Ale...ale..."

"Alebrije Extraordinaire," Olive said.

"So, Olive..." Ari threw out his arms again. "What do you think?"

Olive squinted. "You dressed as an old-fashioned guy?"

"Seriously? You don't recognize me?"

Zeddi crossed her arms. You had to feel bad for him. He was obviously hurt.

Olive huffed out a lungful of air. Annoyed she was being made to interact with a man she hardly knew, on *Halloween* no less, when at that very moment other kids were getting candy that should be hers, she gave him a hard stare. "Ooohhh, I get it."

"What?" Zeddi prompted.

"He's Dr. Henry Walton."

"Doctor...?"

"Indiana Jones?" Olive said testily. "When he's a professor?"

Ari beamed. "Exactly! I knew you'd know."

"Only I'm not Indiana Jones anymore," Olive said.

"She's Indiana Olive!" Isabella blurted. "Badass to the core!"

Olive brandished the newly decorated baseball bat: "Yeah! I have Skull Crusher instead of a whip." She turned to Zeddi. "Now can we go? Please? We've been waiting forever!"

Zeddi shot him an apologetic look. He obviously wasn't used to being around children. "First, a picture for the granddads." She dug her phone from her bag, held it out to Ari. "Would you do the honors?"

"Olive's granddads are gay," Isabella said and twirled around in her Ugg boots.

Amused that Olive had shared this with Isabella, Zeddi affirmed, "Yes, they are, and they would love me to send some photos."

"Cool," Ari said. "Gay dads."

"Yup."

They took a photo with Zeddi and Olive in front of their new front door, then one with Olive and Isabella in front of the fence, then the requisite unattractive selfie of all four of them squeezed into the frame. "Now one with just me and Olive," Ari said, and handed Zeddi his phone. "Since we're the two sides of Indiana Jones."

"Only I'm not Indiana Jones anymore," Olive corrected. "I'm Indiana *Olive*."

"Okay, okay, Indiana Olive," Zeddi said. "Just stand still."

Olive put on her fake smile. Copying her, Ari pinched the edges of the bowtie and fake-smiled too.

The moment the photo was taken, Olive said, "*Now* can we go? *Please?*"

Ari chuckled self-consciously and straightened up. Yes, the poor man was clearly out of his element. Had no idea that when kids hung out together, adults became invisible. Unless, of course, the adults were doling out money or food. Even then. "Let me just lock up," Zeddi said. "And grab an umbrella."

Inside, she stashed Dante's cash in a kitchen drawer, snatched Mags' rainbow umbrella, and took one last look at herself in the mirror. One of the silk flowers in her crown was coming loose. As she fixed it, Mags' painting reflected in the mirror caught her eye. For a millisecond, the crows' feathers appeared to ruffle in the wind. She spun around, but the crows were now static, the illusion gone. Still... "Happy Halloween, Mags," she whispered.

Outside, Ari was still trying to win Olive over. "Are you kidding? There will be tons of candy! More than you'll get knocking on doors, I promise you."

"You telling them about your surprise?" Zeddi asked.

"Yup. And about how they're going to love it."

"As long as there's candy," Olive said. "Can we go now, Mom? *Please?*"

Isabella looked equally desperate.

Zeddi nodded and the girls raced ahead. She was beginning to regret having okayed Ari's surprise. It meant spending the whole evening with him. Hopefully, it would be worth it to hear what he said he needed to warn her about.

From the Miata, he grabbed what was surely an exact replica of Indiana Jones' briefcase, beeped the car lock, and held out his arm for her. "Shall we?"

Damn. Had she misread his motives? Did he think this was a date? She glanced at him. No. He was just being goofy. The Tin Man on the yellow brick road.

She took his arm. Loosely. He'd already had one blow to the ego.

It was too early in the day to be trolling the trailer park for candy, but from the rooftop spiderwebs, the life-sized soft-sculpture witch, the fake gravestones with bony hands reaching up out of the grass, and the tons of jack-o'-lanterns, the residents were rarin' and ready. It was a shame they weren't going to get to trick-or-treat there. Maybe if Ari's surprise didn't take too long, they could.

The closer they got to town, the bigger the crowd grew, and the louder it got.

A swish of costumed skateboarders soared past and nearly hit Isabella's tail.

"Slow down!" Ari yelled.

Zeddi used the moment to nonchalantly let go of his arm.

The strip was cordoned off, the sidewalk filled with costumed kids and adults going from store to store collecting candy. Huge lights were set up for when it got dark, and there were performers everywhere. Buskers, jugglers, break dancers. The local movie theater's marquee announced a midnight showing of *The Rocky Horror Picture Show.*

"This is nothing compared to how it gets at night," Ari explained. "Then the place really blows up."

It was hard to imagine it getting any bigger. "Let's hope it doesn't rain."

"No kidding."

They followed along on the street as the girls charged from store to store collecting candy.

"No kids in your life?" she asked.

"It's that obvious?"

"Kind of."

"Not because I don't like them," he said. "But it's true, I tend to surround myself with adults." He set his briefcase on a planter. Snapped the latch, removed a thermos, unscrewed the top, and poured an amber liquid into it. "To keep us warm."

She took the small plastic cup but held off on drinking. "Um, I just need to say something."

"Okay," he said.

"This is not a date."

"Oh my God, no," he stammered. "I'm sorry if I gave you that impression. I just feel kind of responsible. I mean, I knew when you inherited the trailer you were getting a whole lot more than you bargained for. I know what my mom and her friends are like, and I know what they think about Mags' and Constance's deaths. I just wanted to give you a little history is all, a little perspective. But not here, it's too loud. During my surprise when the girls are occupied—and it's quiet. In the meantime"—he gestured to the scene—"why not take in a little Halloween?"

Why not indeed? She took a swig. Warm, buttery, spicy, sweet, and best of all, infused with alcohol. "What *is* this?"

"Hot buttered rum. I thought it would be the perfect thing on a chilly evening."

She took another pull, felt it slide down her throat. "You thought right. This is a-*mazing*."

"Drink up. I had some while I was making it."

Nearby, a guy with a portable amp was doing a reggae rendition of "The Piña Colada Song," the perfect soundtrack for the parade of people: a family dressed as sailors, a couple of stilt-walkers, a flock of sparkly princesses followed by a harried dad trying to make some business deal on the phone, a terrified little Spider-Man clenching his mother's hand, a murder of sexy witches. Zeddi took another sip of the hot buttered rum. Let it marinate the inside of her mouth. Let it soften the hard edges of the world. She handed the cup back to Ari.

"You sure? There's more."

"I'm good. Thank you, though. That was a needed attitude adjustment."

As they tracked Olive and Isabella's route in and out of the different stores, Ari blathered on about some client who wanted to leave his entire estate to a cat. She could barely hear him over the marimbas. Her mind drifted to the interaction with Dante. If his were the footsteps in the office, then the break-in, which wasn't even really a break-in, had nothing to do with Mags' death—aside from taking advantage of it. She tried to remember the other things that had made her suspect Mags had been murdered. There was the phone call with Mags (which could have been about anything), Barnaby being left outside (there were tons of ways that could have happened), Mags being found in her chair in the same position as her sister (something she'd not seen with her own eyes, and really, not all *that* remarkable), the séance...

"Earth to Zeddi. Earth to Zeddi."

"Sorry. What were you saying?"

"Just that, as it turns out, the cat isn't even his. It's his neighbor's."

"Oh. Wow."

"Mas?"

She waved off the thermos. "Already pretty buzzed, thanks. It's strong."

"What?"

She had to shout to be heard. They were now right by the marimbas where a group of revelers were freestyle dancing to the hypnotic rhythms. "I said it's strong!"

"Too strong?" he shouted back. "Sorry! I got a call while I was brewing it. The guy with the cat! Anyway, I might have doubled up the alcohol by mistake."

"No problem! It's just I still have to drive out to your place later."

"I could drive!"

"The Miata? We wouldn't all fit."

"No. Your van! I'd pick up my car when I dropped you off!"

"Oh. Uh…let's cross that bridge when we get there. We still have dinner between now and then. In the meantime…" She couldn't help herself, she pirouetted into a gaggle of costumed dancers. It felt so good to move! To shake it loose! But where were Olive and Isabella? Had they come out of the frozen yogurt place yet? Should she check on them? No. They were dancing too. When had they come out? Why hadn't she seen them? And where was Ari? She spotted him by a planter looking awkward. So everyone was accounted for. But she'd lost track, that wasn't good. No more hot buttered rum for her. Not on an empty stomach. She danced over to Ari. "How soon to our dinner reservation?"

"We should probably head that way," he said.

❖

The rain arrived with the burgers, and it came hard, drenching the people who weren't fortunate enough to be sitting at a picture window overlooking the street. The restaurant was packed. Wet, costumed people crowded the entryway waiting for a table. Waiters and waitresses held their trays high to get through the rowdy crowd. Zeddi, holding Isabella's detached tail securely between her legs, made a point to smile at the harried waitress as she placed a huge cheeseburger in front of her. Across the small round table, Ari sat with his back to the window. He'd insisted on giving them the view. He really did look like Dr. Henry Walton, now that she remembered who Dr. Henry Walton was, with the parted hair, the wire rims. He'd filled out his chinstrap beard with makeup too. Behind him outside on the street, people huddled under canopies, umbrellas, raincoats, whatever they could find. Some just gave into the rain. A kindred Day of the Dead spirit promenaded methodically through the crowd, laughing, his arms opened wide, his once beautifully decorated face morphing into a scary streaked mask. What a night!

"Anything else?" the waitress asked after placing Ari's veggie burger and salad on the table.

"All good," he said. "Thank you."

"Yes, thank you," Zeddi said. Then to Olive, "Want me to cut your burger in half?"

Olive gave her a withering look. Apparently, unlike regular Olive, badass-to-the-core Indiana Olive took her burgers whole. "Just asking," Zeddi said, amused.

Ari rested an elbow on the back of Olive's chair. "Yeah, only kids need that, right?"

"Right," Olive agreed and bit savagely into the cheeseburger. She was starting to warm up to him. Waiting for their food to arrive, the two had bonded over some obscure Indiana Jones reference and been enthusiastically recounting others since. Zeddi worried that Isabella might feel left out, but the girl was deeply focused on her burger, organizing the lettuce, tomato, and onion into the perfect heap.

Zeddi watched it all through a hot-buttered remove. She was so light-headed! And to be honest, slightly nauseous. Was she coming down with something? Probably not. She was probably just worn out. That, and alcohol on an empty stomach. She bit into her blue cheese burger.

Outside, the rain picked up and more costumed people flooded into the already packed restaurant. They leered at the occupied tables.

"So, this surprise of yours…" Zeddi said, "Is it inside or outside?"

"Inside."

"Good. Maybe there will be a break in the rain, and we can make it back to the trailer without getting soaked."

CHAPTER TWENTY-SEVEN

I'm fine. I just don't want to drive," Zeddi said to Ari. "I'll Uber us over to your place. We can meet you there." Hugging Isabella's detached tail to her chest, she leaned against the van under the carport while the girls crammed in a few last-minute trailer-park trick-or-treats. A break in the rain meant they'd only gotten slightly soggy as they jogged back from the burger joint. That was something. If only she didn't have such a headache. But there was no bowing out of the surprise now. Ari had gotten the girls way too excited about it. And she was determined to get Ari's take on the whole coven thing, and he didn't want to talk until they could do it privately.

"No way," Ari said. "For one thing, good luck getting an Uber tonight. And I'm fine to drive the van. I'll pick up my Miata when I take you home. We'll make it quick since you're not feeling good. Okay? Get you home and into bed."

She nodded. "I'll be fine. I just drank too much." It was embarrassing. She wasn't usually such a lightweight.

"Seriously, let me drive."

Hadn't she already said okay? Maybe not. "Okay," she said aloud, and handed over the keys.

❖

"We want the surprise! We want the surprise!" the girls, pumped to the eyeballs on sugar, chanted.

"Nobody wants anything to drink?" Ari teased "A nice glass of delicious water perhaps?"

"The surprise! The surprise!" they shouted.

Zeddi tried to look enthused, but all she really wanted at this point was to ask him her questions, go home, and flop into bed. She took a deep breath. Made herself focus.

The interior of his house was not what she'd expected. The old Craftsman at the end of the long, weedy, dirt driveway suggested overstuffed chairs with quaint floor lamps, faded Oriental carpets, not this sleek modern open floor plan, not leather furniture, glass tabletops, and granite kitchen counters. Like his office, the color scheme ranged from cream to wheat. In other words, boring. The ocean view, though, had to be fantastic during the day. She wandered over to the picture window. For now just distant lights from a few homes. His minimalist wall clock showed a quarter to eight. Where had the time gone? Suddenly flushed, she peeled off her jacket. Dropped it onto a leather chair.

"Prepare to be amazed!" Ari trumpeted like a ringmaster.

She pasted on a smile and trailed behind him and the girls to a narrow door off the kitchen.

His hand on the doorknob, he taunted, "Are you sure you're ready?"

"Ready!" Olive and Isabella screamed.

"Are you sure?"

"Yes! Yes! Open it! Open it!"

He clearly had no idea how easily stoking this kind of hysteria in nine-year-old girls could backfire and turn into tantrums or tears. She prayed it wouldn't. She didn't have the bandwidth.

Finally, he swung open the basement door and there, taped to the door, was a life-size photo of Indiana Jones. Really? That was the big surprise?

A moment of awkward silence passed before Olive said weakly, "A poster?"

Ari couldn't have been more pleased. "Ah, but it's so much more than that! Downstairs you will find an Indiana Jones obstacle course full of challenges both physical and mental, each designed to test your skill, each offering a generous reward of"—he did a drum roll on his thighs—"c-c-c-candy!"

Olive and Isabella squealed in delight. "Can we do it now, Mom?" Olive pleaded. "Please please please?"

"Yeah, can they, Mom?" Ari echoed and flicked on the light switch.

There was no saying no now. The girls were too excited. Ari was so excited. But this was not going to be the quick thing he'd promised. "Sure."

She followed them halfway down the narrow stairwell to see what all the fuss was about. He really had gone all out. A series of stations, each with a task to be accomplished. A thick knotted rope hanging from a beam, a dangling cargo net, a trash can filled with sandbags, among other *Survivor*-esque challenges.

"But if it gets too late," she amended, "we may have to come back and finish it another time."

"That's right," Ari teased. "Mom's tired and needs to rest."

The girls charged down the stairs. Zeddi tried to think of a polite way to ask him to quit referring to her as Mom. "You really didn't have to do this," she said.

"I had fun. And I wanted to give us plenty of time to talk."

She steadied herself on the railing as they climbed up the steep stairs. "Right." Talking. Just what she felt like doing with a headache from hell. "Do you think I could have a glass of water?" She had some Advil in her bag.

"You can have more than that. More hot buttered rum. Or some tea…"

"Water is fine, thanks."

In the living room, she sank into the leather sofa and shut her eyes. It felt so good to sit.

He brought her a cut glass tumbler of water, and sat directly across from her. "I really should have warned you."

She blinked her eyes into focus. Sat up a little straighter. "About?"

"About what you were inheriting besides the trailer."

"Meaning…" She picked up her bag. Fished around for the Advil. Remembered she'd taken the bottle out to refill. Damn.

"Mags, my mother, Ida, Shakineh."

She set the bag down. Sipped the water. "Mags is dead."

"Well, yes."

"Possibly murdered."

"Look, I know what they think. My dad told me, and it's insane." He took off his fake glasses, set them on the coffee table, rubbed his eyes. "I mean, you knew Mags, she was old. Old people die."

The exact words Jace had used. "But there have been other things."

"There are *always* other things with this bunch. Believe me, I grew up with them. They do this. They latch onto *things*, start building cases around *things*—" He was clearly reining in his anger. Her head hurt too much to care.

"There was a séance."

"A séance."

"Uh-huh."

"And you were invited?"

"Uh-huh."

He shook his head in disgust. Then laughed. "Actually, I don't know why I'm surprised."

"We were trying to communicate with Mags."

"Of course you were. Look, I'm terribly sorry, but my mom and her friends, they're nuts, plain and simple."

"Is that why you're not close to your mom? Because she's nuts?"

He ran his fingers through his hair, seemed to remember it was gelled, then tried to pat the stiffened peaks back into place. Had she gone too far? Said too much? But she had no filters. The hot buttered rum and headache had melted them.

"She said that?"

"Not those exact words."

"I've just been taking some space, that's all. I needed a little break from all the drama."

"Okay, but here's the thing, during the séance—and I know this sounds crazy—but it seemed like we really did connect with Mags."

"And?"

"And your mom fainted."

"And?"

"And we got this creepy voicemail a few days ago, threatening us."

"You got it? Or Mags got it?"

"Well, it was on Mags' answering machine. So technically, Mags got it."

"So, it wasn't necessarily meant for you."

"Well, yeah."

"So Mags probably got herself mixed up in something, and the person leaving the voicemail didn't know she was dead. That wouldn't surprise me. Mags was a meddler, and probably pissed off one of her witchy friends. But I don't see that necessarily pointing to murder, do you? Really?"

"I don't know…"

"And about the séance," he said. "I don't mean to burst your bubble, and I'd be the first to say Shakineh puts on a good show, but who knows what she fed you. Because you ate, right?"

"We did," Zeddi said cautiously.

"Well, there may have been some kind of hallucinogen in there."

Suddenly, she was wide-awake. "*What?*"

"It wouldn't be the first time Shakineh laced the stew, that's for sure, and it wouldn't have been anything strong. Nothing the DEA wouldn't approve of. A salvia maybe, or nutmeg, who knows? Given enough, the senses get a little wonky, I'm telling you. I've experienced it. As for Mom almost fainting, I'm sure she blamed it on her"—he air-quoted—"*autoimmune disease*, which, just so you know, has been thus far completely undiagnosable, and seems to arise at, shall we say, convenient times."

Zeddi tried to process what he was saying. Drug induced? She'd heard about nutmeg in large quantities, but salvia? If only her brain was working better.

"Had I known that my mom and her friends were going to mix you up in their nonsense, I would have put a stop to it," he said. "I'm so sorry. I really am. This is on me. I should have said something."

"I just can't imagine…"

"I get it. They're a charming bunch. Eccentric. Especially that Ida. But I swear, she's the ringleader." He leaned forward. "Hey, you okay?"

"Yeah. I just have this headache." And her makeup was itching like hell.

"You want to nap a little? While the girls do their thing downstairs?" Behind him, two computers on a glass-top desk were in sleep mode, photos hypnotically morphing from one to the next to the next.

"Would that be okay?"

"More than okay," he said kindly.

A peal of laughter floated up from the basement. It seemed miles away.

She gave into her heavy eyelids. "It's just been an intense few days."

He was behind her now, in the kitchen doing something. She didn't care. She just wanted to...

A shrill sound startled her.

"Ariii! Ariii!"

She clawed her way to consciousness. What now? But it was just Olive.

"We're having a little prooo-blem down here," Olive griped.

Zeddi peered over the back of the couch. Olive was standing in the basement doorway, Ari in the kitchen standing by a small round mirror patting his Dr. Henry Walton hair back into place. The fake glasses were back too.

"Oh yeah?" he said.

"The third station?" Olive said. "With the computer? It froze up."

Another pass through his hair. "Whoopsie." He followed her downstairs.

How long had she been sleeping? It couldn't have been long. She fumbled around on the floor for her purse. Found her phone. Just past eight. Not long. Maybe ten minutes.

There was a text from Ida. It had come in an hour ago. *CALL ME AS SOON AS YOU GET THIS!!!*

It was the last thing she felt like doing, but there was no ignoring the capitalization or excessive use of exclamation points. Ida wasn't the type to overdramatize. Or was she? After what Ari had said...

She pulled up her contacts, punched in Ida's number, but there was no cell service. Damn. It really was time to change providers. Maybe outside?

Walking to the door felt like an ordeal, her legs so heavy, the door so massive, but once outside the fresh air was worth the trouble. A copse of eucalyptus trees dripped onto the duff below, otherwise the world was uncannily still. She headed for the van, eyes on the phone, looking for a signal. There were puddles everywhere. Her head still hurt. It was dark. After talking with Ida, she'd call an Uber. Or get Ari to drive them home. No way did she feel safe to drive, and she needed to be home.

A bar. Two bars. Three.

Ida picked up on the first ring. "Thank heavens! I've been so worried! We all have."

"What's up?"

"Yes, yes, it's her," Ida said to someone. Then to Zeddi, "Roni and Shakineh are with me too. We tried again—even Roni, though we counseled against it, but I'm so glad she joined us. Without her... well...oh, it's a heartbreak! For all of us! None of us want to believe it, but we should have known. Maybe we did, but there's no pretending anymore. Not when lives may be at stake. Not when—"

Zeddi leaned against the van. Was Ida speed-talking or was her brain really moving that slowly? "Um...known what exactly? And tried what?"

There was a pause. Then Ida said, "Are you all right? You don't sound like yourself."

"I'm fine. Just tired. So what's all this about?"

"You and Olive are in danger."

"What?"

"Have you had many dealings with Roni's son, Ari?"

"I'm with him right now. Or...I'm at his house. He's in the basement with Olive and her friend. He created an obstacle course for the girls. I'm—"

"You need to get Olive and leave immediately."

"Why?"

"Trust me, you need to leave."

"Ida, I don't think..."

"He's been siphoning. We believe that's what killed Constance and Mags. He wanted their power, tried to steal it!"

"I'm sorry, *what*?"

"I believe that's why Roni's been so sick too. He's been draining her power for his own use—for who knows how long! And now he's after—"

"You think Ari killed Mags and Constance?"

"There really is no other explanation. The vision in tonight's séance was quite clear. It's heartbreaking, but...Zeddi, you really must leave! You say he's in the basement with Olive? You must go get her! He believes her to be a natural. There's no telling—"

"But he's been so nice all evening. It's hard to believe—"

"I'm sorry, dear, but I'm having difficulty understanding you. You're slurring. Has he given you something?"

Slurring? She was? *She was!* Damn! The hot buttered rum! She wasn't sleepy, she'd been drugged! She lurched for the house. "I have to go."

"Wait!" Ida cried.

But there was no waiting. He was alone with the girls—and he'd drugged her. *Drugged* her! She couldn't believe it. Couldn't *not* believe it. She was so pissed, so scared. If he'd put one finger on Olive she'd... she'd...damn! Charging through the dark across the uneven ground, the ankle-twisting vintage lace-up heels were a total liability. But the distance wasn't nearly as long this time, the door not nearly as heavy. Not when she was flooded with adrenaline.

"I heard you walking around up here," Ari said smiling. But he was agitated. Her being up had thrown him off his game—whatever the hell his game was. "It surprised me," he said, and tossed her a quick tight smile.

I bet it did, she shot back mentally. One of the heels of her shoes was coming loose. "I was just getting some fresh air." It took all her power to keep her hands from shaking as she took a glass from the dish drainer, filled it with tap water, gulped it down. Were the girls okay? Why couldn't she hear them? *Speak, damn it. Sound casual.* "I think it's time for us to go."

"There must have been a power surge," he said, ignoring what she'd said. "All fixed now, though. And we still have to talk. You must have more questions."

"I'll Uber, it's cool, but let me get the girls first."

He stepped left, blocking her way. "So it stopped raining?"

She had to be careful. Keep her voice from betraying her panic. "Yeah. It's nice out. You should check it out." Why couldn't she hear the girls?

"You trying to get rid of me?"

"Of course not. It's just..." *Cool. Casual.* "There's supposed to be a lunar eclipse. Maybe you can see it. I looked, but..."

Outside a rogue gust of wind pummeled the large plate glass window with debris. The lights flickered, and in the living room one of the large computer screens clicked on and his screensaver of rotating photos dissolved into a candid photograph of her and Olive outside the Boys and Girls Club. He'd been following them! The look of horror must have crossed her face because he turned around to see what had caused it.

Shit.

"Zeddi," he said.

"Girls?" she called out, her diaphragm refusing to help her lungs. *Try again.* "Girls?" *Louder.* "Time to go!" She took a step toward him.

He didn't budge, said, "But they're having so much fun."

"Yeah, well, I'm not." She was trembling now. "Like I said, I don't feel well. Let me pass, please." Eyes locked on his, legs unsteady beneath her, she prayed for inspiration. "What do you want, Ari? What's this all about?" A knife block on the counter to her right beckoned. She didn't dare actually look at it, but she knew it was there.

"What happened out there?" he said.

"Nothing happened."

"No, something did. I can tell."

"Like I said, I just went out for some fresh air and now I'm ready to go home—with my daughter and Isabella." Oh God, how would she ever explain this to Luciana? "Girls?" she called out a third time. Why weren't they responding? Had he drugged them too? "Girls!"

"I'm a good guy," he said, his perfectly manicured nails clenching the hem of his costume jacket.

"I don't doubt that," she said steadily. "I'm just ready to go home, and I want my daughter and Isabella with me." He seemed like the kind of guy to keep his knives sharp, but the blades were hidden. What if she grabbed a serrated knife? Would that even work? If she slid the serrated edge across his jugular? She'd only get one chance, and the drugs had made her unsteady. That and the broken heel.

"Right," he said, but he was breathing heavily, his muscles taut. Any second now he was going to lunge at her.

"It's true." She tried to casually laugh, but it came out more like a choking sound. "Why wouldn't it be?" Ida knew where they were. That was good. Maybe stalling was the best tactic. But how far away was Ida? Whalers Point? That was over half an hour away. Maybe she should go for the knife.

"I would never hurt Olive," he said. "You've got to trust me."

"*Trust* you?" she blurted. "You drugged me! You've been stalking us!"

His pupils flared. His hands clenched and released, clenched and released. She readied herself to go for the knife, but mercifully, after several seconds of staring her down, he flung his hands in the air and stepped out of her way. "Fine! Go get them. Leave!"

She lurched for the basement doorway. "Girls! Time to go!" There was no response. "Girls!" Then she felt it. The slight push. She grabbed the handrail and started stumbling down the steps, only to hear the door click shut behind her—the snap of the bolt lock gliding into its casing.

CHAPTER TWENTY-EIGHT

For a millisecond, Zeddi weighed racing downstairs to check on the girls against banging on the door and demanding Ari open up, but the decision was a no-brainer. Threading the pole railing through her clammy palm, she fumbled her way down the steep staircase. Until she knew if the girls were okay, she couldn't think straight. Not that she was thinking straight now. Far from it. Pure instinct was driving her now. The stairs were shallow, tall. She had to pay attention. Her broken heel was no help. Nor the lag between thought and action. Each dimly lit, uneven step took concentration. "Girls!" she called out. "Girls!" How had she not realized she was drugged? It was so obvious now.

It wasn't until she reached the bottom step that she spotted Olive and Isabella back in the bowels of the basement sitting happily in front of a computer screen—wearing headphones. They simply hadn't heard her. She indulged herself a second of relief before giving in to anger. Hot buttered rum! What bullshit! And he kept urging her to drink more! And dressing up like Indiana Jones! Making an Indiana Jones obstacle course! All while planning to…what? Steal Olive's supposed power? Was that what Ida had said? It seemed so insane. It *was* insane. *He* was insane.

She had to keep that in mind. There was no negotiating with an insane person.

Now what?

She glanced around the periphery of the basement for possible weapons and spotted an old rusty shovel. It would have to do. Explaining their predicament to the girls was going to be tricky, though. How to do it without scaring them? She shot a silent apology to Luciana. This would likely put the kibosh on Isabella's and Olive's friendship, which made her even angrier. How dare he? How *dare* he?

Above them, the floor squeaked with Ari's pacing. Back and forth, back and forth. He was nervous. He hadn't planned to lock them in the basement. She'd thrown him off when she'd woken up. Did that make him more dangerous, or less? She checked her cell phone on the slim chance she might get service. No dice. She took a deep breath. Time to clue in the girls.

She came up behind them. On the monitor was the question: *What type of animal is Indy scared of?* Even Zeddi knew that. Olive typed in *snakes. Correct!* popped up on the screen, along with a scene of Indiana dangling above a pit of snakes. *Take one piece of candy from the basket.*

"Olive? Isabella?" She tapped Olive on the shoulder.

"Hang on," Olive said.

Zeddi lifted one of the earphones from her ear. "Honey, I need to talk to you. Both of you. It's important."

Olive hit pause. Removed her headphones. "What?"

Isabella removed her headphones too and twisted around to face Zeddi. No longer in the cumbersome alebrije costume, she was now just a sweet little girl in black tights, black turtleneck, and a face made up with stars and rainbows.

Zeddi steadied herself on the backs of the metal fold-out chairs. Crouched down to their level. "We're in some trouble," she whispered. "Nothing we can't get out of, but we need to be very careful, and we need to work together."

Isabella glanced at Olive, checking to see if Zeddi was messing with them or what.

Olive frowned. "Is this part of the obstacle course?"

"No. This is real and I need you to listen to me."

"Mom, you're acting weird. Are you drunk?"

"Ari is not who we thought he was," she continued. "He's not a good man. He may be trying to hurt us. Right now, he's locked us down here. Do you understand?"

Isabella took hold of Olive's hand. She looked terrified. Zeddi yearned to hug her, to tell her everything was going to be all right, but she couldn't risk it. She needed the girls to understand this was serious, to stay alert. At the same time, she needed them to stay calm.

"Also, he put something in my drink that's making it a little hard for me to think clearly and making me a little dizzy."

"So you're not drunk," Olive assessed.

"No. But this is important. Have you eaten anything he's given you? Or drunk anything?"

They shook their heads. "No," Olive said. "His candy prizes are kind of lame."

"*Really* lame," Isabella agreed.

"Does this have to do with who killed Mags?" Olive asked.

"Possibly."

"Remember I told you?" Olive said to Isabella. "About Mags?"

Isabella nodded somberly.

"Okay, here's the deal," Zeddi said. But what was the deal? Wait for Ida or go on the offensive? She wanted to trust Ida, but the truth was she didn't know Ida all *that* well. She didn't know any of these people. And even if she could trust Ida, which she thought she could, Whalers Point was a good forty minutes off. A lot could happen in forty minutes. Would Ida have called the police? No, best not to count on that. Best to count on herself and the girls. "I'm going to head back up there and make him let us out. When he does, we need to make a beeline for Turtle. Wait. My bag is by the couch. The van keys are in it."

Damn.

Think. Think.

"We'll cross that bridge when we get there." *If* we get there.

"We could climb out that window," Isabella said, pointing up.

Olive spun around, Zeddi looked up. Sure enough, a small rectangular window butted up to the ceiling. It hinged at the top. Zeddi would never make it through, but if it indeed opened (it looked ancient), the girls could.

❖

Balanced precariously on the second-to-top step of a rickety wooden ladder, Zeddi whispered, "Please don't break. Please don't break." Below, the girls braced the ladder with their feet. The ladder, missing a rung, had been part of the obstacle course. It had lain flat on the floor with the directions to hop through it. Stupid really, but Zeddi was grateful for it now. It got her high enough to pry at the window with the rusty shovel. She worked quietly, cautiously. Upstairs Ari continued to pace, stopping from time to time, then pacing some more. Every time he stopped, she stopped. The shovel was heavy, and holding it above her head awkward, but she would get the girls out of this hellhole. She had to.

She took a deep breath. Waited for his next step. Pulled down hard on the shovel.

Yes! The rusty window gave way with a crack.

She listened. No pause in his pacing. Yes! He hadn't heard.

She climbed gingerly down the ladder, flimsy rung by flimsy rung, forcing her dopey mind to think preemptively. What if the girls escaped only to find Ari lying in wait while she, still locked in the basement, was unable to help? It was a risk she had to take. His pacing was getting more frantic. "Here's how this is going to work," she whispered. "I'm going to see if I can get him to talk to me through the door. Once you hear that I have him engaged, climb out the window and run to Turtle, lock yourself in, and honk the horn a bunch of times. Flash the lights too. Then I'll know you're safe." She shoved a box of old books against the foot of the ladder to keep it from slipping. "Move quietly and quickly. And, Olive, once you're in the van, grab the pepper spray from the glove box. You remember where we put it?"

Olive nodded.

"Good. And call 9-1-1. Your phone should work out there." It was a crappy flip phone so maybe it wouldn't, but surely if they kept honking the horn and flashing the lights someone would come.

Ari's pacing stopped. There was a loud smash. Was he throwing things now?

She took a hold of Olive's jacket lapels. "And promise me, *promise me*, if it comes to saving yourself or saving me, which it won't, we have a good plan, but if it does, you save yourself. Do you hear me?"

"Mom…"

"I mean it, Olive. Promise me."

"Okay, okay, I promise."

"You too, Isabella. Save yourself. Understand? Ari is a bad bad man."

"Don't worry," Isabella said. "I'm a really fast runner."

"I'm sure you are," she said. She just wished Olive were a little faster. "Okay. I'm going to get him talking. Listen for it. Listen for him talking back to me." Tears were pricking the corners of her eyes, her throat tightening, but she had to be brave for these two sweet girls. They were counting on her. She kissed Olive on the head, gave her a hug. Kissed Isabella too. Gave her a hug. Hugged Olive again. "We can do this."

"Go!" Olive whispered.

"Right."

Turning away from the girls, walking through the hanging strings of plastic spiders, the scary-faced jack-o'-lanterns, the life-size plastic skeleton at the foot of the stairs was the hardest thing life had ever asked of her. She mounted the creaky too-tall, too-shallow stairs, taking the shovel with her. Her mind flashed on Sylvie. If she didn't get this right, she would never see her again. But she would get this right. She would see Sylvie again. In person. She kissed the tattoo on her wrist. *Trust. Believe. Cast the spell.*

At the top of the stairs, she knocked on Paper Indiana Jones' belt buckle. "Ari! Ari! Can we talk, please?" She wiggled the door handle. Waited. Knocked again. "Ari! Please! Why are you doing this?" Again, the wait. *Come on, come on,* she chanted silently, *come to the door.* "Whatever this is," she said aloud, "you don't need to do it. You're a good guy. We can work something out." It wasn't easy, using her good girl voice, her nice voice, but she had to make him come. Him seeing Olive and Isabella running to the van was a risk she couldn't take. She remembered the motion detector light that had flashed on when they first arrived. Prayed it wouldn't catch Ari's eye. *Come on, motherfucker. Come on.*

Finally, the sound of his oxfords striding toward her.

She braced herself against the railing with one hand, gripped the shovel with the other. If he flung open the door, she needed to be ready. He could easily push her down the stairs. But not if she whacked him with the shovel first.

"I would never hurt you," he said, softly.

"What? I didn't hear you?" And neither would the girls if he didn't speak up.

"I *said* I would never hurt you!"

Go! she mentally yelled to the girls. *Go!* It killed her not to be able to go with them, to help them, but she had to keep him talking, that was what would keep them safe. "So why are you doing this?"

There was no response, but she could hear him breathing.

"Please talk to me, Ari. I want to understand. I really do."

"The tradition…"

"Yes?"

"It must be kept alive."

"And that's what you're trying to do by locking us in your basement?"

"Yes. No! Of course not. But you weren't cooperating!"

"Well, maybe if you explained to me what you were trying to do? You're talking about the Keepers, right?"

Again, no response. Was he still there? She listened for footsteps. Didn't hear any. Maybe he was walking quietly. Or about to fling open the door. Her heart thundered in her chest, her breathing jagged, shallow. She had to keep him talking, but her throat was constricting. From below a loud scraping. The ladder? Had the box of books not held it in place? Had he heard? "Ari? Are you still there?" If only she could see the girls. Check on them. If only… "I really want to understand. Talk to me. Please. Maybe we can work something out."

"I wasn't going to hurt Olive," he said quietly.

Yes! He was still there.

"And I never would. I didn't mean to hurt Constance either, or Mags. But Olive, she's young. Strong. It wouldn't drain her the way it did them."

Siphoning. He was talking about siphoning. Nausea rose up in her throat. If only she could record his confession. But to record it, she'd have to reach into her pocket for her phone, to do that she'd have to let go of the shovel. No way.

The door shuddered violently. "Mags chose a nine-year-old over me!"

She gripped the shovel tighter, readied herself in case he somehow actually managed to punch through the door. "Mags what?" she asked nicely. *Come on girls, honk the horn. Honk the horn.*

"Nothing," he said, despondently. "It just hurt, that's all." The door pressed slightly toward her. He had to be leaning on it.

It occurred to her that the van keys were in the living room, in her purse. If she remembered right, they'd left it open. But what if they didn't? What if the girls couldn't get in? Or what if they did get in and he found her purse, found the keys, and— No. She couldn't think this way. It was too late to change plans. Maybe he wouldn't see the purse tucked next to the couch leg. Maybe— No. "Tell me. I want to know." For sure, when he heard the horn, he'd go out to see what was up, but he'd have to come back for the keys. There'd be time for Olive to dig out the pepper spray. If the girls could even get into the van. "Mags chose her for what exactly?"

"To be a Keeper! She was priming her."

"But Ida said she wasn't."

"Ida would say anything to protect Mags. Don't you know that?"

She was making him angry. Not good. Change strategy. "You mean transmission, right? That Mags thought Olive was a natural? But why would Olive need transmission if she's a natural? I just don't see the logic."

"That's just it!" he screamed. "She doesn't! She doesn't need the Gift! But I…" He pounded on the door again.

He was losing it. She was too. The dark stairwell was getting more claustrophobic by the second. She was having trouble breathing. Still, she needed to calm him. But how? *Say something! Say something!* her brain screamed at her frozen vocal cords.

He started pacing again. "Ari! Ari!" Why weren't the girls at the van? "Ari!" Tears welled up in her eyes. The plan wasn't working. Something had gone wrong. "Ari!" Maybe they should have just waited for Ida to come. Would she come? *Was* she coming? Was anyone coming?

"Ari! I didn't mean to upset you. I just don't understand—"

"I'm done talking about this!" he shrieked. "You can't understand! You don't know our ways."

"But I thought you weren't into all this—"

"Shut up! I want to talk to Olive! Now!"

No! "Um. She's too upset right now. Both the girls are. They're down there crying."

"Get her!"

Um…"Yeah. She's too scared. She's—"

"Bring her up! I want to talk to her. *Now!*"

Just then: *HAAANK! HAAANK! HAAANK!* Turtle's ridiculous horn.

Zeddi slumped against the railing in relief. The girls had made it!

❖

"What the hell?" Ari slapped the door so hard she almost jumped off the step.

"Wait!" she called out, then listened helplessly as he crashed through the house. *Damn!* She slapped the door herself. Because she could. Then leaned against it. Took a shaky breath. The girls had made it to Turtle. They were safe. That old van was a tank. He'd have a hell of a time breaking in. And if he did, which he wouldn't, but if he did, if he found the keys in her purse, they had pepper spray, and Olive, she was sure, would be happy to use it. And hopefully, they would have called the cops. And Ida would be there soon. The thoughts did nothing to reassure her. She bashed the blade of the shovel into the door above the doorknob. Did it again. Again. Time to free herself. But old door was stout. One more try—

"FUH!" Ari screamed.

Something had happened. What? She held the shovel mid-swing. Listened. Had he found the girls in the van? No. He sounded closer to the house. Like just outside the door. And like he was in pain? Maybe he tripped?

He began to wail. Pain for sure. Good. Maybe he'd cracked his head. She put her ear to the door, held her breath. A string of expletives, more wailing, then him yelling, "You little bitch!" She froze. Little bitch? Olive! No! Get in the van! Get in the van! Adrenaline pumping, she raised the shovel and prepared to shear the doorknob clean off. Whatever it took to get to her daughter. He screamed again, even louder this time. What was going on? "Olive!" she screamed. "Olive!" His wail turned into a moan, a long, drawn out whimpery moan. "Olive!" she screamed again. "Isabella!"

To hell with the shovel. She grabbed the doorknob. She'd yank the fucking door off its hinges if need be. But wait. Someone was running toward her, someone small, who wasn't wearing oxfords, someone with little girl feet.

"Zeddi! Zeddi!" Isabella called out.

Why wasn't she in the van? And where was Olive? Why wasn't she with Isabella?

The snap of the lock releasing, the door opening. A breathless Isabella in Ugg boots and leotard, her face all rainbows and stars. "We got him!" she said. "We got him!"

Zeddi grabbed her by the shoulders. "Where's Olive?"

She pointed to the open door. "Out there! She—"

Zeddi charged through the kitchen to the door, Isabella hot on her heels. "You should have seen her, Zeddi! She used the skull crusher! She was…"

Zeddi slammed open the front door, charged down the two steps. She had to get to Olive. *Now.* But Ari was in the way. Crouched in the mud, writhing in agony. "Ahh!" he moaned, "Ahh!" He held his head in his hands. "I'm blind! I'm blind!" There was no sign of Olive.

"Olive!" she screamed. If only her eyes would adjust to the dark. "Olive!"

"Over here!"

Yes! Olive was safe! Standing halfway between Ari and the van, the baseball bat held high and ready for action. Zeddi took Isabella's hand and together they made a wide circle around the thrashing Ari.

"I did like Dan told me," Olive said, breathlessly. "I went for the kneecaps!" Her chest was heaving, her eyes wild.

"And I shot him with pepper spray!" Isabella crowed.

"She broke my knee! That little bitch broke my leg!" Ari wailed.

Zeddi dropped to her knees. Pulled Olive and Isabella into a fierce hug, sputtering, "You should have listened to me!"

"But we got him, Mom!"

"Yeah!" Isabella chimed. "Indiana Olive! Badass to the core!"

"Have you called 9-1-1?"

Olive looked momentarily sheepish. "We hadn't gotten to that yet."

She should scold her. Olive had taken a terrible chance confronting Ari, but she was too relieved to care. The girls were okay. They were safe.

"I can't see!" Ari shrieked. Curled up on the ground, face in the crook of his arm, leg at an unnatural angle, he waved a finger wildly in the air. "She blinded me! The little bitch blinded me!"

Zeddi pulled her phone from her pocket. Dialed 9-1-1. "A man has just assaulted my daughters and me. Or...my daughter and her *friend*..." She was talking fast. Too fast. She took a breath.

"Are you in any danger now?"

She stared at Ari in the amber glow of the porch light, mumbling to himself, punching blindly into the dark, falling back into the mud in agony. He wasn't going anywhere. No way. Olive had busted his knee.

"I repeat. Are you in any danger now?"

"I don't think so. But we need someone here, quick. There's a man down. I mean, not down down. He's not dead. He's just...just send someone!"

"What's your location?"

At that moment, the woods exploded in light.

CHAPTER TWENTY-NINE

Ida's car skidded into the driveway. Dazed, Zeddi watched as she, Shakineh, and Roni piled out. Claude, too. The poor man looked terrified.

"I'm sorry, what?" she asked the operator. "Some people—"

"What's your location?"

Zeddi filled her in while watching Roni, arms outstretched, beige raincoat flapping behind her, run to her suffering son as if *he* were the victim. And Shakineh was right behind her! Seriously? She locked eyes with Ida, who was making a beeline for her and the girls.

"Are you all right? What happened?"

Zeddi held up a finger to finish up with the 9-1-1 operator, then hung up. "The police are on their way."

"Because?"

"He tried to kidnap us!" Olive said. "But me and Isabella took him out! He locked us up in the basement, but we escaped and then I bashed him with the skull crusher."

Isabella brandished the small black canister. "And *I* blasted him with pepper spray!"

"Really?" Ida asked Zeddi.

"Really," Zeddi confirmed.

Ida gave Olive's shoulder a squeeze. "Well done."

"She's badass to the core," Isabella said.

"We had to climb through a window," Olive explained. "A tiny one way up high."

Ida turned her attention to Ari in the mud. Lifted her hands to her heart. Heaved a long sigh. "This saddens me beyond measure."

"Not me," Zeddi quipped. "Not after what we've been through."

"Me neither," Olive said. "I hope they lock him up forever!"

Roni dropped to her knees in the muddy driveway and attempted to cradle her son. "Somebody call an ambulance!" she screamed.

Ari pushed her away. "Mom! What are you doing here?"

Shakineh extended her arms toward mother and son. She was obviously aching to join the pathetic mother and son reunion but remained a respectful distance away. A gust snaked its way through the trees, billowing her long black cape.

Zeddi hugged herself. Shifted from foot to foot. Stared aghast at the two women, haloed in the porch light, comforting Ari Miller when not only had he tried to kidnap her and the girls, he'd also probably murdered Mags and her sister. Rage once again rose up in her. Someone had some explaining to do. Now. She squatted next to Ida. "You *knew* Ari was dangerous and didn't do anything about it? You didn't warn me? You didn't go to the police?"

Ida either couldn't or wouldn't look at her. Instead, her eyes stayed on Roni and Ari as she spoke. "I had my suspicions, yes, but I didn't know for sure. Until tonight. And I prayed I was wrong. I had no idea you and Ari had become friends. If I had…well…I didn't, and…" She faced Zeddi. Took her hands. "I'm so sorry." Her eyes were brimming with tears. "But there's no denying it now, for any of us, even Roni, bless her. I suspect Roni's fear of the truth is what's been thwarting our efforts to sort all this out. I'm sure that's what happened in our last séance. That dark cloud was a shield of denial." A pained expression crossed her face. "But things couldn't have been clearer in tonight's séance. Ari killed Mags. I don't think he meant to. But his greed…" She turned away from Zeddi, her shoulders shuddering.

Too angry to comfort Ida, Zeddi stood. "He drugged me! Drugged me, then locked me and my daughter and her friend in the basement! He could have—" She slapped her hands over her mouth. *No. Don't even think it.*

Nearby, Claude began rocking and weeping. Ida wiped her eyes. "It's all right, Claude." She patted his arm. "I'm all right. Everything is all right." She turned to Zeddi next. "I would never have forgiven myself if something—"

"Ow!" Ari howled. "Mom! Stop touching me! My leg is broken. Can't you see?"

"Call an ambulance!" Roni screamed again.

"These people are bonkers," Olive observed.

"Really bonkers," Isabella agreed.

They huddled together on the far side of Ida.

Ida shook her head sadly. "If I'm correct, he's been siphoning Roni's life force for years. I think that's the cause of her autoimmune disease—and no doubt the reason for his good luck over the years. As far as I know, he's never lost a case. But now that she's wearing down, I expect he's been feeling desperate." She sighed. "He's an addict, plain and simple, willing to do anything for another hit of dreaming. He's desperate for the Gift, was willing to abuse his mother to get it. He tried to siphon it from Constance and Mags too, that's what killed them."

"Okay, I know you told me before," Zeddi said. "But what exactly is siphoning?"

Ida looked at her. "Have you ever known someone who seems to suck the life force out of someone else?"

A couple she'd known in Sacramento came to mind. "Sure."

"It's like that, only it's more severe. It's a literal draining of the victim's vitality and can cause serious health issues for the person whose power is being siphoned off. It's dirty magic, greedy magic, and often feeds on love, of all things—which is what made Mags and Constance so vulnerable. They loved Ari, would not have believed him capable. Either one of them would have done anything for him. I suspect too, that he spiked their tea with some mind-numbing herb, then did his dirty magic. He wanted to be a Keeper so badly, wanted the power that came with it, but the Gift just never took with him. He tried for it, I'll give him credit for that, he did try. He was just born with a deaf ear. Some people are." She looked so pained, so old. "It never should have come to this, though, and I'm so sorry for any part I played in it. I truly am. If I hadn't loved him so much myself…"

"I'm going to get my sneakers from the van." It came out sounding more curt than Zeddi had intended, but she needed a moment to digest that Ida loved this monster. She also just needed to sit down, put on some sensible shoes, shed the broken heel. If only she could clean off the makeup. It was itchy as hell. But she would not go back into that house. Ever.

She remembered her purse.

Damn.

Maybe she could talk a police officer into getting it for her? Or they'd escort her in?

She dropped onto the step of the van's open barn door, her head aching from the mix of drugs and adrenaline. Changing out her shoes, she watched the girls recount their big escape to Ida. Then closed her eyes. Breathed in the pungent scent of the damp eucalyptus. She was safe. Olive was safe. The thought didn't do much to cure her headache, but it did help her heart return to its normal rhythm.

It was so obvious now that Ari Miller's nice-lawyer persona was all an act. The guy was a chameleon, morphing into whoever he needed to be to get what he wanted, and he'd taken advantage of Mags—all of them, Ida included. She felt her heart soften toward Ida. She was a victim too. Could very easily have been his next target. She forced back a tremor. Tightened her shoelaces. Made herself to get up and walk over to her and the girls. "Everything okay here?"

The girls nodded innocently. Too innocently. What was up now? Before she could ask, Ida strode into the light where Roni was still trying to comfort Ari and Ari was still pushing her away. Ida collected Shakineh along the way.

"What's going on?" Zeddi asked Olive.

Olive held up Ida's phone. "We're videoing."

"In case he spills the beans," Isabella explained.

Hell no, was Zeddi's first thought. They were just children. Then again, it was better than standing around scared. Proactive magic, Ida would call it.

"Would somebody just call a fucking ambulance?" Roni begged, kneeling in the mud fussing over Ari.

Ida came up behind her. "The police are on their way."

"No!" Roni cried.

"Yes," Ida said. "And you know it's the right thing."

Defeated, Roni fell backward and into the embrace of Ida and Shakineh. She was so limp, she appeared to have no bones at all.

"Police?" Ari wailed. "You called the police on me?"

"Hello, Ari," Ida said.

He glared at her.

She glared back.

"It's all my fault!" Roni interjected.

"Nonsense," Ida snapped. "He's a grown man. He's responsible for himself." Then looking at Roni's tear-streaked face, she softened. "But I suppose in a way we are all of us to blame."

"It's true," Shakineh said, her cape puddling in the mud as she kneeled next to Roni. "We loved him too much."

Wincing, Ari leaned back on his elbows. "Hello? I'm in pain here."

"How could you, Ari?" Shakineh said, voice trembling. "When Dahlia was killed, I gave all my love to you."

"Not this head trip," he said. "Please."

"It's true," Ida said. "We all did. And we did you a disservice. The only child among us, we treated you like a god."

"But you kept the Gift from me."

"Oh, Ari," Roni sobbed. "Why won't you understand? Some people just don't have the ability."

"Have a deaf ear, you mean. Oh, I know you all think that. But it's not true! I've felt it. I've experienced it."

"*We* took you there," Ida said. "As *our* gift."

Much as Zeddi resisted it, she felt a drop of sympathy for the crazed lawyer. After the séance, she'd wanted more too. She'd craved it. Not like this, though. His hunger was destroying him, destroying those he loved.

"It's not true," he said, his chin trembling, his eyes widening. "You just never really believed in me."

"No," Roni wailed. "*I* did."

Ida wasn't buying it. She saw through his act. "You know, Ari, maybe you're right," she said. "Maybe you don't have a deaf ear. Maybe it's your ego that's kept the Gift from you. You want it too badly, but it's a gift—a *gift*, Ari. You can't demand a gift to be given. No one is entitled to a gift—no one."

Suddenly raging, he shouted, "This is all such bullshit!" He thrashed around, tearing at his hair, the thick Henry Walton gel mashing into two little devil horns. "If you had just—" He bent over his twisted knee. "Ow! Damn! I'm in pain. Doesn't anyone care?"

Ida didn't let up. "But to *siphon*..." she said with disgust. "How *could* you?"

"Yes," Roni blubbered. "How could you? I gave you everything. But it was never enough. Never ever enough. And now..."

"And now you've killed two women who loved you," Ida said point-blank. "Mags and Constance."

"I didn't mean to!" he sniveled. "I just wanted to trance with them, and then…"

"What?" Ida prodded. "You thought you could just siphon a little of their Gift? Come on, Ari. At least have the decency to admit what you've done."

"They wanted to."

"Did they? Or did you persuade them? They both loved you, Ari, would have done anything for you. Especially Mags." Ida was sobbing herself now. "You knew that, and you used her!"

"Okay! Okay!" he howled while covering his ears. "I killed them! But I didn't mean to. I didn't! I just wanted—"

"To take what wasn't yours."

"Yes," he said, and lowered his head.

"And you knew the risks. You knew that siphoning was dangerous."

"I did."

"Especially when they were in trance. You know how unsafe that is! And at their age!"

"Yes."

"And yet, you were still going to try with Olive. Weren't you?"

Zeddi felt Olive's shoulder tense. Felt her own stomach tighten. Maybe it was time to send Olive and Isabella to the van. Ida had gotten the confession, wasn't that enough? But fulfilling the job Ida had given her was obviously giving Olive a sense of control in this horrid situation, some agency. She needed that.

"And what foolishness," Ida persisted accusingly, "was it to arrange them in the same position, sitting in their chairs, hands folded in their laps? What was that about?"

"That was just random," Ari said. "I swear."

"Was it? Or is this another of your lies?"

Ari glared at her, his eyes swollen and red from the pepper spray.

Zeddi wasn't sure if Ida heard the car crunching down the long driveway or saw its flashing blue and red lights dancing on the trees as it switchbacked through the eucalyptus grove. She didn't think so. But unexpectedly, she realized that she herself had a question she needed answered, and this might be her only chance. She stepped around Olive and into the glow of the porch light. "Are you the one who left that scary message on Mags' answering machine?" If there was some other crazed witch out there, she wanted to know about it. She couldn't feel safe in the trailer until she did.

He looked her right in the eye. "Mags was priming Olive, you know that, right?"

"She wasn't," Ida countered.

"But she planned to."

"Maybe. But we'll never know that now, *will* we?"

"Did you?" Zeddi pushed.

"So what if I did?" he said. "It was just a phone call."

A sudden gust of wind let loose a hailstorm of eucalyptus seed pods. They hit the ground around him like bullets. She turned her back on him. *Bastard!*

"I want to ask him something too," Olive said, looking up from the phone.

The request punched Zeddi smack in the solar plexus. She didn't want Olive anywhere near this deranged man, and was about to say so when she had a second thought: Confronting the monster might be just the proactive magic Olive needed. And really, Ari Miller was no danger to anyone in his current state. She took a moment to circle Olive in white light, then said, "Okay. One question. But don't get too close."

Olive handed the phone to Isabella, adjusted her glasses, and took a few steps forward. "What about the crystal skull? What did you do with that? Because we know the one in the shed isn't the real one."

Zeddi almost laughed. After all they'd been through, Olive's mind was still on that damn skull.

"I can't help you there," he said. "Sorry, kid. Mags wouldn't let me near it."

"If not you, then who?" Shakineh asked, accusingly. "Who has the skull?"

A car door slammed, then a second one, but the headlights stayed on, flooding the gruesome scene in blinding light.

"Who called the police?" a pudgy male officer barked.

Squinting, Zeddi raised a hand. "I did. This man"—she gestured to Ari—"drugged me, then locked me, my daughter, and her friend in his basement."

"He needs an ambulance!" Roni wailed.

Zeddi looked to the other officer, hoping to connect with her woman to woman, but the burly lady cop was not the warm and fuzzy type. Not at all. Or maybe it was just the bizarre nature of the scene that had her hackles up: the costumes, the old women, a middle-aged man lying there in the mud moaning.

The pudgy officer turned to Ari, spoke to him man-to-man. "Is this true, sir?"

Ari used his lawyer voice. "No, it is not, Officer."

What?! "Liar!" Zeddi spat.

Ida approached the officer. "It's more than that. This man just confessed to murdering Constance and Mags McKenzie. We have his video confession."

"What?" Ari said angrily. "You were taping me?" He tried to get up to defend himself but fell back into the mud. "This is bullshit! I'm the victim here." He pointed at Zeddi and the girls. "They shot me with pepper spray and attacked me! That one there, she broke my knee! And anything on that phone will not be admissible in court, you can be sure of that."

"He needs an ambulance," Roni said. "Would someone please call an ambulance?"

"Mom, would you just shut up and let me take care of myself?"

Roni stared at him, incredulous, then said softly, "Don't you see? I've tried, but you made a mess of everything."

Shakineh helped Roni to her feet and embraced her, but Roni barely seemed aware of it. "Where's Jace?" she said through tears. "He should be here."

"He's on his way," Shakineh consoled.

In the distance coyotes howled.

The tough woman officer walked back to the patrol car to call in an ambulance. Pudgy spoke to Zeddi. "If you were trapped in the basement, how did you get out?"

"My daughter and her friend escaped out a window, then came and got me. Then I called you."

"And you are the one who incapacitated him?"

"Ah, no. My daughter did that too."

"With the skull crusher!" Olive said and held up her bat.

"I did the pepper spray," Isabella boasted.

The officer cocked an eyebrow. "You're not very big to be fighting off bad guys."

Isabella gestured to Olive. "It was her idea."

Olive beamed. "You can just call me Indiana Olive."

He scratched his head. "Okay then, good to know."

Jace's Tesla skidded in behind the police car. "What's going on here?" he demanded after slinging the car door open. He looked like he'd just come from the gym: hoodie and sweats.

"And you are?" the police officer inquired.

"Jace Miller. This man's father."

"Looks like your son has gotten himself in some trouble, sir. After we get that knee looked at, we're going to be bringing him in for some questioning, along with these ladies."

Jace strode over to Ari and crouched. "Are you all right, son? What happened?"

Ari glared at him. "Really, Dad? You're going to start caring now?"

"What's that supposed to mean?" Jace turned to Roni. "Babe? Could you fill me in, please? Could *someone* please fill me in?"

Shakineh stepped away, giving the Millers some space.

"You gave up on me," Ari said finally.

"I *what*?"

"You heard me."

"How did I—"

"No, Ari," Roni said. "He didn't. He never stopped believing in you, ever."

"Then why did you stop practicing?" Ari demanded of Jace. "Why did you quit the coven?"

"He stopped practicing," Roni explained, "to show you that a person didn't need the Gift to lead a worthwhile life. He stopped practicing because he loves you."

"Exactly what I said, he stopped practicing because poor little Ari, the son of two Keepers, the treasure of them all, just didn't have what it took to enter dreamtime. Poor little Ari—"

"Shut up!" Roni screamed. "Just shut up! You have no idea what he gave up for you!"

Zeddi gripped Olive's hand. The police had to think they were all out of their minds. But who cared? Just lock the lying maniac up.

"Look, Mom, Ari's crying," Olive whispered.

"I see," she whispered back, reflecting on what Ida had said. *The only child among us, we treated him like a god.* And look how he turned out. Was it possible to love a child too much?

Her musing was interrupted by Claude, who pointed up to a break in the clouds and cried, "Moon!" She'd completely forgotten about him standing over there in a clearing in his snappy trench coat, alone, looking cold, confused, scared—good old Claude, the only one of them who'd noticed.

Everyone looked up, including the two officers. Sure enough, the eclipse was underway, the moon partially hidden by the earth's shadow. And for a second the sounds of the night, the chirping of the crickets, the rustle of leaves as the breeze twisted through the canopy, the gentle sucking of the underground roots as they fed on the recent rain, the swish of some unseen bird's wingbeats roared in Zeddi's ears.

"That explains all the kooks out tonight," Burly uttered to Pudgy.

He laughed. "Yeah, whoever scheduled a full moon eclipse on Halloween sure didn't have us in mind."

CHAPTER THIRTY

"Would you get the door, please?" Zeddi asked Olive. "I've got pancake batter on my hands."

It was probably Dan. Olive had requested they invite him over for brunch. She wanted to tell him in person how she'd gone for the kneecaps.

Zeddi yawned. It had been late by the time they'd returned to the trailer, and they were all wired to hell, but after some warm milk laced with cinnamon and honey, the girls, unlike her, had dropped off. For a long while, she'd stood in the bedroom doorway watching them sleep, worrying about how the night's horror would affect the two little warriors in the one large bed, a fat, snoring Barnaby between them. She'd wished she could curl up next to Olive like she did sometimes in the van, but Olive was growing up, would soon have her own room, her own bed. It was time for Zeddi to let go a little, let her have a life. Go sleep on the couch.

She looked over at the girls now, still in their pajamas, playing with a tarot deck by the fire. They seemed to be doing okay. She just hoped the incident wouldn't put the kibosh on their friendship. Who knew how Luciana was going to respond when she heard about what had happened.

"Olive? Did you hear me? Olive?"

"Okay, okay." Olive tore herself away from Isabella and the cards. Went to answer the door.

Just the memory of those minutes locked in Ari's basement made Zeddi's skin crawl. What if they hadn't escaped? What if she'd drunk more of the hot buttered rum? What if Ari had come down into the basement and found them trying to escape? What if she'd lost Olive? What if? What if? What if? She ladled pancake batter onto the skillet of sizzling butter. Watched it pop. That she'd misread Ari made her mistrustful of herself. And if you couldn't trust yourself who could you trust?

"It's that woman you have a crush on," Olive said.

The spatula flew from Zeddi's hand and clattered onto the floor "What?"

"Sylvie," Olive clarified, like Zeddi didn't know which woman she had a crush on.

Zeddi dropped to her knees, swiped up the spatula, peered over the kitchen bar.

"Hey," Sylvie said, giving her a little wave. "I've been trying to reach you all morning."

Damn! Here she was still in her sweats. She hadn't even brushed her teeth. "You have?" She wiped the batter from her hands, grabbed her phone. Dead. "Oops. I guess after last night—"

"I worried."

"So you drove down to check on us?"

"Well…" Sylvie dug the toe of her tie-dyed Doc Marten into the welcome mat. Ran her fingers self-consciously through her mop of black hair. She looked a little rumpled herself. Like she'd slept in her clothes.

One of the pancakes made a loud sputtering sound and started to smoke. Oops. "It's fine!" She ran the spatula under the faucet. "Come in!"

"Olive, this is Sylvie," she said, flipping the first of the seriously burned pancakes.

"Uh…I know?" Olive said. "I just *told* you it was Sylvie."

Oh. Right.

Sylvie laughed. Held out her hand. "Nice to meet you, Olive, the real you. Not just the FaceTime you."

"You too," Olive said, giving her the once-over. "I thought you were taller."

Sylvie laughed again. "Sorry to disappoint. Hey. I heard you had quite a night last night."

Olive clicked her fingers. Struck a pose. "Taking out the bad guys, one by one."

Sylvie raised an appreciative eyebrow. "I guess."

She was obviously good with kids. Another thing to adore about her.

After a bit more banter, and being introduced to Isabella, the girls went back to playing with the tarot cards, and Sylvie joined Zeddi in the kitchen. "Could I have a word?" she said quietly.

"Sure…um…" Zeddi fumbled a pie pan from the cabinet and slid the pancakes onto it. "I'll just…um…toss these pancakes in the oven. Dan's coming over. He should be here soon. I mean, we can still talk. I just…what are you doing here? I'm mean, I'm so glad! But…"

"There's just something I need to say to you, and I was afraid I'd lose my nerve if I didn't say it today. And then you weren't picking up, so I hopped in the car."

Apprehensive, Zeddi led her outside. Was this it? Was she too much for Sylvie? She knew she'd blathered on last night on the phone— and there Sylvie was breaking down the set, closing up the theater. Had she talked too much? Sounded as unhinged as she felt? Was the crying too much?

"The thing is," Sylvie said the moment Zeddi shut the door. "When we talked last night, after you told me what had happened, all I could think was, what if I'd lost you? What if this thing between us—"

Relief flooded Zeddi's veins.

"I know! Me too! When I was locked in that basement, and a million things were going through my head, one of them was what if Sylvie and I never get to—"

"Even though we're still so new—" Sylvie said.

"Even though—"

"It just seems like—"

"I know," Zeddi said softly.

Sylvie's eyes were so green. The light spray of freckles so adorable. "It's just so wild," she said. "But see, when I did manage to finally sleep, Mags showed up in my dreams. I don't even know what she looked like in real life, but in my dream she had huge antlers, and her face was wrinkled like the bark of an ancient tree. I don't remember what the dream was about. It was all colors, abstract, I remember that.

But I woke up with this intense sense of urgency. Like, *do something!* And…and…this part is really wild. I got on my computer and started looking at job opportunities in Tres Ojos. Just to see. And there's an opening for a librarian. It was just listed. And I thought…"

Zeddi took her hands. "Seriously?"

"Is this too fast?"

"Yes. No. Yes. But you'd have to give up—"

"I thought about that. But honestly, the only reason I started working with the burlesque was so I could meet you. I mean, I didn't know I was going to meet you. But I was looking for you. I know that now."

Zeddi realized she was vice-gripping Sylvie's hands. She let up a little. "You'd really move down here? If you got the job?"

Sylvie lifted her shoulders all the way to her ears. "I'm willing to see where this leads."

"You realize, it's not just me. It's Olive."

"I get that. And who knows if I'll even get the job. But it just seems so—"

"Like if we don't—"

"Then we'll never—"

"Exactly."

Zeddi wrapped her arms around Sylvie's neck.

Sylvie drew her in closer.

"So," Zeddi whispered, her lips pressed to Sylvie's ear. "Are you staying for pancakes?"

❖

Over breakfast in the living room, and in between bites of pancakes, Olive and Isabella recounted to Dan and Sylvie their harrowing escape from the bad guy's basement. "And I did just like you said," Olive said to Dan. "Went for the kneecaps!"

Zeddi was only half listening. Sylvie, on the couch next to her, was so distracting. Not that Sylvie was doing anything distracting. Just her being there was distracting. The voltage between them was off the charts—*so* much better than FaceTime pillow cuddling. So much better than her fantasies. She ached to scoot over next to Sylvie, but she had to play it cool for now. Let Olive warm up to the idea of sharing her.

Dan, sitting in Mags' favorite chair, the one Zeddi had found her in, set his empty plate on the side table next to him. "Let me get this straight. He was after you because he thought you had"—he fluttered his fingers—"special powers?"

"The Gift," Olive clarified. "It's what the Keepers of the Sacred Song have. It's how they dream together. They weave sound into a magic spell, and it's…um…it's magic."

"It's what they did in the séance," Isabella added. "She told me all about it."

This was news. Olive had talked to Isabella about the séance? She hadn't said one word about it to Zeddi.

"Wow," Dan said. "Do *you* think you have the Gift, Olive?"

Olive contemplated, a pancake crumb stuck to her lower lip. "I think so. Yeah. I'm pretty sure I do."

Was it possible that Olive was a natural? What did being a natural even mean? Zeddi got up to put on more water for coffee. She'd ask Ida. She wanted to keep Ida in her life. She'd come to really care for her. And if it was true that Olive *did* have some kind of gift, she'd need Ida to help them figure out what to do with it.

Olive licked the syrup from her fork, slurped down the last of her orange juice, said, "Can I show Izzy the shed now? You promised I could."

Izzy. When had Isabella Graciela Mendez turned into just Izzy? Who knew? Kids were like that: trying on new personas like sweaters. "Sure," Zeddi said. "But put your shoes on. And jackets over your PJs, please. It's cold out."

The girls raced to the bedroom.

"And you know what?" Zeddi called after them. "You should each choose something from in there to remind you of how brave you were yesterday. We can ask Ida, Roni, and Shakineh if they want anything too, but first, you each pick something. You deserve it after last night."

"Cool!" Olive shouted.

Zeddi returned to the couch, daring to sit a little closer to Sylvie. "So, you were right about Ari," she said to Dan.

Barnaby jumped up onto his lap. "How so?"

"You told me you didn't get a good hit off him."

Dan gave Barnaby a pat. "A lucky guess."

"Well, I should have listened."

"Nah. If you listened to me about every dude I got a bad hit off of, you'd become like me, bitter and afraid to leave the house." He turned to Sylvie. "Can you imagine?"

Sylvie shot Zeddi a winning smile. "Nah."

Zeddi felt herself flush.

"So," Dan said, "are you making more coffee? Because at this hour, I should really be sleeping."

"Close the door behind you!" Zeddi yelled to the girls as they rocketed down the hall and out into the backyard.

When they didn't, Dan said, "I got it," and set a disgruntled Barnaby onto the floor.

"So do *you* think she has some kind of magic powers?" Sylvie asked. "This Gift thing?"

"Beats me," Zeddi said, sneaking a pinkie across the couch to Sylvie's thigh. "After the past two weeks, I'd believe anything."

The kettle whistled.

"Mom!" Olive screamed from the backyard. "You gotta see this!"

So much for having a moment. Zeddi got up to turn off the kettle. "I'm almost afraid to look."

"But you know you have to," Dan said, goading her on.

"Yeah," Sylvie said. "You know you do."

In the backyard, Olive pointed to a large, broken ceramic herb pot by the shed's entrance. "Look."

A pile of dirt? An uprooted rosemary bush? A mess of blue pot shards she'd have to sweep up? Then she saw it. "Holy…"

"Holy is right," Dan said.

"It that?" Sylvie began.

"The crystal skull," Olive whispered in awe.

And there was no Tijuana vibe with this skull, not at all. It had an aura. It had stories. You could feel it. "A raccoon must have knocked the pot over," Zeddi said. "Or…" *Or what?* The skull, in its desire to be free of its potted grave, had tipped itself over? No, that was crazy thinking. A carryover from last night's drugging.

"I wonder how long it's been buried?" Isabella said.

"And why?" Zeddi said. To keep it safe? Hide it?

Olive squatted to get a closer look then reached a single tentative finger out to the muddy skull, just the way she'd touched Mags two weeks ago, the day they'd found her sitting in her chair, dead.

"What do you think?" Zeddi asked once Olive's finger was safely back in her puffy jacket pocket.

"It's exactly like the ones in Indiana Jones," Olive breathed. "And it's glad we found it."

"How about I hose it off," Zeddi said, and swooped down to pick it up. "Just so you don't get mud all over your clean pajamas." It was heavier than she expected. And cold. She carried it over to the damp garden table and set it down. The truth was, she didn't want Olive anywhere near it. The thing gave her the creeps. No wonder Mags had buried it.

Olive followed her over. "That's what I'm keeping."

Sylvie stifled a laugh.

Zeddi shot Sylvie a look, then said, "Really? After all this?"

"*Because* of all this."

"A trophy," Dan said. "Makes sense."

"Yeah," Isabella said, framing her hands into an imaginary movie placard. "Indiana Olive and the Crystal Skull."

Great. They were ganging up on her. She peeled a thin red worm from the skull's eye socket. "Olive, I'm just not sure."

"You *said* we could each choose something."

"But this skull…"

"What about it?"

What about it, indeed?

A gust rattled the wind chime.

Ducks on the river squawked.

Zeddi pulled her sweater tight around her. Spotted her tattoo. Smiled.

Trust.

About the Author

Clifford Mae Henderson (cliffordhenderson.net), also writing under the name Clifford Henderson, was named after her grandmother Clifford, who once wore a nightgown to a formal event because she liked it better than any of the dresses she could find. Clifford Mae has attempted to follow in her renegade grandmother's footsteps, spending as much time as possible trying to shake things up. Her novels have received various awards, including a Foreword Review Book of the Year Award, an Independent Publisher Book Award, Golden Crown Literary Awards, Rainbow Awards, and Lesbian Fiction Reader Choice Awards. When not writing, Clifford Mae and her life partner of over a quarter century run the Fun Institute, an improv school in Northern California where they teach the art of collective pretending.

Books Available From Bold Strokes Books

A Talent Ignited by Suzanne Lenoir. When Evelyne is abducted and Annika believes she has been abandoned, they must risk everything to find each other again. (978-1-63679-483-9)

All Things Beautiful by Alaina Erdell. Casey Norford only planned to learn to paint like her mentor, Leighton Vaughn, not sleep with her. (978-1-63679-479-2)

An Atlas to Forever by Krystina Rivers. Can Atlas, a difficult dog Ellie inherits after the death of her best friend, help the busy hopeless romantic find forever love with commitment-phobic animal behaviorist Hayden Brandt? (978-1-63679-451-8)

Bait and Witch by Clifford Mae Henderson. When Zeddi gets an unexpected inheritance from her client Mags, she discovers that Mags served as high priestess to a dwindling coven of old witches—who are positive that Mags was murdered. Zeddi owes it to her to uncover the truth. (978-1-63679-535-5)

Buried Secrets by Sheri Lewis Wohl. Tuesday and Addie, along with Tuesday's dog, Tripper, struggle to solve a twenty-five-year-old mystery while searching for love and redemption along the way. (978-1-63679-396-2)

Come Find Me in the Midnight Sun by Bailey Bridgewater. In Alaska, disappearing is the easy part. When two men go missing, state trooper Louisa Linebach must solve the case, and when she thinks she's coming close, she's wrong. (978-1-63679-566-9)

Death on the Water by CJ Birch. The Ocean Summit's authorities have ruled a death on board its inaugural cruise as a suicide, but Claire suspects murder, and with the help of Assistant Cruise Director Moira, Claire conducts her own investigation. (978-1-63679-497-6)

Living For You by Jenny Frame. Can Sera Debrek face real and personal demons to help save the world from darkness and open her heart to love? (978-1-63679-491-4)

Ride with Me by Jenna Jarvis. When Lucy's vacation to find herself becomes Emma's chance to remember herself, they realize that everything they're looking for might already be sitting right next to them—if they're willing to reach for it. (978-1-63679-499-0)

Rivals for Love by Ali Vali. Brooks Boseman's brother Curtis is getting married, and Brooks needs to be at the engagement party. Only she can't possibly go, not with Curtis set to marry the secret love of her youth, Fallon Goodwin. (978-1-63679-384-9)

Whiskey and Wine by Kelly and Tana Fireside. Winemaker Tessa Williams and sex toy shop owner Lace Reynolds are both used to taking risks, but will they be willing to put their friendship on the line if it gives them a shot at finding forever love? (978-1-63679-531-7)

Hands of the Morri by Heather K O'Malley. Discovering she is a Lost Sister and growing acquainted with her new body, Asche learns how to be a warrior and commune with the Goddess the Hands serve, the Morri. (978-1-63679-465-5)

I Know About You by Erin Kaste. With her stalker inching closer to the truth, Cary Smith is forced to face the past she's tried desperately to forget. (978-1-63679-513-3)

Mate of Her Own by Elena Abbott. When Heather McKenna finally confronts the family who cursed her, her werewolf is shocked to discover her one true mate, and that's only the beginning. (978-1-63679-481-5)

Pumpkin Spice by Tagan Shepard. For Nicki, new love is making this pumpkin spice season sweeter than expected. (978-1-63679-388-7)

Sweat Equity by Aurora Rey. When cheesemaker Sy Travino takes a job in rural Vermont and hires contractor Maddie Barrow to rehab a house she buys sight unseen, they both wind up with a lot more than they bargained for. (978-1-63679-487-7)

Taking the Plunge by Amanda Radley. When Regina Avery meets model Grace Holland—the most beautiful woman she's ever seen— she doesn't have a clue how to flirt, date, or hold on to a relationship. But Regina must take the plunge with Grace and hope she manages to swim. (978-1-63679-400-6)

We Met in a Bar by Claire Forsythe. Wealthy nightclub owner Erica turns undercover bartender on a mission to catch a thief where she meets no-strings, no-commitments Charlie, who couldn't be further from Erica's type. Right? (978-1-63679-521-8)

Western Blue by Suzie Clarke. Step back in time to this historic western filled with heroism, loyalty, friendship, and love. The odds are against this unlikely group—but never underestimate women who have nothing to lose. (978-1-63679-095-4)

Windswept by Patricia Evans. The windswept shores of the Scottish Highlands weave magic for two people convinced they'd never fall in love again. (978-1-63679-382-5)

A Calculated Risk by Cari Hunter. Detective Jo Shaw doesn't need complications, but the stabbing of a young woman brings plenty of those, and Jo will have to risk everything if she's going to make it through the case alive. (978-1-63679-477-8)

An Independent Woman by Kit Meredith. Alex and Rebecca's attraction won't stop smoldering, despite their reluctance to act on it and incompatible poly relationship styles. (978-1-63679-553-9)

Cherish by Kris Bryant. Josie and Olivia cherish the time spent together, but when the summer ends and their temporary romance melts into the real deal, reality gets complicated. (978-1-63679-567-6)

Cold Case Heat by Mary P. Burns. Sydney Hansen receives a threat in a very cold murder case that sends her to the police for help, where she finds more than justice with Detective Gale Sterling. (978-1-63679-374-0)

Proximity by Jordan Meadows. Joan really likes Ellie, but being alone with her could turn deadly unless she can keep her dangerous powers under control. (978-1-63679-476-1)

Sweet Spot by Kimberly Cooper Griffin. Pro surfer Shia Turning will have to take a chance if she wants to find the sweet spot. (978-1-63679-418-1)

The Haunting of Oak Springs by Crin Claxton. Ghosts and the past haunt the supernatural detective in a race to save the lesbians of Oak Springs farm. (978-1-63679-432-7)

Transitory by J.M. Redmann. The cops blow it off as a customer surprised by what was under the dress, but PI Micky Knight knows they're wrong—she either makes it her case or lets a murderer go free to kill again. (978-1-63679-251-4)

Unexpectedly Yours by Toni Logan. A private resort on a tropical island, a feisty old chief, and a kleptomaniac pet pig bring Suzanne and Allie together for unexpected love. (978-1-63679-160-9)

Crush by Ana Hartnett Reichardt. Josie Sanchez worked for years for the opportunity to create her own wine label, and nothing will stand in her way. Not even Mac, the owner's annoyingly beautiful niece Josie's forced to hire as her harvest intern. (978-1-63679-330-6)

Decadence by Ronica Black, Renee Roman & Piper Jordan. You are cordially invited to Decadence, Las Vegas's most talked about invitation-only Masquerade Ball. Come for the entertainment and stay for the erotic indulgence. We guarantee it'll be a party that lives up to its name. (978-1-63679-361-0)

Gimmicks and Glamour by Lauren Melissa Ellzey. Ashly has learned to hide her Sight, but as she speeds toward high school graduation she must protect the classmates she claims to hate from an evil that no one else sees. (978-1-63679-401-3)

Heart of Stone by Sam Ledel. Princess Keeva Glantor meets Maeve, a gorgon forced to live alone thanks to a decades-old lie, and together the two women battle forces they formerly thought to be good in the hopes of leading lives they can finally call their own. (978-1-63679-407-5)

Peaches and Cream by Georgia Beers. Adley Purcell is living her dreams owning Get the Scoop ice cream shop until national dessert chain Sweet Heaven opens less than two blocks away and Adley has to compete with the far too heavenly Sabrina James. (978-1-63679-412-9)

The Only Fish in the Sea by Angie Williams. Will love overcome years of bitter rivalry for the daughters of two crab fishing families in this queer modern-day spin on Romeo and Juliet? (978-1-63679-444-0)